EXTRAVAGANT PRAISE FOR

Rainbows End

"No one has written as insightfully about the consequences of the deep future of the Internet (the next twenty years) as Vernor Vinge in his sprightly science fiction tale, *Rainbows End.* Everyone from Web professionals to intelligence analysts are studying it closely."

—Stewart Brand, creator of the *Whole Earth Catalog* and cofounder of The Long Now Foundation

"Nobody sees the future with more keen a visionary eye than Vernor Vinge. Follow him into *Rainbows End* . . . and come out amazed by the possibilities. What a great book."

—David Brin, Hugo and Nebula Award–winning author

"The near future is less alien here than in some of Vinge's other work, but no less fascinating and well-constructed. Some surprisingly savvy, well-rounded teen characters make this a winner." —*Booklist*

"A computational [dis|u]topia that perfectly captures the roaring hilarity of out-of-control technological change. Vinge's blazing a new trail toward the Singularity, turning cypherpunk paranoia into cracking adventure stories that combine technical rigor and a keen eye for the social impact of technology."

—Cory Doctorow, author of *Someone Comes to Town, Someone Leaves Town* and coeditor of Boing Boing

"This is definitely a must read book, and I am willing to predict that it will receive a Hugo nomination in the next year. For an enthralling look at our near future, you need to pick up *Rainbows End*."

—Colleen R. Cahill, *Fast Forward*

"Vernor Vinge has done it again: He has foreseen the human implications of new technologies long before anyone else. In *True Names,* it was cyberspace. In *Rainbows End*, it is—among other things—the superhuman intelligence that can result from cleverly connecting vast numbers of people electronically. Not only is this a good yarn, but it had my neurons popping with new ideas every few pages."

—Thomas W. Malone, the Patrick J. McGovern Professor of Information Systems and director of MIT Center for Coordination Science

"This may well be Vernor Vinge's best novel—adept, well told, with great new ideas leaping from the page. Vernor anticipates our future like nobody else, and even better, makes you believe it."

—Gregory Benford, Nebula Award–winning author of *Timescape*

"In a world of lightning-fast intrigue, Vinge puts dangerous technology and Big Brother snooping in the hands of ordinary people. Both frightening and fun. A real winner."

—Wil McCarthy, author of *Collapsium*

"The plot is deliciously intricate, and it's all I can do to hold back from spoiling its more exciting treats and colorful characters. *Rainbows End* is a feverishly entertaining next-gen tech thriller."

—SF Reviews.net

"Nobody sees the near future as clearly as Vernor Vinge. His notion of the 'Singularity' was one of the few genuinely new tropes in science fiction. Now *Rainbows End* is a glimpse of the shifting strangeness of a tech-drenched future. So plausible it's barely fiction at all."

—Stephen Baxter, author of *The Time Ships*

"*Rainbows End* is a spy thriller, a coming-of-age novel and an academic comedy. Vinge is on the cutting edge of technology, and it's a delight when tomorrow's wonders are displayed with humor."

—*Denver Post*

"Vernor Vinge is the Aldous Huxley of the computer age. His science fiction is satisfying in part because it's well-written and gripping. But more importantly, he knows how to tell a politically-informed fable about what happens—good, bad, and neutral—when we use technology to transform our ways of knowing the world."

—Wired.com

Books by Vernor Vinge

Tatja Grimm's World
The Witling
The Peace War
Marooned in Realtime
True Names and Other Dangers (collection)
Threats . . . and Other Promises (collection)

ACROSS REALTIME
comprising:
The Peace War
"The Ungoverned"
Marooned in Realtime

A Fire Upon the Deep
A Deepness in the Sky
True Names and the Opening of the Cyberspace Frontier
The Collected Stories of Vernor Vinge
Rainbows End

*Available from Tor Books

RAINBOWS END

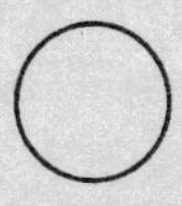

Vernor Vinge

A TOM DOHERTY ASSOCIATES BOOK
NEW YORK

This is a work of fiction. All the characters, organizations, and events portrayed in this book are either products of the author's imagination or are used fictitiously.

RAINBOWS END

Edited by James Frenkel

A Tor Book
Published by Tom Doherty Associates, LLC
175 Fifth Avenue
New York, NY 10010

www.tor-forge.com

ISBN 978-0-8125-3636-2

First Edition: May 2006
First Mass Market Edition: April 2007

Printed in the United States of America

0 9 8 7 6 5 4

To the Internet-based cognitive tools that are changing
our lives—Wikipedia, Google, eBay,
and the others of their kind, now and in the future

ACKNOWLEDGMENTS

I am grateful for the advice and help of:
Jeff Allen, David Baxter, Ethan Bier, John Carroll, Randy Carver, Steven Cherry, Connie Fleenor, Robert Fleming, Peter Flynn, Mike Gannis, Harry Goldstein, Thomas Goodey, Barbara Gordon, Judith Greengard, Dipak Gupta, Patricia Hartman, Patrick Hillmeyer, Cherie Kushner, Sifang Lu, Sara Baase Mayers, Keith Mayers, Terry McGarry, Sean Peisert, William Rupp, Peter H. Salus, Mary Q. Smith, Charles Vestal, Joan D. Vinge, Gabriele Wienhausen, and William F. Wu.

I am very grateful to James Frenkel for the wonderful job of editing he has done with this book. Jim and Tor Books have been very patient with me in the long process of creating *Rainbows End.*

CONTENTS

RAINBOWS END

Prologue

DUMB LUCK AND SMART THINKING

The first bit of dumb luck came disguised as a public embarrassment for the European Center for Defense Against Disease. On July 23, schoolchildren in Algiers claimed that a respiratory epidemic was spreading across the Mediterranean. The claim was based on clever analysis of antibody data from the mass-transit systems of Algiers and Naples.

CDD had no immediate comment, but in less than three hours, public-health hobbyists reported similar results in other cities, complete with contagion maps. The epidemic was at least one week old, probably originating in Central Africa, beyond the scope of hobbyist surveillance.

By the time CDD got its public-relations act together, the disease had been detected in India and North America. Worse yet, a journalist in Seattle had isolated and identified the infectious agent, which turned out to be a Pseudomimivirus. That was about as embarrassing a twist as the public-relations people could imagine: Back in the late teens, CDD had justified its enormous budget with a brilliant defense against the New Sunrise cult. The Sunrise Plague had been the second-worst Euroterror of the decade. Only CDD's leadership had kept the disaster from spreading worldwide.

The Sunrise Plague had been based on a Pseudomimivirus.

There were still good people at CDD. They were the same specialists who had saved the world in 2017. They quickly resolved the July 23 issue. Public Relations could now spin a more or less accurate statement: Yes, this Pseudomimi had evaded the standard announcement protocols. The failure was a simple software error at the Center's "Current Events" website. And yes, this Pseudomimi might be a derivative of the Sunrise Plague. Denatured strains of the original, death-optimized, virus continued to echo around the world, a permanent addition to the background noise of the biosphere. Three had already been sighted that year, one just five days before, on July 18.

Furthermore (and here the public-relations people regained their usual élan), *all* such events were subclinical, having essentially no perceptible symptoms. The Pseudomimiviruses had an enormous genome (well, enormous for a virus, small for almost anything else). The New Sunrise cult had transformed that genome into a Swiss Army knife of death, with a tool to counter almost every defense. But without such optimization, the Pseudomimis were clunky bags of DNA junk. "And so, in conclusion, we at CDD apologize for failing to announce this routine event."

A week passed. Two weeks. There were no further captures of the organism. Antibody surveys showed that the epidemic never got much farther than the rim of the Mediterranean. CDD's claims for the outbreak were absolutely correct. This kind of "subclinical respiratory epidemic" was almost a contradiction in terms. If not one victim in a thousand even gets the sniffles, the virus is almost dependent on charity to make its way in the world.

The CDD explanations were accepted. The public-health hobbyists had been scaremongering a commonplace event.

In fact, there was only one misrepresentation in the CDD story, and that successfully eluded public notice: The failure to announce the virus had not been a mess-up at the public website. Instead, it had been a glitch in the Center's just-revised internal alert system. So the responsible specialists had been as ignorant of the event as the general public; it was the hobbyists who had alerted both.

In the inner circles of EU intelligence, there were people who were not forgiving of such lapses. These were people who countered terror on a daily basis. These were people whose greatest successes were things you never heard about—and whose failures could be bigger than the Sunrise Plague.

Understandably, these people were both paranoid and obsessive. The EU Intelligence Board assigned one of its brightest agents, a young German named Günberk Braun, to oversee a quiet reorganization at CDD. In those parts of intelligence where Braun was known, he was somewhat famous—as the most obsessing of the obsessive. In any case, he and his teams quickly revamped the internal reporting structure of the CDD, then undertook a Center-wide review that was to last six months and consist of random "fire drills" that would probe threats and conjectures more bizarre than the epidemiologists had ever imagined.

For CDD, those six months promised to be a torment for the incompetent and a revelation for the brilliant. But Braun's fire-drill regime lasted less than two months, and was ended by an advertisement at a soccer match.

The first meeting of the Greece-Pakistan Football Series was held in Lahore on September 20. The Greece-Pakistan Series had some tradition behind it—or perhaps the supporters were just old-fashioned. In any case, the advertising was very much a blundering, twentieth-century affair. There were commercials where each advert was seen by everyone. Display space was sold on the inner barricades of the stadium, but even that was not targeted per viewer.

A remarkable thing happened at the match (two remarkable things, if you count the fact that Greece won). At halftime a thirty-second advert for honeyed nougats was shown. Within the hour, several freelance marketing analysts reported a spike-surge of nougat sales, beginning three minutes after the advert. That single advertisement had repaid its sponsor one hundred times over. Such was the stuff of dreams—at least for those unwholesomely fixated on the marketing arts. Throughout the afternoon, these millions debated the remarkable event. The advertisement was analyzed in every detail. It was an uninspired thing, quite in keeping with the third-rate company that produced it. Importantly, it contained no subliminal messing about (though finding such was the main hope of those who studied it). The delay and abruptness of the surge were quite unlike a normal advertisement response. Within hours, all reasonable participants agreed that the Honeyed Nougat Miracle was just the kind of mirage that came from modern data-dredging capabilities: if you watch trillions of things, you will often see one-in-a-million coincidences. At the end of the day, the whole affair had canceled itself out, just another tiny ripple in the myriad conversations of public life.

Certain observers did not lose interest. Günberk Braun, like most in the inner circles of the EUIB, had an enormous (let's be frank: an *apprehensive*) respect for the power of open intelligence analysis. One of his teams noticed the Honeyed Nougat Miracle. They considered the discussion. True, the event was almost surely a mirage. And yet, there were additional questions that could be asked; some were questions that governments had a special knack for answering.

And that brings us to the second bit of dumb luck. On a whim, Braun called for a fire drill: the analytical resources of the CDD would be pointed at the *public-health* significance of the Honeyed Nougat Miracle. Whatever the practical content of the mystery, this would exercise the Center in the conduct of a secret, real-time, emergency investigation. At that, it wasn't much crazier than his previous drills. By now, the brighter of the CDD's specialists were very much in the swing of such festivities. They quickly generated a thousand conjectures and imagined half a million tests. These would be seeds for the search trees of the investigation.

Over the next two days, the CDD analysts proceeded down their trees, extending and pruning—all the time exercising statistical restraint; this sort of work could generate more mirages than the marketing hobbyists had ever dreamed. Just the topic list would fill an old-time phone book. Here are the good parts, dramatically arranged:

There was no connection between the buying surge and the honeyed-nougat advert. This conclusion was not based upon theoretical analysis: CDD showed the advertisement to small response groups. All of the halftime publicity was similarly tested. One of the stadium displays—an advertisement for a dating service, which had aired only briefly—caused occasional interest in nougats. (The dating-service advert was a bit of design-artist excess, its background of intersecting lines a distracting moiré pattern.) Proceeding down the test tree, the dating-service advertisement was played for a number of specialized audiences. For instance, it had no enhanced effect on persons with antibodies to the July 23 Pseudomimivirus.

The dating-service advertisement did provoke nougat lust when shown to those who'd been infected by the earlier, *July 18 Pseudomimi, the one that CDD had properly reported.*

As a child, Günberk Braun had often daydreamed of how, in

an earlier time, he might have prevented the firebombing of Dresden, or stopped the Nazis and their death camps, or kept Stalin from starving the Ukraine. On off days, when he couldn't move nations, little Günberk imagined what he might have done in 1941 December 7 at a radar outpost in Hawaii, or as an American FBI agent in the summer of 2001.

Perhaps all young boys go through such a phase, largely ignorant of historical context, simply wanting to be savior heroes.

But when Braun considered this latest report, he knew he was in the middle of something as big as his childhood fantasies. The July 18 Pseudomimi and the advertising at the football match—together they amounted to an extremely well disguised test of a new weapon concept. In its developed form, such a weapon would make the Sunrise Plague look like a malignant toy. At the least, biological warfare would become as precise and surprising as bullets and bombs: slyly infect a population with the slow random spread of disease, all but undetected, and then *bam,* blind or maim or kill—singly with an email, or by the billions with a broadcast, too quickly for any possible "defense against disease."

If Braun had been a CDD person, this discovery would have precipitated immediate alarums to all the disease defense organizations of the Indo-European Alliance, as well as to the CDC in America and the CDCP in China.

But Günberk Braun was not an epidemiologist. He was a spook, and he was paranoid even for that. Braun's fire drill was under his personal control; he had no trouble suppressing the news there. Meantime, he used his resources in the EUIB and the Indo-European Alliance. Within hours, he was deep into a number of projects:

He brought in the best cult expert in the Indo-European intelligence community and set her loose on the evidence. He reached out to the military assets of the Alliance, in Central Africa and all the failed states at the edge of the modern world. There were solid clues about the origin of the July 18 Pseudomimi. Though this research was not bioscientific, Braun's analysts were very similar to the best at CDD—only smarter, more numerous, with far deeper resources. Even so, they were lucky: over the next three days, they put two and two (and two and two and two . . .) together. In the end, he had a good idea who was behind the weapons test.

And for the first time in his life, Günberk Braun was truly terrified.

01

MR. RABBIT VISITS BARCELONA

Within the intelligence services of the Indo-European Alliance, there were a handful of bureaucratic superstars, people such as Günberk Braun of the EUIB. Hopefully, their identities were unknown—or a mass of contradictions—to the general public. The superstars had their own heroes. In particular, when people like Günberk Braun were confronted with the most desperate problems, there was a place to get help. There was a certain department in India's External Intelligence Agency. It didn't show up in EIA organization charts, and its purpose was happily undefined. Basically, it was whatever its boss thought it should be. That boss was an Indian national known (to those very few who knew of him at all) as Alfred Vaz.

Braun took his terrifying discovery to Vaz. At first, the older man was as taken aback as Braun himself had been. But Vaz was a fixer. "With the proper human resources, you can solve almost any problem," he said. "Give me a few days. Let's see what I can dig up."

IN DOWNTOWN BARCELONA, three days later:

The rabbit hopped onto the unoccupied wicker chair and thence to the middle of the table, between the teacups and the condiments. It tipped its top hat first at Alfred Vaz and then at Günberk Braun and Keiko Mitsuri. "Have I got a deal for you!" it said. Altogether, it was an unremarkable example of its type.

Alfred reached out and swiped his hand through the image, just to emphasize his own substance. "We're the ones with the deal."

"Hmph." The rabbit plunked its ass down on the table and pulled a tiny tea service out from behind the salt and pepper. It poured itself a drop or two—enough to fill its cup—and took a sip. "I'm all ears." It wiggled two long ones to emphasize the point.

From the other side of the table, Günberk Braun gave the creature a long stare. Braun was as ephemeral as the rabbit, but he projected a dour earnestness that was quite consistent with his real personality. Alfred thought he detected a certain surprised disappointment in the younger man's expression. In fact, after a moment, Günberk sent him a silent message.

Braun --> Mitsuri, Vaz: <sm>*This* is the best you could recruit, Alfred?</sm>

Alfred didn't reply directly. Instead, he turned to the creature sitting on the table. "Welcome to Barcelona, Mr. Rabbit," he said. He waved at the towers of the Sagrada Familia, which soared up and up from just across the street. The cathedral was best seen without virtual elaboration; after all, the reality of Gaudí architecture was gaudy beyond the imagination of modern revisionists. "Do you have any idea why we selected this location for our meeting?"

The rabbit sipped its tea. Its gaze slid in a very un-rabbity way to take in the noisy crowds that swept past the tables, to scan the costumes and body-plans of tourists and locals. "Ah, is it that Barcelona is a place for the beautiful and the bizarre, one of the few great cities of the twentieth century whose charm survives in the modern world? Could it be that on the side, you and your families are taking touchy-feely tours through Parc Güell and writing it all off on your expense accounts?" He stared at Braun and at Keiko Mitsuri. Mitsuri was frankly masked. She looked a bit like Marcel Duchamp's nude, built from a shifting complex of crystal planes. The rabbit shrugged. "But then again, maybe you two are thousands of kilometers away."

Keiko laughed. "Oh, don't be so indecisive," she said, speaking with a completely synthetic accent and syntax. "I'm quite happy to be in Parc Güell right now, feeling reality with my very own real hands."

Mitsuri --> Braun, Vaz: <sm>In fact, I'm in my office, admiring the moonlight on Tokyo Bay.</sm>

The rabbit continued, ignorant of the silent-messaging byplay: "Whatever. In any case, the real reasons for meeting here: Barcelona has very direct connections to wherever you're really from, and modern security to disguise what we say. Best of all, it has laws banning popular and police snooping . . . unless of course you *are* the EU Intelligence Board."

Mitsuri --> Braun, Vaz: <sm>Well, that's one-third of a correct guess.</sm>

Braun --> Mitsuri, Vaz: <sm>Mr. Rabbit himself is calling from some distance.</sm> An EU real-time estimate hung in the air above the little creature's head: seventy-five percent probability that the mind behind the rabbit image was in North America.

Alfred leaned toward the rabbit and smiled. As the agent with physical presence, Vaz had limitations—but some advantages, too. "No, we're not the secret police. And yes, we wanted some secure communication that was a bit more personal than text messaging." He tapped his chest. "In particular, you see me physically here. It builds trust." *And should give you all sorts of invalid clues.* Vaz waved to a waiter, ordered a glass of Rioja. Then, turning back to the creature on the tablecloth: "In recent months, you have bragged many things, Mr. Rabbit. Others brag similarly nowadays, but you have certificates that are difficult to come by. Various people with notable reputations have endorsed your abilities."

The rabbit preened. This was a rabbit with many implausible mannerisms. Physical realism did not rank high in its priorities. "Of course I am highly recommended. For any problem, political, military, scientific, artistic, or amorous—meet my terms, and I will deliver."

Mitsuri --> Braun, Vaz: <sm>Go ahead, Alfred.</sm>

Braun --> Mitsuri, Vaz: <sm>Yes, the minimal version of course. Nothing more till we see some results that we couldn't make for ourselves.</sm>

Alfred nodded as if to himself. "Our problem has nothing to do with politics or war, Mr. Rabbit. We have only some scientific interests."

The rabbit ears waggled. "So? Post your needs to the answer boards. That may get you results almost as good as mine, almost as fast. And for certain, a thousand times cheaper."

Wine arrived. Vaz made a thing of sniffing the bouquet. He glanced across the street. The bidding on physical tour slots to the Sagrada Familia was closed for the day, but there was still a queue of people near the cathedral entrance, people hoping for no-shows. It proved once again that the most important things were those you could touch. He looked back at the gray rabbit. "We have needs that are more basic than picking the brains of a few thousand analysts. Our questions require serious, um, experimentation. Some of that has already been done. Much remains. All together, our project is the size you might imagine for a government crash research program."

The rabbit grinned, revealing ivory incisors. "Heh. A government crash program? That's twentieth-century foolishness. Market demands are always more effective. You just have to fool the market into cooperating."

"Maybe. But what we want to do is . . ." The hell of it was, even the cover story was extreme. "What we want is, um, administrative authority at a large physical laboratory."

The rabbit froze, and for an instant it looked like a real herbivore, one suddenly caught in a bright light. "Oh? What kind of physical lab?"

"Globally integrated life sciences."

"Well, well, well." Rabbit sat back, communing with itself—hopefully with itself alone. EU Intelligence set a sixty-five percent probability that Rabbit was not sharing the big picture with others, ninety-five percent that it was not a tool of China or the U.S.A. Alfred's own organization in India was even more confident of these assumptions.

The rabbit set down his teacup. "I'm intrigued. So this is not an information-provision job. You really want me to subvert a major installation."

"Just for a short time," said Günberk.

"Whatever. You've come to the right fellow." Its nose quivered. "I'm sure you know the possibilities. In Europe there are a scattering of top institutions, but none is totally integrated—and for now they remain in the backwash of sites in China and the U.S.A."

Vaz didn't nod, but the rabbit was right. There were brilliant researchers the world over, but only a few data-intensive labs. In the twentieth century, technical superiority of major labs might last thirty years. Nowadays, things changed faster, but Europe was a little behind. The Bhopal complex in India was more integrated, but lagging in micro-automation. It might be several years before China and the U.S.A. lost their current edge.

The rabbit was chuckling to itself: "Hm, hm. So it must be either the labs in Wuhan or those in Southern California. I could work my miracles with either, of course." That was a lie, or else Alfred's people had totally misjudged this fine furry friend.

Keiko said, "We'd prefer the biotech complex in San Diego, California."

Alfred had a smooth explanation ready: "We've studied the San Diego labs for some months. We know they have the resources we need." In fact, San Diego was where Günberk Braun's terrible suspicions were focused.

"Just what are you planning?"

Günberk gave a sour smile. "Let us proceed by installments, Mr. Rabbit. For the first installment, we suggest a thirty-day deadline. We'd like from you a survey of the San Diego labs' security. More important, we need credible evidence that you can provide a team of local people to carry out physical acts in and near those labs."

"Well then. I will hop right on it." The rabbit rolled its eyes. "It's obvious you're looking for an expendable player, somebody to shield your operation from the Americans. Okay. I can be a cutout. But be warned. I am very pricey and I *will* be around to collect afterwards."

Keiko laughed. "No need to be melodramatic, Mr. Rabbit. We know of your famous skills."

"Quite right! But so far you don't believe in them. Now I'll go away, sniff around San Diego, and get back to you in a couple of weeks. I'll have something to show you by then, and—more important for me—I'll have used my enormous imagination to specify a first payment in this installment plan that Mr. So-German-Seeming has proposed." He gave a little bow in Günberk's direction.

Mitsuri and Braun were radiating bemused silence, so it was Alfred who carried on the conversation. "We'll chat again then. Please remember that for now we want a survey only. We want to know whom you can recruit and how you might use them."

The rabbit touched its nose. "I will be the soul of discretion. I always know much more than I reveal. But you three really should improve your performances. Mr. So-German is just an out-of-date stereotype. And you, señora, the work of impressionist art reveals nothing and everything. Who might have a special interest in the San Diego bio labs? Who indeed? And as for you—" Rabbit looked at Vaz. "That's a fine Colombian accent you're hiding."

The creature laughed and hopped off the table. "Talk to you soon."

Alfred leaned back and watched the gray form as it dodged between the legs of passersby. It must have a festival permit, since other people were evidently seeing the creature. There was no *poof* of vanishment. The rabbit remained visible for twenty meters up Carrer de Sardenya, then darted into an alley and was finally and quite naturally lost to sight.

The three agents sat for a moment in apparently companionable silence, Günberk bent over his virtual wine, Vaz sipping at his real Rioja and admiring the stilted puppets that were setting up for the afternoon parade. The three blended well with the normal touristy hurly-burly of the Familia district—except that most tourists paying for café seating on C. de Sardenya would have had more than a one-third physical presence.

"He is truly gone," Günberk said, a bit unnecessarily; they could all see the EU signals analysis. A few more seconds passed. The Japanese and Indian intelligence agencies also reported in: Rabbit remained unidentified.

"Well that's something," said Keiko. "He got away clean. Perhaps he can function as a cutout."

Günberk gave a weary shrug. "Perhaps. What a disgusting twit. His kind of dilettante is a cliché a century old, reborn with each new technology. I wager he's fourteen years old and desperately eager to show off." He glanced at Vaz. "Is this the best you could come up with, Alfred?"

"His reputation is not a fraud, Günberk. He has managed projects almost as complex as what we have in mind for him."

"Those were research projects. Perhaps he is a good—what's the term?—'weaver of geniuses.' What we want is more operational."

"Well, he correctly picked up on all of the clues we gave

him." There had been Alfred's accent, and the network evidence they had planted about Keiko's origin.

"Ach ja," said Günberk, and a sudden smile crossed his face. "It's a bit humiliating that when I am simply myself, I'm accused of overacting! Yes, so now Mr. Rabbit thinks we are South American drug lords."

The shifting crystal mists that were Keiko's image seemed to smile. "In a way, that's more plausible than what we really are." The heirs of drug wars past had been in eclipse this last decade; access to "ecstasy and enhancement" was so widespread that competition had done what enforcement could never accomplish. But the drug lords were still rich beyond the dreams of most small countries. The ones lurking in failed states might be crazy enough to do what they three had hinted at today.

Günberk said, "The rabbit is manageable, I grant that. Competent for our needs? Much less likely."

"Having second thoughts about our little project, Günberk?" This was Keiko's real voice. Her tone was light, but Alfred knew she had her own very serious misgivings.

"Of course," said Günberk. He fidgeted for a moment. "Look. Terror via technical surprise is the greatest threat to the survival of the human race. The Great Powers—ourselves, China, the U.S.—have been at peace for some years, mostly because we recognize that danger and we keep the rest of the world in line. And now we discover that the Americans—"

Keiko: "We don't know it's the Americans, Günberk. The San Diego labs support researchers all over the world."

"That is so. And a week ago I was as dubious as you. But now . . . consider: The weapons test was a masterpiece of cloaking. We were incredibly lucky to notice it. The test was a work of patience and professionalism, at the level of a Great Power. Great Powers have their own inertia and bureaucratic caution. Field testing must necessarily be done in the outside world, but they do not run their weapons development in labs they do not own."

Keiko made a sound like faraway chimes. "But why would a Great Power plot a revolution in plague delivery? What profit is there in that?"

Günberk nodded. "Yes, such destruction would make sense for a cult, but not for a superpower. At first, my conclusion was a nightmare without logic. But my analysts have been over this again and again. They've concluded that the 'honeyed-nougat symptom' was not simply a stand-in for lethal disease. In fact, it was an essential feature of the test. This enemy is aiming at something greater than instant biowarfare strikes. This enemy is close to having an effective YGBM technology."

Keiko was completely silent; even her crystals lost their mobility. YGBM. That was a bit of science-fiction jargon from the turn of the century: You-Gotta-Believe-Me. That is, mind control. Weak, social forms of YGBM drove all human history. For more than a hundred years, the goal of *irresistible* persuasion had been a topic of academic study. For thirty years it had been a credible technological goal. And for ten, some version of it had been feasible in well-controlled laboratory settings.

The crystals shifted; Alfred could tell that Keiko was looking at him. "Can this be true, Alfred?"

"Yes, I'm afraid so. My people have studied the report. Günberk's luck was extraordinary, since this was really a simultaneous test of *two* radical innovations. The honeyed-nougat compulsion was far more precise than needed for a test of remote disease triggering. The perpetrators knew what they were coding for—consider the cloaking advertisement for nougats. My analysts think the enemy may be capable of higher semantic control in as little as a year."

Keiko sighed. "Damn. All my life, I've fought the cults. I thought the great nations were beyond the most monstrous evils . . . but this, this would make me wrong."

Günberk nodded. "If we are right about these labs and if we fail to properly . . . deal . . . with them, that could be the end of history. It could be the end of all the striving for good against evil that has ever been." He shook himself, abruptly returning to the practical. "And yet we are reduced to working through this damned rabbit person."

Alfred said gently, "I've studied Rabbit's track record, Günberk. I think he can do what we need. One way or another. He'll get us the inside information, or he'll create enough chaos—*not* attributable to us—that any evil will be clearly visible. If the worst is true, we'll have evidence that we and China and even the nonculpable parties in the U.S.A. can use to stamp this out." Suppression attacks on the territory of a Great Power were rare, but there was precedent.

All three were silent for a moment, and the sounds of the festival afternoon swept around Vaz. It had been so many years since his last visit to Barcelona. . . . Finally, Günberk gave a grudging nod. "I'll recommend to my superiors that we proceed."

Across the table, Keiko's prismatic imagery shimmered and chimed. Mitsuri's background was in sociology. Her analyst teams were heavily into psychology and social institutions—much less diversified than the teams working for Alfred, or Günberk. But maybe she would come up with some alternative that the other two had missed. Finally she spoke: "There are many decent people in the American intelligence community. I don't like doing this behind their back. And yet, this is an extraordinary situation. I have clearance to go ahead with Plan Rabbit—" she paused "—with one proviso. Günberk fears that we've erred in the direction of employing an incompetent. Alfred has studied Rabbit more, and thinks he's at just the right level of talent. But what if you are both wrong?"

Günberk started in surprise. *"The devil!"* he said. Alfred guessed that some very quick silent messaging passed between the two.

The prisms seemed to nod. "Yes. What if Rabbit is significantly *more* competent than we think? In that unlikely event, Rabbit might hijack the operation, or even ally with our hypothetical enemy. If we proceed, we must develop abort-and-destroy plans to match Rabbit's progress. If he becomes the greater threat, we must be prepared to talk to the Americans. Agreed?"

"Ja."

"Of course."

O

KEIKO AND GÜNBERK stayed a few minutes more, but a real café table on C. de Sardenya in the middle of the festival was not the proper place for virtual tourists. The waiter kept circling back, inquiring if Alfred needed anything more. They were paying table rent for three, but there were crowds of real people waiting for the next available seating.

So his Japanese and European colleagues took their leave. Günberk had many loose ends to deal with. The inquiries at CDD must be gracefully shut down. Misinformation must be layered carefully about, concealing things both from the enemy and from security hobbyists. Meantime, in Tokyo, Keiko might be up the rest of the night, pondering Rabbit traps.

Vaz stayed behind, finishing his drink. It was amazing how fast his table space shrank, accommodating a family of North African tourists. Alfred was used to virtual artifacts changing in a blink of the eye, but a clever restaurateur could do almost as well with physical reality when there was money involved.

In all Europe, Barcelona was the city Alfred loved the most. The Rabbit was right about this city. But was there time to be a real tourist? Yes. Call it his annual vacation. Alfred stood and bowed to the table, leaving payment and tip. Out on the street, the crowds were getting rather extreme, the stilt people dancing wildly about among the tourists. He couldn't see the entrance of the Sagrada Familia directly, but tourism info showed the next certain tour slot was ninety minutes away.

Where to spend his time? Ah! Atop Montjuïc. He turned down an alley. Where he emerged on the far side, the crowds were thin . . . and a tourist auto was just arriving for him. Alfred sat back in the single passenger cockpit and let his mind roam. The Montjuïc fortress was not the most impressive in Europe, and yet he had not seen it in some time. Like its brethren, it marked the bygone time when revolutions in destruction technology took decades to unfold, and mass murder could not be committed with the press of a button.

The auto navigated its way out from the octagonal city blocks of the Barcelona basin and ran quickly up a hillside, grabbing the latch of a funicular that dragged them swiftly up the side of Montjuïc. No tedious switchback roadway for this piece of automation. Behind him, the city stretched for miles. And then ahead, as they came over the crest of the hill, there was the Mediterranean, all blue and hazy and peaceful.

Alfred got out, and the tiny auto whipped around the traffic circle, heading for the cable-car installation that would take its next customer in an overflight across the harbor.

He was at just the spot he had ordered on the tourist menu, right where twentieth-century guns faced out from the battlements. Even though these cannon had never been used, they were very much the real thing. For a fee, he could touch the guns and climb around inside the place. After sundown there would be a staged battle.

Vaz strolled to the stone barrier and looked down. If he blocked out all the tourism fantasy, he could see the freight harbor almost two hundred meters below and a kilometer away. The place was an immensity of freight containers rambling this way and that, chaos. If he invoked his government powers, he could see the flow of cargo, even see the security certificates that proclaimed—in ways that were validated by a combination of physical and cryptographic security—that none of the ten-meter boxes contained a nuke or a plague or a garden-variety radiation bomb. The system was very good, the same as you would find for heavy freight anywhere in the civilized world. It had been the result of decades of fear, of changing attitudes about privacy and liberty, of technological progress. Modern security actually worked most of the time. There hadn't been a city lost in more than five years. Every year, the civilized world grew and the reach of lawlessness and poverty shrank. Many people thought that the world was becoming a safer place.

Keiko and Günberk—and certainly Alfred—knew that such optimism was dead wrong.

Alfred looked across the harbor at the towers beyond. Those hadn't been here the last time he visited Barcelona. The civilized world was wealthy beyond the dreams of his youth. Back in the 1980s and 1990s, the rulers of modern states realized that success did not come from having the largest armies or the most favorable tariffs or the most natural resources—or even the most advanced industries. In the modern world, success came from having the largest possible educated population *and* providing those hundreds of millions of creative people with credible freedom.

But this utopia was a Red Queen's Race with extinction.

In the twentieth century, only a couple of nations had the power to destroy the world. The human race survived, mostly by good luck. At the turn of the century, a time was in view when dozens of countries could destroy civilization. But by then, the Great Powers had a certain amount of good sense. No nation-state could be nuts enough to blow up the world—and the few barbaric exceptions were Dealt With, if necessary with methods that left land aglow in the dark. By the teens, mass death technology was accessible to regional and racial hate groups. Through a succession of happy miracles—some engineered by Alfred himself—the legitimate grievances of disaffected peoples were truly addressed.

Nowadays, Grand Terror technology was so cheap that cults and small criminal gangs could acquire it. That was where Keiko Mitsuri was the greatest expert. Even though her work was hidden by cover stories and planted lies, Keiko had saved millions of lives.

The Red Queen's Race continued. In all innocence, the marvelous creativity of humankind continued to generate unintended consequences. There were a dozen research trends that could ultimately put world-killer weapons into the hands of anyone having a bad hair day.

Alfred walked back to the nearest cannon, paying the touch fee with a wave of his hand. He leaned against the warm metal, sighting out over the blue mediterranean haze, and imagining a simpler time.

Poor Günberk. He had the truth exactly backward. Effective YGBM would not be the end of everything. In the right hands, YGBM technology was the one thing that could solve the modern paradox, harnessing the creativity of humankind without destroying the world in the process. In fact, it was humankind's only hope for surviving the twenty-first century. *And in San Diego, I am so close to success.* He had insinuated his project into the bio labs three years earlier. The great breakthrough had come less than a year ago. His test at the soccer match had proven the delivery system. In another year or so, he'd have developed higher semantic controls. With that, he could reliably control those immediately around him. Much more important, he could spread the new infection across whole populations and engineer a few universally viewed transmissions. Then he would be in control. For the first time in history, the world would be under adult supervision.

That had been the plan. Now incredibly bad luck had jeopardized it. *But I should look at the bright side; Günberk came to me to fix the problem!* Alfred had spent a lot of effort digging up "Mr. Rabbit." The fellow was clearly inexperienced, and every bit the egotistical fool that Günberk believed. Rabbit's successes were just barely impressive enough to make him acceptable. They could manage Rabbit. *I can manage Rabbit.* From inside the labs, Alfred would feed the Rabbit just the right misinformation. In the end neither Rabbit nor Alfred's colleagues in the Indo-European Alliance would realize they had been fooled. And afterward, Alfred could continue undisturbed with what might well be the last, best chance for saving the world.

Alfred climbed into the gun turret and admired the fittings. The Barcelona tourist commission had spent some real money on rebuilding these artifacts. If their mock battle this evening meshed with this physical reality, it would be very impressive. He glanced at his Mumbai schedule—and decided to stay in Barcelona a few more hours.

02

THE RETURN

Robert Gu should be dead. He knew that, he truly did. He had been a long time dying. He wasn't really clear on how long. In this unending present, he could see only blurs. But that didn't matter, since Lena had turned the lights down so low that there was nothing to see. And the sounds: for a while he had worn things in his ears, but they were devilishly complicated and always getting lost or worn out. Getting rid of them had been a blessing. What sounds remained were vague mumblings, sometimes Lena complaining at him, pushing and poking. Following him into the john, for God's sake. All he really wanted was to go home. Lena wouldn't let him do that simple thing. If it really was Lena at all. Whoever, she wasn't very nice. *I just want to go home. . . .*

O

AND YET, HE never did quite die. The lights were often brighter now, though blurry as ever. There were people around and voices, the high-pitched tones he remembered from home. They talked as if they expected to be understood.

Things had been better before, when everything was a mumbling blur. Now he hurt all over. There were long drives to see the doctor, and afterward the pain was always worse. There was some guy who claimed to be his son, and claimed that wherever he was *now* was home. Sometimes they rolled him outside to feel the bright sun on his face and listen to the birds. No way was this home. Robert Gu remembered home. There had been snow on big mountains he could see from his folks' backyard. Bishop, California, U.S.A. That was the place, and this wasn't it.

But even though this wasn't home, his little sister was here. Cara Gu had been around before, when things were dark and mumbling, but she'd always been just out of sight. This was different. At first he was just aware of her high, piping voice, like the wind bells his mother kept on the porch at home. Finally, one day he was out on the patio, feeling the sunlight brighter and warmer than it had seemed in a long time. Even the blurs were sharp and colorful. There was Cara's high little voice asking him "Robert this" and "Robert that" and—

"Robert, would you like it if I showed you around the neighborhood?"

"What?" Robert's tongue felt all sticky, his voice hoarse. It suddenly occurred to him that with all the mumbling and darkness maybe he hadn't spoken in some time. And there was something else that that was even more strange. "Who are you?"

There was silence for a moment, as if the question were foolish or had been asked many times before. "Robert, I'm Miri. I'm your grand—"

He jerked his hand as much as it would move. "Come closer. I can't see you."

The blur moved directly in front of him, into the middle of

the sunlight. This was not some hint of presence behind his shoulder or in his memory. The blur became a face just inches from his own: he could see the straight black hair, the small round countenance smiling at him as if he were the greatest guy in the world. It really was his little sister.

Robert reached forward, and her hand was warm in his. "Oh, Cara. It's so good to see you." He wasn't home, but maybe he was close. He was quiet for a moment.

"I'm . . . I'm glad to see you, too, Robert. Would you like to go for a ride around the neighborhood?"

". . . Yes, that would be nice."

Things happened fast then. Cara did something and his chair seemed to spin around. It was dark and gloomy again. They were inside the house and she was fussing like she always did, this time getting him a hat. She still teased though, as in asking him if he needed to go to the bathroom. Robert sensed that the thug who claimed to be his son was lurking just to one side, watching it all.

And then they were out—what, the front door?—and onto a street. Cara stayed beside his wheelchair as they strolled and rolled down an empty street lined with tall, thin trees . . . palm trees, that's what they were. This wasn't Bishop. But this was Cara Gu—though on her very best behavior. Little Cara was a good kid, but she could only be good for so long and then she would find some devilish tease and have him chasing her all over the house, or vice versa. Robert smiled to himself and wondered how long the angelic phase would last this time. Maybe she thought he was sick. He tried unsuccessfully to turn in his chair. Well, maybe he was sick.

"See, we live on Honor Court. Over there, that's the Smithsons' house. They transferred here from Guam last month. Bob thinks they're growing five—oops, but I'm not supposed to talk about that. And the boyfriend of the base commander lives in that house by the corner. I'm betting they'll be married by the end of the year. . . . And there are some kids from school I don't want to talk to just now." Robert's wheelchair took an abrupt turn, and they were heading down a side street.

"Hey!" Robert tried again to turn in his chair. Maybe those kids were friends of *his*! Cara was teasing after all. He slumped down in the chair. There was the smell of honey. Bushes seemed to hang low above them. The houses were gray and greenish blurs. "Some tour!" he groused. "I can't see a Dam Ned thing."

The wheelchair abruptly slowed. "Really?" The little wretch was all but chortling. "Don't worry, Robert! There's some devious twiddling that can fix your eyes."

Grump. "A pair of glasses would fix them, Cara." Maybe she was hiding them from him.

There was something about the brightness and the dry wind that swept these streets—wherever this was. It made him wonder what he was doing tied down to a wheelchair. They toured around a couple more blocks. Cara fussed endlessly over him. "Are you too warm, Robert? Maybe you don't need that blanket." "The sun is going to burn your head, Robert. Let me tilt your cap down a little bit." At one point there were no houses. It seemed that they were on the edge of a long slope. Cara claimed they were looking off toward the mountains—but all Robert could see was a hazy line of tan and faded ochre. They were nothing like the mountains that shouldered into the sky above Bishop, California, U.S.A.

Then they were back indoors, in the house they had started from. Things were as dark and gloomy as ever, the room lights swallowed up in darkness. Cara's bright voice was gone. She was off to study for her classes, she said. No classes for Robert. The thug was feeding him. He still claimed to be Robert's son. But he was so big. Afterward there was another ignominious potty stop, more like a police interrogation than a trip to the can. And then Robert was left mercifully alone, in the darkness. These people didn't even have television. There was just the silence, and the dim and faraway electric lights.

I should be sleepy. He had a vague memory of nights fading off into nights fading off into years, of drowsing sleep that came right after dinner. And then later waking, walking through strange rooms and trying to find home. Arguing with Lena. Tonight was . . . different. He was still awake. Tonight he was thinking of things that had just happened. Maybe that was because he had made it partway home. *Cara.* So he hadn't found his folks' house on Crombie Street and the bedroom that looked out on the old pine tree and the little cabin he had built in its branches. But Cara was part of all that, and she was here. He sat for a long time, his thoughts slowly crunching forward. Across the room, a single lamp was kind of a whirlpool in the darkness. Barely visible, the thug was sitting by the wall. He was talking to someone, but Robert couldn't see who.

Robert ignored the guy, and thought hard. After a while he remembered something very scary. Cara Gu had died in 2006. They hadn't said a word to each other for years before that.

And when she died, Cara had been fifty-one years old.

WEST FALLBROOK HAD been a handy place in the early years of the century. Busy too. Right next to Camp Pendleton, it had been the base's largest civilian community. A new generation of marines had grown up here . . . and prosecuted a new generation of war. Robert Gu, Jr., had seen the tail end of that frenzy, arriving at a time when Chinese-American officers were welcomed back to positions of trust. Those had been high and bittersweet days.

Now the town was bigger, but the marines weren't nearly such a large part of it. Military life had become a lot more complicated. Between little bits of war, Lieutenant Colonel Gu found that West Fallbrook was a nice place to raise a daughter.

"I still think it's a mistake for Miri to call him 'Robert.'"

Alice Gu looked up from her work. "We've been over this before, dear. It's how we've brought her up. We're 'Bob' and 'Alice,' not 'Ma' and 'Pa' or whatever silliness is currently approved. And Robert is 'Robert,' not 'Grandpapa.'" Colonel Alice Gong Gu was short and round-faced and—when she wasn't deadly stressed—motherly. She had graduated numero uno from Annapolis, back when being short and round-faced and motherly were definite career minuses. She'd be a general officer by now except that higher authority had discovered more productive and dangerous work for her. That accounted for some of her kookie ideas. But not this one; she had always insisted that Miri address her parents as if they were all just pals.

"Hey, Alice, I've never minded that Miri calls us by our first names. There'll come a time when besides loving us, the Little General will also be our peer, maybe our boss. But this is just confusing my old man—" Bob jerked a thumb at where Robert Senior sat, half slumped and staring. "Play back the way Dad was acting this afternoon. See how he lit up. He thinks Miri is my aunt Cara, when they were little kids!"

Alice didn't answer right away. Where she was, it was mid-morning. Sunlight glittered off the harbor behind her. She was running support for the U.S. delegation in Jakarta. Indonesia was joining the Indo-European Alliance. Japan was already a member of that bizarrely named club. The joke was that the "Indo-Europeans" would soon have the world surrounded. There was a time when China and the U.S.A. would not have taken that as a joke. But the world had changed. Both China and the U.S. were relieved by the development. It left them with more time to worry about real problems.

Alice's eyes flickered this way and that as she nodded at an introduction, laughed at some witty comment. She walked a short distance with a couple of self-important types, chattering all the while in Bahasa and Mandarin and Goodenuf English, of which only the English was intelligible to Bob. Then she was alone again. She leaned a little toward him, and gave him a big grin. "Well that sounds like a good thing!" she said. "Your father has been beyond all rational discourse for how many years? And now suddenly he's engaged enough to have a good time. You should be thrilled. From here, he'll only get better. You'll have your father back!"

". . . Yes." Yesterday, he'd said goodbye to the last of the in-home caregivers. Dad should improve very fast now. The only reason he was still in a wheelchair was that the docs wanted to make sure his bone regeneration was complete before they let him loose in the neighborhood.

She saw the expression on his face, and cocked her head to one side. "Are you chicken?"

He glanced at his father. The Paraguay operation was just a few weeks away. A covert op at the edge of the world. The prospect was coming to seem almost attractive. "Maybe."

"Then let our Little General do her thing and don't worry."

She turned and waved at someone beyond his vision. "Oops." Her image flickered out and there was only silent messaging—

Alice --> Bob: <sm>Gotta go. I'm already covering for Secretary Martinez, and local custom does *not* approve of time-sharing.</sm>

Bob sat for a moment in the quiet living room. Miri was upstairs, studying. Outside, the late afternoon slid into evening. A peaceful time. Back when he was a kid, this was when Dad would bring out the poetry books, and Dad and Mom and little Bobby would have a readalong. Actually, Bob felt a happy nostalgia for those evenings. He looked back at his father. "Dad?" No answer. Bob leaned forward and tried to shout diffidently. "Dad? Is there enough light for you? I can make it lots brighter."

The old man shook his head distractedly. Maybe he even understood the question, but he gave no other indication. He just sat there, slumped to the side. His right hand rubbed again and again at the wrist of his left. And yet, this was a big improvement. Robert Gu, Sr., had been down to eighty pounds, a barely living vegetable, when UCSF Medical School took him on for their new treatment. It turned out the UCSF Alzheimer's cure worked where the years of conventional treatment had failed.

Bob did a few errands on base, checked the plans for the upcoming Paraguay operation . . . and then sat back and just watched his father for a few minutes.

I didn't always hate you.

As a child, he had never hated his old man. Maybe that wasn't surprising. A kid has very little to compare to. Robert was strict and demanding, on that little Bobby had been very clear. For even though Robert Senior had often and loudly blamed himself for being such an easygoing parent, sometimes that seemed to contradict what Bob saw at his friends' homes. But it had never seemed mistreatment to Bob.

Even when Mom left Dad, even that hadn't turned Bob against the old man. Lena Gu had taken years of subtle abuse and she couldn't take any more, but little Bobby had been oblivious of it all. It wasn't till later, talking to Aunt Cara, that he realized how much worse Robert treated others than he had ever treated Bob.

For Lieutenant Colonel Robert Gu, Jr., this should be a joyous time. His father, one of America's most beloved poets, was returning from an extended campout in the valley of the shadow of death. Bob took a long look at Robert's still, relaxed features. No, if this were cinema, it would be a Western and the title would be *The Return of the SOB.*

03

A MINEFIELD MADE IN HEAVEN

"My eyeballs are . . . fizzing!"

"This shouldn't be painful. Do they actually hurt?"

". . . No." But the light was so bright that Robert saw fiery color even in the shadows. "It's all still a blur, but I haven't seen this well in . . ." he didn't know how long; time itself had been a darkness ". . . in years."

A woman spoke from right behind his shoulder. "You've been on the retinal meds for about a week, Robert. Today we felt we had a working population of cells present, so we decided to turn them on."

Another woman's voice: "And we can cure your blurred vision even more easily. Reed?"

"Yes, Doctor." This voice came from the man-shaped blur directly in front of him. The figure leaned near. "Let me put this over your eyes, Robert. There'll be a little numbness." Big gentle hands slipped glasses across Robert's face. At least this was familiar; he was getting new lenses fitted. But then his face went numb and he couldn't close his eyes.

"Just relax and look to the front." Relaxing was one thing, but there was no choice about looking to the front. And then . . . *God,* it was like watching a picture come up on a really slow computer, the blurs sharpening into finer and finer detail. Robert would have jerked back, but the numbness had spread to his neck and shoulders.

"The cell map in the right retina looks good. Let's do the left." A few more seconds passed, and there was a second miracle.

The man sitting in front of him eased the "glasses" off Robert's head. There was a smile on his middle-aged face. He wore a white cotton shirt. The pocket was embroidered with blue stitching: "Physician's Assistant Reed Weber." *I can see every thread of it!* He looked over the man's shoulder. The walls of the clinic were slightly out of focus. Maybe he'd have to wear glasses out-of-doors. The thought set him laughing. And then he recognized the pictures on the walls. This was not a clinic. Those wall hangings were the calligraphy that Lena had bought for their house in Palo Alto. *Where am I?*

There was a fireplace; there were sliding glass doors that opened onto a lawn. Not a book in sight; this was no place he had ever lived. The numbness in his shoulders was almost gone. Robert looked around the room. The two female voices—they weren't attached to anything visible. But Reed Weber wasn't the only person in sight. A heavyset fellow stood on his left, arms akimbo, a broad smile on his face. Robert's look caught his, and the smile faltered. The man gave him a nod and said, "Dad."

". . . Bob." It wasn't so much that memory suddenly returned as that he noticed a fact that had been there all along. Bobby had grown up.

"I'll talk to you later, Dad. For now I'll let you wrap things up with Dr. Aquino and her people." He nodded at the thin air by Robert's right shoulder—and left the room.

The thin air said, "Actually, Robert, that's about all we intended to do today. You have a lot to do over the next few weeks, but it will be less chaotic if we take things one step at a time. We'll be keeping watch for any problems."

Robert pretended to see something in the air. "Right. See you around."

He heard friendly laughter. "Quite right! Reed can help you with that."

Reed Weber nodded, and now Robert had the feeling that he and Weber were truly alone in the room. The physician's assistant packed away the glasses, and various other pieces of loose equipment. Most were plain plastic boxes, prosaic throwaways except for the miracles they had made. Weber noticed his look, and smiled. "Just tools of the trade, the humdrum ones. It's the meds and machines that are floating around inside you that are really interesting." He stowed the last of the bricklike objects and looked up. "You're a very lucky guy, do you know that?"

I am in daylight now, where before it was night since forever. I wonder where Lena is? Then he thought about the other's question. "How do you mean?"

"You picked all the right diseases!" He laughed. "Modern medicine is kind of like a minefield made in heaven. We can cure a lot of things: Alzheimer's, even though you almost missed the boat there. You and I both had Alzheimer's; I had the normal kind, cured at earliest onset. Lots of other things are just as fatal or crippling as ever. We still can't do much with strokes. Some cancers can't be cured. There are forms of osteoporosis that are as gruesome as ever. But all your major infirmities are things we have slam-dunk fixes for. Your bones are as good as a fifty-year-old's now. Today we did your eyes. In a week or so we'll start reinforcing your peripheral nervous system." Reed laughed. "You know, you've even got the skin and fat biochemistry that responds to Venn-Kurasawa treatments. It's not one person in a thousand who steps on that heavenly landmine; you're even going to *look* a lot younger."

"Next you'll have me playing video games."

"Ah!" Weber reached into his equipment bag and pulled out a slip of paper. "We can't forget that."

Robert took the paper and unfolded it all the way. It was really quite large, almost the size of foolscap. This appeared to be letterhead stationery. At the top was a logo, and in a fancy font the words "Crick's Clinic, Geriatrics Division." The rest was some kind of outline, the main categories being: "Microsoft Family," "Great Wall Linux," and "Epiphany Lite."

"Eventually you'll want to use 'Epiphany Lite,' but in the meantime, just touch the computer type you're most familiar with."

The items listed under "Microsoft Family" were the brand names of Microsoft systems all the way back to the 1980s. Robert stared uncertainly.

"Robert? You—you do know about computers, right?"

"Yes." The memory was there, now that he thought about it. He grinned. "But I was always the last to get on board. I got my first PC in 2000." And that was because the rest of the English Department was brutalizing him for not reading his email.

"Whew. Okay, you can imitate any of those old styles with that. Just lay it out flat on the arm of your chair. Your son has this room set to play the audio, but most places you'll have to keep your fingers touching the page if you want to hear output." Robert leaned forward to get a close view of the paper. It didn't glow; it didn't even have the glassy appearance of a computer display. It was just plain, high-quality paper. Reed pointed at the outline items. "Now press the menu option that corresponds to your favorite system."

Robert shrugged. Over the years, the department had upgraded through a number of systems, but—he pressed his finger to the line of text that said "WinME." There was no pause, none of the boot-up delays he recalled. But suddenly a familiar and annoying musical jingle was in the air. It seemed to come from all around, not from the piece of paper. Now the page was full of color and icons. Robert was filled with nostalgia, remembering many frustrating hours spent in front of glowing computer screens.

Reed grinned. "A good choice. WinME has been a simple rental for a long time. If you picked Epiphany, we'd be whacking through their licensing jungle. . . . Okay, now the rest should be almost exactly what you know. Crick's Clinic even has some of the modern services filtered down so they look like browser sites. This isn't quite as good as what your son and I use, but you won't have any more trouble with 'invisible voices'; you'll see Rachel and Dr. Aquino on the page here, if you want. Be cool, Robert."

Robert listened to Weber's mix of probably dated slang and tech talk, to the joviality and the phrase structures that might suggest sarcasm. Once upon a time, all that would have been enough for Robert to calibrate this fellow. Today, just out of the murk of senility, he couldn't be sure. So he probed a little. "I'm all young again?"

Reed sat back, and gave an easy laugh. "Wish I could tell you that, Robert. You're seventy-five years old, and there are a lot more ways for the body to break down than the MDs have even imagined. But I've been on your case for six months. You've come back from the dead, man. You've almost got the Alzheimer's licked. It makes sense to try these other treatments on you now. You're going to have some surprises, mostly for the good. Just take it easy, roll with the punches. For instance, I noticed that you recognized your son just now."

"Y-Yes."

"I was here just a week ago. You didn't recognize him then."

It was strange to poke into that dimness, but . . . "Yes. I knew I couldn't have a son. I wasn't old enough. I just wanted to go home, I mean to my parents' home in Bishop. And even now, I was surprised to see that Bob is so old." Consequences were crashing down upon him. "So my parents are dead—"

Reed nodded. "I'm afraid so, Robert. There's a whole lifetime that you're going to start remembering."

"As a patchwork? Or oldest memories first? Or maybe I'll get stuck at some point—"

"The MDs can give you the best answers on that." Reed hesitated. "Look, Robert. You used to be a professor, right?"

I was a poet! But he didn't think Reed would appreciate which was the more valued rank. "Yes. Professor—well, Professor Emeritus—of English. At Stanford."

"Okay then. You were a smart guy. You have a lot to learn, but I'm betting you'll get those smarts back. Don't panic if you can't remember something. Don't push too hard, either. Practically every day the docs are going to restore some additional capability. The theory is that this will be less disturbing for you. Whether that's right or wrong won't matter if you keep cool. Remember you have a whole loving family here."

Lena. Robert lowered his head for a moment. Not a return to childhood, but a kind of second chance. If he could come all the way back from the Alzheimer's, if, if . . . then he might have another twenty years left, time to make up for what he had lost. So two goals: his poetry, and . . . "Lena."

Reed leaned closer. "What did you say, sir?"

Robert looked up. "My wife. I mean my ex-wife." He tried to remember more. "I bet I'll never remember what happened after I lost my marbles."

"Like I say, don't worry about it."

"I remember being married to Lena and raising Bobby. We split up years ago. But then . . . I also remember her being with me when the Alzheimer's really started to shut me down. And now she's gone again. Where is she, Reed?"

Reed frowned, then leaned forward and zipped up his equipment case. "I'm sorry, Robert. She passed away two years ago." He stood and gave Robert a gentle pat on the shoulder. "You know, I think we've made really good progress today. Now I've got to run."

O

IN HIS FORMER life, Robert Gu had paid even less attention to technology than he had to current events. Human nature doesn't change, and as a poet his job was to distill and display that unchanging essence. Now . . . well, *I'm back from the dead!* That *was* something new under the sun, a bit of technology somewhat too large to ignore. It was a new chance at life, a chance to continue his career. And where he should continue his art was obvious: with *Secrets of the Ages*. He had spent five years on the cantos of that sequence, poems such as "Secrets of the Child," "Secrets of the Young Lovers," "Secrets of the Old." But his "Secrets of the Dying" had been an arrant fake, written before he really started to die—no matter that people seemed to think it was the most profound canto of the sequence. But now . . . yes, something new: "Secrets of the One Who Came Back." The ideas were coming and surely verse would follow.

Every day there were new changes in himself, and old barriers suddenly removed. He could easily accept Reed Weber's advice to be patient with his limitations. So much was changing and all for the better. One day he was walking again, even if it was a lurching, unstable gait. He fell three times that first day, and each time, he just bounced back to his feet. "Unless you fall on your head, Professor, you'll be fine," Reed said. But his walking got steadily better. And now that he could see—really *see*—he could do things with his hands. No more pawing around in the dark. He had never realized how important sight was to coordination. There are uncountable ways that things can lie and tangle and hide in three dimensions; without vision you're condemned to compromise and failure. *But not me. Not now.*

And two days after that . . .

. . . he was playing Ping-Pong with his granddaughter. He remembered the table. It was the one that he'd bought for little Bobby thirty years ago. He even remembered Bob taking it off his hands when he finally gave up his home in Palo Alto.

Today Miri was pulling her punches, lobbing the ball high and slow across the table. Robert moved back and forth. Seeing the ball was no problem, but he had to be very careful or he'd swing too high. Careful, careful went the game—until Miri had him down fifteen to eleven. And then he won five points, each stroke a kind of spastic twitch that somehow smashed the white plastic into the far edge of the table.

"Robert! You were just fooling me!" Poor, pudgy Miri raced from one corner of the table to the other, trying to keep up with him. Robert's slams had no spin, but she wasn't an expert player. Seventeen to fifteen, eighteen, nineteen. Then his powerful swings got out of tune, and he was back to being a staggering spastic. But now his granddaughter showed no mercy. She racked up six straight points—and won the game.

And then she ran around the table to hug him. "You are great! But you'll never fool me again!" It didn't do any good to tell her what Aquino had said, that the reconstruction of his nervous system would cause randomly spiky performance. He might end up with the reflexes of an athlete; more likely the endpoint would be something like average coordination.

IT WAS FUNNY, how he paid attention to the day of the week. That had stopped mattering even before he lost his marbles. But now, on the weekends, his granddaughter was around all day.

"What was Great-Aunt Cara like?" she asked him one Saturday morning.

"She was a lot like you, Miri."

The girl's smile was sudden and wide and proud. Robert had guessed that this was what she wanted to hear. *But it's true, except that Cara was never overweight.* Miri was like Cara, right in those last years of preadolescence when her hero worship for her older brother had been replaced by other concerns. If anything, Miri's personality was an exaggeration of Cara's. Miri was very bright—probably smarter than her great-aunt. And Miri was already into the extreme independence and moral certainty of the other. *I remember that persistent arrogance,* thought Robert. That had been an enormous irritation; breaking her of it had been what drove them apart.

Sometimes Miri had her little friends over. The boys and girls mixed pretty indescriminately at this age and in this era. For a few brief years they were almost matched for muscle. Miri loved to play doubles at Ping-Pong.

He had to smile at the way she bossed her friends around. She had them organized into a tournament. And though she was scrupulously honest, she played to *win.* When her side got behind, her jaw set in angry determination, and there was steel in her eyes. Afterward she was quick to acknowledge her own failures, and just as quick to critique her playmates.

Even when her friends were gone physically, they were often still around, invisible presences like Robert's doctors. Miri walked around the backyard talking and arguing with nobody—a parody of all the cellphone discourtesy that Robert remembered from his later years at Stanford.

Then there were Miri's grand silences. Those didn't match anything in his recollection of Cara. Miri would push gently back and forth on the swing that hung from the only good-sized tree in the backyard. She would do that for *hours,* speaking only occasionally—and then to the empty air. Her eyes seemed to be focused miles away. And when he asked her what she was doing, she would start and laugh and say that she was "studying." It looked much more like some kind of pernicious hypnosis to Robert Gu.

Weekdays, Miri was off at school; a limo pulled up for her every morning, always at the moment that the girl was ready to go. Bob was gone nowadays, "to be back in a week or so." Alice was home part of each day, but she was in a distinctly short-tempered mood. Sometimes he would see her at lunch; more often, his daughter-in-law was at Camp Pendleton until mid-afternoon. She was especially irritable when she came back from the base.

Except for Reed Weber's therapy sessions, Robert was left much to his own devices. He wandered around the house, found some of his old books in cardboard boxes in the basement. Those were almost the only books in the house. This family was effectively illiterate. Sure, Miri bragged that many books were visible any time you wanted to see them, but that was a half truth. The browser paper that Reed had given him could be used to find books online, but reading them on that single piece of foolscap was a tedious desecration.

It was remarkable foolscap, though. It really did support teleconferencing; Dr. Aquino and the remote therapists were not just invisible voices anymore. And the web browser was much like the ones he remembered, even though many sites couldn't be displayed properly. Google still worked. He searched for Lena Llewelyn Gu. Of course, there was plenty of information about her. Lena had been a medical doctor and rather well known in a limited, humdrum way. And yes, she had died a couple of years ago. The details were a cloud of contradiction, some agreeing with what Bob told him, some not. It was this damn Friends of Privacy. It was hard to imagine such villains, doing their best to undermine what you could find on the net. A "vandal charity" was what they called themselves.

And that eventually got him into the News of the Day. The world was as much a mess as ever. This month, it was a police action in Paraguay. The details didn't make sense. What were "moonshine fabs" and why would the U.S. want to help local cops close them down? The big picture was more familiar. The invading forces were looking for Weapons of Mass Destruction. Today they had found nuclear weapons hidden beneath an orphanage. The pictures showed slums and poor people, ragged children playing inscrutable games that somehow seemed to deny the squalor all around. There was an occasional, almost lonely-looking, soldier.

I'll bet this is where Bob is, he thought. Not for the first time—or the thousandth—he wondered how his son could have chosen such an ugly, dead-end career.

○

EVENINGS THEY HAD something like a family meal, Alice and Robert and Miri. Alice seemed happy to do the cooking, though tonight she looked like she hadn't slept for a couple of days.

Robert hung around the kitchen, watching mother and daughter slide trays from the fridge. "TV dinners, that's what we used to call this sort of thing," he said. In fact, this stuff had the appearance and texture of delicious food. It all tasted like mush to him, but Reed said that was because his taste buds were ninety-five percent dead.

Miri hesitated the way she often did when Robert tossed out some idea she hadn't heard before. But as usual, her response was full of confidence. "Oh, these are much better than TV junk food. We can mix and match the parts." She pointed at the unmarked containers sizzling in—well, it looked like a microwave. "See, I got the ice-cream dessert and Alice got . . . angel-hair blueberries. Wow, Alice!"

Alice gave her a brief smile. "I'll share. Okay, let's get this into the dining room."

It took all three of them to carry everything, but no second trip was needed. They set the food on the long dining table. The tablecloth was an intricate damask that seemed to be different every night. The table itself was familiar, another hand-me-down. Lena's presence was still everywhere.

Robert sat down beside Miri. "You know," he said, more to probe reactions than anything else. "This all seems a bit primitive to me. Where are the robot servants—or even the little automatic hands to put the TV dinners in the 'wave and take them out?"

His daughter-in-law gave an irritated shrug. "Where it makes sense, we have robots."

Robert remembered Alice Gong when she had married Bob. Back then, Alice had been an impenetrable diplomat—so smooth that most people never realized her skill. In those days, he had still had his edge both with verse and with people; he took such a personality as a challenge. And yet, his former self had never been able to find a chink in her armor. The new Alice only *imitated* the composure of the old, and with varying success. Tonight was not one of her better nights.

Robert remembered the news about Paraguay and took a stab in the dark. "Worried about Bob?"

She gave him an odd smile. "No. Bob is fine."

Miri glanced at her mother and then chirped, "Actually, if you want mechs, you should see my doll collection."

Mechs? Dolls? It was hard to dominate people when you didn't know what they were talking about. He backed up: "I mean, there are all the things that future freaks have been predicting for a hundred years and that never happened. Things such as air cars."

Miri looked up from her steaming food. At one corner of the tray there really was a bowl of ice cream. "We have air taxis. Does that count?"

"That gets partial credit." Then he surprised himself: "When can I see one?" The Robert of old would have dimissed mechanical contrivances as beneath any mature interest.

"Any time! How about after dinner?" This last question was directed at Alice as much as Robert.

That brought a more natural smile to Alice's face. "Maybe this weekend."

They ate in silence for a moment. *I wish I could taste this stuff.*

Then Alice was onto the topic she must have been saving up: "You know, Robert, I've been looking at the medics' reports on you. You're almost up to speed now. Have you considered resuming your career?"

"Why, of course. I'm thinking about it all the time. I've got new writing ideas—" He gestured expansively, and was surprised by the fear that suddenly rose in him. "Hey, don't worry, Alice. I've got my writing. I've got job offers from schools all around the country. I'll be out of your way as soon as I get my feet solidly on the ground."

Miri said, "Oh no, Robert! You can stay with us. We *like* having you here."

"But at this point don't you think you should be actively reaching out?" said Alice.

Robert looked back mildly. "How is that?"

"Well, you know that Reed Weber's last session with you is next Tuesday. I'll bet there are still new skills you'd like to master. Have you considered taking classes? Fairmont High has a number of special—"

Colonel Alice was doing pretty well, but she was handicapped by the thirteen-year-old at Robert's side. Miri piped up with "Yecco. That's our vocational track. A few old people and lots of teenage dumbheads. It's dull, dull, dull."

"Miri, there are basic skills—"

"Reed Weber has done a lot of that. And *I* can teach Robert to wear." She patted his arm. "Don't worry, Robert. Once you learn to wear, you can learn anything. Right now, you're in a trap; it's like you're seeing the world through a little hole, just whatever your naked eye sees—and what you can get from *that.*" She pointed at the magic foolscap that was tucked into his shirt pocket. "With some practice you should be able to see and hear as good as anyone."

Alice shook her head. "Miri. There are lots of people who don't use contacts and wearables."

"Yes, but they're not my grandfather." And there was that defiant little thrust of her jaw. "Robert, you should be wearing. You look silly walking around with that view-page clutched in your hand."

Alice seemed about to object more forcefully. Then she settled back, watching Miri with a neutral gaze that Robert couldn't fathom.

Miri didn't seem to notice the look. She leaned her head forward, and stuck a finger close to her right eye. "You already know about contacts, right? Wanna see one?" Her hand came away from her eye. A tiny disk sat on the tip of her middle finger. It was the size and shape of the contact lenses he had known. He hadn't expected anything more, but . . . he bent close and looked. After a moment, he realized that it was not quite a clear lens. Speckles of colored brightness swirled and gathered in it. "I'm driving it at safety max, or you wouldn't see the lights." The tiny lens became hazy, then frosty white. "Uk. It powered down. But you get the idea." She popped it back into her eye, and grinned at him. Now her right eye was fogged with an enormous cataract.

"You should get a fresh one, dear," said Alice.

"Oh no," said Miri. "Once it warms up, it'll be good for the rest of the day." And in fact the "cataract" was fading, Miri's dark brown iris showing through. "So what do you think, Robert?"

That it's a rather gross substitute for what I can do simply by reading my view-page. "That's all there is to it?"

"Um, no. I mean, we can fix you up with one of Bob's shirts and a box of contacts right away. It's learning to use them that's the trick."

Colonel Alice said, "Without some control it's like old-time television, but much more intrusive. We wouldn't want you to be hijacked, Robert. How about this: I'll get you some trainer clothes and that box of contacts that Miri mentioned. Meantime, give some thought to attending Fairmont High, okay?"

Miri leaned forward and grinned at her mother. "Betcha he's wearing inside of a week. He won't need those loser classes."

Robert smiled benignly over Miri's head.

○

IN FACT, THERE *had* been job offers. His return had percolated onto the web, and twelve schools had written him. But five were simply speaking invitations. Three were for semester artist-in-residence gigs. And the others weren't from first-rank schools. It was not exactly the welcome Robert expected for one of "the century's literary giants" (quoting the critics here).

They're afraid I'm still a vegetable.

So Robert kept the offers on ice and worked on his writing. He would show the doubters he was as sharp as ever—and in the doing, he would overleap them, to the sort of recognition he deserved.

But progress was slow on the poetry front. Progress was slow on a lot of fronts. His face actually looked young now. Reed said such complete cosmetic success was rare, that Robert was a perfect target for the "Venn-Kurasawa" process. Wonderful. But his coordination remained spastic and his joints ached all the time. Most ignominious, he still had to hike down to the john several times each night to take a leak. *That* was surely the Fates reminding him he was still an old man.

Yesterday had been Weber's last visit. The guy had a menial

mind, but it was exactly matched to the menial aid he provided. *I'll miss him, I suppose.* Not least because now there was another empty hour in every day.

And progress was especially slow on the poetry front.

For Robert, dreams had never been an important source of inspiration (though he had claimed otherwise in several well-known interviews). But wide-awake attempts at creativity were the last resort of pedestrian minds. For Robert Gu, real creativity most often came after a good night's sleep, just as he roused himself to wakefulness. That moment was such a reliable source of inspiration that when he was having problems with writing he would often go the pedestrian route in the evening, stock up his mind with the intransigencies of the moment . . . and then the next morning, drowsing, review what he knew. There in the labile freshness of new consciousness, answers would drift into view. In his years at Stanford, he'd run the phenomenon past philosophers, religionists, and the hard-science people. They'd had a hundred explanations, from Freudian psychology to quantum physics. The explanation didn't matter; "sleeping on it" worked for him.

And now, coming out of years of dementia, he still had that morning edge. But his control of the process was as erratic as ever. Some mornings, his mind was awash with ideas for "Secrets of the One Who Came Back" and his revision of "Secrets of the Dying." Yet none of these morning brainstorms contained poetical detail. He had the ideas. He had concepts down to the level of verse blocks. But he didn't have the words and phrases that made ideas into beauty. Maybe that was okay. For now. After all, making the words sing was the highest, purest talent. Didn't it make sense that such would be his very last talent to return?

In the meantime, many of his mornings were wasted on garbage insights. His subconscious had turned traitor, fascinated by *how* things worked, by technology and math. During the day, when he was surfing his view-page, he was constantly diverted by topics unrelated to any artistic concern. He had spent one whole afternoon on a "child's introduction" to finite geometry, for God's sake . . . and the big insight he wakened with the next morning had been a proof of one of the harder exercises.

Robert's day time was a grinding bore, an endless search for the right words, all the while trying to ignore the lure of his view-page. His evenings were spent putting off Miri and her attempts to stick foreign objects onto his eyeballs.

Finally, morning insight came to his rescue. Rising toward wakefulness, thinking dispassionately about his failure, he noticed the green junipers beyond his window, the yard painted in soft pastels. There was a world outside. There were a million different viewpoints there. What had he done in the past when progress hit roadblocks? *You take a break.* Do something different; almost anything. Going back to "high school" would get him out of this, get Miri out of his hair. It would certainly expose him to different, even if narrow, viewpoints.

Alice would be so pleased.

04

AN EXCELLENT AFFILIANCE

Juan Orozco liked to walk to school with the Radner twins. Fred and Jerry were a Bad Influence, but they were the best gamers Juan knew in person.

"We got a special scam for today, Juan," said Fred.

"Yeah," said Jerry, smiling the way he did when something really fun or embarrassing was on the way.

The three followed the usual path along the flood control channel. The concrete trough was dry and bone white, winding its way through the canyon behind the Mesitas subdivision. The hills above them were covered with iceplant and manzanita; ahead, there was a patch of scrub oaks. What do you expect of San Diego North County in early October?

At least in the real world.

The canyon was not a deadzone. Not at all. County Flood

Control kept the whole area improved, and the public layer was just as fine as on city streets. As they walked along, Juan gave a shrug and a twitch just so. That was enough cue for his Epiphany wearable. Its overlay imagery shifted into Hacek's *Dangerous Knowledge* world: The manzanita morphed into scaly tentacles. Now the houses that edged the canyon were large and heavily timbered, with pennants flying. High ahead was a castle, the home of Grand Duke Hwa Feen—in reality, the local kid who did the most to maintain this belief circle. Juan tricked out the twins in the leather armor of Knights Guardian.

"Hey, Jer, look." Juan radiated, and waited for the twins to slide into consensus with his view. He had been practicing a week to get these visuals in place.

Fred looked up, accepting the imagery that Juan had conjured. "That's old stuff, Juanito." He glanced at the castle on the hill. "Besides, Howie Fein is a dwit."

"Oh." Juan released the vision in an untidy cascade. The real world took back its own, first the landscape, then the sky, then the creatures and costumes. "But you liked it last week." Back when, Juan now remembered, Fred and Jerry had been maneuvering to oust the Grand Duke.

The twins looked at each other. Juan could tell they were silent messaging. "We told you today would be different. We're onto something special." They were partway through the scrub oaks now. Coming out the far side, you could see ocean haze; on a clear day—or if you used Clear Vision—you could see all the way to the ocean. On the south were more subdivisions, and a patch of green that was Fairmont High School. On the north was the most interesting place in Juan Orozco's neighborhood:

Pyramid Hill Amusement Park dominated the little valley that surrounded it. The underlying rock was more a pointy hill than a pyramid, but the park's management thought "pyramid" was the sexier adjective. Once upon a time it had been an avocado orchard, dark green trees clothing the hillsides. You could see it that way if you used the park's logo view. To the naked eye, there were still lots of trees. But there were also lawns, and real mansions, and the launch tower. Among other things. Pyramid Hill claimed to have the longest freefall ride in California.

The twins were grinning at him. Jerry waved at the hill. "How would you like to play *Cretaceous Returns,* but with real feeling?"

Pyramid Hill managers knew exactly what to charge for different levels of touchy-feely experience. The low end was pretty cheap; "real feeling" was at the top. "Ah, that's too expensive."

"Sure it is. If you pay."

"And, um, don't you have a project to set up before class?" The twins had shop class first thing in the morning.

"That's still in Vancouver," said Jerry.

"But don't worry about us." Fred looked upward, somehow prayerful and smug at the same time. " 'UP/Express will provide, and just in time.' "

"Well, okay. Just so we don't get into trouble." Getting into trouble was the major downside of hanging with the Radners. A couple of weeks earlier, the twins had shown him how to avoid a product safety recall on his new wikiBay bicycle. That had left him with a great martial-arts weapon—and a bike that was almost impossible to unfold. Ma had not been pleased.

"Hey, don't worry, Juan." The three left the edge of the flood channel and followed a narrow trail along the east edge of Pyramid Hill. This was far from any entrance, but the twins' uncle worked for County Flood Control and they had access to CFC utilities support imagery—which just now they shared with Juan. The dirt beneath their feet became faintly translucent. Fifteen feet down, Juan could see graphics representing a ten-inch runoff tunnel. Here and there were pointers to local maintenance records. Jerry and Fred had used such omniscience before and not been caught. Today they were blending it with a map of the local network nodes. The overlay view was faint violet against the sunlit day, showing communication blind spots and active high-rate links.

The two stopped at the edge of a clearing. Fred looked at Jerry. "Tsk. Flood Control should be ashamed. There's not a localizer node within thirty feet."

"Yeah, Jer. Almost anything could happen here." Without a complete localizer mesh, nodes could not know precisely where they and their neighbors were. High-rate laser comm could not be established, and low-rate sensor output was smeared across the landscape. The outside world knew only mushy vagueness about this area.

They walked into the clearing. They were deep in a network blind spot, but from here they had a naked-eye view up the hillside, to ground that must surely be within Pyramid Hill. If they continued that way, the Hill would start charging them.

But the twins were not looking at the Hill. Jerry walked to a small tree and squinted up. "In fact, this is an interesting spot. They tried to patch the coverage with an airball." He pointed into the branches and pinged. The utility view showed only a faint return, an error message. "It's almost purely net guano at this point."

Juan shrugged. "The gap will be fixed by tonight." Around twilight, when aerobots flitted around the canyons, swapping out nodes here and there.

"Well, why don't we help the county by patching things right now?" Jerry held up a thumb-sized greenish object. He handed it to Juan.

Three antenna fins sprouted from the thing's top. It was a typical ad hoc node. The dead ones were more trouble than bird poop. "You've perv'd this thing?" The node had BreakIns-R-Us written all over it, but perverting networks was harder in real life than in games. "Where did you get the access codes?"

"Uncle Don gets careless." Jerry pointed at the device. "All the permissions are loaded. Unfortunately, the bottleneck node is still alive." He pointed upward, into the sapling's branches. "You're small enough to climb this, Juan. Just go up and knock down the node."

"Hmm."

"Hey, don't worry. Homeland Security won't notice."

In fact, the Department of Homeland Security would almost certainly notice, at least after the localizer mesh was patched. But just as certainly they wouldn't care. DHS logic was deeply embedded in all hardware. "See All, Know All" was their motto, but what they knew and saw was for their own mission. They were notorious about not sharing with law enforcement. Juan stepped out of the blind spot and took a look at the Sheriff's Department view. The area around Pyramid Hill had its share of arrests, mostly for enhancement drugs . . . but there had been nothing hereabouts for several weeks.

"Okay." Juan came back to the tree and scrambled up about ten feet, to where the branches spread out. The old node was hanging from rotted Velcro. He knocked it free and the twins caused it to have an accident with a rock. Juan shinnied down from the tree. They watched the diagnostics for a moment. Violet mists sharpened into bright spots as the nodes figured out where they and their perved sibling were, and coordinated up toward full function. Now point-to-point, laser routing was available; they could see the property labels all along the boundary of Pyramid hill.

"Ha," said Fred. The twins started uphill toward the property line. "C'mon, Juan. We're marked as county employees. We'll be fine if we don't stay too long."

PYRAMID HILL HAD all the latest touchy-feely gear. These were not just phantoms painted by your contact lenses on the back of your eyeballs. On Pyramid Hill there were games where you could ride a Scoochi salsipued or steal the eggs of raptors—or games with warm furry creatures that danced playfully around, begging to be picked up and cuddled. If you turned off all the game views, you could see other players wandering through the woods in their own worlds. Somehow the Hill kept them from crashing into each other.

In *Cretaceous Returns,* the sound of the free-fall launcher was disguised as thunder. The trees were imaged as towering ginkgoes, with lots of places you couldn't see through. Juan played the pure visual *Cret Ret* a lot these days, in person with the twins, and all over the world with others. It had not been an uplifting experience. He had been "killed and eaten" three times so far this week. It was a tough game, one where you had to contribute or maybe you got killed and eaten every time. So Juan had joined the Fantasists Guild—well, as a junior wannabe member. Maybe that would make him clueful. He had already designed a species for *Cret Ret.* His saurians were quick, small things that didn't attract the fiercest of the critics. The twins had not been impressed, though they had no alternatives of their own.

As he walked through the ginkgo forest, he kept his eye out

for critters with jaws lurking in the lower branches. That's what had gotten him on Monday. On Tuesday it had been some kind of paleo disease.

So far things seemed safe enough, but there was no sign of his own contribution. They had been fast breeding and scalable, so where were the little monsters? Sigh. Sometime he should check out other game sites. They might be big in Kazakhstan. Here, today . . . nada.

Juan stumped across the Hill, a little discouraged, but still uneaten. The twins had taken the form of game-standard velociraptors. They were having a grand time. Their chicken-sized prey were Pyramid Hill game bots.

The Jerry-raptor looked over its shoulder at Juan. "Where's your critter?"

Juan had not assumed any animal form. "I'm a time traveler," he said. That was a valid type, introduced with the initial game release.

Fred flashed a face full of teeth. "I mean where are the critters you invented last week?"

"I don't know."

"Most likely they got eaten by the critics," said Jerry. The brothers did a joint reptilian chortle. "Give up on making creator points, Juan. Kick back and use the good stuff." He illustrated with a soccer kick that connected with something that scuttled across their path. That got lots of classic points and a few thrilling moments of quality carnage. Fred joined in and red splattered everywhere.

There was something familiar about this prey. It was young and clever-looking . . . a newborn from Juan's own design! And that meant its mommy would be nearby. Juan said, "You know, I don't think—"

"The Problem Is, None Of You Think Nearly Enough." The sound was premium external, like sticking your head inside an old-time boom box. Too late, they saw that the tree trunks behind them grew from yard-long claws. Mommy. Drool fell in ten-inch blobs from high above.

This was Juan's design scaled up to the max.

"Sh—" said Fred. It was his last hiss as a velociraptor. The head and teeth behind the slobber descended from the ginkgo canopy and swallowed Fred down to the tips of his hind talons. The monster crunched and munched for a moment. The clearing was filled with the sound of splintering bones.

"Ahh!" The monster opened its mouth and vomited horror. It was so good—Juan flicker-viewed on reality: Fred was standing in the steaming remains of his raptor. His shirt was pulled out of his pants, and he was drenched in slime—real, smelly slime. The kind you paid money for.

The monster itself was one of the Hill's largest mechanicals, tricked out as a member of Juan's new species.

The three of them looked up into its jaws.

"Was that touchy-feely enough for you?" the creature said, its breath a hot breeze of rotting meat. For sure it was. Fred stepped backward and almost slipped on the goo.

"The late Fred Radner just lost a cartload of points"—the monster waved its truck-sized snout at them—"and I'm still hungry. I suggest you move off the Hill with all dispatch."

They backed away, their gaze still caught on the monster's teeth. The twins turned and ran. As usual, Juan was an instant behind them. Something like a big hand grabbed him. "You, I have further business with." The words were a burred roar through clenched fangs. "Sit down. Let's chat."

¡Caray! I have the worst luck. Then he remembered that it had been Juan Orozco who had climbed a tree to perv the Hill entrance logic. Stupid Juan Orozco didn't need bad luck; he was already the perfect chump. And now the twins were gone.

But when the "jaws" set him down and he turned around, the monster was still there—not some Pyramid Hill rent-a-cop. Maybe this really was a *Cret Ret* player! He edged sideways, trying to get out from under the pendulous gaze. This was just a game. He could walk away from this four-story saurian. Of course, that would trash his credit with *Cretaceous Returns,* maybe drench him in smelly goo. And if Big Lizard took its play seriously, it might cause him trouble in other games. *Okay.* He sat down with his back to the nearest ginkgo. So he would be late another day; that couldn't make his school situation any worse.

The saurian settled back and slid the steaming corpse of Fred Radner's raptor to one side. It brought its head close to the ground, to look at Juan straight on. The eyes and head and color were exactly Juan's original design, and this player had the moves to make it truly impressive. He could see from its battle scars that it had fought in several *Cretaceous* hot spots.

Juan forced a cheerful smile. "So, you like my design?"

It flashed yard-long fangs. "I've been worse." The creature shifted game parameters, bringing up critic-layer details. This was a heavy player, maybe even a game cracker! On the ground between them was a dead and dissected example of Juan's creation. Big Lizard nudged it with a foreclaw. "But the skin texture is from a Fantasists Guild example library. The color scheme is a cliché. The plaid kilt would be cute if it weren't in all the Epiphany Now ads."

Juan drew his knees in toward his chin. This was the same crap he had to put up with at school. "I borrow from the best."

The saurian's chuckle was a buzzing roar that made Juan's skull vibrate. "That might work with your teachers. They have to eat whatever garbage you feed them—at least till you graduate and can be dumped on the street. This design is so-so. There have been some adoptions, mainly because it has good mechanics. But if we're talking real quality, it just don't measure up." The creature flexed its custom battle scars.

"I do other things."

"Yes, and if you never deliver, you'll fail with them, too."

That was a point that occupied a lot of Juan Orozco's internal worry time. More and more it looked like he was going to end up like his pa—only Juan might never even get a job to be laid off from! "Try your best" was the motto of Fairmont High. But trying your best was only the beginning. Even if you tried your best, you could still be left behind.

These were not things he'd confess to another gamer. He glared back at the slitted yellow eyes, and suddenly it occurred to him that—unlike teachers—this guy was not being paid to be nice. And it was wasting too much time for this to be some humiliating con. *It actually wants something from me!* Juan sharpened his glare. "And you have some suggestions, O Mighty Virtual Lizard?"

"That . . . could be. Besides *Cret Ret,* I have other things going. How would you like to take an affiliate status on a little project?"

Except for local games, no one had ever asked Juan to affiliate on anything. His mouth twisted in bogus contempt. "Affiliate? A percent of a percent of . . . what? How far down the value chain are you?"

The saurian shrugged and there was the sound of ginkgoes creaking against its shoulders. "My guess is I'm way, way down. That's how it is with most affiliances. But I can pay real money for each answer I pipe upward." The creature named a number; it was enough to ride the freefall every day for a year. A payoff certificate floated in the air between them, showing the named amount and a bonus schedule.

Juan had played his share of finance games. "I get twice that or no deal." Then he noticed the subrights section. The numbers were not visible. That could be because anyone he recruited would get a lot more.

"Done!" said the Lizard, before Juan could correct his bid upward.

And Juan was sure it was smiling!

". . . Okay, what do you want?" *And what makes you think a dwit like me can supply it?*

"You're at Fairmont High, aren't you?"

"You already know that."

"It's a strange place, isn't it?" When Juan did not reply, the critter said. "Trust me, it is strange. Most schools, even charter schools, don't schedule Adult Education students in with the children."

"Yeah, the vocational track. The old farts don't like it. We don't like it."

"Well, the task from my upstream affiliate is to snoop around, mainly among these old guys. Make friends with them."

Yecco. But Juan glanced at the payoff certificate again. It tested valid. The payoff adjudication was more complicated than he wanted to read, but it was backed by Bank of America. "Who in particular?"

"Ah, that's the problem. Whoever is at the top of my affiliance is coy. We're just collecting information. Basically, some of these senior citizens used to be big shots."

"If they were so big, how come they're in our classes now?" It was just the question the kids asked at school.

"Lots of reasons, Juan. Some of them are just lonely. Some of them are up to their ears in debt, and have to figure how to make a living in the current economy. Some of them aren't good for much but a healthy body and lots of old memories. They can be very bitter."

"Unh, how do I make friends with people like that?"

"If you want the money, you figure out a way. Anyway, here are the search criteria." The Big Lizard shipped him a document. He browsed through the top layer.

"This covers a lot of ground." Retired San Diego politicians, bioscientists, parents of persons currently in such job categories. . . .

"There are qualifying characteristics in the links. Your job is to interest appropriate people in my affiliance."

"I . . . I'm just not that good at talking people up." Especially people like this.

"Stay poor then. Chicken."

Juan was silent for a moment. His pa would never take a job like this. Finally, he said, "Okay, I'll go affiliate with you."

"I wouldn't want you doing anything you feel un—"

"I *said,* I'll take the job!"

"Okay! Well then, what I've given you should get you started. There's contact info in the document." The creature lumbered to its feet, and now its voice came from high above. "Just as well we don't meet again on Pyramid Hill."

"Suits me." Juan stood up. He made a point of slapping the creature's mighty tail as he walked off downhill.

THE TWINS WERE way ahead of him, standing by the soccer field on the other side of campus. As Juan came up the driveway, he grabbed a viewpoint in the bleachers and gave them a ping. Fred waved back, but his shirt was still too gooey for comm. Jerry was looking upward at the UP/Ex shipment falling toward his outstretched hands. Just in time, for sure. The twins were popping the mailer open even as they walked into the shop tent.

Unfortunately, Juan's first class was at the end of the far wing. He ran across the lawn, keeping his vision tied to unimproved reality: The buildings were mostly three stories today. Their gray walls were like playing cards stacked in a rickety array.

Inside, the choice of view was not entirely his own. Mornings, the school administration required that the Fairmont News show all over the interior walls. Three kids at Hoover High had won IBM career fellowships. Applause, applause, even if Hoover was Fairmont's unfairly advantaged rival, a charter school run by the Math Ed Department at SDSU. The three young geniuses would have their college education paid for, right through grad school, even if they never worked a day at IBM. *Big deal,* Juan thought, trying to comfort himself. Someday those kids might be very rich, but a percentage of their professional fortunes would always go back to IBM.

He followed the little green nav arrows with half his attention . . . and abruptly realized he had climbed two flights of stairs. School admin had rearranged everything since yesterday. Of course, they had updated his nav arrows, too. It was a good thing he hadn't been paying attention.

He slipped into his classroom and sat down.

○

MS. CHUMLIG HAD already started.

Search and Analysis was Chumlig's main thing. She used to teach a fast-track version of this at Hoover High, but well-documented rumor held that she just couldn't keep up. So the Department of Education had moved her to the same-named course here at Fairmont. Actually, Juan kind of liked her. She was a failure, too.

"There are many different skills," she was saying. "Sometimes it's best to coordinate with lots of other people who together can make the answers." The students nodded. Be a coordinator. That's where the biggest and most famous money was. But they also knew where Chumlig was going with this. She looked around the classroom, nodding that she knew they knew. "Alas, you all intend to be top agents, don't you?"

"It's what some of us will be." That was one of the Adult Ed students. Winston Blount was old enough to be Juan's great-grandfather. When Blount had a bad day he liked to liven things up by harassing Ms. Chumlig.

The Search and Analysis instructor smiled back. "It's about as likely as being a major league baseball star. The pure 'coordinating agent' is a rare type, Dean Blount."

"Some of us must be the administrators."

"Oh." Chumlig looked kind of sad for a moment, like she was figuring out how to pass on bad news. "Administration has changed a lot, Dean Blount."

Winston Blount sat back in his chair. "Okay. So we have to learn some new tricks."

"Yes." Ms. Chumlig looked out over the class. "That's an important point. This class is about search and analysis, the heart of the economy. We obviously need search and analysis as consumers. In almost all modern jobs, search and analysis are how we make our living. But, in the end, we must also know something about something."

"Meaning those courses we got C's in, right?" That was a voice from the peanut gallery, probably someone who was physically truant.

Chumlig sighed. "Yes. Don't let those skills die. You've been exposed to them. Use them. Improve on them. You can do it with a special form of preanalysis that I call 'study.' "

One of the students actually held up a hand. She was that old.

"Yes, Dr. Xiang?"

"I know you are correct. But—" The woman glanced around the room. She looked about Chumlig's age, not nearly as old as Winston Blount. But there was kind of a frightened look in her eyes. "But some people are better than others. I'm not as sharp as I once was. Or maybe others are just sharper. . . . What happens if we try our hardest, and it just isn't good enough?"

Chumlig hesitated. *How will she answer this!* thought Juan. It was the real question. "That's a problem that affects everyone, Dr. Xiang. Providence gives each of us our hand to play. In your case, you've got a new deal and a new start on life." Her look took in the rest of the class. "Some of you think your hand in life is all deuces and treys." At the front of the room were some really dedicated students, not much older than Juan. They were wearing, but they had no clothes sense and had never learned ensemble coding. As Chumlig spoke, you could see their fingers tapping away, searching on "deuces" and "treys."

"But I have a theory of life," said Chumlig, "and it is straight out of gaming: *There is always an angle.* You, each of you, have some special wild cards. Play with them. Find out what makes you different and better. Because it is there, if only you can find it. And once you do, you'll be able to contribute answers to others and others will be willing to contribute back to you. In short, synthetic serendipity doesn't just happen. By golly, *you* must create it."

She hesitated, staring at invisible class notes, and her voice dropped down from oratory. "So much for the big picture. Today, we're going to talk about morphing answerboard solutions. As usual, we're looking to ask the right questions."

O

JUAN LIKED TO sit by the outer wall, especially when the classroom was on the third floor. You could feel the wall sway gently back and forth as the building kept its balance. That sort of thing made his ma real nervous. "One second of system failure and everything will fall apart!" she had complained at a PTA meeting. On the other hand, house-of-cards construction was cheap—and it could handle a big earthquake almost as easily as it did the morning breeze.

He leaned away from the wall and listened to Chumlig. That was why the school made you show up in person for most classes; you had to pay a little bit of attention just because you were trapped in a real room with a real instructor. Chumlig's lecture graphics floated in the air above them. She had the class's attention; there was a minimum of insolent graffiti nibbling at the edges of her imagery.

And for a while, Juan paid attention, too. He really did. Answerboards could generate solid results, usually for zero cost. There was no affiliation, just kindred minds batting problems around. But what if you weren't a kindred mind? Say you were on a genetics board. If you thought transcription was a type of translation, it could take you months to get anywhere.

So Juan tuned her out and wandered from viewpoint to viewpoint around the room. Some were from students who'd set their viewpoints public. Most were just random cams. He browsed Big Lizard's task document as he paused between hops. In fact, the Lizard was interested in more than just the old farts. Some ordinary students made the list, too. This affiliance must be as wide as the California Lottery.

He started some background checks. Like most kids, he kept lots of stuff saved on his wearable. He could run a search like this very close to his vest. He didn't route to the outside world except when he could use a site that Chumlig was talking about. She was real good at nailing the mentally truant. But Juan was good at ensemble coding, driving his wearable with little gesture cues and eye-pointer menus. As her gaze passed over him, he nodded brightly and replayed the last few seconds of her talk.

As for the old students . . . competent retreads would never be here; they'd be rich and famous, the people who owned most of the real world. The ones in Adult Education were the has-beens. These people trickled into Fairmont all through the semester. The oldfolks hospitals refused to batch them up for the beginning of classes. They claimed that senior citizens were "socially mature," able to handle the jumble of a midsemester entrance.

Juan went from face to face, matching against public records: Winston Blount. The guy was a saggy mess. Retread medicine was such a crapshoot. Some things it could cure, others it couldn't. And what worked was different from person to person. Winston Blount had not been a total winner.

Just now the old guy was squinting intensely, trying to follow Chumlig's answerboard example. He had been in several of Juan's classes. Juan couldn't see the guy's med records, but he guessed that his mind was mostly okay; he was as sharp as some of the kids in class. And once upon a time he had been an important player at UCSD. Once upon a time.

Okay, put him on the "of interest" list.

And then there was Xiu Xiang. PhD physics, PhD electrical engineering; 2010 Winner of the President's Medal for Secure Computation. Overall the hotstuff index on her was almost Nobel-quality. Dr. Xiang sat hunched over, looking at the table in front of her. She was trying to keep up on a *view-page!* Poor lady. But for sure she would have connections.

Chumlig was still going on about how to morph results into new questions, oblivious of Juan's truancy.

Who's next? Robert Gu. For a moment, Juan thought he had the wrong viewpoint. He sneaked a glance to his right, toward where the Adult Education crocks hung out. Robert Gu, PhD literature. A poet. He was sitting with the crocks, but he looked about seventeen years old! Juan brought his apparent attention back to Ms. Chumlig and inspected the new arrival close up. Gu was slender, almost scrawny, and tall. His skin was smooth and unblemished. But he looked like he was sweating. Juan risked a peek at outside medical references. *Aha!* Symptoms of the Venn-Kurasawa treatment. Dr. Robert Gu was a lucky man, the one in a thousand who fully responded to that piece of retread magic. On the other hand, it looked to Juan like the guy had run out of luck after that. He was fully unpingable. There was a crumpled piece of view-page on his desk, but he wasn't using it. Years ago, this guy had been more famous than Xiu Xiang, but he was an even bigger loser now. . . . What was "Deconstructive Revisionism" anyway? Oh. Definitely not something on the Big Lizard's list. Juan slid the name into the trashcan. But wait, he hadn't checked out Gu's family connections. He queried—and suddenly there was silent messaging hanging in letters of silent flame all across his vision:

Chumlig --> Orozco: <sm>You have all day to play games, Juan! If you won't pay attention here, you can darn well take this course over.</sm>

Orozco --> Chumlig: <sm>Sorry. Sorry!</sm> He suspended his question queue and dropped the external session. At the same time, he played back the last few minutes of her talk, desperately trying to summarize. Most times, Chumlig just asked embarrassing questions; this was the first she'd sminged him with a threat.

And the amazing thing was, she'd done it in a short pause,

when everyone else thought she was just looking at her notes. Juan eyed her with new respect.

O

"YOU WERE A little hard on the boy, don't you think?" Rabbit was trying out new imagery today, this based on classic *Alice in Wonderland* illustrations, complete with engraving lines. The effect was fully silly on a three-dimensional body.

Big Lizard did not seem impressed. "You don't belong down here. Juan is my direct affiliate, not yours."

"A bit overly sensitive, aren't you? I'm simply spot-checking the depths of my affiliance."

"Well, stay out. Juan needs this class."

"Of course I share your charitable motives." The rabbit gave the lizard his most dishonest leer. "But you cut him off just when he was looking at someone especially interesting to me. I have provided you with a most excellent affiliance. If you want my continued support, you must cooperate."

"Listen you! I want the boy to reach out for himself, but I don't want him to be hurt." Lizard's voice trailed off, and Rabbit wondered if Chumlig was finally having second thoughts. Not that it mattered. Rabbit was having fun, spreading out across the Southern California social scene. Sooner or later, he would figure out what this job was all about.

05

DR. XIANG'S SHE

Shop class. It was by far Juan Orozco's favorite class. Shop was like a premium game; there were real gadgets to touch and connect. That was the sort of thing you paid money for up on Pyramid Hill. And Mr. Williams was no Louise Chumlig. He let you follow your own inclinations, but he never came around afterward and complained because you hadn't accomplished anything. It was almost impossible not to get an A in Ron Williams's classes; he was wonderfully old-fashioned.

Shop class was also Juan's best opportunity to make progess on Big Lizard's project, at least with the old farts and the do-not-call privacy freaks. He wandered around the big gadget tent looking like an utter idiot. Juan had never been any good at diplomacy games. And now he was schmoozing oldsters. Well, trying to.

Xiu Xiang was really a nice lady, but she just sat at the equipment bench and read from her view-page. She had the parts list formatted like some kind of hardcopy catalog. "Once I knew these things," she said. "See that." She pointed at a section in the museum pages: *Xiang's Secure Hardware Environment.* "I designed that system."

Juan came up with "You're world-class, Dr. Xiang."

"But . . . I don't understand even the principles of these new components. They look more like pond scum than self-respecting optical semiconductors." She read one of the product descriptions, stopped at the third line. "What's redundant entanglement?"

"Ah." He looked it up, saw pointers into jungles of background concepts. "You don't need to know about 'redundant entanglement,' ma'am. Not for this class." He waved at the product descriptions on Xiang's view-page. The image sat like carven stone, not responding to his gesture. "Go forward a few pages, you'll find the stuff we have available here in class. Look under"—jeez this was a pain, spelling out navigation in words—"look under 'fun functional compositions,' and go from there." He showed her how to use her view-page to ID local parts. "You don't need to understand everything."

"Oh." In a few moments she was playing with the possibilities, had downloaded half a dozen component gadgets. "This is like being a child. Doing, without understanding." But then she started putting BuildIt parts together, doing pretty well after Juan showed her how to find the interface specs. She laughed at some of the descriptions. "Sorters and shifters. Solid-state robots. I bet I could make a cutter out of this."

"I don't see it." Cutter? "Don't worry, you can't hurt anything." That wasn't quite true, but close enough. He sat and watched, made a few suggestions, even though he wasn't really sure what she was up to. Enough of establishing rapport; he marked that box in his diplomacy checklist and moved on to the next stage. "So, Dr. Xiang, do you keep in touch with your friends at Intel?"

"That was a long time ago. I retired in 2010. And during the war, I couldn't even get consulting jobs. I could just feel my skills rusting out."

"Alzheimer's?" He knew she was *much* older than she looked, even older than Winston Blount.

Xiang hesitated, and for a moment Juan was afraid he had made the lady really angry. But then she gave a sad little laugh. "No Alzheimer's, no dementia. You—people nowadays don't know what it was like to be old."

"I do so! All my grandparents are still alive. And I have a great-grandpa in Puebla. He plays a lot of golf. Great-Grandma, she does have dementia—you know, a kind they still can't fix." In fact, Great-Grandma had looked as young as Dr. Xiang. Everyone thought she had really lucked out. But in the end that only meant she lived long enough to run into something they *couldn't* cure.

Dr. Xiang just shook her head. "Even in my day, not everyone went senile, not the way you mean. I just got behind in my skills. My girlfriend died. After a while I just didn't care too much. I didn't have the energy to care." She looked at the gadget she was building. "Now, I have at least the energy I had when I was sixty. Maybe I even have the same native intelligence." She slapped the table. "And all I'm good for is playing with jacked-up Lego blocks!"

It almost looked like she was going to start crying, right in the middle of shop class. Juan scanned around; no one seemed to be watching. He reached out to touch Xiang's hand. He didn't have the answer. Ms. Chumlig would say he didn't have the right question.

O

THERE WERE STILL a few others to check out: Winston Blount, for instance. Not a jackpot case, but he ought to be worth something to the Lizard. In shop class, Blount just sat in the shade of the tent, staring off into space. The guy was wearing, but he didn't respond to messages. Juan waited until Williams went off for one of his coffee breaks. Then he sidled over and sat beside Blount. Jeez, the guy really *looked* old. Juan couldn't tell exactly where he was surfing, but it had nothing to do with shop class. Juan had noticed that when Blount wasn't interested in a class, he just blew it off. After a few minutes' silence, Juan realized that he wasn't interested in socializing either.

So talk to him! It's just another kind of monster whacking. Juan morphed a buffoon image onto the guy, and suddenly it wasn't so hard to cold-start the encounter. "So, Dean Blount, what do you think of shop class?"

Ancient eyes turned to look at him. "I couldn't care less, Mr. Orozco."

O-*kay!* Hmm. There was lots about Winston Blount that was public record, even some legacy newsgroup correspondence. That was always good for getting a grown-up's, um, attention.

Fortunately, Blount continued talking on his own. "I'm not like some of the people here. I've never been senile. By rights, I shouldn't be here."

"By rights?" Maybe he could score points just by imitating an old-time shrink program.

"Yes. I was Dean of Arts and Letters through 2012. I was on track to be UCSD Chancellor. Instead I was pushed into academic retirement."

Juan knew all that. "But you . . . you never learned to wear."

Blount's eyes narrowed. "I made it a point never to wear. I thought wearing was a demeaning fad." He shrugged. "I was wrong. I paid a heavy price for that. But things have changed." His eyes glittered with deliberate iridescence. "I've taken four semesters of this 'Adult Education.' Now my résumé is out there in the ether."

"You must know a lot of important people."

"Indeed. Success is just a matter of time."

"Y-You know, Dean, I may be able to help. No wait—I don't mean by myself. I have an affiliance you might be interested in."

"Oh?"

He seemed to know what affiliance was. Juan explained Big Lizard's deal. "So there could be some real money in this." He showed him the payoff certificates, and wondered what amount his recruit would see there.

Blount squinted his eyes, no doubt trying to parse the certificates into a form that Bank of America could validate. After a moment he nodded, without granting Juan numerical enlightenment. "But money isn't everything, especially in my situation."

"Well, um, I bet whoever's behind these certs would have a lot of angles. Maybe you could get a conversion to help-in-kind. I mean, to something *you* need."

"True." They talked a few minutes, till the place got busy. Some of the shop projects were finally showing results. At least two teams had made mobile nodes, swarm devices. Tiny paper wings fluttered all around. The other swarmer crawled in the grass and up the legs of the furniture and chairs. It stayed out of clothes, but it was awfully close to being intrusive. Juan zapped a few of them, but the others kept coming.

Orozco --> Blount: <sm>Can you read me?</sm>

"Of course I can," replied the old man.

So despite Blount's claims of withittude, he couldn't manage silent messaging, not even the finger tapping most grown-ups used.

The class period was almost over anyway. Juan looked up at the billowing tent fabric. He was a little discouraged. He had covered almost everyone on the list, and Winston Blount was the best he'd found: someone who couldn't even sming. "Okay. Well, keep my offer in mind, Dean Blount. And remember, there are only a limited number of people I'm allowed to take in." Blount rewarded this sales jabber with a thin smile. "Meantime, I-I have other possibilities." Juan nodded in the direction of the weird new guy, Robert Gu.

Winston Blount didn't follow Juan's gaze, but you could tell he was sneaking a peek sideways. For a moment the skin on his face seemed to tighten. Then the smile returned. "May God have mercy on your soul, Mr. Orozco."

○

JUAN DIDN'T GET his chance at Robert Gu till Friday, right after Ms. Chumlig's *other* class. Creative Composition was almost always the low point of Juan's school week. Chumlig was flexible as to media, but students had to stand up and perform their own work. That was bad enough when you had to watch some other kid mess up, but unbearable when *you* were the performer. Order of appearance was decided at Ms. Chumlig's whim. Normally worrying about that would have occupied most of Juan's attention. Today, he had other concerns that mercifully blotted out the usual panic.

Juan skulked to the back of the class and slumped down, covertly watching the others. Winston Blount was here, which was a surprise. He blew off this class almost as often as he did shop. *But he took me up on my offer.* The Lizard's account showed that the old man had taken his first step toward signing on.

On the far side of the room, Robert Gu was surfing with his view-page. Even that looked like a struggle for the guy. But it turned out that Gu was part of a particular Marine Corps family—and when Juan had reviewed all of the affiliation instructions he had found that *that* was a big plus. If he could just interest Robert Gu in affiliation, he'd hit the top bonus level.

Chumlig's voice cut across his thought. "No volunteers for first up? Well—" she looked off into the air, and then turned to Juan.

¡Caray!

06

SO MUCH TECHNOLOGY, SO LITTLE TALENT

Chumlig's "Creative Composition" class was shaping up to be the low point of Robert Gu's first week at Fairmont High. Robert remembered his own high-school years very well. In 1965, school had been easy, except for math and science, which he didn't care about anyway. Basically, he never did homework in anything. But the poems he wrote, almost without conscious effort, were already in a different world from what his poor teachers normally encountered. They considered themselves blessed to be in his presence—and rightly so.

But in this brave new world he could see only a fraction of the "compositions" the students allegedly created, and he had no doubt they could appreciate very little about his work.

Robert sat at the edge of the class, doodling on his view-page. As usual, the children were on the left side of the room, and the Adult Ed students were on the right. Losers. He had learned a few names, even talked to the Xiang woman. She said she was going to have to drop Chumlig's composition class. She just didn't have the courage to perform in front of others. The only talent she had was in obsolete engineering, but at least she was smart enough to know she was a loser. Not like Winston Blount, the biggest loser of all. Occasionally he caught Winnie looking his way, and Robert would smile to himself.

At the front of the class, Ms. Chumlig was coaxing today's first performer. "I know you've been practicing, Juan. Show us what you can do."

"Juan" stood and walked to center stage. This was the kid who had been chatting up the Adult Ed students in shop class. Robert remembered his earnest sales-rep behavior. At a guess, the boy was on the low side of average, the kind that high schools of Robert's time graduated pro forma. But here, in the twenty-first century, incompetence was no excuse: Chumlig seemed to have serious expectations. The boy hesitated and then began waving his arms. Without any visible effect. "I don' know, Ms. Chumlig, it's still not, um, fully ready."

Ms. Chumlig just nodded patiently, and gestured for him to continue.

"Okay." The boy squinted his eyes and his armwaving became even more chaotic. It wasn't dance, and the boy wasn't speaking. But Chumlig leaned back against her desk, and nodded. Much of the class watched the random mime with similar attention, and Robert noticed that they were nodding their heads as if in time to music.

Crap. More invisible nonsense. Robert looked down at his magic foolscap and played with the local browser selections. Internet Explorer was much as he remembered, but there were dropdowns that allowed him to "Select View." Yes, the fantasy overlays. He tapped on "Juan Orozco Performs." The first overlay looked like graffiti, rude commentary on Juan's performance. It was the sort of thing you might see on a note passed furtively from child to child. He tapped the second view selection. Ah. Here the boy stood on a concert stage. The classroom windows behind him opened onto a vast city as seen from a high tower. Robert held his hand along the margin of the page, and there was sound. It was tinny and faint compared with the room audio back in the house, but . . . yes, it was music. It was almost Wagner, but then it rambled off into something that might have been a marching song. In the window on Robert's view-page, rainbows formed around the boy's image. Fluffy white—*ferrets?*—hopped into existence at every jerk of his hands. Now all the other kids were laughing. Juan was laughing too, but his handwaving became desperate. Ferrets covered the floor, shoulder-to-shoulder, and the music was frenetic. The creatures misted together into snow and lifted on miniature tornadoes. The boy slowed his rhythm, and the sound became something like lullaby music. The snow glistened, sublimating into invisibility as the music faded. And now Robert's browser window showed the same unmagical child who stood in reality at the front of the room.

Juan's peers applauded politely. One or two yawned.

"Very good, Juan!" said Ms. Chumlig.

It was as impressive as any advertising video that Robert had seen in the twentieth century. At the same time it was essentially incoherent, a garbage dump of special effects. So much technology, so little talent.

Chumlig talked the class through the components of Orozco's effort, gently asking the boy where he was going to take his work, suggesting that he collaborate (collaborate!) with other students in putting words to the composition.

Robert looked surreptitiously about the room. The windows were opened onto the brown and sere hillsides of North County autumn. Out there, sunlight was everywhere, and a slow breeze brought in the smell of honeysuckle. He could hear kids playing on the far side of the lawn. Inside, the classroom was a cheap plastic construction, utterly without esthetic sensibility. Yes, school was easy, but it could also be mind-numbingly boring; he'd have to reread his own poems about that. The forced confinement. The endless days of sitting still and listening to witless talk, while the whole world waited outside.

Most of the students were actually looking in Chumlig's general direction. Was that just an artful scam? But when the woman asked a random child a snap question, she got relevant—if halting—answers.

And then, much sooner than he had imagined:

". . . quitting early today, so we have time for only one more presentation," said Ms. Chumlig. *What has she been saying? Damn.* Chumlig was looking directly at him now. "Please show us your composition, Professor Gu."

JUAN SLUNK BACK to his seat, barely listening to Chumlig's analysis. She was always gentle in these public critiques, but the bad news was obvious all around him. Only the Radner twins had posted something nice. Someone who looked like a rabbit was grinning at him from the peanut gallery. *Who was that?* He turned and plunked himself down in his chair.

". . . so we have time for only one more presentation," finished Ms. Chumlig. "Please show us your composition, Professor Gu."

Juan looked back at where Gu was sitting. What sort of presentation could he make?

Robert Gu seemed to wonder the same thing: "I really don't have anything that the class would . . . appreciate. I don't do audiovisuals."

Chumlig smiled brightly. When she smiled like that at Juan, he knew his excuses would count for nothing. "Nonsense, Professor Gu. You were—you are a poet."

"Indeed."

"And I made an assignment."

Gu looked young, but when he cocked his head and eyed Ms. Chumlig, there was such power in his gaze. *Jeez, if only I could look like that when Chumlig has me on the hot seat.* The young-old man was silent for a second, and then he said calmly. "I have written a short piece, but as I said it has none of—" his gaze swept the class, nailing Juan for an instant "—the pictures and sound that seem expected."

Ms. Chumlig gestured him forward. "Your words will do splendidly today. Please. Come down."

After a second, Gu stood and came down the steps. He moved fast, with kind of a spastic lurch. Gossipy notes flew back and forth. For the moment, the class's attention was focused like Ms. Chumlig always wanted.

Chumlig stepped out of his way, and Robert Gu turned to face the class. Of course, he couldn't call a up word display. But he didn't look at his view-page either. He just looked at the class and said, "A poem. Three hundred words. I tell you about the land of North County as it really is, here and beyond." His arm twitched outward, toward the open windows.

Then he just . . . talked. No special effects, no words scrolling through the air. And it couldn't really be a poem since his voice didn't get all singsong. Robert Gu just talked about the lawn that circled the school, the tiny mowers that circled and circled across it. The smell of the grass, and how it squeezed down moist in the morning. How the slope of the hills took running feet to the creek brush that edged the property. It was what you saw here every day—at least when you weren't using overlays to see somewhere else.

And then Juan wasn't really aware of the words anymore. He was *seeing*; he was there. His mind floated above the little valley, scooted up the creek bed, had almost reached the foot of Pyramid Hill . . . when suddenly Robert Gu stopped talking, and Juan was dumped back into the reality of his place at the rear end of Ms. Chumlig's composition class. He sat for a few seconds, dazed. Words. That's all they were. But what they did was more than visuals. It was more than haptics. There had even been the smell of the dry reeds along the creek bed.

For a moment no one said anything. Ms. Chumlig looked glassy-eyed. Either she was very impressed or she was surfing.

But then a classic Pompous Bird flew up from the old farts' side of the room. It swooped across the room to drop a huge load of wet birdshit on Robert Gu. Fred and Jer burst out laughing, and after a moment the whole class responded.

Of course, Robert Gu couldn't see the special effects. For a second he looked puzzled, and then he glared at the Radners.

"Class!" Ms. Chumlig sounded truly pissed. The laughter choked off and everyone applauded politely. Chumlig held them to it for a moment, then lowered her own hands. Juan could see she was scanning them all. Normally she ignored graffiti. This time she was searching for someone to crucify. Her gaze ended up in the old farts' section, and she looked a little surprised.

"Very well. Thank you, Robert. That is all we have time for today. Class, your next assignment is to collaborate and improve on what you have already done. It's up to you to find local partners for this step. Send me the teamings and your game plan before we meet next time." The Ignominious Details would be in the mail by the time they got home.

Then the class bell—triggered by Chumlig, in fact—rang out. By the time Juan got himself out of his chair, he was in the tail end of the mad rush for the door. It didn't matter. He was a little dazed by the strange form of *virtual* virtual reality that Robert Gu had created.

Behind him he could see that Gu had finally figured out the class was over. He would be outside with the rest of them in a few seconds. *My chance to enlist him for the Lizard.* And maybe something else. He thought on the old man's magic words. Maybe, maybe, they could collaborate. Everybody had laughed at Robert Gu. But before the Pompous Bird had been launched, before they had laughed, Juan Orozco had felt the awed silence. *And he did that with words alone. . . .*

When robert walked to the front of the class, he was more irritated than nervous. He had wowed students for thirty years. He could wow them with the bit of verse he had composed for today. He turned, and looked out the class. "A poem," he said. "Three hundred words. I tell you about the land of North County as it really is, here and beyond." The poem was a pastoral cliché, composed last night and based on his memories of San Diego and what he saw on the drive to Fairmont. But for a few moments, his words held them, just as in the old days.

When he was done there was a moment of absolute silence. What impressionable children. He looked over at the Adult Ed people, saw the jagged, hostile smile on Winston Blount's face. *Envious as ever, eh, Winnie?*

Then a pair of oafs near the front started laughing. That precipitated scattered giggles.

"Class!" Chumlig stepped forward and everyone applauded, even Blount.

Chumlig said a few more words. Then the class bell rang and the students were all rushing for the door. He started after them.

"Ah, Robert," said Ms. Chumlig. "Please stay a moment. That bell 'did not toll for you.'" She smiled, no doubt pleased by her command of literary allusion. "Your poem was so beautiful. I want to apologize to you, for the class. They had no right to put the—" She gestured at the air above his head.

"What?"

"Never mind. This is not a truly talented class, I fear." She look at him quizzically. "It's hard to believe you're seventy-five years old; modern medicine is working miracles. I've had a number of senior students. I understand your problems."

"Ah, you do."

"Anything you do in this class will be a favor for the others here. I hope you'll stay, help them. Rework your poem with some student's visuals. They can learn from you—and you can learn the skills that will make the world a more comfortable place for you."

Robert gave her a little smile. There would always be cretins like Louise Chumlig. Fortunately, she found something else to focus on: "*Oh!* Look at the time! I've got to start Remote Studies. Please excuse me." Chumlig turned and walked to the center of the classroom. She jabbed a hand toward the top row of seats. "Welcome, class. Sandi, stop playing with the unicorns!"

Robert stared at the empty room, and the woman talking to herself. So much technology . . .

OUTSIDE, THE STUDENTS had dispersed. Robert was left to ponder his reencounter with "academia." It could have been worse. His little poem had been more than good enough for these people. Even Winnie Blount had applauded. To impress someone even when he hates you—that was always a kind of triumph.

"Mr. Gu?" The voice was tentative. Robert gave a start. It was the Orozco kid, lurking by the classroom door.

"Hello," he said, and gave the boy a generous smile.

Maybe too generous. Orozco came out of the shadows and walked along with him. "I—I thought your poem was wonderful."

"You're too kind."

The boy waved at the sunlit lawn. "It made me feel like I was actually out here, running in the sunlight. And all without haptics or contacts or my wearable." His gaze came up to Robert's face and then flickered away. It was a look of awe that might have really meant something if the speaker had been anyone worthwhile. "I'll bet you're as good as any of the top game advertisers."

"I'll bet."

The boy dithered for an inarticulate moment. "I notice you're not wearing. I could help you with that. Maybe, maybe we could team up. You know, you could help me with the words." Another glance at Robert, and then the rest of the kid's speech came out in a rush. "We could help each other, and then there's another deal I can get you in on. It could be a lot of money. Your friend Mr. Blount has already come on board."

They walked in silence for a dozen paces.

"So, Professor Gu, what do you think?"

Robert gave Juan a kindly smile, and just as the kid brightened, he said, "Well, young man, I think it will be a cold day in hell before I team with an old fool like Winston Blount—or a young fool such as yourself."

Zing. The boy stumbled back almost as if Robert had punched him in the face. Robert walked on, smiling. It was a small thing, but like the poem, it was a start.

07

THE EZRA POUND INCIDENT

There was a dark side to Robert's morning insights. Sometimes he would wake not to a grand solution but to the horrid realization that some problem was real, immediate, and apparently unsolvable. This wasn't worrywart obsessiveness, it was a form of defensive creativity. Sometimes the threat was a total surprise; more often it was a known inconvenience, now recognized as deadly serious. The panic attacks normally led to real solutions, as when he had withdrawn his earliest long poem from a small press, hiding its naive shallowness from public view.

And very rarely, the new problem was truly unsolvable and he could but flail and rail against the impending disaster.

Last night, coming away from his presentation at Fairmont High, he'd been feeling pretty good. The groundlings had been impressed, and so had the likes of Winston Blount—who was a more sophisticated kind of fool. *Things are getting better. I'm coming back.* Robert had drifted through dinner, pretty much ignoring Miri's pestering about all the things she could help him with. Bob was still absent. Robert had halfheartedly badgered Alice with questions about Lena's last days. Had Lena asked for him at the end? Who had come to her funeral? Alice was more patient than usual but still not a great source of information.

Those were the questions he'd gone to sleep with.

He woke with a plan for finding answers. When Bob returned, they would have a heart-to-heart talk about Lena. Bob would know some of the answers. And for the rest . . . in Search and Analysis, Chumlig had been talking about the Friends of Privacy. There were methods of seeing through their lies. Robert was getting better and better at S&A. One way or another, he would recover his lost times with Lena.

That was the good news. The bad news floated up as he lay there drowsing through his scheme for turning technology into a searchlight on Lena. . . . The bad news was an absolute, gut certainty that replaced the vague uneasiness of earlier days. *Yesterday, my poetry impressed the groundlings.* That was no reason for joy, and he'd been a fool to be warmed by it for even an instant. Any blush of pleasure should have vanished when little Juan Whosits had announced that Robert was as brilliant as an advertising copywriter. *Lord!*

But Winston Blount had applauded Robert's little effort. Winston Blount was certainly competent to judge such verse. And here Robert's morning insight came up with the memory of Winnie applauding, the measured beat of Blount's hands, the smile on his face. That had *not* been the look of an enemy bested and awed. Never in the old days would Robert have confused it for that. No, Winnie had been *mocking* him. Winston Blount was telling him what he should have known all along. His outdoorsy poem was shit, good only for an audience accustomed to eating shit. Robert lay still for a long moment, a groan trapped in his throat, remembering the banal words of his little poem.

That was the genius insight of this dark morning, the conclusion he had evaded every day since he was brought back from the dead: *I've lost the music in the words.*

Every day he was awash with ideas for new poetry, but not the smallest piece of concrete verse. He had told himself that his genius was coming back with his other faculties, that it was coming back slowly, in his little poems. All that was a mirage. And now he knew it for a mirage. He was dead inside, his gifts turned into vaporous nothingness and random mechanical curiosity.

You can't know that! He rolled out of bed and went into the bathroom. The air was cool and still. He stared out the half-open bathroom window at the little gardens and twisted conifers, the empty street. Bob and Alice had given him an upstairs room. It had been fun to be able to run up and down stairs again.

In truth nothing had changed about his problems. He had no new evidence that he was permanently maimed. It was just that suddenly—with the full authority of a Morning Insight—he was certain of it. *But hell. For once this could be just panic without substance!* Maybe obsessing on Lena's death was spilling over, making him see death in all directions.

Yes. No problem. There was no problem.

HE SPENT THE morning in a panicked rage, trying to prove to himself that he could still write. But the only paper was the foolscap, and when he wrote on it, his scrawling penmanship was re-formed into neat, fontified lines. That had been an irritation in days past, but never enough to force him to dig up real paper. Today, now . . . he could see that his soul was sucked out of the words before he could make them sing! It was the ultimate victory of automation over creative thought. Everything was beyond the direct touch of his hand. That was what was keeping him from finally connecting with his talents! And in the entire house there were no real paper-and-ink books.

Aha. He rushed to the basement, pulled down one of the moldering cartons that Bob had brought from Palo Alto. Inside, there were real books. When he was a kid, he had practically camped out on the living-room sofa the whole summer. They had no television, but every day he'd bring home a new pile of books from the library. Those summers, lying on the sofa, he had read his way through frivolous trash and deep wisdom—and learned more about truth than in an entire school year. Maybe that was where he had learned to make words sing.

These books were mostly junk. There were school catalogs from before Stanford went all online. There were handouts that his TAs had painfully Xeroxed for the students.

But, yes, there were a few books of poetry. Pitifully few, and read only by silverfish these last ten years. Robert stood up and stared at the boxes farther back in the basement dimness. Surely there were more books there, even if selected by brute chance, whatever was left after Bob auctioned off the Palo Alto place. He looked down at the book in his hand. Kipling. Damned jingoistic elevator music. *But it's a start.* Unlike the libraries that floated in cyberspace, this was something he could hold in his hands. He sat down on the boxes and began to read, all the while pushing his mind ahead of the words, trying to remember—trying to *create*—what should rightly be the rest of the poem.

An hour passed. Two. He was vaguely aware that Alice came down to announce lunch, and that he waved her off impatiently. This was so much more important. He opened more boxes. Some contained Bob and Alice's own junk, even more vacuous than what they had retrieved from Palo Alto. But he found a dozen more books of poetry. Some of them were . . . good stuff.

The afternoon passed. He could still *enjoy* the poetry, but the enjoyment was also pain. *I can't write a jot of the good stuff, except where I happen to remember it.* And his panic grew. Finally, he stood and threw Ezra Pound into the basement wall. The spine of the old book split and it sprawled on the floor, a broken paper butterfly. Robert stared for a moment. He had never harmed a book before, not even if it bore the ugliest writing in the world. He walked across the room and knelt by the ruin.

Miri chose that moment to come bouncing down the stairs. "Robert! Alice says I can call an air taxi! Where would you like to go?"

The words were noise, scraping on his despair. He picked up the book and shook his head. "No." *Go away.*

"I don't understand. Why are you digging around here? There are easier ways to get what you want."

Robert stood, his fingers trying to put Ezra Pound back together again. His eyes found Miri. Now she had his attention. She was smiling, so sure of herself, in maximum bossiness mode. And for the moment she didn't understand the light in his eyes. "And how is that, Miri?"

"The problem is that you can't access what's all around us. That's why you're down here reading these old books, right? In a way you're like a little kid—but that's good, that's *good!* Grown-ups like Alice and Bob have all sorts of bad habits that hold them back. But you're starting almost fresh. It'll be easy for you to learn the new things. But not from dumbhead vocational classes. See? Let me teach you how to wear." It was the same wearisome nag as always, but she thought she'd found a clever new angle.

This time, he would not let it pass. Robert took a step toward her. "So you've been watching me down here?" he said mildly, building up to what he intended.

"Um, just in a general way. I—"

Robert took another step toward her and shoved the mutilated book toward her face. "Have you ever heard of this poet?"

Miri squinted at the broken spine. " 'E,' 'z'—oh, 'Ezra Pound'? Well . . . yes, I've got all her stuff. Let me show you, Robert!" She hesitated, then saw the foolscap lying atop a box. She picked it up and it came to life. Titles streamed down the page, the cantos, the essays—even, God help us, later criticism from the mindless depths of the twenty-first century. "But seeing it on this page is like looking through a keyhole, Robert. I can show you how to see it all around you, with—"

"Enough!" said Robert. He slid his voice down till it was quiet, cutting, overtly reasonable. "You simpleton. You know nothing and yet you presume to run my life, just as you run the lives of your little friends."

Miri had backed up a step. There was shock on her face, but that had apparently not yet connected with her mouth. "Yes, that's what Alice says, that I'm too bossy—"

Robert took another step, and Miri was against the stairs. "You've spent your whole life playing video games, convincing yourself and your friends that you're worth something, that you're some kind of beautiful thing. I'll bet your parents are even foolish enough to tell you how clever you are. But it's not a pretty thing to be bossy when you're a fat, brainless brat."

"I—" Miri's hand rose to her mouth and her eyes grew wide. She took an awkward step backward, up the steps. His words were connecting now. He could see the veneer of self-confidence and bright cheeriness collapsing.

And Robert pursued: " 'I,' 'I'—yes, that's probably what your self-centered little mind thinks about most. It would be hard to bear your worthlessness otherwise. But think about that before you come again trying to run *my* life."

Tears welled in the girl's eyes. She turned and sprinted up the stairs, her footsteps not a pounding of childish force, but soft—almost as if she didn't want anything about herself to be sensed.

Robert stood for a moment, looking up the empty stairway. It was like standing at the bottom of a well, with a patch of daylight across the top.

He remembered. There had been a time, when he was fifteen and his sister Cara was about ten . . . when Cara became independent, bothersome. At the time Robert had had his own problems—totally trivial from the altitude of seventy-five years, but they'd seemed significant at the time. Getting past his sister's newfound ego, making her realize how little she counted in the general scheme of things, that had given him such a rush of pleasure.

Robert stared up into the patch of daylight and waited for the rush.

O

BOB GU GOT out of debrief late on Saturday. He had been delinquent about tracking events at home; the Paraguay operation had been all-absorbing. Okay, that was an excuse. But it was also the truth. There had been hot launchers under that hostage orphanage. There in Asunción, he had seen the abyss.

So it wasn't until he arrived home that he got the *local* bad news. . . .

His daughter was too big and grown-up to sit on his lap, but she sat close on the sofa and let him take her hands in his. Alice sat on the other side; she looked calm, but he knew she was totally freaked. Training jitters plus this problem at home were almost too much for her.

So it was past time to face up to family responsibilities:

"It's nothing you did, Miri."

Miri shook her head. There were dark rings around her eyes; Alice said she had stopped crying only an hour ago. "I was trying to help him and . . ." The sentence dribbled off. Her voice held none of the confidence that had grown in it over the last two or three years. *Damn.* In the corner of his eye, Bob could see that his father was still ensconced in his room upstairs, silently sticking it to them all. Visiting Dad was next on the agenda. The old man was going to have a surprise.

For now, there was something more important to set right. "I know you were, Miri. And I think you have helped Grandpa a lot since he came to live with us." The old man would still be trying to find his shoes if she hadn't. "You remember, we talked about this when Grandpa came? He is not necessarily a nice fellow" *—except when he wants a favor, or he's setting you up for a fall; then he can charm almost any human ever born.*

"Y-Yes. I remember."

"What he says when he's trying to hurt you doesn't have any connection with whether you've been good or bad, clever or stupid."

"B-But maybe I was too pushy. You didn't see him this morning, Bob. He was so sad. He thinks I don't notice, but I do. His pulse was way up. He's so afraid that he can't write anymore. And he misses Grandma, I mean Lena. *I* miss Lena! But I—"

"It's not your responsibility to solve this problem, Miri." He glanced over Miri's head at Alice. "It's mine, and till now I've messed up. Your job, well, that's at Fairmont Junior High."

"Actually, we call it Fairmont High."

"Okay. Look. Before Grandpa came, school was just about all you thought about. That and your friends and your projects. Didn't you tell me you're going to transform the place this Halloween?"

Some shred of her past enthusiasm lit Miri's face. "Yeah. We've got the backstory on all the SpielbergRowling stuff. Annette's going to—"

"Then that and your regular schoolwork is what you should concentrate on. That's your mission, kiddo."

"But what about Robert?"

Robert can go to hell. "I'll talk to him. I think you're right that he's got a problem. But, you know sometimes, well . . . there's something you have to learn as you grow up. Some people make their own problems. And they never stop hurting themselves and messing up the people around them. When that's the case, then you shouldn't keep hurting yourself for them."

Miri's head bowed and she looked very sad. And then she looked back at him. Her jaw came up in that familiar, stubborn way. "Maybe that's true about other people . . . but this is *my* grandfather."

08

NO USER-SERVICEABLE PARTS WITHIN

After that remarkable Saturday, Robert Gu spent considerably less time at his son's home. He slept there, still in the upstairs room. Sometimes he even ate in the dining room. Miri was always somewhere else. Alice was as impassive as stone. When Bob was around, the hospitality was even more sparse. Robert was living on borrowed time, and it had nothing to do with his medical condition.

He hung out in empty rooms at school, reading from his old books. He surfed the web more than ever. Chumlig showed him some modern utilities that hid in his view-page, things that could not even pretend to be WinME programs.

And he drove around town. That was as much to play with the automatic cars as it was to see what San Diego had become; in fact, the suburban sprawl was just as drab as in the past. But Robert discovered that his new, maimed personality had a thing about gadgets. Cryptic machines were everywhere nowadays. They lurked in walls, nestled in trees, even littered the lawns. They worked silently, almost invisibly, twenty-four hours a day. He began to wonder where it all ended.

One day after school, Robert drove into the far East County, past the endless, ordinary suburbs. The housing didn't thin out until he was well into the mountains. But twenty miles beyond El Cajon, he came to a gap in the housing and what looked like a war in progress. Dust plumes spouted from buildings several hundred yards back from the highway. When he rolled down the window, he heard what might have been artillery fire. A frontage road ran along a high fence. A rusted sign said "UP/Express" something or other.

And then the strange firing range was behind him.

The highway was a long straight climb now, up past four thousand feet. It was farther and farther between off-ramps. The auto slowly accelerated. According to the awkward little dashboard display that he'd found in his WinME game folder, they were doing better than 120 miles per hour. The boulders and scrub along the shoulder were a blur, and the window rolled itself closed. He passed the manual vehicles in far right lanes as though they were standing still. *Someday, I have to learn to drive again.*

Then he was over the crest. The auto slowed, taking the curves at a mere fifty miles per hour. He remembered driving this way with Lena, on a much smaller Highway 8, maybe in 1970. Lena Llewelyn was new to California, new to the U.S.A. She had boggled at the size of the place compared with her native Britain. She'd been so open then, so trusting. That was even before she decided to specialize in psychiatry.

The hills shed their faded green and stood as piles of rounded boulders. The desert spread endlessly below and beyond. He came down from the mountains, turned off Highway 8, and drove slowly along old desert roads toward Anza Borrego State Park. The last of the suburbs were up on the ridgeline. Down here, things were as they had been when he'd been in grad school—even as they had been for centuries before that.

There were plenty of traffic signs on these smaller roads. Some were rusted and tilted, but they were real. His gaze turned to watch a bullet-punctured stop sign dwindle behind him. It was beautiful. A little farther on he came upon a dusty path that ran off across endless desert. The automobile balked at following it: "Sorry, sir, there's no guidance that way, and I notice you don't have a driver's license."

"Ha. In that case, I'm taking a little walk." Surprisingly, there was no objection to that. He opened the door and stepped out into the breezy afternoon. He could feel his spirit unlimber. He could see forever. Robert walked east along the rutted dirt road. *Here* at last he had reached the natural world.

His foot kicked something metallic. A spent round? No. The gray lump had a triple antenna sticking out of the top. He tossed it into the bushes. He was not beyond the web even here. He pulled out his magic foolscap, surfed the local area. The picture showed the ground around him, from some kind of camera built into the paper; little signs floated above every weed—*Ambrosia dumosa* this and *Encelia farinosa* that. Ads for the park's gift shop scrolled across the top of the page.

Robert pressed 411. The expense meter at the corner of the page was running now, almost five dollars a minute. That sort of money meant there was a human at the other end. Robert talked to the paper. "So how far am I from—" *from the natural world* "—how far am I from unimproved land?"

A tag changed color; his request had been subcontracted. A woman's voice replied, "You're almost there; it's another . . . two miles in the direction you are heading. If I might suggest, sir, you don't really need 411 to answer questions like this. Just—"

But Robert had already stuffed the paper back in his pocket. He set out eastward, his shadow breaking the trail ahead of him. It had been a very long time since he had walked two miles. Even before the Alzheimer's, walking two miles would have been the stuff of an emergency. But today he was not even out of breath, and the pain in his joints was muted. *The most important thing about me is broken, while almost everything else works.* Reed Weber was right, it was a heavenly minefield. *I am so lucky.*

Over the wind, he heard the sound of electric motors torquing up. His car was driving off to do business elsewhere. Robert did not look back.

His shadow grew longer, the air cooler. And finally he had reached the beginning of nature. A little voice spoke in his ear, announcing that he was leaving the tagged section of the park. Beyond this point, only "low-rate emergency wireless" was guaranteed. Robert walked on, across the unlabeled wilderness. *So this is the closest thing to being alone these days.* It felt good. A cold, clean purity.

For a moment, the recollection of Saturday's confrontation with Bob swept over him, more real than the desert evening. There had been times, years ago, when he raged at his son, trying to shame him for wasting his talents in the military. But last Saturday, the rage had flowed in the other direction.

"Sit!" the boy grown up had said to his father, in a tone that Robert had never heard from him before.

And Robert had dropped onto the sofa. His son towered over him for a moment. Then Bob sat down opposite him and leaned close. "Miri won't talk about the details, but it's clear what you did this afternoon, mister."

"Bob, I was just—"

"Shut up. My little girl has enough problems, and you *will not* add to them!" His glare was long and steady.

". . . I didn't mean any harm, Bob. I had a bad day." Some distant part of him realized that he was *whining*, and that he couldn't stop. "Where is Lena, Bob?"

Bob's eyes narrowed. "You've asked me that before. I wondered if it was an act." He shrugged. "Now I don't care. After today, I just want you out of here, but . . . have you looked at your finances, Dad?"

It was going to come down to that. "Yes . . . there's a finance package in my WinME. My savings, I was a multimillionaire in 2000."

"That's three bubbles back, Dad. And you guessed wrong on every one. But at this point you're nearly certified as self-sufficient. You'd have a hard time scaring up any public assistance. The taxpayers are not kind to seniors; old people run too much of the country already." He hesitated. "And after today, my generosity has run out. Mom died two years ago—and dumped you decades before that. But maybe you should wonder about other things. For instance, where are all your old pals from Stanford?"

"I—" Faces rose up in Robert's mind. He'd been in the English Department at Stanford for thirty years. There were lots of faces. Some of them belonged to people who were years younger than he was. Where were they now?

Bob nodded at his silence. "Right. Not one has visited you, nor even tried to contact you. I should know. Even before today, I figured that when you got your strength back you'd start hurting whoever was nearest—and that would be Miri. So I've been trying to farm you out to one of your old buddies. And you know what, Dad? There's not one who wants anything to do with you. Oh, there are newsies. You won't have to look far to find as many fans as ever—but among them all there's not a single friend." He paused. "Now you don't have any options. Finish the semester; learn what you can. *And then get out of our house.*"

"But Lena. What about Lena?"

Bob shook his head. "Mom's dead. You had no use for her except when you needed a servant or a kickball. Now it's too late. She's dead."

"But—" There were memories, but they clashed with one another. The last decade at Stanford. The Bollingen Prize and the Pulitzer. Lena had *not* been there to share them. She had divorced him just about the time Bob joined the Marines. And yet—"You remember. Lena got me into that rest home, Rainbows End. And then she was *here*, when things got really dark. She was here with Cara"—his little sister, still ten years old, and dead since 2006. His words stumbled to a halt.

Something glittered in his son's eyes. "Yes, Mom was here, just like Cara. A shame attack won't work on me, Dad. I want you out of this house. End of the semester at the latest."

And that was the longest conversation Robert had had with anyone since Saturday.

It was cold. He'd walked a long way into the desert. The night had risen partway up the sky. Stars hung over a flat land that stretched forever beyond him. Maybe that should be the "Secret of the One Who Came Back" . . . that he just wanted to go away again, walking forever into the bluish dark. He walked a bit farther, then slowed, stopped beside a huge rough rock—and stared into the night.

After some minutes, he turned and started back into the bright twilight.

JUAN GOT SIDETRACKED from Big Lizard's quest. School began to seriously intrude. Chumlig wanted them to complete their projects and she wanted real results. Worst of all, the school board had suddenly decided the class must demo their creative compositions at Parents' Night—in place of the final exam. Low grades and Chumlig's disappointment in him were bad enough; Juan already knew he was a loser. But such public humiliation was something he desperately wanted to avoid.

So for a while he was on a different quest: finding someone to team with in composition class. The problem was, Juan was no good at writing. He wasn't more than so-so with math or answerboards. Ms. Chumlig said the secret of success was "to learn to ask the right questions." But to do that she also said you had "to know something about something." That wisdom and "everyone has some special talent" were the drumbeats of her classes. But it didn't help. Maybe the best he could hope for was a team so big the losers would shield each other.

Today he sat at the back of the shop tent with Fred and Jerry. The twins had missed their proper shop class that morning, so now they were wasting the rest of the day here rather than in study hall. It was kind of fun. The two were pretending to work on a magnetic orrery—a plagiarism so obvious that their plans still had the source URLs written on them. About half the class had completed something. Doris Schley's paper airplanes were flying, but just this afternoon her team had discovered terrible stability problems. They didn't know about Fred and Jerry's unofficial project: The twins had hijacked the tent's air-conditioning. While they kicked back and fooled with the orrery, they were using the fans to tumble Schley's fliers.

Xiu Xiang sat hunched over the transport tray she had been working on lately. She didn't look so blank and despairing these days, even if she had warped the transport surface to where it wasn't good for anything. Xiang practically had her nose buried in the equipment. Every so often she drew back and studied her view-page, then returned to the unmoving wreck she had created.

Winston Blount had been scarce since Juan had put him onto the Lizard's quest. Juan counted that as encouraging; maybe Mr. Blount was working on the affiliance.

Juan leaned into the cool air from the fans. Back here it was nice. It was hot and noisy over by the outside entrance, but that's where Robert Gu sat. Earlier, the guy had been watching Dr. Xiang. Sometimes she seemed to be watching him back, but even more secretly. Now Mr. Gu mainly stared at the traffic circle, watching the cars that occasionally pulled up, picked up or dropped off passengers, and then departed. The table in front of the fake teenager was littered with BuildIt fragments, and several rickety-looking towers. Juan zoomed in on a couple of them from a viewpoint in the tent above Gu's head. Huh. The gadgets had no motors, not even any control logic.

So Gu was going to crash in this class just as sure as Juan was in Composition. It suddenly occurred to him that maybe he could resume the Lizard's game, and take one last whack at finding a teammate for Ms. Chumlig's project. *But I tried him last week.* Robert Gu was the best writer Juan had ever known. He was so good he could kill you with his words. Juan tucked his chin in and tried to forget last week.

And then he thought, *The guy isn't wearing, so he's staring at nothing. He must be bored out of his skull.* Juan dithered for another ten minutes, but shop class had thirty minutes more to run and the Radners were way too focused on their anti-aircraft guns.

Jerry --> Juan: <sm>Hey, where you going?</sm>

Juan --> Radners: <sm>Gonna make one more try with Gu. Wish me luck.</sm>

Fred --> Juan: <sm>It's unhealthy to want a grade that bad.</sm>

Juan meandered across the pavilion, walking along the lab benches as if he were studying the other projects. He ended up beside the strange old man. Gu turned to look at him, and Juan's casual cover evaporated. Gu's sweaty face looked almost as young as Fred Radner's. But the eyes looked right into Juan, cold and cruel. Last week, the guy had seemed friendly—right up to the moment he ripped Juan apart. Now all Juan's clever opening lines were gone; even the dumb ones were hiding. Finally he managed to point at the crazy towers Robert Gu had been working on. "What's the project?"

The young-old man continued to stare at Juan. "A clock." Then he reached into a parts box and dropped three silver balls into the top of the tallest tower.

"Oh!" The balls bounced down connecting stairways. The first tower was directly in front of Juan. Going to the right, each tower was a bit shorter and more complex than the last. Mr. Gu had used most of the "classic parts" that Ron Williams kept in stock. This was a clock? Juan tried to match it against old-time clock patterns. There were no perfect fits, though the thing did have levers that clicked back and forth against a whatchamagoogle . . . an escape wheel. Maybe the balls tipping down the stairways were like the hands on a clock.

Gu continued to stare at him. "But it's running fast," he said.

Juan leaned forward and tried to ignore that stare. He captured about three seconds of the contraption's motion, enough to identify stationary points and dimensions. There was an old mechanics program that came in handy for medieval gadget games; he fed the description into it. The results were easy to interpret. "You just gotta make that lever a quarter-inch longer." He poked a finger at a tiny spar.

"I know."

Juan looked back at him. "But you're not wearing. How did you figure that out?"

Gu shrugged. "A medical gift."

"That's pretty neat," Juan said uncertainly.

"For what? To do what any child can do already?"

Juan didn't have any answer for that. "But you're also a poet."

"And now I'm good with gadgets." Gu's hand twitched out, smashing through the levers and wheels. Parts sprayed in all directions, some of them breaking under the force of his blow.

That got everyone's attention. The class was suddenly quiet—and blazing with sming.

It was time to back off. But Juan really really needed help with Creative Composition. And so he said, "You still know about words, though, right?"

"Yes, I still know about words. I still know about grammar. I can parse sentences. I can even spell—hallelujah, without mechanical aid. What's your name?"

"Juan Orozco."

"Yes, I remember. What are you good for, Mr. Orozco?"

Juan tucked his chin in. "I'm learning how to ask the right questions."

"Do so, then."

"Um." Juan looked at the other parts Gu had collected, things he hadn't used in his clock. There were rotary motors, there were wireless synchs, there were programmable gear trains. There was even a transport tray like the one Dr. Xiang had messed up. "So how come you don't use any of these gadgets? That would be lots easier."

He expected Gu to spout some Chumliggy thing about solving a problem within constraints. Instead, the other poked angrily at the components. "Because I can't see inside them. Look." He flipped a rotary motor across the table. " 'No user-serviceable parts within.' It's stamped right in the plastic. Everything is a black box. Everything is inscrutable magic."

"You could look at the manuals," said Juan. "They show internals."

Gu hesitated. His hands were gathered into fists. Juan edged back a few inches. "You can see internals? You can change them?"

Juan watched the fists. *He's flipping crazy.* "You can see them easy. Almost everything serves up its own manual. If it doesn't, just Google on the part number." The look on Gu's face sent Juan into fast mode: "As for changing the internals . . . often they're programmable. But otherwise, the only changes you can make are when you order, back at the design and fab stage. I mean, these are just *components.* Who'd want to change them once they're made? Just trash 'em if they're not working like you want."

"Just components?" Gu looked out from under the fringes of the shop-class tent. An automobile was tooling up Pala Avenue, heading for the school's traffic circle. "What about the fucking cars?"

"Unh." The whole class was staring. Almost the whole class: Mr. Williams was on break and out of contact.

Mr. Gu twitched for a few seconds. Then suddenly he was standing. He grabbed Juan by the collar. "By God I'm going to have a look."

Juan bounced along just ahead of Robert Gu's angry, pushing hands. "Break open a car? Why would you want to do that?"

"That's the wrong question, kid." At least they were walking *away* from the traffic circle. Even if he went after an automobile, what damage could he do? The car bodies were a trashy composite, easy to recycle, but strong enough to take a fifty-mile-per-hour crash. Visions of battle lasers and monster sledgehammers came to mind. But this was the real world.

Jerry --> Juan: <sm>What is the goofball up to?</sm>

Juan --> Radners: <sm>I dunno!</sm>

Robert Gu marched him across the tent to where Xiu Xiang was sitting. By the time he arrived, the only evidence of madness was the faint twitchiness in his face. "Dr. Xiang?"

The crazy man actually sounded relaxed and friendly, but Xiang hesitated a long moment. "Yes," she said.

"I've been admiring your project. Some kind of mass mover?"

Xiang tilted the warped surface up toward him. "Yes. It's just a toy, but I thought I could get a leverage effect by warping the surface." Talking about the gadget seemed to distract her from Gu's weirdness.

"Very nice!" There was nothing but charm in Gu's voice. "May I?" He picked up the panel and studied the ragged edge.

"I had to cut out gores so the microgrooves wouldn't bind," she said, standing up to point at her work.

Transport trays were for shedding dirt or sliding small containers. For most things, they were better than robot hands, even if they didn't look as impressive. Juan's mother had remodeled their kitchen with fake-marble transports; afterward, everything she wanted was where it should be, in the fridge or oven or on the cutting board, just when she needed it. Usually, the microgrooves couldn't slide anything faster than a couple of inches a second.

What Xiang was saying gave Juan an idea. Maybe the warped board was not broken. He started to put the dimensions into a mechanics program—

But Robert Gu already seemed to know what the thing could do. "You could triple the delivered force if you adjusted it, here." He twisted the tray. It creaked the way ceramics do when you've bent them *almost* to the breaking point.

"Wait—" She reached for her project.

"I didn't break it. This is even better. Come on over and I'll show you." His words were all so open and friendly. But he was already walking away.

Xiang chased after him, but she didn't act like a kid would when someone grabs their property. She walked along beside Gu, her head tilted to get a look at the wrecked transport tray.

"But there's no way to use that mechanical advantage with just the batteries it's rated for—" The rest of what she said was mathematical; Juan just saved it.

As Gu swept by the Radner twins, his right arm flicked out, grabbing a jar of metal beads that Fred and Jerry were using for their orrery.

"Hey!" The Radners jumped to their feet and followed him, not saying much out loud. The Adult Ed students were like untouchables. You didn't mess with them and vice versa.

Jerry --> Juan: <sm>What did we miss, Juan?</sm>

Fred --> Juan: <sm>Yeah. What did you say to him?</sm>

Juan danced backward, lifting his hands to say that he was an innocent bystander.

Almost an innocent bystander. As Gu walked past his workbench, he jerked his chin toward the tent entrance. "Make yourself useful, Orozco. Get me some line current."

Juan scooted ahead. There were 110VAC sources on campus, though most were indoors. He looked up public utilities and saw a big arrow pointing down into the lawn. This outlet was used to power building reconfiguration when they needed an extra auditorium. It had a thirty-foot extension reel. He ran to the spot and pulled the line up from the fresh-cut grass.

Now all the kids—minus Schley's team, which was suddenly overjoyed by the improvement in their fliers' performance—were following them out of the tent.

The car coming up the traffic loop was gliding to a stop at the curb behind him. It was Ms. Chumlig, back from lunch.

Robert Gu caught up, Xiang right behind him and looking upset. Gu was no longer making nice noises. He grabbed the power cord from Juan and plugged it into the transport tray's universal, bypassing the teeny battery pack that Dr. Xiang had used. He tilted the tray on edge and poured the metal beads from the Radners' project into the top-edge opening.

Chumlig was out of the car. "What's going on—"

The crazy man smiled at her. "My shop project, Louise. I've had enough of 'no user-serviceable parts within.' Let's take a look." He leaned over the car's front hood and ran his finger down the printed words forbidding customer maintenance. The kids stood in clusters, awed. Juan had never heard of anyone at Fairmont High going wacko. Robert Gu was making history. The old man set the transport tray against the automobile. *So where is your battle laser, Mr. Spaceman?* Gu sighted along the edge of the tray, then glanced to his right, at the Radner brothers. "You really don't want to be standing there."

Xiu Xiang was frantic, shouting at the twins. "Get back, get back!"

And now Juan was getting way unbelievable answers from his mechanics program. He hopped back from the transport tray. Robert Gu didn't need a battle laser. For this job, he had something just as good.

Gu powered up the tray. The noise was like tearing cloth but *loud*, a crack-of-doom sound. Real sparks sprayed from where the transport tray touched the car's hood. Twenty feet ahead of the car, where the Radners had been standing, there was an oleander hedge. Some of the branches were as thick as Juan's arm. Now the white flowers were dancing like there was a breeze; one of the largest branches snapped and fell on the sidewalk.

Gu slid the tray along the curve of the automobile, driving dozens of metal beads per second into the hood, cutting an eighth-inch-wide slit in the composite. He turned the tray—the *cutter*—and made a corner. Now the lawn near his feet was ripped by the invisible ricochets.

In less than ten seconds, Gu had brought the cut around to itself. The carved section fell into the dark of the car's drive compartment.

Gu tossed Xiu Xiang's project onto the lawn. He reached into the drive compartment and flipped out the loose hull section. A ragged and maybe disdainful cheer rose from the kids behind him. "Hey, dork! There has to be a latch. Why didn't you scam the lock?"

Gu didn't seem to hear. He leaned forward to look into the interior. Juan edged closer. The compartment was in shadow, but he could see well enough. Not counting damage, it looked just like the manual said. There were some processor nodes and fiber leading to the dozens of other nodes and sensors and effectors. There was the steering servo. Along the bottom, just missed by Gu's cutting, was the DC bus to the left-front wheel.

The rest was empty space. The capacitor and power cells were in the back.

Gu stared into the shadows. There was no fire, no explosion. Even if he had chopped into the back, the safeties would have prevented any spectacular outcome. But Juan saw more and more error flags float into view. A junk wagon would be coming real soon.

Gu's shoulders slumped, and Juan got a closer look at the component boxes. Every one had physical signage: NO USER-SERVICEABLE PARTS WITHIN.

The old guy stood and took a step away from the car. Behind them, Chumlig and now Williams were on the scene, herding the students back into the tent. For the most part, the kids were fully stoked by all the insanity. None of them, not even the Radner brothers, ever had the courage to run amok. When they committed something major, it was usually done in software, like what the guy had shouted from the crowd.

Xiu Xiang gathered up her weird, Gu-improved, project. She was shaking her head and mumbling to herself. She unplugged the gadget and took a step toward Robert Gu. "I object to your appropriation of my toy!" she said. There was an odd expression on her face. "Though you did improve it with that extra bend." Gu didn't respond. She hesitated. "And I *never* would have run it with line power!"

Gu waved at the guts of the dead car. "It's Russian dolls all the way down, isn't it, Orozco?"

Juan didn't bother to look up "Russian dolls." "It's just throwaway stuff, Professor Gu. Why would anyone want to fool with it?"

Xiu Xiang leaned around him, saw the nearly empty compartment, and the boxes with their stamped-on labels. She look up at Gu. "You're worse off than I am, aren't you?" she said softly.

Gu's hand twitched up and for a moment Juan thought he was going to punch her out. "You worthless bitch. You were never more than an engineer, and now you have to reeducate even for that." He turned and walked away along the traffic circle, down the hill toward Pala Avenue.

Xiang took a step or two after Gu. From inside the school,

Chumlig was demanding that everyone come indoors; Juan reached out to touch Xiang's arm. "We gotta go back inside, Dr. Xiang."

She didn't argue, but turned and walked back toward the tent, her transport tray held close. Juan followed her, all the time watching the crazy man as he departed in the opposite direction.

O

EVEN WITH ROBERT Gu off campus, the rest of the afternoon was fairly exciting. The school board invoked cloture. Well, they tried to invoke cloture. But they had to allow the students contact with home, and most kids regarded this as an opportunity to grab a journo affiliance. Juan had been close enough to provide some of the best pictures of the "great automobile wrecking"; his mother was not happy about that. She'd be even less happy when she noticed that "the madman" was in three of Juan's classes.

So anyway the campus was famous in San Diego and beyond, competing with the billion other bizarrities of the day, all over the planet. Students from other classes played hookey and came over. Juan saw a young, kind of plump kid talking in person with Ms. Chumlig. Miri Gu.

By 3:00 P.M. the excitement had faded. This was past the end of classes for most students. The Radners' betting pool on Gu's punishment had been bought out by some guys in LA. Lucky for the twins. The trouble with instant fame was that there was always something new coming to distract everyone's attention.

Overall, it had been a wild day, but kind of sad.

Juan was almost home when he got a phone call.

A phone call? Well, Classic IM Lite was what Epiphany called it. This must be his great grandpa. "Yes?" he replied, without thinking.

The call came as a window view from a synthetic camera. He was looking upward, into a small bedroom. Bizarre decorations, though: hardcopy books stacked in cardboard boxes. A distorted face filled most of the screen. Then the caller sat back. It was Robert Gu, calling from his view-page.

"Hi kid."

"Hi, Professor." In person, Robert Gu was fully scary. In this cheap flat view, he just looked small and crumpled.

"Look, kid . . ." The picture twisted and jerked. Gu was fidgeting with the page. When it settled, the other's face filled the screen again. "What you were talking about last week. I think I could help out with your writing."

Yes! "That would be tragic, Professor Gu."

Gu gave him a blank look.

"I mean, that would be way cool. And I'd be happy to show you how to wear." He was already thinking how he would explain this to his ma.

"Right." Gu's face retreated, and he gave a shrug. "I suppose that would be fine too. If they let me back in school, I'll see you there."

09

CARROT GREENS

Make no mistake about it, this job of saving the world was no bed of roses.

Alfred glared at Günberk Braun's latest report: "Covert Search for Grand Terror in San Diego." Things had been hard enough before Günberk spotted Alfred's YGBM project, but since the Barcelona meeting, Alfred's duplicity had become steadily more difficult to maintain. He had never expected that Braun could keep such a careful watch on the San Diego labs. Alfred had had to shut down almost all his activity there, even canceling his regular specimen outshipments; this affair had set his schedule back by months.

The only bright spot was that Günberk and Keiko were going ahead with Plan Rabbit. In fact, Rabbit had resurfaced a week ago, along with his initial survey and his payment demands. The demands had been laughable, basically a wholesale shopping list of enhancement drugs, just what you might think South American drug lords could supply to a bright young businessman. As for his survey—Rabbit had come up with a list of contacts in San Diego and a complicated plan for getting direct surveillance equipment into the labs. Günberk and Keiko had been respectively irritated and amused by the scheme, but all three of them agreed they could make it work. The Americans would know they had been probed, but unless things went very wrong, the operation would be deniable.

Of course, what Günberk and Keiko saw was the easy part. The hard part was what Alfred was hiding beneath Plan Rabbit. When this magnificent intrusion/inspection was complete, there would be no evidence of his research program. Working as the trusted leader of the operation, Alfred was confident that he could accomplish that much. The *triumph* would be to leave credible evidence that would point bird-dog Günberk somewhere far across the world—and leave Alfred's operation intact in San Diego. Failing that, Alfred would have to rebuild his research setup—and his security—at second-rate sites. He could lose a year or two of development time.

Would such a delay really matter? He had completed the hard part. The honeyed-nougat test had demonstrated that he had a delivery system. In fact, his Pseudomimi viral was far more robust that Günberk realized. If Grand Terror had been Alfred's goal, he was already in the winner's circle; he could trigger devastating psychosis, even customize for particular targets. The way to develop higher mental controls was clear. But meantime, the human race was still careening down a mountain road, with no one at the wheel. The Saturday-night specials, the cheap delivery systems, the plagues—there was always the next precipice, the Next Very Bad Thing. What if the Next Very Bad Thing was the final, fatal Bad Thing, and what if they ran into it before he could take control?

So yes, anything he could do to save a few months was worthwhile. He pushed away Günberk's report and returned to planning just what he would do during the brief hours when this operation put Günberk and Keiko and himself in control of the San Diego labs.

He was so absorbed in his scheming that he almost didn't

hear the sound behind him. There was a small popping noise and a little whoosh of air, typical game sound effects. They were sounds that absolutely did not belong here. Alfred flinched and turned.

Rabbit had grown. "Hi there!" it said. "I thought I'd pop up and give you a special progress report, maybe ask for your help with some details." Rabbit gave Alfred a bucktoothed grin and sat back to enjoy a carrot. Sat back in the big leather visitor's chair across from Alfred's desk. In Alfred's office. His inner office, the one here in the bombproof catacombs under Mumbai, at the heart of India's External Intelligence Agency.

Alfred had managed covert operations for almost seventy years. It had been decades since he had been so rudely upset. It was like being young again—not a good feeling. He stared at Rabbit for a moment, absorbing the terrible implications of the creature's presence. *Perhaps it would be best to ignore those for now.* And so his reply was a random flail: "A progress report? We've seen your progress. I personally was somewhat disappointed. You've accomplished little—"

"That you can see."

"—beyond creating a fog of foolishness, self-defeating as often as not. The 'local agents' you've recruited are incompetent. For example—" Alfred made a show of fetching records. Meantime, the people in the EIA analyst pool were tracing Rabbit's intrusion. They opened a graphics window above the creature's head. Rabbit was coming through routers on three continents.

"For example," Alfred continued, picking a name almost at random, "take this 'Winston Blount.' Years ago, he was a top administrator at UCSD. But he never had any personal connection with the founders of the bio labs, and today . . ." He waved his hand in dismissal. "These people have so little connection with the San Diego labs that I might validly ask what we are getting for our money."

The Rabbit leaned across Alfred's mahogany desk. Its reflection in the deep varnish moved in perfect synchrony. "You might ask. And what great ignorance that would reveal. *You* know what to look for and still this is all you have discovered. Think how invisible this must be to the Americans. I am a phantom that shows as brownian noise until—viola!—the jaws of my operation spring shut."

A smile stretched across Rabbit's face. It gave its ears a wiggle, and gestured around Alfred's inner sanctum. "In a very small way—just a proof of principle, really—those jaws closed on you today. You, the Japanese, the Europeans, you all thought you had me fooled. What of your anonymity now, eh? Eh?"

Alfred glowered at the animal. No need to disguise his upset. *But pray God this is all he has discovered.*

Rabbit settled its elbows on Alfred's desk and continued chattily, "Don't worry, I'm not being so open with your pals in Japanese and EU Intelligence. I figure it might panic them—and this is a project I've come to enjoy, meeting new people, learning new skills. You understand."

It cocked its head as if expecting some confidence in return.

Alfred pretended to consider the matter and finally gave Rabbit a judicious nod. "Yes. Knowing our cover was blown—even to an insider such as yourself—they would likely abort the mission. You did the right thing."

The numbers above Rabbit's ears were changing. The available routing information was mostly bogus, but the network latencies—the delays—made his analysts eighty percent confident that Rabbit was coming from North America. Without help from the European signals intelligence people, he wasn't going to get any better estimate. But telling Günberk about this visit was the last thing Alfred wanted to do.

So I must treat this son of a bitch as a respected colleague. Alfred sat back and essayed a mild demeanor. "Between us then. What has been your progress?"

The rabbit tossed the butt end of his carrot onto Vaz's desk and crossed his paws behind his head. "Heh. I've almost completed assembling the operational team. That file you're looking at probably lists some of them, including the esteemed Dean Blount. I can pay off most of these people with my own resources. One of them may play ball in a spirit of good-natured adventure. The others need inducements that the wealth of nations can satisfy. And the one thing the Indo-European Alliance has is the wealth of nations."

"As long as it is totally untraceable and doesn't look like the wealth of nations."

"Trust me. If these loons think about it at all, they'll figure we really are South American drug lords. Anyway, I'll have their wish list for you in a week or so. If all goes according to plan, you'll have full access to the San Diego bio labs for almost four hours, sometime in late December."

"Excellent."

"And then maybe you'll tell me just what you're looking for in those labs."

"We believe the Americans are up to something there."

Rabbit's eyebrows raised. "A Great Power betraying its own kind?"

"It's happened before," though not since the early part of the century, the Sino-American misunderstanding.

"Hmm." For a brief moment, Rabbit seemed almost thoughtful. "I trust you'll let me in on what you discover."

Alfred nodded. "If we can can keep this between the two of us." In fact, Rabbit learning about Alfred's YGBM project would give new meaning to the phrase "worst-case outcome."

Fortunately, Rabbit did not push the issue. "There is one other thing," said the creature. "One last contact, an interesting fellow—in a way more interesting to me than all your espionage hugger-mugger."

"Very well." Alfred resolved to accept whatever foolishness the other was spouting.

A picture of a youngish Chinese fellow hung in the air. Vaz's gaze swept through the attached bio. No, this chap wasn't young. "That's Bob Gu's father? You're going to fiddle with—" He spluttered into silence, remembering recent events in Paraguay. For a moment he forgot the need for placid acceptance; some types of foolishness were very hard to swallow. "See here, this operation was to be discreet. How could you—"

"Not to worry. I have zero interest in Junior. It's just one of those crazy coincidences. See, Bob Gu's father is Alice Gu's father-in-law."

Hmm? Alfred parsed the contorted language. Then he realized that Rabbit was talking about Alice Gong. *Oh.* Rabbit had left the land of the foolish and was trekking deep into madness. Alfred was speechless.

"Ah, you know about Alice then? Did you know that she is tooling up for a full-scale audit of San Diego bio-lab security? Just think! Real soon now, the Americans are gonna go ask Alice to tighten up the guard there. Tracking her is *muy importante,* old man."

". . . Yes." The EU and Japan would bail out if they knew Alice Gong Gu was on this case. *And Alice will surely detect what I'm doing at the bio labs.* "So what are you proposing?"

"I want to make sure Alice is not guarding the labs when we go in. I've had Gu Senior on a line for several days. But that's going too slowly. Besides—" another challenging, toothy grin "—I'm dying to talk to the guy directly. We need a zombie contact." Another picture/bio popped up.

"An Indian national?"

"Subtle, am I not? Yes, though for the last two years Mr. Sharif has been living in the U.S.A. He really has no connection with any Indo-European intelligence service. I'll contact him like the gentle cloud of coincidence that I am. If the Americans identify him, he will be a perfect red herring. Your EU and Japanese friends would be too cowardly to go for this. *You,* I think, have more courage. So I'm here to give you a heads-up. Cover me on this. Keep your people out of Sharif's way. Sometimes he will really be me."

Vaz was silent for a long moment. He had not known that Alice Gong Gu was training for an audit of the San Diego labs. That was bad news. Very bad news. It wasn't enough that Gong be kept away one night. Then inspiration struck. Alice's genius came at a terrible sacrifice. He had stumbled on her secret several years ago; in her own way, she risked more than Alfred ever had. *And my weapon, incomplete as it is, could stop her cold.* He looked back at Rabbit. "Indeed, you have my support in this. It should involve just the two of us."

Rabbit preened.

"But if I may make a suggestion," Alfred continued, one colleague to another. "It may be best if we schedule things so that Alice Gu *is* on duty the night we go in. With proper preparation, we may be able to turn her presence to our advantage."

"Really?" Rabbit was literally bug-eyed with curiosity. "How is that?"

"I'll have the details for you in a few days." In fact, there were lots of details, but not for Rabbit's ears. Alfred was already posting the mission requirements to his inner teams. How long would it take to build a Pseudomimivirus appropriate to Alice's special weakness? What was the surest delivery method? Indirect infection was probably not practical here.

And what cover story would work best with this wretched rabbit?

Said rabbit was still looking at him expectantly.

"Of course," Vaz continued, "there are aspects of the matter that I should best keep to myself."

"Heh. Of course. World-shaking plans, and so forth? Never mind, I am content to remain your Great Cutout from Heaven. I'll be in touch. Meantime—" Suddenly he was wearing a gray uniform studded with medals and draped with aiguillettes. He stuck his arm out in a hitlerian salute. "Long live the Indo-European Alliance!"

With that, the rabbit's image vanished like the cheap theatrics it was.

Alfred sat motionless for almost two minutes, not responding to the shrill alarms that pounded through the office network, not responding to the various staff analyses that were already being generated. Alfred was rearranging his priorities. He hadn't known about Alice Gong Gu, but now he did and with enough time to turn her presence into an advantage. It was a sad thing that he would harm this woman who was actually fighting on his side, who had done more than almost anyone to keep the world safe.

He forced his attention back on track. Besides dealing with Alice, there was another new priority: to learn more about Rabbit, to learn how to destroy him.

O

ALFRED VAZ HAD no official rank in the External Intelligence Agency, but he had immense power there. Even with modern compartmentalization techniques, he never could have cloaked his research programs otherwise. Now . . . well, Rabbit's visit to EIA headquarters was arguably the most spectacular intelligence failure of the decade—but only if outsiders knew to argue about it! Alfred used all his power in the Agency and all the secret political levers he had accumulated over seventy years to keep the news within his own teams. If the EIA inspector general had got a whiff of it, all Alfred's plans would have unraveled. It was a sad fact that his own government would probably count him as a traitor if it knew of his efforts to save the world.

All this made investigating Rabbit's jape a delicate affair. Somehow this enemy had penetrated the most secure isolation firewall known. Rabbit had even coopted hi-res localizer support (evident from his perfectly positioned imagery). The obvious explanation was that Rabbit had succeeded in subverting the Secure Hardware Environment. If that were so, then the foundation of all modern security was suspect—and Rabbit's visit was a clap of doom.

Surely Armageddon would not be announced by a silly rabbit? There followed almost eighty hours of uncertainty as Alfred's inner teams pounded away at the mystery. Finally, his EIA analysts discovered the true explanation, something at once comforting and deeply embarrassing to them: Rabbit had—admittedly with extraordinary cleverness—exploited a combination of buggy software and foolish registry settings, the kind of flaws that bedevil careless consumers. The bottom line: Rabbit was far more dangerous than Alfred had originally thought, but he was *not* the Next Very Bad Thing.

Vaz suffered through every moment of the suspense. But in the end, the most infuriating aspect of the incident was the piece of carrot that Rabbit left on his desk. With all the resources and expertise of the modern Indian state, it took EIA signals intelligence almost three days to obliterate the logic that injected that image into his office network.

10

AN EXCELLENT THESIS TOPIC

Miri kept a low profile around the house, even though that bothered Alice—which was kind of contradictory, since Bob didn't want her talking with Robert anytime soon. Either way, they both seemed to think that given the chance, Robert would just hurt her again.

Okay. She let Robert have the living room whenever he pleased. She made sure she was outside when he was in. But she also snooped on him whenever she honorably could.

Halloween was just around the corner. She should be over at her friends' sites, deep into final planning. She and Annette and Paula had done so much prep with SpielbergRowling. Now it all seemed kind of dumb.

So Miri hung out with farther-away friends. Jin's parents were shrinks in the Provincial Medical Care Group in Hainan. Jin didn't speak very good English, but then Miri's Mandarin was worse. Actually, language wasn't a problem. They'd get together on his beach or hers—depending on which side of the world was daylight or had the nicest weather—and chatter away in Goodenuf English, the air around them filled with translation guesstimates and picture substitutions. Their little clique had contributed lots to the answerboards; it was the most "socially responsible" of Miri's hobbies.

Jin was full of theories about Robert: "Your grandfather was way gone-dead before the doctors bring him back. No surprise he feel bad now." He floated a couple of academic papers in support of his point. Today Jin was hosting several other kids who had senile or otherwise damaged old folks living at home. Mostly they just listened, as sand crabs or simply presence icons. A few presented human forms, maybe their real-world appearance. Now one of those—she looked about ten years old—spoke up. "My great-great-aunt is like that. Back in the twentieth, she was an account executive." Hmm, account executive didn't mean anything like the English words might make you think. "By the teens she was all crippled up. I've seen pictures. And she got drifty and depressed. My grandma said she lost her edge and then she lost her job."

One of the sand crabs reared back, a lurker drawn into the open. "So what's new in that? My brother is all unemployed and depressed, and he's only twenty. It's hard to keep up."

The ten-year-old ignored the interruption. "Gee-grantie was just old-fashioned. Grandma got her a job as a landscape artist—" The little girl slipped into pure picturing, showing old-time cellphone advertisements for background scenery you could rent for when people call and you're in the bathroom. "Grantie was good at that, but she never made as much money as before. And then video landscapes went fully irrelevant. Anyway, she lived with my grandma for twelve years. It sounds just like what you're talking about, Miri."

Twelve years! I'll go bonkers after even a year of this. She glared at the little girl. "So what happened then?"

"Oh, everything turned out fine in the end. My mom found a treatment site. They specialize in upgraded specialties. Forty-eight hours at their clinic and Gee-grantie had the skills of an ad manager." Which was about the modern equivalent of "account executive."

Silence. Even some of the crabs looked a little shocked.

After a moment, Jin said, "That sound like JITT to me."

"Just-in-time training? What if it is?"

"JITT is illegal," said Miri. *This is not something I want to talk about.*

"It wasn't illegal back then. And this JITT wasn't so bad. Gee-grantie lives pretty well as long as she keeps taking her upgrades. She seems happy, 'cept that she cries a lot."

"Sound like mind control to me," said Jin.

The little girl laughed. "It is not. You should know that, Jin Li! You, Chinese, with two shrink parents." Her eyes danced about, searching on things the others could not see. "Your parents were in the army, weren't they? They must know all about mind control. That's what you Han tried in Myanmar!"

Jin came to his feet, and kicked sand through the little girl's image. "No! I mean, that is year and year ago. Nobody do anything like that now. *We* certainly don't!"

Miri decided she didn't like the little girl. What she said was more or less true, but . . . Bob had talked to her once about the Myanmar Restoration, back when she was doing a history project in the fifth grade. She had quoted him as "an unnamed source high in the American military"; in fact, he said the same thing as most websites. You-Gotta-Believe-Me technology had been a Big Nightmare possibility for years. Myanmar was the only place where YGBM had been tried on a large scale. "It all comes down to the delivery problem," Bob had said. "The Chinese army had some new drugs, things that were very persuasive in a research lab. But in the field? The Chinese sank half their budget into YGBM and they didn't get as much payoff as a good propaganda campaign." Humans had a million years of evolution learning to resist the power of suggestion; there was no magic way to beat that!

Now Miri came to her feet, too. *"Hey!"* she said, in the tone Alice occasionally used. "I didn't come here to talk politics! I came for help with my grandfather."

The little girl stared at her for a moment, her face quirked in an odd smile. The air was full of support for Miri, unanimous minus one. After a moment, the little girl shrugged. "I was just trying to help. Hey, I'll be good. I'm all ears." And she demonstrated with a graphical exaggeration, growing wiggly rabbit ears.

So they all sat down again and had a quiet moment. Miri looked out along the beach. She knew this was the true view even though she had never been to Hainan in person. It was beautiful, a lot like the Cove in La Jolla, but this beach was much bigger, with correspondingly more real people. Out near the horizon there were three white peaks, icebergs on their way to coastal cities farther north. Just like in California.

"Okay, then," said Jin. "How we help Miri Gu? But no JITT. That's a dead end. Is your grandpa good at anything now day?"

"Well, he's always been great with words, better than anyone I know. He has poor clothes sense, but he's become very quick with numbers and mechanical things." That brought a wave of interest; some of the crabs opened up with little stories about numeracy. "But that just seems to send him into a rage." She showed them the story of the disemboweled automobile. If Louise Chumlig hadn't stood up for him, that would have gotten him expelled.

The little girl's big ears had shrunk back to normal size. Of course, she had more opinions: "Heh. I'm reading about him, what he was like before. He had a track record back in the twentieth century. 'Famous Poet,' blah blah blah. But he was only beloved by people who never met him."

"That's not true! Robert never suffered fools gladly, b-but—" She ran out of steam, remembering Lena and the stories about Graunty Cara. And remembering the Ezra Pound Incident.

Jin dug his toes into the sand. "Let's get back to track. Does he have any friends in school?"

"N-No. He's been matched up with Juan Orozco. That kid is like most in those classes, a dumbhead."

"What about friends from before?" said the little girl.

Miri shook her head. All the people Robert had known and helped when he was a great poet, none of them had made contact. Was being a friend such a temporary thing? "There are other old people in the class, but they're on different projects. They hardly talk at all."

"Go for a personality match. There must be hundreds of people with complementary problems." The little girl smiled. "Then arrange for an accidental collision? See, if your grandpa doesn't know you're working behind the scenes, he can't be resentful." She looked up, as if surprised by insight: "Better yet—once upon a time your grandpa stirred up a lotta critical interest. I bet there are still graduate students who would love to fawn on him. Sell one of them a truly excellent thesis topic!"

O

AFTERWARD, MIRI DID a number of character searches. One of the guys in Robert's Fairmont classes had known him for years! She should have noticed that before. The two had so much in common! If she could just get them together. Hmm. Too bad that dummy Orozco was teaming with Robert. . . . But Winston Blount was into something outside of school, and that involved at least one other person who had been in grad school with Robert way back in the 1970s.

How to set up something to bring them all together?

She also searched for graduate students who might want to talk with Robert. She was confident that no grandparent of Miri Gu would be susceptible to false flattery, but it would be nice for Robert to meet an outsider who obviously respected him. If it was somebody with weak data skills . . . well, that might be good, too; she might be able to help out directly.

She did a world search, the kind of thing that drags in yak herders desirous of learning English. But this time—hey, she got a near perfect match in less than five minutes. And this Sharif fellow was in Oregon, just far enough away that most contact would be virtual and tweakable. For all her snottiness, the little girl had made some really good suggestions.

Miri hesitated. In fact, all the really successful suggestions had been due to the little girl. Maybe the "little girl" persona was covering something. Miri started a query replicating out through everyone and everything that might provide identity clues. But even if the kid were really ten years old, it wouldn't prove anything. Some fifth graders were scary.

O

THE WOMAN WAS tall, and dressed in black. "I understand you're looking for some help," she said.

Huh? Zulfikar Sharif looked up from his beef taco. He hadn't heard her approach. Then he realized that he was still alone at his table in the back of the OSU caf. He frowned at the apparition, "I'm not accepting fantasies." *God protect me. I've been perverted still again.*

The woman looked at him severely. She wasn't more than thirty, but he couldn't imagine her on a date. "Young man, I am not your fantasy. You are looking for help with a thesis topic, are you not?"

"Oh!" Zulfi Sharif was no lover of high technology, but now in his second year in the OSU Literature Department, he'd become a bit desperate. His thesis advisor was no help; Professor Blandings seemed most interested in having a permanent, unpaid research assistant. So way back in January, Sharif had put out feelers for help. That had provoked endless adverts for plagiarized and custom-writ material. Annie Blandings was so obnoxious that Sharif was almost tempted by some of the early offers—till his geekier friends pointed out how badly that could go wrong.

Sharif had filtered out the plagiarists and the sarcastic jerkoffs. That left very little. So much for high technology. He had spent the last two semesters propping up Blandings's career in Deconstructive Revisionism. In the remaining time, he worked at a 411 job for the American Poetry Association and did his best to craft a thesis out of vapor. He had come to America hoping for old-world insight into the literature that he loved. Lately, he was beginning to wonder if he should have stayed home in Kolkata.

And now, suddenly, this woman. *The answer to my prayers. Yes, sure.* He waved her to be seated; at least that would embarrass her.

But the apparition knew exactly where it stood. It slid into the chair across the table with scarcely an overlap of body and furniture.

"I was really expecting an email," he said.

The woman in black just shrugged. Her imperious glance did not waver. After a moment, Sharif continued, "In fact, I *am* looking for a thesis topic. But I'll have you know, I'm not interested in fraud, or plagiarism, or collaboration. If you're selling that, then please shove off. I simply want the sort of pointers"—*and support*—"that a good thesis advisor would give a student."

The lady smiled a cruel smile, and it suddenly occurred to Sharif that she might be connected to Annie Blandings. The old fart didn't even wear—but maybe she had friends who did.

"Nothing whatsoever illegal, Mr. Sharif. I simply saw your ad. I have a tremendous opportunity for you."

"And I don't have much money!"

"I'm sure we can come to an arrangement. Interested?"

"Well . . . possibly."

The lady in black leaned forward. Even her shadow matched the cafeteria lighting. Sharif hadn't realized that such precision was possible. "I don't suppose you know that Robert Gu is alive and well and living in Southern California?"

"Huh? Bullshit! He died some years ago. There hasn't been . . ." His words dribbled off before her silent stare. He tapped briefly at his phantom keypad, calling up a standard search. Since he started working 411, he'd become rather good at this kind of ultra-fast research. Results streamed across the tabletop. "Okay. He just stopped writing. Alzheimer's . . . and *he's come back!*"

"Indeed. Does this suggest possibilities?"

"Um." Sharif continued his guppy imitation for a second or two. *If I had just looked for the right facts, I would have known this a month ago.* "It does suggest possibilities." Interviewing Robert Gu would run a close second to chatting up William Shakespeare.

"Good." The lady in black tented her fingers. "There are complications, however."

"Like what?" An opportunity this good must be a scam.

"Robert—" The woman's image seem to freeze for an instant, maybe a communications jitter. "—Professor Gu has never suffered fools gladly. And never less so than now. I can give you access capability in his private enum. It will be up to you to intrigue him."

Without the enum, getting through to the great man could be very difficult.

"How much?" he said. He had twenty thousand dollars in the student credit union. Perhaps his brother in Kolkata could be hit up for one more loan.

"Ah, my price is not in dollars. I simply ask to tag along, occasionally to make a suggestion or ask a question."

"But I'll have first use?"

"Of course."

"I, well—" Sharif wavered. *Robert Gu!* "Okay, you've got a deal."

"Very good." The lady gestured for his hand. "Give me a moment of full access."

Epiphany Rule Number One, what they pound on in all the instructions: *Full access is only for parents and spouses—and then only if you like to take chances.* Whether it was her tone or his need Sharif was never sure, but he reached out and touched the empty air. He matched the pointing gesture with a lowering of security. The tingle in his fingers was surely his imagination, but now the air between them was full of binding certificates.

Then the paperwork was done. What remained in the air was a single enum. Sharif stared at the identifier with sudden apprehension. "So I just *call* him?"

She nodded. "Now you have that capability. But remember what I said about his . . . his intolerance for fools. Do you know his works?"

"Of course."

"Do you admire them?"

"Yes! I honestly and intelligently admire the hell out of them." It was a claim that worked with all the profs Sharif knew. In this case, it was also the truth.

The lady nodded. "That may be enough. Keep in mind that Professor Gu is not feeling well. He is still recovering from his illness. You may have to be directly useful to him."

"I'll empty the man's chamber pot if that will help."

Again a brief freeze of expression. "Ah! I don't think that will be necessary. But he misses things from the past. He misses the way books used to be. You know, those clunky things you have to carry around."

Who is this creature? But he nodded. "I know all about, um, physical books. I can show him plenty, and in person." He was already looking up taxi services.

"Very good." The apparition smiled. "Good luck, Mr. Sharif." And it was gone.

Sharif sat for almost a minute, staring blankly into the space lately occupied by the woman in black. And then he was consumed by the desire to share this news with others. Fortunately, the caf was nearly empty this late at night, and Sharif was not one of those who could message as quickly as they were overcome by the whim. No, after a moment he realized that this was likely something he should keep under his hat, at least until he'd established a connection with Robert Gu.

Besides . . . second thoughts were percolating up. *How could I be so stupid as to let her into my wearable?* He ran the Epiphany integrity check a couple of times. Widgets of purity floated in the air above his taco. Epiphany said he was clean; of course, if he'd been totally perverted that's exactly what it would say. *Damnation. I don't want to fry-clean my clothes. Not again!*

Especially in this case. He looked at the golden enum: Robert Gu's own direct identifier. If he took the right approach, he would finally have his thesis. Not just any ordinary thesis. Sharif considered Robert Gu to be from the highest rank of modern literature, up there with Williams and Cho.

And Annie Blandings thought Gu was God.

11

INTRODUCTION TO THE LIBRAREOME PROJECT

Wearable computers, what a concept. IBM PC meets Epiphany-brand high-fashion. In fact, Robert might have mistaken his new wardrobe for ordinary clothes. True, the shirts and pants were not a style he favored. There were embroidered patterns both inside and out. But the embroidery was more noticeable to the touch than the eye; Juan Orozco had to show him special views to reveal the net of microprocessors and lasers. The main problem was the damn contact lenses. He had to put them on every morning and then wear them all day. There were constant twinkles and flashes in his eyes. But with practice, he got control of that. He felt a moment of pure joy the first time he managed to type a query on a phantom keyboard and view the Google response floating in the air before him. . . . There was a feeling of *power* in being able to draw answers out of thin air.

And then there was what Juan Orozco called "ensemble coding."

A week passed. Robert was practicing with his beginner's outfit, trying to repeat the coding tricks Juan had shown him. For the most part, even the simplest gestures didn't work when he first tried them. But he would flail and flail—and when the command did work, the success gave him a pitiful spike of joy and he worked even harder. Like a boy with a new computer game. Or a trained rat.

When the phone call came, he thought he was having a stroke. There were bright flashes before his eyes, and a faraway buzzing sound. The buzzing broke into words: ". . . very mu*zzzz* like to . . . interview you *zzzz*ir . . ."

Aha! Spam, or some kind of reporter.

"Why would I want to give an interview?"

"B*zzz*t a short int . . . view."

"Even a short one." Robert's reply was a reflex. It had been years since he'd had the opportunity to dump on a journalist.

The light was still a glaring shapelessness, but when Robert straightened his collar, the voice became sharp and perfect. "Sir, my name is Sharif, Zulfikar Sharif. The interview would be for my Lit-in-English thesis."

Robert squinted and shrugged, squinted again. And then suddenly he got it right: his visitor was standing in the middle of the bedroom. *I have to tell Juan about this!* It was his first real three-dimensional success, and everything that the kid had claimed about retinal painting. Robert stood and stepped to the side, looking behind the visitor. The image was so solid, so complete. *Hmm.* And yet the visitor cast shadows contrary to the real lighting. *I wonder whose fault that is?*

His dark-skinned visitor—Indian? Pakistani? his voice held a South Asian lilt—was still talking. "Please don't say no, sir! Interviewing you would be my great honor. You are a resource for all humanity."

Robert walked back and forth in front of the visitor. He was still boggled by the medium of the message.

"Just a small amount of your precious time, sir! That's all I ask. And—" He looked around Robert's room, probably seeing what was truly there. Robert had not had a chance to set up false backgrounds. Juan had been going to show him that yesterday, but they had gotten sidetracked by Robert's side of the bargain—tutoring the kid in English. Poor, subliterate Juan. This Sharif fellow on the other hand: *How bright are graduate students these days?*

This particular graduate student was looking more and more desperate. His gaze caught on something behind Robert. "Ah, books! You are one who still treasures the real thing."

Robert's "bookcases" were made from plastic slats and cardboard boxes. But they held all the books he had rescued from the basement. Some of them—the Kipling—he would never have bothered with in the old days. But these were all he had now. He looked back at Sharif. "Indeed I do. Your point, Mr. Sharif?"

"I just thought—it means we share the same values. By helping me, you'll be advancing those noble passions." He paused—listening to some inner voice? Since his lessons with Juan, Robert had become suspicious of people listening to their inner voices. "Perhaps we could strike a bargain, sir. I would give almost anything for a few hours of your opinions and reminiscence. I would be happy to be your personal 411 agent. I'm an expert at such services; it's how I pay my way at OSU. I can guide you through the contemporary world."

"I already have a tutor." And when he considered the flippancy, he felt a twinge of surprise. In a sense it was true: he had Juan.

Another significant silence. "Oh. Him." Sharif—his image, perfect except for the misplaced shadows and the shoes that disappeared a quarter inch into the floor—walked around Robert. To get a closer look at the books? Suddenly, Robert had even more questions for Juan Orozco. But Sharif was talking again: "These are permanently printed? Not just-in-time chapbooks?"

"Of course!"

"Wonderful. You know . . . I could show you around the UCSD library."

Millions of volumes.

"I can go down there myself, anytime." But so far he hadn't quite dared. Robert looked at his little library. In the middle ages, a rich man might have so many books. Now people with books were rare once again. But at UCSD, there was a real, physical library. And going with his graduate student . . . that would be a little like the old days.

He looked back at Sharif. "When?"

"Why not now?"

Robert would have to let Juan Orozco know this afternoon's session was off. He felt an instant of uncharacteristic embarrassment. Juan was going to show him how to do glance searches, and Robert had promised Juan scansion. Robert pushed the regrets aside. "Let's go, then," he said.

O

ROBERT TOOK A car down to campus. For some reason, he couldn't get a clear image of Sharif inside the automobile. There was just his voice chattering away, asking Robert for his opinion of everything they saw, offering opinions and facts whenever Robert seemed even faintly puzzled.

Robert had driven past the outskirts of campus before; today he would see what the place had finally become. Coming out of Fallbrook, there were the usual subdivisions, unexceptional and dull. But just north of campus, he drove past endless gray-green buildings. Here and there, windowless walkways stretched across the canyons.

"Bioscience labs," Sharif cheerfully explained. "They're mostly underground." He fed Robert's Epiphany with pointers to images and details. Ah. So these doorless, windowless structures were not some twenty-first-century experiment in communal living. In fact, there weren't more than a few dozen people inside them. The connecting corridors were for biosample transport.

Monstrous things might gestate in these buildings and in the caverns below. But salvation, too. Robert gave them a little salute. Reed Weber's heavenly minefield was created in places like these.

These were the anterooms to UCSD. He braced himself for unintelligible futurism: the main campus. His car drove down Torrey Pines Road. The intersections were almost as he remembered, though there were no traffic lights and no stopping. Cross traffic interleaved with smooth and eerie grace. *Someday I must write a lighthearted piece about the secret life of automobiles.* He had never seen one stop for much longer than it took passengers to get off and on. Out in the desert, his car had departed almost immediately, stranding him. But by the time he got back to the road, another had pulled up. The devices were always moving. He imagined them circling the county, forever maneuvering so that no customer ever need wait more than a few moments. *But what do they do at night, when business is scarce?* That would be the topic of his poem. Were there hidden garages, hidden car parks? There had to be garages for repair work—or at least equipment swapouts. But maybe there was no other stopping. This was the stuff of both poetry and futurism: Maybe at night when demand fell and they otherwise would have to sleep without profit in some empty lot, maybe then they conspired to clump together like Japanese transformer toys . . . to become freight trucks hauling cargo that was too big for UP/Express.

In any case, the old parking lots on the north side of campus were gone, replaced by gaming fields and house-of-cards-style office buildings. Robert had the car drop him at the edge of the old campus, near where Applied Physics and Math used to be.

"Nothing looks the same, even where there were buildings before." In fact, there seemed to be more open space than he remembered from the seventies.

"Don't worry about it, Professor." Sharif was still audio only. It sounded as if he were reading from a brochure: "UCSD is an unusual campus, less traditional than any other in the UC system. Most of the buildings were rebuilt after the Rose Canyon earthquake. Here's the official view." Suddenly the buildings were sturdy, reinforced concrete, much as he remembered.

Robert waved the fakery away, a gesture Juan had showed him early on. "Hands off the main view, Mr. Sharif."

"Sorry."

Robert walked eastward across campus, sampling the ambience. On the gaming fields, there was just as much rushing around as in the 1970s, half a dozen separate games of touch football and soccer. Robert had never participated in those, but one thing he'd admired about UCSD was that the students *played* sports that were semi-pro spectator events at other schools.

Up close . . . well, the people he passed looked ordinary enough. There were the familiar backpacks, with the handles of tennis rackets sticking out the top like assault rifles.

Many people were talking to themselves, sometimes gesturing into the empty air, or jabbing fingers at unseen antagonists.

Nothing new in that; cellphone addicts had always been one of Robert's pet peeves. But these folks were more blatant about it than the kids at Fairmont High. There was something foolish about a fellow walking along, suddenly stopping to tap at his belt, and then talking to the air.

The new, numerate Robert couldn't resist keeping count of what he saw—and he soon noticed something the old Robert might not have: There were many college-age kids running around, but there were too many old people. One person in ten looked really old, old as Robert truly was. One in three were lean and spry, the twentieth-century cliché of "active senior citizens." And some . . . it took him a while to spot the few where modern medicine was all on target. Their skin was firm and their stride was strong; they almost looked young.

Then the most encouraging sight of all: a pair of old duffers coming his way—and both of them carrying books! Robert felt like grabbing their free hands and dancing a jig. Instead he gave them a broad grin as they walked by.

O

SHARIF AGREED THAT stepping into an ordinary building—or even the campus bookstore—wouldn't be an effective way to find real books. "The university library is your best bet, Professor."

Robert walked down a gentle slope. The eucalyptus grove was more overgrown than he remembered. The dry crowns rustled in the breeze above. The debris of bark and twigs and branches crunched under his feet. Somewhere ahead of him, a choir sang.

Then, through the trees, he saw the Geisel Library. Unchanged after all the years! Well, the pillared supports were covered with ivy—but there was nothing virtual about it. He walked out from under the trees and stared.

Sharif's voice popped up, "Professor, if you'll bear to the right, the sidewalk goes to the main—"

That was the way Robert remembered, but he hesitated when the other's voice dropped away. "Yes?"

"Oops, heh. Just detour around to the left. There's a mob of singers blocking the main entrance."

"Okay. What is all the singing about, anyway?"

Sharif made no reply.

Robert shrugged and followed his invisible guide's suggestion, walking around the north side of the building, down to what had been a lower-level parking lot. From here the library towered above him. He remembered when it was built, the criticisms: "It's an expensive white elephant," "We've been hijacked by space cadets." In fact, it did look like something brought down from outer space: the six aboveground stories formed a huge octahedron, touching ground on one vertex and clasped by fifty-foot pillars. In Robert's time, the structure had been concrete and sweeping glass. Now the vines extended past the fifth story, obscuring the concrete. The library still looked like it came from heaven, but now it was an ancient gem-mountain, and the clasp was the green of a supporting earth.

The singers were louder. It sounded as if they were singing "La Marseillaise." But there were also chants that sounded like a good old-fashioned student protest.

He was well under the overhang now. He had to look straight up to see the undersides of the fourth, fifth, and sixth floors, to see where the concrete finally emerged from the ivy.

Strange. The edges of each floor were straight as ever, but the concrete was laced with irregular lighter lines. In the sunlight those lines glinted like silver wedged in stonework.

"Sharif?"

No answer. *I should look up the explanation.* Juan Orozco could do such searches almost without thinking. Then he smiled: the silvery crack lines were a kind of playful mystery—and that might be their explanation. UCSD had a tradition of weird and wonderful campus art.

Robert started toward the short stairway that led to a loading dock. This looked like the most direct way into the library. There was a faded AUTHORIZED STAFF ONLY sign painted on the wall. The freight door was rolled down shut, but a second, smaller door was ajar. From within he could hear some kind of power saw—carpentry? He remembered what Juan had said about getting Epiphany's default local views. He waggled his hand tentatively. Nothing. He gestured again, a little differently: *Oops.* The loading dock was plastered with KEEP OUT signs. He glanced up the hillside; somewhere beyond the crest would be the main entrance. Epiphany showed him a mauve nimbus pulsating in time with the singing. Words floated above the music *"À bas la Bibléotome!"*—"Down with the Librareome Project!" Now that he was hearing both real and remote voices, the music was close to cacophony.

"What's going on, Sharif?"

This time there was an answer: "It's just another student protest. You'd never get in through the front door."

He stood still for a moment, filled with mild curiosity about what students demonstrated against nowadays. *No matter.* He could look that up later. He stepped nearer the half-opened door, looked down a dimly lit hallway. Despite the phantasmic storm of warnings and rules, he saw no obstacle to free passage. But now the strange sound was louder than the choir: rough, tearing growls spaced by silence.

Robert stepped through the doorway.

12

GUARDIANS OF THE PAST, HANDMAIDENS OF THE FUTURE

From its beginning, the Elder Cabal had met on the sixth floor of the Geisel Library. Winston Blount, calling in favors from his years at Arts and Letters, had made that possible. For a while, he had even had a nice clubroom in the staff lounge up here. That had been after the Rose Canyon quake, when the bright young future freaks had been briefly leery of their own technological fixes and floor space was available to those willing to risk the heights.

In the first years, there were almost thirty regulars. The membership had changed from year to year, but they were mostly faculty and staff from the turn of the century, almost all retired or laid off.

Time passed and the cabal dwindled. Blount himself had drifted away from the group, discovering that there weren't many more favors left for him to call in. His plans for a resumed career had centered on the Fairmont Adult Ed program. Then the Orozco boy had unintentionally pointed him at a magnificent shortcut: the Librareome protest movement. And the inner circle of the cabal was perfect for that. Perhaps it was just as well that the inner circle was exactly the cabal's entire remaining membership.

Tom Parker was sitting right beside the window wall. He and Blount peered down upon the protesters. Parker chuckled. "So, Dean, are you going to preach to the choir?"

Blount grunted. "No. But they can see us up here. Give the folks a wave, Tommie." Blount followed his own advice, raising his arms in a kind of blessing upon the singers at the main entrance and the slightly smaller mob on the terrace by the Snake Path. In fact, he had offered to speak at the demonstration. In the old days he would have been a featured speaker. Now he was still a critical player, but of zero publicity value. He flickered through some of the images that glowed above the crowd. "My, this event *is* big. Layered in fact." But some of the layers were counterdemonstrations, obscene ghosts that capered through the crowd to mock them. *Damn them.* He turned off all enhancements, and noticed that Parker was grinning at him.

"Still trying to use those contact lenses, aren't you Dean?" He patted his laptop computer lovingly. "It just goes to show, you can't beat the genius of a mouse-and-windows environment." Parker's hands slid across the keyboard. He was working through the layers of enhancement that Blount had been seeing directly with his contacts. Tom Parker might be the sharpest fellow left in the cabal, but he was hopelessly fixated on old ways. "I've customized my laptop to pick out what's really important." Images flickered on his tiny screen. There were things Winston Blount had not noticed in his contacts: someone had set a kind of nimbus over the demonstrators. Impressive.

Tommie was still chuckling. "I can't tell about that purple halo. Is it supposed to be pro- or anti-Librareome?"

On the other side of Parker, Carlos Rivera leaned back from the window and stretched. "Anti, according to the journalists.

They say the halo is to bless the guardians of the past." The three watched silently for a moment. The sound of the choir came through the high glass windows, but also from protesters around the world. The combined effect was more symbolic than beautiful, since the voices were so far out of synch.

After a moment, Carlos Rivera spoke again. "Almost a third of the physical visitors are from out of town!"

Blount grinned back at him. Carlos Rivera was a strange young fellow, a disabled veteran. He hardly met the cabal's informal age requirements, but in some ways he was almost as old-fashioned as Tommie Parker. He wore small thick glasses, the kind that had been popular in the early teens. He had typer rings on all his fingers and both thumbs. His shirt was one of the old displayables. Right now it showed white letters on black: "Librarians: Guardians of the Past, Handmaidens of the Future." But the most important thing about Carlos Rivera was that he was on the Library staff.

Parker was studying the numbers on his laptop. "Well, we've got the world's attention. We spiked at two million viewers a few moments back. And lots more will be watching this asynchronously."

"What does UCSD Public Relations say?"

Parker typed briefly on his laptop. "They're lying low. The PR people would just as soon that this be a non-event. Ha. But they're getting pounded by the popular press. . . ." Parker leaned back and shifted into reminiscence. "There was a time, I would have hidden my own cameras down on the lower floors. And if they deadzoned me, I'd've broken into the PR site and pasted pictures of burning books all across their press releases!"

"Duì," said Rivera, nodding his head. "But that would be difficult nowadays."

"Yup. Worse, it would take courage." Tommie patted his laptop. "And that's the trouble with people nowadays. They've traded freedom for security. When I was a young man, the cops didn't live in every widget, and there wasn't some clown collecting royalties on every keystroke. Back then there was no 'Secure Hardware Environment' and it didn't take ten thousand transistors to make a flipflop. I remember in '91, when I took down the"—and he was off on one his stories. Poor Tommie. Modern medicine had not cured him of his need to tell about old adventures again and again.

But Carlos Rivera seemed to love these stories. He nodded every few seconds, his expression rapt. Blount sometimes wondered whether Rivera's enthusiasm should be held for or against the young fellow.

"—so anyway, by the time they thought to check for crimps in the fiber, we had dumped all the files and—"

Now, for a wonder, Rivera was no longer listening. He had turned toward the stacks, and his expression was full of surprise. He rattled off something in Chinese, then thankfully slipped back into English: "I mean, please wait a moment."

"What?" Parker glanced at his laptop. "Have they started the shredders?"

Damn, thought Blount. He had been hoping that terrible moment could be marked by the protesters.

"Yes," said Rivera, "but that was several minutes ago, while you were talking. This is something different. Someone has gotten into the loading area."

Winston bounced to his feet—bounced as much as semirejuvenated joints could be made to bounce. "I thought you said there was security down there?"

"I thought there was!" Rivera came to his feet, too. "I can show you." Images popped into Blount's eyes, views from cameras on the north and east sides of the building, more views than he could make sense of.

Blount waved the images away. "I want to see this for myself." He plunged into the library stacks, Rivera close behind.

"If we had known about this, we could have put some of our people down there." That was the problem nowadays. Security was so good that when it broke down, no one was around to take advantage! In the back of Blount's mind, something marveled at his new priorities. There had been a time when Dean Winston C. Blount had been the fellow on the establishment side, doing his best to make sure that the know-nothings didn't bust things up. Now . . . well, now, a certain amount of hell-raising might be the only way to set the establishment right.

"Has the choir seen this?"

"Dunno. The best views were quarantined." Rivera sounded out of breath.

They detoured around the elevators and staff rooms that occupied the middle of the floor. Now they were moving at right angles to the stacks. Far down the book-lined shelves he glimpsed the sky beyond the windows. "You said there was chance that Max Huertas might show up today."

"*Duì.* Yes. There's some chance he might come. Several libraries begin the project this week, but UCSD is the star." Huertas was more than just the money behind the Librareome. He was also a major investor in the biotech labs near campus. He had turned the university scene upside down with his Librareome insanity, ultimately greasing it past an administration that should have fought him to the death.

Blount's jog slowed as they approached the windows. The UCSD campus had suffered a revolution in the last decades. The vibrant building campaign of his time as dean had been swept away by the Rose Canyon quake and the facile logic of the modern university administrations. The campus had reverted to a woodsy, low-density style, with buildings that might just as well have been prefab Quonsets. In a sad, sad way it reminded him of the campus's earliest years, of his grad-school years. *We built such a beautiful place here, and then we let opportunism and remote learning and the damn labs dissipate it all.* What shall it profit a university, if it shall enroll five hundred thousand, and lose its own soul?

He reached the northeast windows and looked down. The sixth floor was at the building's maximum overhang. You could see almost straight down—to a stretch of cracked concrete, the library loading dock. And there was a guy down there, furtively looking around. Carlos Rivera caught up with Blount and for a moment they were both staring downward. Then Blount noticed that the younger man was actually staring through the floor; he'd found some camera on the lower levels. "That's not Max Huertas," said Carlos. "He'd come with a gang of lackeys."

"Yeah." But it was someone who could persuade the Library rent-a-cops to let him go down there. Blount tapped the glass.

"Look up here, you jerk!" It was amazing what little he could see from straight up. The stranger carried himself with a twitchy awkwardness, like an old-timer coping with a regrown nervous system. . . . Blount was beginning to get a very bad feeling. And then the stranger turned his gaze upward. It was like finding a large rat at your feet.

"Oh, Christ." A strange combination of disgust and curiosity forced him to say: "Just get him up here."

○

AFTER THE SUNNY loading dock, the hallway seemed very dark. Robert hesitated, adjusting to the light. The walls were streaked with scuff and scrape marks. The floor was naked concrete. This was not a public area. It reminded him of years ago when he and certain undergrads would sneak around in the utility cores of these buildings.

Epiphany hung tiny labels on the doors and ceiling, and even the cracks in the walls. They weren't terribly informative, ID numbers and maintenance instructions, the sort of thing that might have been paint-stenciled in the old days. But—if he wanted to take the time—he could search through the signs and get background information. And there were mysteries. A large, silver-puttied crack in the wall was marked "cantileverLimitCycle < 1.2mm:25s." Robert was about to search on that when he noticed a door decorated with a larger banner, one that ticked out the seconds:

00:07:03 Librareome Equipment in Operation: KEEP OUT!

What the hell, this door was open too.

On the other side, the power-saw racket was louder. He walked fifty feet, past plastic crates—"Rescued Data," the labels said. At the end, behind some kind of legged forklift, there was another unlocked door. And now he was on familiar ground: he was at the bottom of the library's central stairwell. He looked up and up, into the foreshortened spiral of steps. Tiny flecks of white floated and swirled in the column of light. Snowflakes? But one landed on his hand: a fleck of paper.

And now the ripping buzz of the saw was still louder, and there was also the sound of a giant vacuum cleaner. But it was the irregular ripping buzz that echoed down the stairwell and beat him about the head. There was something familiar about that, but it wasn't an *indoors* kind of sound. He started up the stairs, pausing at each landing. The dust and the noise were worst at the fourth floor, labeled "Catalog Section PZ." The door opened smoothly. Beyond would be the library stacks. All the books you could ever want, miles of them. The beauty of ideas waiting in ambush.

But this was like no stacks he had ever seen. The floor was draped in white tarpaulin. The air was hazy with drifting debris. He took a breath, smelled pine pitch and burnt wood—and for a moment he couldn't stop coughing.

Brap, painfully loud now, coming from four aisles to his right. There were empty shelves here, a littering of paper scraps and deep dust.

Brrap. Against logic, sometimes recognition comes hard. But finally, Robert remembered the exact sound which that abrupt roar must be. He had heard it occasionally throughout his life, but always the machine had been outdoors.

Brrrap! A tree shredder!

Ahead of him, everything was empty bookcases, skeletons. Robert went to the end of the aisle and walked toward the noise. The air was a fog of floating paper dust. In the fourth aisle, the space between the bookcases was filled with a pulsing fabric tube. The monster worm was brightly lit from within. At the other end, almost twenty feet away, was the worm's maw—the source of the noise. Indistinct in the swirling haze, Robert could see two white-suited figures, their jackets labeled "Huertas Data Rescue." The two wore filter masks and head protectors. They might have been construction workers. In fact, this business was the ultimate in deconstruction: first one and then the other would pull books off the racks and toss them into the shredder's maw. The maintenance labels made calm phrases of the horror: The raging maw was a "NaviCloud custom debinder." The fabric tunnel that stretched out behind it was a "camera tunnel." Robert flinched from the sight—and Epiphany randomly rewarded his gesture with imagery from within the monster: The shredded fragments of books and magazines flew down the tunnel like leaves in tornado, twisting and tumbling. The inside of the fabric was stitched with thousands of tiny cameras. The shreds were being photographed again and again, from every angle and orientation, till finally the torn leaves dropped into a bin just in front of Robert. Rescued data.

BRRRRRAP! The monster advanced another foot into the stacks, leaving another foot of empty shelves behind it. Almost empty. Robert stepped into the aisle and his hand caught on something lying on a shelf. It wasn't dust. It was half a page, a remnant of all the thousands of books that had already been sucked into the "data rescue" equipment. He waved it at the white-suited workers and screamed words that were lost in the noise of their shredder and the worm tunnel fans.

But the two looked up and shouted something back.

If the body of the glowing worm hadn't been between him and them, Robert might have rushed the pair. As it was, they just waved impotently at each other.

Then a third guy appeared, behind Robert. This one was an overweight thirty-something wearing Bermuda shorts and a huge black T-shirt. The young man was shouting at him in—what, Mandarin? He waved pleadingly for Robert to follow him back toward the stairwell, away from the nightmare.

O

THE SIXTH FLOOR of the library was not part of the nightmare. In fact, it looked pretty much as Robert remembered from the early 1970s. The guy with the big T-shirt led him through the stacks to a study area on the south side of the building. There was a short fellow with an ancient laptop computer, sitting right by the windows. The little guy stood and stared. Then suddenly he laughed, and stuck out his hand. "I'll be damned. You really *are* Robert Gu!"

Robert took the proffered hand, and stood uncertainly for a moment. Book shredders below, mystery man up here. And the crazy choir. He could finally see the singers in the plaza.

"Ha. You don't recognize me, do you, Robert?" *No.* The guy had lots of blond hair, but his face was as old as the hills. Only his laughter was familiar. After a second, he shrugged and waved for Robert to sit down. "I don't blame you," he chattered on. "But recognition the other way is easy. You lucked out,

Robert, didn't you? I'd guess the Venn-Kurasawa treatment worked a hundred percent for you; your skin looks better than when you were twenty-five years old." The old man slid an age-spotted hand across his own features and smiled ruefully. "But how's the rest of you? You look a little twitchy."

"I—I lost my marbles. Alzheimer's. But—"

"Hey, right. I can tell."

It was the heedless frankness that Robert suddenly recognized. Behind the stranger's face, Robert recognized the freshman who had made his UCSD years significantly more exciting. "Tommie Parker!" The young squirt who could never be put down, who had been a computer-science jock at UCSD before he had even graduated from high school, before there had even been such a major. The little guy who couldn't wait for the future.

Tommie nodded, chuckling. "Yup. Yup. But it's been 'Professor Thomas Parker' for a long time. You know I got my doctorate from MIT? Then I came back here and I taught for almost forty years. You're looking at a Member of the Establishment."

And seeing what time had done . . . for a moment Robert was silent. *I should be immune by now.* He looked out the window at the crowds, away from Parker. "So what's going on, Tommie? You're camped up here like some grand commander."

Parker laughed and typed at his keyboard. From what Robert could see of the display, it was some ancient system, worse than his view-page—and nothing like what he could get from Epiphany. But there was enthusiasm in Tom Parker's voice. "It's this protest demonstration we set up. Against the Librareome Menace. We didn't stop the shredding, but—jeez, look at that. I got your break-in on video." Tommie's display showed what looked like a telephoto image shot from north of campus. A tiny figure that might have been Robert Gu was entering the library's freight area. "I don't know how you got past security, Robert."

"Management wonders that too," said the young man who rescued Robert. He had sat down behind the front desk and brushed flakes of paper dandruff off of his hair and T-shirt. Suddenly the "Chad is Bad" slogan on his shirt made a lot of sense. He noticed Robert's regard and gave him a little wave. "Hi, Professor Gu. I'm Carlos Rivera, library staff." His T-shirt morphed to white, which at least made the little bits of paper less obvious.

"You're part of this destruction?" He suddenly noticed the half page he had saved from the shredder. He laid it gently on the table. There were words there; maybe he could figure out what they had been part of.

"No, no," said Parker. "Carlos is helping us. In fact, all the librarians oppose the shredding—excepting the administrators. And seeing that you got past library security, I think we have allies even there. You're a famous guy, Robert. And we can use the video you got."

"But I—" Robert started to say he didn't have a camera. Then he thought of the clothes he was wearing. "Okay, but you'll have to show me how to give it to you."

"No problem—" began Rivera.

"You're using that Epiphany junk, aren't you, Robert? Yeah, you'll have to get some wearer to help you. Wearables are supposed to be such a convenience, but mainly they're an excuse for other people to run your life. Me, I'll stick with the proven solutions." He patted his laptop. Through some fluke of memory, Robert recognized the model. Twenty-some years ago, this gadget had been at the cutting edge of power and miniaturization, barely eight inches by ten, with a brilliant, millimeters-thin screen and a fancy camera. Now . . . even to Robert it was a ponderous behemoth. *How can it even talk to the modern magic?*

Parker's glance slid across to the librarian. "How did he make it into the building, Carlos?"

Rivera said, "*Wǒ bù zhīdào.*"

Tommie groaned. "You're talking Chinese, Carlos."

"Oops, sorry." He glanced at Robert. "I was an army translator during the war," he said, as if that explained everything. "I don't know how he got in, Professor Parker. I saw him walking down from Warschawski Hall. I was using the same viewpoints as our security does. But you notice that even after he got to the shredders, there was still no one to stop him." He turned, looked expectantly into the stacks. "Maybe the dean has other people working on this."

After a moment, an old man stepped out from behind the books. "You know I don't, Carlos." He walked to the window without looking at Robert. *Aha,* thought Robert, *so this is where Winnie's disappeared to the last couple of weeks.* Blount stared down at the plaza for several seconds. Finally he said, "The singing has stopped. They know about Gu's arrival, don't they?"

"Yes, sir. Even though we haven't published our own video, there's plenty of journalists floating around. At least three popular sources have IDed him." Outside, the crowd was cheering.

Robert tried the little shrug that Juan said would bring up local news. All he got was advertising.

And Sharif was still silent.

After a moment, Blount walked back to the head of the table and sat down with a wheeze. He hadn't looked directly at Robert; Winnie didn't seem nearly as confident as in Chumlig's class. *How long has it been since we last played our little political games?* Robert gave Blount a steady look. That should cause Epiphany to search on him. Also, in the old days, that look had always unnerved the guy.

"Okay," Blount nodded at Tom Parker, "tell our protestors to start the windup. You know, the interviews and opinion pieces."

"What about Mr. New Development here?" Tommie jerked a thumb in Robert's direction.

Blount finally looked at Robert. And Epiphany began streaming information across his view: *Google BioSource: Winston C. Blount, MA English from UCSD 1971, PhD English Literature from UCLA 1973, Associate Professor of English at Stanford 1973–1980, Professor of Literature and later Dean of Arts and Letters at UCSD 1980–2012. [Biblio, Speeches, Favorite things]. . . .*

"So, Winnie," he said, "you still wheeling and dealing?"

The other's face paled, but his reply was evenly worded. "Call me Winston, or Dean Blount. If you please." There was a time when he had gone by "Win." It was Robert who had cured him of that.

They stared at each other silently for another second. Finally, Blount said, "Do you have an explanation for how you got in the service entrance?"

Robert gave a little laugh. "I just walked in. I'm the most ignorant of all, Winston." What had become of Zulfi Sharif?

Tommie Parker looked up from his laptop. "There is recent public information on Robert Gu. Robert's been in deep Alzheimer's for almost four years. He's one of the late cures." He glanced up at Robert. "Jeez, man, you almost died of old age before you got well. On the other hand, it looks like you've had great medical luck otherwise. So what brought you to UCSD on this of all days?"

Robert shrugged. It was surprising how much he did *not* want to go into his problems with Bob and Miri. "The timing is just coincidence. I came down to UCSD because . . . because I wanted to see the books."

A not-so-friendly smile came to Blount's face. "How very like you, that you come the day we start burning them."

Rivera protested, "It's shredding, Dean. I mean, technically speaking. Except for the chad, all the shredda is preserved."

Robert looked at the torn paper he had brought from downstairs: shredda that had escaped its final resting place? He held up the forlorn slip of paper. "Honestly, I don't know what's going on. What was this? What madness explains destroying the book this was part of?"

Winnie didn't answer immediately; he waved at Rivera to pass him the fragment. He set it on the table and stared for a second. His bitter smile grew a little wider. "What pleasant irony. They're starting in the PZ's, aren't they, Carlos?"

"Duì," the young man replied, hesitantly.

"This," Winnie waved the paper in the air, "is from a science-fiction book!" A grim chuckle. "Those sci-fi bastards are just getting what they deserve. For thirty years they had literature education hijacked—and this is what all their reductionism has gotten them. Good riddance." He crumpled the paper and tossed it back at Robert.

Tommie grabbed the little ball of paper and tried to resuscitate it. "It's just an accident that science fiction came first, Dean."

"Actually," said Rivera, "there are rumors the shredders started with science fiction because there would be fewer complainers among the geeks."

"It doesn't matter," said Tommie. "They were scheduled to be well into other stuff by the end of today."

Winnie leaned forward. "What do you mean '*were* scheduled'?"

"You didn't know?" Parker patted his laptop again; was he in love with the ancient device or what? "The shredding ran into a minor technical problem. They've shut down for the day." He grinned. "The popular press says the 'minor technical problem' is the sudden appearance of Robert in the middle of their operation."

Rivera hesitated, and light glinted in the depths of his thick eyeglasses. "Yes," he said. So the crowd outside had something to celebrate after all. Winnie got up, looked out the window again, and sat down. "Very good, we've earned our first victory! Relay our congratulations to the troops, Tommie."

Robert raised his hands, "Will somebody please explain this madness to me? There may be nothing burning, but this does seem like *Fahrenheit 451*. That's another science-fiction story, Winston."

Rivera waved vaguely. "Search on keyword Librareome, Professor Gu."

Robert gestured and tapped. *How does Juan manage to do this without looking like an idiot?*

"Here, use my laptop. You'll never figure out how to drag news out of Epiphany."

Winston Blount slapped the table. "He can do that on his own time, Tommie. We have serious work to do."

"Okay, Dean. But Robert has changed things. We can use his reputation."

Rivera nodded. "Yes. He's won practically every literary prize there is."

"Stuff it," said Blount. "We already have five Nobelists on board. Compared to them, Gu is nothing special." Blount's glance flickered across Robert's face. The putdown he directed at Robert was accompanied by a minute hesitation, probably too short for the others to notice.

The most important things about Winston Blount were not in his Google bio. Once upon a time, Winnie had thought himself a poet. But he wasn't; he was merely articulate and the owner of a large ego. By the time they both arrived as junior faculty at Stanford, Robert had lost patience with the poseur. Besides, committee meetings would have been deadly dull if not for his hobby of needling Winnie Blount. The guy had been an unending source of amusement because he seemed to think he could outwit Robert. Semester after semester, their verbal duels became more pointed, Winnie's failure more obvious. It hadn't helped the other's cause that Blount had no talent for what he wanted most, to create significant literature. Robert's lighthearted campaign had been devastating. By the late 1970s, Poor Winnie was the laughingstock—quietly the laughingstock—of the department. All that was left of his claims to significance was his pomposity. He had departed Stanford, and Robert remembered feeling the satisfaction of having done the world a good deed when Blount found his proper place in the scheme of things, becoming an administrator. . . .

But he was probably just as good a poet as the new Robert Gu. *I wonder if Winnie really knows that?*

Of course, Tommie Parker was oblivious of such undercurrents. He responded to Blount's comment as though it were a neutral statement of fact. "*Someone* thinks he's important, Dean. Someone who had the power to slip him past some fairly good commercial security." He turned to Gu. "Think back, Robert. I know you're new to the information scene—and Epiphany obscures an awful lot—but did you notice anything strange today? I mean, before you got to the library?"

"Well—" He looked into the air above them. His web search was just beginning to show results, text and pics about the "Librareome Project: rescuing prehistory for the students of today." That *was* certainly strange stuff. Otherwise . . . there were the floating lights that meant various things. He tried to remember Juan's explanations. *Ah.* Sharif was back, a ruby icon that hovered just around the corner of the stacks. "I've had some help, a grad student named Zulfikar Sharif."

"Were you in contact with him as you came down toward the library?"

"Yes. Sharif thought I could get in easier if I didn't try to walk through the crowd at the main entrance."

Rivera and Parker exchanged glances. "You didn't see the security ribbons? They should have guided you to the south side of building."

"Professor, I think you were hijacked."

Parker nodded. "Don't feel bad about it, Robert. That sort of thing happens a lot with wearables. We should track down this 'Zulfikar Sharif' character."

Robert pointed to the ruby light. "I think he's still here."

The gesture must have been taken as a cue by his Epiphany—somehow making the light a public thing: Rivera looked in the direction he was pointing. "Yes! See that, Professor Parker?"

Tommie looked down at his laptop and massaged the touchpad. "Of course I see him. I'll bet he's been listening via Robert. What say we invite him out for a chat?"

Blount was squinting around, hopelessly. Evidently, he couldn't see the ruby glow. Nevertheless he took the question as directed at him. "Yes. Do it."

Robert tapped a release. A second passed. The ruby tinkerbell floated down to the edge of the table—and abruptly became a full-sized human being, dark-skinned, with earnest eyes. Sharif smiled apologetically, and shuffled through the edge of the table to "sit" on a chair on the other side. "Thank you so much for invoking me, Professor Gu. And yes," nodding to the others, "I have been listening. Apologies for my various communication problems."

"I call that taking advantage of a beginner's ignorance," said Parker.

Blount nodded emphatically. "I would say so! I—" He hesitated, seemed to think it over. "Ah, hell. What does it matter, Tommie? Everything we're doing today is perfectly open."

Tommie grinned. "True! But one thing I've learned is you *always* look a gift horse in the mouth. Sometimes they turn out to be the Trojan variety." He looked at the image in his laptop. "So, Mr. Sharif, I don't care if you've been eavesdropping or not. Just tell us what you've been doing with Robert Gu. Someone led him down to the service entrance and through all sorts of security."

Sharif smiled hesitantly. "In all honesty, I was as surprised as you about that. Professor Gu and I were talking freely when he arrived on campus. He got rather quiet as we came down the slope from your Warschawski Hall. And then for no apparent reason, he turned left and we went around the north side of the library. The next thing I knew he was walking into the freight entrance—and I lost contact. I don't know what more I can say. My own wearable security is of the highest order, of course. Um." He hestitated a moment and then changed topic. "Aren't you taking this whole thing in the wrong way? I mean, the Librareome Project will open up all past literature to everyone—and faster than any other project could do it. What is wrong with that?"

This last was met with total silence. Winston Blount smiled thinly. "I don't suppose you've seen our website?"

"Ah, not as yet." He paused and his eyes seemed to be looking far away. "Okay, I see what you're saying." He smiled. "I suppose I should be on your side—what you want will keep my 411 job safe! See here, I love the old poets, but old-time literature is so hard to get at. If your interest is in post-2000 topics, critical sources are everywhere and research gets *results*. But for the rest, you have to search through *that*." Sharif waved at the orderly ranks of books, the stacks that filled the library's sixth floor. "It can take days to gain even trivial insights."

Lazy bum, thought Robert, and wondered at Sharif's earlier enthusiasm for "real books." But he had noticed the trend even in his own teaching days. It wasn't just the students who refused to get their hands dirty. Even so-called researchers ignored the universe of things that weren't online.

Winnie glowered at the young man. "Mr. Sharif, you don't understand the purpose of the stacks. You don't go into the stacks expecting the precise answer to your burning-question-of-the-moment. It doesn't work that way. In all the thousands of times that I've gone hunting in the stacks, I've seldom found exactly what I was looking for. You know what I did find? I found the books on close-by topics. I found answers to questions that I had never thought to ask. Those answers took me in new directions and were almost always more valuable than whatever I originally had in mind." He glanced at Rivera. "Isn't that so, Carlos?"

Rivera nodded, a little weakly, Robert thought.

But Winnie was absolutely right, so right that Robert had to say something on the same side. "This is insanity, Sharif. Apparently, the Librareome Project is someone's idea for photographing and then digitizing the Library. But—" suddenly he was remembering things from his last years at Stanford "—didn't Google already do that?"

"That's true," said Rivera. "In fact, that was our first argument, and perhaps still the best one. But Huertas is a great salesman, and he does have arguments in his favor. What he has in mind is fast and very, very cheap. Past digitizations have not been as global or as unified as this will be. And Huertas has lawyers and software that will allow him to render microroyalty payments across all the old copyright regimes—without any new permissions."

Winnie vented a sour laugh. "The real reason the administration people bought into this is that they like Huertas's money, and maybe even the publicity. But let me tell you, Mr. Sharif, shredding destroys the books. That is the bottom line. We will be left with a useless jumble."

"Oh, no, Professor Blount. Read the overview. The pictures coming from the camera tunnel are analyzed and reformatted. It's a simple matter of software to reorient the images, match the tear marks and reconstruct the original texts in proper order. In fact—besides the mechanical simplicity of it all—that's the reason for the apparent violence. The tear marks come close to being unique. Really, it's not a new thing. Shotgun reconstructions are classic in genomics."

"Oh, yeah?" Robert picked up the much-abused page that he had rescued from the PZ stacks. He held it out like some limp murder victim. "So what perfection of software is going to recover something that was torn from its binding and never photographed?"

Sharif started to shrug and then saw the expression on

Robert's face. "Sir, it's really not a problem. There will be some loss, true. Even where everything is properly photoed, the programs will make some mismatches. Potentially, the error rate can be less than a few words per million volumes, far better than even hardcopy republishing with manual copyediting. That's why other major libraries are participating in the project, to get accurate cross-checking."

Other major libraries? Robert realized that his mouth was hanging open. He shut up; he couldn't think of anything to say.

Tommie stared into his laptop. "You seem suddenly well informed, Mr. Sharif."

"But . . . well, I am wearing," the young man said.

"Hmpf. And all you really want is to pursue your love of literature."

". . . Yes! My thesis advisor has based her entire career on Gu's *Secrets of the Ages.* And now I find out that the great poet is back from Alzheimer's! It's the opportunity of a lifetime. . . . Look. If you don't believe the Google bio, check in the 411 directories. I have lots of satisfied customers, many of them literature students at UCSD—not that I give them an unethical degree of help! Not at all." Aha. Maybe ghostwritten homework was still a no-no, even in this brave new world. "I don't know what happened with Professor Gu today, but didn't it slow down the Librareome Project? Isn't that what you want?"

Blount and Rivera were both nodding agreement.

"Yup," said Tommie. "You're a horse of some kind."

"I am simply a Lit-in-English student!"

Tommie shook his head. "You could be almost anything. You could be a committee. When you want to sound like a lit-lover, we get chat from a member who knows about poetry." Tommie tilted back his chair. "There's an old saying: The beginning of trust has to be an in-person contact. I don't see any usable chain of trust in your biography."

Sharif stood and walked partway through the table. He looked upward, waving his arms at the sky. "You want in-person? That I can supply. Look down here, at the bench by the footpath."

Tommie tilted his chair still farther back and glanced over

his shoulder. Robert walked to the window and looked down. Much of the crowd had dispersed, leaving just a few knots of die-hard demonstrators. The footpath was a tiled serpent that wound its way up the hillside, its head reaching just to the edge of the library terrace. It was a very real mosaic, new artwork since Robert's years at UCSD.

"I came all the way from Corvallis just to see Professor Gu. Please don't turn me away now."

And there by the path was a second Zulfi Sharif, this one not virtual at all. He was looking up at them and waving.

13

THE MIRI GANG IS BORN

For as long as Miri could remember, she'd had this problem with grandparents. Alice's parents—and Alice's grandparents, too—had all been living in Chicago; not one of them had survived. On Bob's side of the family, Robert had been almost dead, but then he came back! Now Miri was afraid she was losing him all over again.

And then there was Lena. . . .

Lena Gu was only dead on the record. Lena had persuaded Bob to set up that lie with the Friends of Privacy. Lena even ordered him to keep the details from Miri. But Bob had told Miri what he was doing. That was smart, because Miri would have figured it all out anyway. This way, Miri was imprisoned by her promises to Bob. She hadn't breathed a whisper of the truth to Robert, even when they were still talking and he had been so desperate.

But now *Miri* was getting desperate. She hadn't seen Lena in five months. Almost, she had called Lena after the Ezra Pound Incident. But that would have only confirmed Lena's opinions of Robert. Bob just wanted to ignore Robert's problems; coward. Alice was no coward, but she was deep in training these days and it wasn't going well. *Okay, I can handle this on my own,* Miri had told herself. She conceived a clever rehabilitation plan, working with Zulfi Sharif. At first, that had been great. Sharif's wearable had been easy to subvert; she had direct access to Robert. But after Robert's trip to UCSD, she realized that someone *else* was using Sharif, too.

It was definitely time to visit Lena.

Miri waited till the weekend and took a car down to Pyramid Hill. The place was really busy on Saturdays. Bob said it reminded him of the arcades of his childhood. You had to travel physically to the park, but once you got there you could do touchy-feely with all the best games. It was run by Baja Casinos, but for kids not old enough to legally gamble. The important thing for Miri was that the park had pretty good security. Even if Robert got curious about where she was going, it was unlikely he could follow her through to Lena.

She unhooked her bicycle from the rack on the back of the car, and imaged it as a small jackass. Her own persona was classic anime: big eyes, spiky hair, and tiny mouth. That should turn off anyone who might otherwise try to play with her.

Miri walked her jackass along a path that circled the hill. She overruled the anime imagery to view what was most popular today. Ugh. It was mostly Scooch-a-mouti nonsense. Salsipueds and baba llagas were everywhere. A year ago, no one had heard of the Scoochis, and now they were bigger than some of the corporate names. They had even dented the mega release of the latest *Cretaceous Returns.* There were hundreds of different *types* of Scoochi characters. Some were slyly stolen intellectual property. The rest were from folklores at the edge of the world. The imagery was very, very cheap, without any creative center. Maybe that's why little kids were the biggest fans.

Near the top of the hill, a Lesser Scooch-a-mout roared into the sky. That sound was not watts from some synthesizer. The departing Scooch-a-mout was how her view imaged the park's high ride. The ride capsule blasted from deep in the hill, hit four gees before it coasted into the sky, giving its passengers almost a minute of zero-gee before touching down in the park annex. It was the most spectacular ride in Southern California. Nowadays Miri's friends sniffed at it: "Might as well be a UP/Ex package." But when Miri was little, she had spent more than one afternoon bouncing back and forth across the sky.

Today, she got halfway to the east exit without choosing a particular game. She was careful not to touch, much less ride, the mechs. She especially avoided the furry cuddly critters. Except at the exits, "You touch, you pay" was the rule at Pyramid Hill. Maybe she should buy into a game just to shed some of the marketing pressure.

She paused, looked across the hillside. There was lots of noise and action, but if you listened carefully, you could tell that the kids in the bushes were actually playing in other universes, all choreographed so neither players nor equipment would get in each other's way. She had picked the right cover; classical anime was just too highbrow for these dorks.

"How about *Twin Spirits?* You only need two physicals for that."

"Eep!" Miri almost tripped over her jackass. She twisted around, putting the bike between her and the voice. There was a real person, also tricked out in anime costume. Miri dropped down into the true view: *Juan Orozco.* Talk about bad luck. She had never imagined he would be into classic anime.

She found her voice, a trilly high-pitched English thing that Annette Russell had given her. "Not today, I'm afraid. I'm looking for something grander."

Orozco—and the spiky-haired critter he presented—cocked his head questioningly. "You're Miri Gu, aren't you?"

This was majorly bad etiquette, but what do you expect from an fourteen-year-old loser? "So? I still don't want to play." She turned away and pushed her bike along the path. Orozco followed right along. He had a fold-up bike that didn't get in his way at all.

"You know I've teamed with your grandpa in Ms. Chumlig's composition class?"

"I knew that." *Boogers!* If Juan learned what Miri was up to, then *Robert* might too. "Have you been tracking me?"

"That's not against the law!"

"It's not polite." She didn't look at him, just stomped along very quickly.

"I haven't been watching second-by-second. I just was hoping to run into you, and then I saw you coming in the west gate. . . ." So maybe he had just set up proximity alerts. "You know, your grandpa is trying to help me. Like with my writing. I think I'm getting better at it. And I'm teaching him to wear. But . . . I feel sorry for him. He seems to be angry all the time."

Miri kept walking.

"Anyway, I was thinking . . . if he could get some of his old friends back . . . maybe he would feel better."

Miri whirled on him. "Are you recruiting?"

"No! I mean, I have an affiliance that could benefit seniors, but that's not what this is about. Your grandpa is helping me at school, and I want to help him."

They were coming down the Hill, approaching the east gate. This was the last chance for Pyramid Hill to make money. The closer you got to the gate, the harder the sell, across all park-supported realities. Furries danced playfully around them, begging to be picked up. The critters were real mechanicals; if you reached out to touch them, you'd find plush, deep fur under your hands, and real heft to their bodies. Near the gate, management wanted to sell these little robots, and a free feel goodbye had swayed thousands of otherwise resistant children. When Miri was younger, she'd bought about one doll a month. Her favorites still played in her bedroom.

She rolled her poor jackass through the crowd, avoiding the talking bears and the miniature Scooch-a-mouts, and the real children. Then they were out the gate. For a moment, Miri fumbled and lost her imagery. Now she was a plain fat girl, and her bike was a dumb machine. Orozco just looked skinny and nervous. He had a shiny new bike, but he couldn't seem to get it unfolded.

I don't want him to find out about Lena.

She jabbed a finger at the boy's chest. "My grandfather is fine. He doesn't need to be recruited into some payoff scheme. Outside of school, you stay away from him." She flashed imagery that Annette had created for their Avengers clique. The boy flinched.

"But I just want to help!"

"And furthermore, if I catch you tracking me . . ." She

switched to a deniable mode, a delayed delivery he wouldn't see for several hours. Anonymous --> Juan Orozco: <sm>If you really anger me, your school transcripts will look like you tried to scam them.</sm>

Juan's eyes widened slightly at the sudden silence. He would have some time to stew over what was coming.

It was all empty threat of course; Miri believed in obeying the law, even if she might pretend otherwise.

She ran her bike a couple of steps and hopped on, and almost fell off. Then she recovered and coasted down the hill, away from Orozco.

THE RAINBOWS END retirement community was in a valley northeast of Pyramid Hill. The place was very old and famous. It had been founded sixty years ago, ages before the suburbs ever got out this far. It hit its peak in the early twenty-first century, when a wave of newly rich old people had arrived here.

Miri pedaled along the bike path, doing her best to stay out of everybody's way. Her guest pass was still valid, but kids were mostly second-class citizens at Rainbows End. When she was young, visiting Lena here, she had thought the village was magical. The real lawns were as beautiful as the fake ones in West Fallbrook. There were real bronze statues. The colonnades and brickwork were real too, finer than all but the most expensive of the shopping malls.

Since then, she had studied senior issues in school—and there was no way to avoid certain cynical conclusions: There was still some real money in Rainbows End, but it was money spent by people who couldn't do any better. Most of those who remained were living on vapor and biotech promises, unlucky in investment and/or medicine.

Orozco had not tried to follow or cover his tracks; she had traced him eastward. He'd finally gotten his bike unfolded and was pedaling toward the Mesitas subdivision. She watched with narrowed eyes. Could Juan Orozco be the punk who'd briefly hijacked Sharif at UCSD? No way. That had been a loud smart-aleck who insisted on bragging. More important, Mr. Smart-

Aleck really was competent, maybe as sharp as Miri herself.

Okay. There were more important things to think about. Lena's house was at the far end of the second street up. It was time to image and imagine. She had thought a lot about this meeting, thinking all the things she might say, all the sad things she might see. Miri had constructed a special vision. It was based on things she had been working on in some form since the second grade, when she learned the personal significance of "variant-12 intractable osteoporosis."

First, she made the trees along her path taller and wider, nothing like palms. As she climbed the hill, their high leafiness was replaced by overarching boughs of long-needled evergreens. Of course, Miri didn't have any *physical* support for this. She didn't have game stripes in her shirt; she didn't have micro-cooling. The sun still beat on her, even if she made the sky overcast and the trees bend low. Maybe she should think of the heat as some sort of spell. She had thought of doing that before, but there were always other improvements that seemed more important. After all the months of daydreaming, this vision was not beholden to any commercial art. It borrowed from a hundred fantasies, but the effect was Miri's very own, for her concept of Lena. She had not put any of it public. Most visions were much more fun when they were shared, but not this one.

Finally, she lurched to a stop and got off the bike. The last couple hundred feet had to be on foot. There were a few other people around, but in her vision they were unremarkable peasants. She saw the sidewalks and wheelchair ramps as forest paths and mossy, timeworn steps. She stumbled more than once on the inconsistencies, but that seemed only fair for a humble petitioner such as herself.

And then she was in the inner grove. There were occasional side paths, evidence of cabins hidden deeper in the forest. Her trees were very old here, their huge branches high above her head. Miri walked the bike along the ancient path. The people of the inner grove were higher rank—not in the category of Lena, but still powers to be respected. Miri kept her eyes on the ground and hoped that none of them would talk to her.

She made the final turn, walked another fifty feet, to a wide, timbered cabin. When she looked up, she could see breaks in the tree cover, but they didn't reveal sky. Instead she was looking up into sun-touched green. The highest crown of the forest canopy stood right above this place. The witchery of witches. The source of elder wisdom. She leaned her bike against the timbers and reached up to hit the massive brass knocker. The sound boomed loud in her ears. She ignored the junky twentieth-century melody that actually played; that was the old doorbell that Lena had brought from Palo Alto.

A moment passed. Miri heard footsteps from within. Footsteps? The huge door creaked inward, and Miri's envisioning was confronted with a significant challenge: a woman, not much older-looking than the teachers at school. *What are you doing here!* Miri stared for a moment, speechless. She rarely hit surprises this big. After a moment she recovered herself and nodded respectfully. "Xiu Xiang?"

"Yes. You're Miri, aren't you? Lena's granddaughter?" She stepped aside and gestured Miri in.

"Um, I didn't know you'd recognize me." Miri stepped indoors, imagining madly. Xiu Xiang looked too young to be a real witch. *Okay, I'll make her be Lena's apprentice, a watchamagoogle—a newbie witch!*

Newbie Xiang smiled. "Lena has shown me pictures of you. We even saw you at school once. Lena told me you would come around, um, sooner or later."

"So . . . she'll see me?"

"I'll ask her."

Miri gave a little bow. "Thank you, ma'am."

Newbie Xiang led Miri to an upholstered chair next to a book-laden desk. "I'll be right back."

Miri settled in the chair. Oops. It was hard plastic. As for the desk . . . well those were real books, the kind some people used for just-in-time reading. The pages were whatever you wanted, but they were real pages. Of course these were not the thick and hoary things of Miri's imaging, but they were piled deep. There was a view-page on top, very much out of place, and a confession of ineptitude. Miri quickly morphed it into a glowing grimoire. She edged forward in her chair and looked at the books. Mechanics and electrical engineering. These would be Newbie

Xiang's; Miri had studied the background of all the students in Robert's classes. The box of toys under the desk must be things she had built in shop class. Miri recognized the warped transport tray from the news.

What an incredible coincidence that Xiu Xiang was rooming with Lena. . . .

There were sounds behind her. The inner door was opening. It was Newbie Xiang, with the senior witch right behind her. Miri was ready with imagery for this. Lena's real chair had six small wheels on articulated axles, very practical and dull. But Mistress Gu's chair had tall wooden wheels, sheathed in silver, and canted outward. Little blue sparks chased each other around the rims as it moved. And Miri imaged Lena dressed in heavy black, a black that absorbed the room's light in the classical magical way. A black that obscured the details of what it clothed. Lena's pointy, brimmed hat was hung jauntily from the chair's high backpost. And that was where Miri's special effects ended. The rest she always kept the way that Lena really was. In fact, *all* her vision was to give her grandmother the proper frame, one that would reveal how wonderful she truly was.

The senior witch looked Miri up and down and then said, "Didn't Bob tell you to let me be?" But she didn't sound as angry as Miri had feared.

"Yes. But I miss you so much."

"Oh." She leaned forward slightly. "How is your mom, Miri? Is she okay?"

"Alice is fine." Lena knew way too much about Alice, but she had no need-to-know. Besides, she couldn't help Alice. "I wanted to talk to you about some other things."

Mistress Gu sighed, and closed her deep-set eyes. When she opened them, she might have been smiling. "Well, I'm glad to see you, kiddo. It's just that I don't want to argue with you or Bob. And most of all, I don't want You-Know-Who to know that I'm still around."

"I'll only argue a little bit, Lena." *As much as will make positive headway and still leave me welcome to come visit again.* "You don't have to worry about You-Know-Who." Mistress Gu's own wording was straight out of fantasy tradition, though it was sad that Robert should be cast as ultimate evil. "I promise I won't reveal you to him." *At least, not without your permission.* "I took precautions coming here. Besides, You-Know-Who is no good at snooping."

Lena shook her head. "That's what you think."

Newbie Xiang sat down beside the wheelchair and watched them silently. Maybe she could help. "You see You-Know-Who every day, don't you, ma'am?" Miri said.

"Yes," said Xiang, "in shop class and Louise Chumlig's Search and Analysis."

"Ms. Chumlig's not so bad"—*at least for the bonehead classes.* Miri was fast enough to squelch the additional comment, but she felt herself blush even so.

Newbie Xiang didn't seem to notice. "In fact, she's quite good. I've been telling Lena." She glanced at the senior witch. "Louise knows things about asking questions that took me a lifetime to understand. And more than anyone, she's shown me the importance of analysis packages." She pointed at the old grimoire. Miri was a little taken aback. Yes, Ms. Chumlig was a nice person, but she was full of clichés, and she *droned.*

But even a junior witch is not someone you contradict, and Miri was very anxious to be congenial. She dipped her head, "Yes, ma'am. Anyway, you see a lot of You-Know-Who. Is he really such a terrible person?"

Xiu Xiang shook her head. "He is strange. He looks so *young.* Robert—I mean 'You-Know-Who'—can be very gracious, and then suddenly cut you dead. I've seen him do that to several children. The old people steer clear of him. I think Winston Blount hates him."

Yes. Miri had watched Winston Blount in the UCSD library last Saturday. Most of her attention had been absorbed in the battle for the persona of Zulfikar Sharif, but she had not missed Blount's hostility.

Newbie Xiang glanced at the frail lady in the wheelchair. "I'm afraid Lena is right about him. He uses people. He admired my shop project and then walked off with it."

Lena cackled. That was something an elderly person could do well. In Miri's opinion it was the only positive thing about old age. "Xiu, Xiu. You told me you were thrilled to see him chop that car."

Newbie Xiang looked embarrassed. "Well, yes. I got into science with model rockets and homemade RF controllers. I'd have been nothing without hands-on experience. Nowadays, our access to real things is muffled by layers of automated bureaucracy—and I guess my own SHE is partly to blame. So both Robert and I wanted to break something, and I cheered him for *acting*. But what I wanted was of no concern to him. I was just a convenient tool."

Lena laughed again. "You're so lucky. You learned in days what took me years." She raised a clawed hand to wipe at her hair. Modern medicine had not completely failed Lena Gu. Five years ago she'd had Parkinson's. Miri remembered the tremors. Modern medicine had reversed her Parkinson's, kept her mind sharp, stopped various ills large and small. But her abnormal osteoporosis was still beyond cure. As far back as the second grade, Miri had been able to understand the technical "why" of that. The moral "why" was something even Alice couldn't explain.

Miri looked into the wizened face of the senior witch. "I-I'm glad it took you years to see through You-Know-Who. Otherwise you two would never have had Bob and raised him to marry Alice . . . and I would never be."

Lena looked away. "Yes," she grumped. "Bobby was the only reason I stayed with your grandfather. We gave Bobby a good home. And he was halfway human with the boy, at least till it was clear he couldn't run Bob's adult life. By that time, Bob had escaped to the Marine Corps." Her gaze flickered back to Miri. "I congratulate myself on that. I made a terrible mistake marrying your grandfather, but it brought two lovely lives into existence—and it only cost me twenty years."

"Don't you ever miss him?"

Mistress Gu's eyes narrowed. "That's coming perilously close to arguing with me, young lady."

"Sorry." Miri came over to kneel on the floor beside Lena's wheelchair. She reached out to hold Lena's hand. The old woman smiled. She knew what was coming, but she didn't have completely effective defenses. "You had all those years apart from him. I remember you visiting, back when You-Know-Who was well and never visited." Even then, Lena had been a little old lady, a busy doctor who smiled the most when she was talking to Miri. "Were you happy then?"

"Of course! After all those years, I was free of the monster!"

"But when You-Know-Who began to lose his mind, then you helped him."

Lena rolled her eyes and looked at Newbie Xiang. "When I say the word, you kick this brat back on the street."

Xiang looked uncertain. "Um, okay."

"But that's not . . . just yet." Lena looked back at Miri. "We've been over this ground before, Miri. Bob came here to Rainbows End and begged me to help. Remember? He brought you along with him. Bob has never understood how things were between Robert and me. God bless him, he doesn't realize that all the affection he saw was just for him. But between his pleading and your cute little face, I agreed to help out with the monster's final years. . . . And you know, sometimes dementia softens a person up. There was a year or so, when Robert was nearly helpless, but he could still recognize people and remember our years together—there was a time when he was tractable. We actually got along for a while!"

Miri nodded.

"And then they figured how to cure Robert's brand of dementia. By then your grandfather had declined from tractability into a kind of veggie state. Miri, I would have stuck with him through the end if there hadn't been the miracle cure. But I could see what was coming. The monster would be back." Lena punched a crooked finger in her granddaughter's direction. "Burn me once, shame on him. Burn me twice, shame on me. So I stay out of the picture. Understand?"

But her other hand remained in Miri's; the girl gave it a squeeze. "But couldn't this be different? By the time they cured Grandfather, part of him had already died." That had been Jin Li's theory, not Miri's. "I know he's often angry now, but that's because he's lost a lot. Maybe the bad things you remember are gone too."

Lena waved her free hand in the direction of Newbie Xiang.

"Did you hear what Xiu just said about his new nobleness of character?"

Miri thought fast: It never worked with Alice, but sometimes a quick change of subject could distract Bob. She glanced at Newbie Xiang. "Lena, you've been living here since Grandfather's been sick. You could have moved anywhere since you don't visit us anymore, but you're still just ten miles away."

Lena's chin came up. "I've lived in San Diego for years. I'm not going to give up seeing my friends, shopping the old stores, hiking—well I have given up the hiking. The point is that, even resurrected, You-Know-Who is not going to run my life!"

"But—" *very thin ice here!* "—did you know Dr. Xiang before?"

The senior witch's lips thinned. "No. And now you're going to point out, or let plaintive silence imply, that since there are twenty-five hundred oldfolks here at Rainbows End, this matchup couldn't be coincidence."

Miri was silent.

Finally Newbie Xiang spoke up. "It was my choice. I moved down here this summer, about the time I got my get-up-and-go back. I'm one of the older people living at Rainbows End, but I'm so bright and bubbly—" a strange sad smile "—they don't know what to do with me. So I volunteered to be a roommate. It's worked out well. Your grandma is ten years younger than I am, but that doesn't mean so much at our age." She gave Lena's shoulder a pat.

Miri remembered that Lena Llewelyn Gu had done years of psychiatric consulting here at Rainbows End. If anyone could arrange a matchup with Xiu Xiang, it was her. She opened her mouth to remark on this—and noticed the warning glare in Lena's eyes, as clear as any silent messaging could ever be.

After a moment, Lena shifted in her chair. "See, my girl? Pure coincidence. But I do admit it's been useful. Xiu keeps me advised of You-Know-Who's adventures in modern education." She gave a nasty witchy smile that needed no help from Miri's special effects.

"Yes," said Xiang. "We, we have our collective eyes on him."

"The monster is not going to catch up with me this time around."

Miri rocked back. "You're running a joint entity!" She hadn't dreamed the two witches could be so truly, modernly magical.

"A what?" said Newbie Xiang.

"A joint entity. Partners with complementary strengths and weaknesses. In public you are one, represented by the mobile partner. But what you can do and understand is the best of each of you."

Xiang stared at her without comprehension.

Oh. Miri pinged both women. Except for Lena's medicals, they were fully offline. Miri had been too distracted by her own imagining. "You aren't wearing, are you?"

Xiu gestured at her desk. "I have my view-page and these books. I'm trying to learn so many serious things, Miri. I don't have time to bother with wearing."

Miri almost forgot her mission. "Dr. Xiang, you're so wrong about wearables. I mean, hasn't Ms. Chumlig talked about that? Some analysis packages don't have traction if you run them with static video."

Newbie Xiang gave a reluctant nod. "She showed me BLAST9. But that just seems to be molecular design dressed up in game toy nonsense."

"But you've only run them on your view-page!"

The younger witch hunched down. "I have so much to learn, Miri. I'm working through the simpler things, what I can run on the view-page."

Lena watched the other woman for a second and then she seemed to wilt back into her wheelchair. She looked down at her granddaughter. "Poor Miri. You don't understand. You live in a time that thinks it can ignore the human condition." She cocked her head. "You never read *Secrets of the Ages,* did you?"

"Of course I've read it!"

"I'm sorry, Miri, I'm sure you have. After all, it's my beloathed ex-husband's most famous achievement. And I'll give him this; those poems are a work of genius. Their 'implacable weight' is all his hurtfulness turned to support great truths. But you can't see that, can you, Miri? You are surrounded by medical promises and halfway cures. It distracts you from the bedrock of reality." She paused and her head bobbed. It was almost like her old palsy, but maybe this was simply indecision, wondering whether to say more. "Miri, the truth is, if we are careful and lucky we live to be old, and weak, and very very tired. There comes an end to striving."

"No! You'll get better, Lena. You've just had bad luck. It's just a matter of time."

There was a whisper of a witchly cackle, and Miri remembered that "It's just a matter of time" was the mantra of Robert's poem cycle.

For a moment, grandmother and granddaughter glared certainty at each other. Then Lena said, "And this is about where I figured our chat would come. I'm sorry, Miri."

Miri bowed her head. *But I just want to help!* Strange. That had been the Orozco kid's whine. To Miri. Okay, maybe he wasn't a complete jerk. And maybe he could help. But there was something else he'd said, and right now it was much more important. . . . Yes! Suddenly Miri saw how she could turn defeat into victory. She looked up into her grandmother's face and smiled innocently. "Did you know, Lena . . . that You-Know-Who is learning to wear?"

14

THE MYSTERIOUS STRANGER

Even after three weeks, Robert and Juan still did most of their studying in person, right after classes let out. They would walk out to the bleachers and one ignoramus would endeavor to teach the other.

Occasionally Fred and Jerry Radner would tag along, unofficial third and fourth ignoramuses. The twins had teamed with each other in Chumlig's composition class, but they seemed to take innocent pleasure in following Robert's progress, offering advice that was more colorful than Juan's, but rarely as useful.

Then there was the fifth ignoramus. Xiu Xiang had chickened out of Creative Composition, but she was still taking her other courses at Fairmont. And like Robert, she was learning to wear; nowadays she wore a frilly, beaded blouse—another kind of Epiphany beginner's outfit. She was there the afternoon when Robert and Juan ran into the Chileans. This was out on the track that circled the athletics field. No one else seemed to be around; the varsity teams wouldn't be here for a while yet.

Miri --> Juan: <sm>Hey! Wake up, Orozco. Flag down <enum/>. </sm>

Juan --> Miri: <sm>Sorry, I didn't see them.</sm>

Miri --> Juan: <sm>You missed them yesterday, too. Flag them before they shift to the Radners. I told you these guys would make good practice.</sm>

Juan --> Miri: <sm>Okay, okay!</sm>

"Hey," Juan said abruptly, "Dr. Gu, Xiu. Look!" He shipped an enum capability to Robert's Epiphany. It was just like the targets they'd been working with the last few days. The kid claimed that if you practiced, this kind of interaction was as natural as looking at where another person was pointing. It wasn't that easy for Robert Gu. He stopped and squinted at the icon. By default that should force access. Nothing. He tapped on his phantom keypad. He noticed Xiang, a few feet away, doing the same.

. . . And then suddenly there were a half-dozen students in evidence, all jabbering in Spanish.

Miri --> Juan, Lena, Xiu: <sm>Okay, I think Robert sees them.</sm>

Lena --> Juan, Miri, Xiu: <sm>I see them! Can you, Xiu?</sm>

Xiu --> Juan, Lena, Miri: <sm>no yet i must—</sm>

Miri --> Juan, Lena, Xiu: <sm>Don't try to message back, Dr. Xiang. You're not fast enough yet; Robert will get suspicious. Just talk out loud, as if to him and Juan.</sm>

Xiang was silent for a moment, her fingers still tapping. She was even worse at wearing than he was. But then she said, "Yes, I do see them!" She glanced at Juan Orozco. "Who are they?"

"Friends of Fred and Jerry, from way south. Chile."

Miri --> Juan: <sm>Tell them to play synch monster.</sm>

Juan --> Miri: <sm>Okay.</sm>

Juan rattled Spanish at the visitors, almost too fast for Robert to understand. Something about helping beginners with a monster.

The others' Spanish was even less intelligible. But maybe that didn't matter. The visitors stepped back, and the space was filled with a shambling purple *something.*

Xiang laughed. "I see that too. But the creature . . . it's not even pretending to be real."

Robert leaned close to the lopsided vision. "It's pretending to be a stuffed animal," with crudely stitched seams and tufts of stuffing peeking from between the joints. But the vision was almost seven feet tall, and when Robert approached, it shambled back from him.

Robert laughed, "I've read about these things."

Lena --> Juan, Miri, Xiu: <sm>I looked it up, Xiu. You move, it moves. But each of you can only control a part of it.</sm>

"Oh." Xiu Xiang stepped forward, blocking the creature's retreat. Its rear legs stopped but the front kept pushing, and it almost tipped over.

Miri --> Juan: <sm>Say the goal is to make it do a graceful dance.</sm>

Juan said, "The goal is we all cooperate to make it move. Dance around it, Xiu."

She did. Music followed her motion. The creature's rear legs reengaged, and its butt end seemed to track her march. The children from Chile thought that was hilarious.

When Robert cocked his wrist and wiggled a beat, the music came up. Juan began clapping, and the beast's shoulders twitched to the music. The children from the Far South watched silently for a moment. They looked as solid as the real Juan and Xiu Xiang, but they were no more expert than most San Diego users. Their shadows went the wrong way, and their feet had only a casual acquaintance with the surface of the lawn. But after an instant, the Chileans seemed to hear the music and began clapping too. And now the critter's tail—their domain in this game?—began pumping up and down.

Robert expanded on his gestures, grabbing control of the

creature's floppy claws. For a moment, the monster danced in synch with the music, each gesture consistent. But the network delay was about half a second, and worse, it varied randomly from a tiny fraction of a second to well over a second. The dance got wilder as errors were corrected and overcorrected, until the tail was whacking at the heel claws. The creature rotated onto its back and its legs flailed in random directions.

Lena --> Juan, Miri, Xiu: <sm>That was fun!</sm>

"Damn!" said Robert.

But everybody was laughing, and not at any particular victim. One by one, the faraway children disappeared, till only the real people were left, Robert and Juan and Xiu Xiang.

"We could have done better, Juan!"

Lena --> Xiu: <sm>See? He's always complaining. Give him another minute and he'll be making sly claims that *you* are to blame for everything that went wrong.</sm>

Juan was still laughing. "I know, I know. But the network link was *basura más odiosa.* There are game companies who give you cheapnet for free, because it makes everyone so mad they upgrade to paying status."

"Well then why did we try?"

"Hey, to practice. For fun."

Robert remembered the inept international choir down at UCSD. "We should have used a metronome. Can you bring these kids back?"

"Nah, we were just . . . like waving to each other. You know, in passing."

In passing. "I didn't see them at all until you showed them to me. How busy is the aether?" Robert slashed the air with his hand. How many realities burbled immanent?

"Out here in public, it's lots too busy to view all at once. There's probably three or four hundred nodes in line of sight of your Epiphany. Each of those could manage dozens of overlays. In a crowd there'd be hundreds of active realities, and bazillions potentially—"

Miri --> Juan: <sm>Don't go there. My grandfather is smart enough to add up teeny clues and guess at us invisibles.</sm>

Juan --> Miri: <sm>Yeah? Well you're making one clue

yourself. Showing Mrs. Gu visible to Xiu just confuses her. Look how she avoids where you have Lena standing.</sm>

The boy seemed to lose his train of thought. "Of course, when there are just two or three people around, the laser traffic is mostly just a potential."

They walked farther along the track, the boy demonstrating how to surf through the public views. Robert and Xiu Xiang practiced at his direction, sometimes achieving a consensus view. Xiang seemed more relaxed than at the beginning of the walk; at least she was walking a bit closer to Juan and Robert.

But Xiu didn't respond when Robert joked, "I'd say we're getting to be truly awful."

Lena --> Xiu: <sm>See!</sm>

Robert wondered at what a weird duck this Xiang woman was.

O

XIU XIANG WAS weird in other ways. Though she had dropped the composition class because she was too shy to perform in front of others, she loved the shop class. Every day she seemed to be playing with something new from the class inventory. That was the only time she was clearly happy, smiling and humming to herself. Some of her projects were obvious to the new Robert, some he could make good guesses about. She was happy to explain them. "Maybe there aren't any 'user-serviceable parts' inside," she said, "but what I've built, I understand!" She was doing the equivalent of a student semester project every day, and enjoying every minute of it.

Xiu wasn't entirely crazy; normally she didn't show up when Robert Gu was teaching Juan. Robert had never taught children, and he didn't like incompetents. For all Juan's good intentions, he was both. And now Robert was pretending to teach him to write.

"It's easy, Juan," Robert heard himself say. *Lies on top of pretense!* Well, maybe not: writing crap was easy. Twenty years of teaching graduate poetry seminars had shown him that. Writing well was a different thing. Writing beauty that sings was something that no amount of schooling could teach. The geniuses must take care of themselves. Juan Orozco was distinctly less able than the students of Robert's experience. By twentieth-century standards he was subliterate . . . except where he needed words to access data or understand results. Okay, perhaps he was not subliterate. Maybe there was some other word for these crippled children. Paraliterate? *And I bet I can teach him to write crap, too.*

So they sat high in the bleachers, pounding words across the sky, Juan Orozco oblivious of the runners below and the games far away. There came a time when he didn't play with his fonts anymore.

There came a day when he wrote something that had affect and image. It was not utter crap. It was almost up to the standards of muddled cliché. The boy stared into the sky for half a minute, his jaw slack. "That is so . . . bitchin'. The words, they make me see things." His gaze flickered sideways, to Robert. A smile spread across his face. "You with wearing, me with writing. We're getting really good!"

"Perhaps equally so." But Robert couldn't help smiling back.

A WEEK PASSED. Most evenings, Robert had interviews with Zulfi Sharif. After school and sometimes on weekends, he and Juan worked together. Much of that was remote now. They were still flailing around for a semester project. More and more, Robert was intrigued with the problem of far coordination. Games, music, sports, it all got jittery beyond a few thousand miles and a couple dozen routers. The boy had bizarre plans for how they might put everything together. "We could do something with music, *manual* music. That's lots easier than game synchronization." Robert went for hours at a time without thinking about his demented, maimed condition.

These school projects were more interesting to the new Robert Gu than Sharif's admiring interviews—and far more interesting than his occasional visits to UCSD. The library shredding had been temporarily suspended, apparently due to the demonstration and his own unintendedly dramatic appearance there. But without the demonstrators, the library was a dead place. Modern students didn't have much use for it. There was just Winnie's "Elder Cabal" up on the sixth floor, rebels whose cause was suddenly on hold.

Robert and Xiu Xiang had mastered most of the Epiphany defaults. Now when he looked at a real object in "just that way," explanations would pop up. With the proper squint or stare at attendant icons, he got the added detail he wanted. Look at the object a different way, and he often could see through and beyond it! Xiu wasn't as good as Robert with the visuals. On the other hand, if she didn't get flustered, she was better at audio searches: when you heard a word you didn't know, if you could tag it, then search results would appear automatically. *That* explained the marvelous vocabulary—and equally marvelous screwups—he noticed in the children's language.

Miri --> Juan: <sm>You should tell him that the nondefaults are a lot harder.</sm>

Juan --> Miri: <sm>Okay.</sm>

"You know, Dr. Gu, you and Xiu are, um, really good with the defaults. But we should work on the nondefaults, too."

Xiang nodded. She was remote today, too, though not as realistically as Juan Orozco. Her image was perfectly solid, but her feet were melted into the bleacher bench in front of her, and occasionally he got glimpses of—background? Her apartment? He kidded her about that, but as usual when he made a joke, it just made her even more quiet.

Lena --> Juan, Miri, Xiu: <sm>What! What did he see?</sm>

Miri --> Juan, Lena, Xiu: <sm>Not to worry. Xiu has a good background filter. Besides, you're in the kitchen and she's sitting in the living room.</sm>

Robert turned back to Juan. "So what are the most useful nondefaults?"

"Well, there's silent messaging. The bit rate is so low, it works when nothing else does."

"Yes! I've read about sming. It's like the old instant messaging, except no one can see you're communicating."

Juan nodded. "That's how most people format it."

Lena --> Juan, Miri, Xiu: <sm>No! Let the SOB learn sming on his own!</sm>

Miri --> Juan, Lena, Xiu: <sm>Please, Lena!</sm>

Juan --> Lena, Miri, Xiu: <sm>It's something everyone uses, ma'am.</sm>

Lena --> Juan, Miri, Xiu: <sm>I said no! He's already sneaky enough.</sm>

The boy hesitated. ". . . but it takes a lot of practice to do it smoothly. It can be more trouble than it's worth when you get caught." Maybe he was remembering run-ins with his teachers?

Xiang sat forward on the bench. She was leaning on some invisible piece of furniture. "Well, what are some other things?"

"Ah! Lots of stuff. If you override the defaults you can see in any direction you want. You can qualify default requests—like to make a query about something in an overlay. You can blend video from multiple viewpoints so you can 'be' where there is no physical viewpoint. That's called ghosting. If you're really slick, you can run simulations in real time and use the results as physical advice. That's how the Radners do so well in baseball. And then there's the problem of faking results if you hit a network soft spot, or if you want a sender to look more realistic—" The boy rattled on, but now Robert was able enough to record the words; he would have to come back to this.

Lena --> Juan, Miri, Xiu: <sm>The monster's eyes are glazing over. I think you've distracted him, Juan.</sm>

Xiu said, "Okay, let's start with the easiest, Juan."

"That would be moving attention from face front." The boy talked them through some simple exercises. Robert had no idea how this looked to Xiu Xiang. After all, she was already remote. For himself, looking directly backward was easy, especially if he took the view off his own shirt. But Juan didn't want him to use mirror orientation; he said that would just be confusing once he moved on to other angles.

Without the defaults, things got very tedious. "I'll spend my whole life just tapping in commands, Juan."

"Maybe if we use the eye menus," Xiang said.

Robert gave her an irritated look. "I am, I am!"

Lena --> Xiu: <sm>Never criticize him. He'll get back at you when it hurts the most.</sm>

Xiang's gaze dropped from his. He looked at Juan. "I never see *you* tapping your fingers."

"I'm a kid; I grew up with ensemble coding. Hey, even my mom mostly uses phantom typing."

"Well, Xiu and I are retreads, Juan. We have learning plasticity and all that. Teach us the command gestures or eyeblinks or whatever."

"Okay! But this is not like the standard gestures you've already learned. For the good stuff, everything is custom between you and your wearable. The skin sensors pick muscle twinges that other people can't even see. You teach your Epiphany and it teaches you."

Robert had read about this. It turned out to be just as weird as it sounded, a cross between learning to juggle and teaching some dumb animal to help you juggle! He and Xiu Xiang had about twenty minutes to make fools of themselves before the soccer teams came out to play. But that was long enough that now Robert could look all around himself with just a subtle shrug.

Juan was smiling. "You guys are really good, for—"

"—for oldfolks?" said Xiu.

Juan's smile broadened. "Yeah." He looked at Robert. "If you can do this maybe I can learn to put words together. . . . Look, I gotta go help my ma. She's running a tour this afternoon. See you all tomorrow, okay?"

"Okay," said Xiang. "I should leave too. How is that most gracefully accomplished?"

"Ha! Most graceful takes practice—but I want it to look cool to anyone watching." He pointed at the teams rowdying about on the soccer field. "For them, I mean. So how about if I iconify-and-guide you, Dr. Xiang?"

"Very good."

Xiang's image collapsed into a ruby point of light.

The boy stood and grinned at Robert. "I think I have the geometry good enough that no one has to cooperate on the receiving side." His image climbed down the bleachers. His shadow matching was much better than Sharif normally managed. Xiang's icon tagged along right above his shoulder. He reached the grass and walked away along the edge of the bleachers, his figure shortening in perspective.

And then abruptly, golden letters hung across Robert's vision.

Xiang --> Gu: <sm>See you tomorrow!</sm>

Huh. So that's what silent messaging looked like. Robert watched the two till they were out of sight.

Lena --> Miri, Xiu: <sm>Wow! I can't tell Juan's image from the real people. That boy is clever.</sm>

Miri --> Lena, Xiu: <sm>He did okay.</sm>

Robert had no more classes. He could go home now, too. There were plenty of rides available; the cars flocked to the traffic circle when the children were going home. But just now, Robert wasn't keen on getting back to Fallbrook. He saw that Miri would be arriving home in a few minutes. Bob was on watch duty tonight—whatever that meant. Any run-in with Miri would bring Alice Gu into action. Robert was amazed that he'd ever thought his daughter-in-law was smooth and diplomatic. In a subtle way, she was scary. Or maybe it was simply that Robert realized that if Alice ever became determined, he would be exiled to "Rainbows End." (He'd never been able to decide if that spelling was the work of an everyday illiterate or someone who really understood the place.)

Okay, so hang around school and watch. There were dynamics here that were unchanged since his childhood, perhaps unchanged since the beginning of human history. He would rebuild his sense of superiority. He climbed to the south corner of the bleachers, far above the kids forming up soccer teams, and even clear of the secretive children who sat at the other end making barely veiled jokes about everyone else.

Miri --> Lena, Xiu: <sm>He should be going home now.</sm>

Lena --> Miri, Xiu: <sm>Not my monster. See the far look in his eyes? He's thinking about everything that's happened, figuring out just how to cause Xiu grief.</sm>

Xiu --> Lena, Miri: <sm>He has seemed pretty normal since he went crazy in shop class.</sm>

Xiu --> Lena, Miri: <sm>No, Lena, please use silent messaging. I know I just sat down by you at the kitchen table. But I want to get some practice.</sm>

Lena --> Miri: <sm>Sigh. Xiu's a dear, but she can be so obsessive.</sm>

Xiu --> Lena: <sm>Yoo-hoo, Lena! What are you typing to Miri?</sm>

The sun was lowering behind him, and the shadow of the bleachers extended partway onto the field. He had a naked-eye view of most of the campus. In fact, the buildings looked like junk, the sort of thing you used to buy mail-order if you needed some extra storage in your backyard. But it wasn't all new junk. The school's main auditorium was wood, rebuilt here and there with plastic. According to the labels he called up on overlay, it had originally been a pavilion for showing horses!

Xiu --> Lena, Miri: <sm>I think he's just training his Epiphany.</sm>

Focus on the soccer field. That looked like something from Bobby's school years—if you didn't mind the fact that there were no line marks or goals. Robert brought up the sports view, and now he could see the usual field layout. The soccer kids moved out onto the field. They wore crash equipment, real helmets, quite unlike what he remembered. The kids' high-pitched voices wafted direct to him without any magic of modern electronics. They circled around midfield, seemed to be listening to someone.

With a whoop, the teams rushed toward each other, chasing—what? An unseen ball? Robert searched frantically through his options, saw a flickering parade of possible overlays. *Aha!* Now the teams had spectacular uniforms, and there were umpires. In the bleachers, there was a scattering of adults—teachers? parents?—what you'd expect for a contest that was more a class event than varsity sport.

Xiu --> Lena, Miri: <sm>What is that game?</sm>

Miri --> Lena, Xiu: <sm>Egan soccer.</sm>

Xiu --> Lena, Miri: <sm>He's just watching the game, Lena.</sm>

Lena --> Miri, Xiu: <sm>Maybe.</sm>

Xiu --> Lena, Miri: <sm>I think Juan is right about him, Lena. Let me talk to him. You'd still be covered.</sm>

Xiu --> Lena: <sm>Don't be that way.</sm>

Robert still couldn't see the soccer ball. Instead, the field was now covered by a golden fog. In places it came almost to the players' waists. Tiny numbers floated within the mist, changing with the thickness and brightness of the glow. When the players of opposing teams rushed into close contact, the glow flared brightly, and the children would angle around each other as if trying to line up a kick. And then the light would erupt like an arc of wildfire across the field.

Xiu --> Lena, Miri: <sm>What about Sharif, Miri? You use him to talk to Robert, right?</sm>

Miri --> Lena, Xiu: <sm>Yes. I thought Sharif would be a perfect cat's-paw. He has the right academic background to talk to Robert. And he has terrible personal hygiene! It was easy to take him over. Trouble is, so did somebody else. Mostly we're getting in each other's way. Hey!</sm>

Xiu --> Lena, Miri: <sm>I've lost all the close-up views on your grandfather.</sm>

Miri --> Lena, Xiu: <sm>We've lost local audio, too. That was seamless. I didn't know Robert was that swift.</sm>

Lena --> Miri, Xiu: <sm>I warned you.</sm>

One child broke away from the others and raced along the golden fire, somehow guessing just where and when it would flare up. The girl gave an odd, flailing kick—and landed on her rear. For an instant there was a light in the nearest goal, so sharp and intense it was as if all the fog had suddenly coalesced into the fuzzy image of a soccer ball. Everybody was shouting, even the phantom adults in the bleachers.

Robert made a grumpy noise. Even something as simple as a schoolyard game didn't make sense. He pulled at his cuff, trying to get a clearer view.

"It's not your fault, my man. You're seeing properly." The voice seemed to be coming from right beside him. Robert glanced over, but there was no body to keep the voice company. He stared into the empty space, and after a moment, the voice continued. "Just look at the scoreboard. Everything is fuzzy about this game, even the score." On the big scoreboard facing the bleachers, the goal was recorded as 0.97. "I do think that should be rounded to one. That was an excellent, near-certain goal the girl kicked." On the field, the teams had retreated to their sides. Another phantom kickoff was in progress.

Robert kept his eyes on the action below. He didn't reply to the helpful voice. "You don't recognize the game, do you, Professor? It's Egan soccer. See—" A reference floated across his vision, everything anyone could want to know about Egan soccer. Out on the field, three kids had fallen over, and two had collided. "Of course," the voice continued, "it's really just an approximation to the ideal."

"I'll bet," said Robert, and he almost smiled. The stranger's tone was confiding, the speech affected—and almost every sentence was a mild putdown. It was a pleasure to run into a type he understood so well. He turned and looked into the empty space. "Run along, kid. You're a long way from being able to play head games with me."

"I don't play games, my man." The reply started out angry, segued back to patronizing good humor. "You are an interesting case, Robert Gu. I'm used to manipulating people, but usually through intermediaries. I'm much too busy to chat with bottom dwellers directly. But you intrigue me."

Robert pretended to watch the game, but the voice continued, "I know what's eating you up inside. I know how much it bothers you that you can't make poetry anymore."

Robert couldn't suppress a start of surprise. The invisible stranger gave a little chuckle; somehow he had distinguished the movement from Robert's natural twitchiness. "No need to be coy. You can't disguise your reactions here. The medical sensing on school grounds is so good that you might as well be hooked up to a lie detector."

I should just walk away. Instead he watched the "soccer" match for a few moments. When he was sure he had proper control of his voice, he said, "You are admitting to a crime, then."

Another chuckle. "Of sorts, though it's the crime of superior network skills. You can think of me as something of a higher being, empowered by all the tools with which mortal men have chosen to smarten the landscape."

This must be a kid. Or maybe not. Maybe the visitor was invisible because even his virtual presence on school grounds was a violation of law. Robert shrugged. "I'd be happy to report your 'superior network skills' to interested parties."

"You won't do that. Primus, because the police could never identify me. Secundus, because I can return to you what you have lost. I can give you back your poetical voice."

This time, Robert was in control and managed a creditable chuckle of his own.

"Ah," said the other, "such suspicion. But also the beginning of belief! You should read the news, or just loosen up your ad filters. In olden times, you had athletes on steroids and students on amphetamines. Those drugs were largely false promises. Nowadays, we have things that really work."

A drug dealer, by God! Robert almost laughed for real. But then he considered himself, his smooth skin, his ability to run and jump and scarcely feel out of breath. *What's already happened would be magic by the standards of my past life.* Yes, this might be a drug dealer, but so what? "Where's the profit in drugs for recovering world-class poesy?" Robert spoke the words with proper flippancy, then realized how much he was revealing. Maybe that didn't matter.

"You are so old-fashioned, Professor." The stranger paused. "See those hills to the south of you?" Hills covered with endless housing. "A few miles beyond them is one of the few places on Earth where physical location is still important."

"UCSD?"

"Close. I mean the biotech labs that surround the campus. What goes on in those labs is nothing like twentieth-century medical research. Modern cures are awesome things, but often they are unique to the individual patient."

"You can't finance research that way."

"Don't get me wrong. Broad-spectrum cures are still the big moneymakers. But even those use custom analysis to guard against side effects. Yes, you are a singleton case. The Alzheimer cures are sometimes incomplete, but the failures are idiosyncratic. There is no other great poet who's had your problem. As of *today,* there is no cure." This clown knew how to mix the brutal putdowns with flattery. "But we live in an age of enhancement drugs, Professor, and many of them are singleton hits. There is a chance, a very good chance, that the labs can be *caused* to find you a cure."

Magic. *But what if he can do it? This is The Future. And I am alive again, and maybe—* Robert felt the hope growing within him. He couldn't help it. *This SOB has me. I know it's manipulation, but that doesn't matter.*

"So who am I dealing with, O Mysterious Stranger?" It was a losing question, but it just slipped out.

"Mysterious Stranger? Um—" There was a pause, no doubt as this paraliterate looked up the reference. "Why yes, you got my name on the very first try! Mysterious Stranger. That is good."

Robert gritted his teeth. "And I take it that getting your help involves something dangerous or illegal."

"Definitely illegal, Professor. And somewhat dangerous—for you, that is. Whatever might cure you would be pushing into unknown medical territory. But at the same time, very much worth it, don't you think?"

Yes! "Maybe." Robert kept the tension out of his voice, and glanced mildly at the empty space beside him. "What's the price? What do you want from me?"

The stranger laughed. "Oh, don't worry. I simply want cooperation with a project you're already involved in. Keep seeing your pals at the UCSD library. Go along with their plans."

"And keep you up-to-date on them?"

"Ah, no need for that, my man. I am an all-encompassing cloud of knowingness. No, what I need is your hands. Think of yourself as a droid who was once a poet. So, Professor, do we have a deal?"

"I'll think about it."

"Once you do, I'm sure you'll sign."

"In blood, I suppose?"

"Oh, you're so old-fashioned, Professor. No blood. Not yet."

LIEUTENANT COLONEL ROBERT Gu, Jr., had brought work home from the office. That's how he thought of it anyway, when he worked in the time that both he and Alice thought should be theirs and Miri's. But Miri had her own studying to do tonight, and Alice . . . well, her latest assignment was the worst yet. She wandered about, stony-faced and terse. Anyone else in her position would be dead by now, or a raving lunatic. Somehow she hung on, often simulating something like her natural self, and successfully managing the prep for her latest assignment. *That's why the Corps keeps driving her harder and harder.*

Bob pushed the thought away. There was a reason for such sacrifice. Chicago was more than a decade past. There hadn't been a successful nuclear attack on the U.S. or any of the treaty organization countries in more than five years. But the threat was always there. He still had nightmares about the launchers at that orphanage in Asunción, and what he had almost done to shut them down. And as always, the web oozed with rumors of new technologies that would make the classical weapons obsolete. Despite ubiquitous security, despite the efforts of America, China, and the Indo-Europeans, the risks kept growing. There would still be places that would come to glow in the dark.

Bob sifted through the latest threat assessments. Something was in the wind, and it might be closer than Paraguay. The really bad news was two paragraphs further on: An analyst pool at CIA thought the Indo-Europeans might be somehow *collaborating* with bad guys. *Christ! If the Great Powers can't stand together, how can humanity make it through this century?*

There was motion behind him. It was his father, standing in the doorway.

"Dad," he acknowledged politely.

His old man stared for a second. Bob made the general form of his paperwork visible.

"Oops. Sorry, Son. You're working?" He squinted at Bob's desk.

"Yeah, some stuff from the office. Don't worry if it looks blurry; it's not on the house menu."

"Ah. I, I was wondering if I could ask you some questions."

Bob hoped he didn't look too surprised; this diffident approach was a first. He waved for his father to take a seat. "Sure."

"At school today, I was talking to someone. Voice only. The caller could have been on the other side of the world, right?"

"Yes," said Bob. "If it was from far away, you might notice."

"Right. Jitter and latency."

Is he just parroting jargon? Before he lost his mind, Dad had been a technical ignoramus. Bob remembered once in the days of very-dumb-phones when Dad insisted that his new cordless handset was a cheap substitute for a cellphone. Mother had proven him wrong by having Bob take the cordless down the street and try to call her home-business number. She'd rarely made mistakes like that; the old man had been hell on her for weeks afterward.

Dad was nodding to himself. "I suppose timing analysis could reveal a lot."

"Yes. Your average high-school student is good at both sides of that game." *If you hadn't ruined things, you could learn all this from Miri.*

His old man looked away, introspective. Worried?

"Is someone hassling you at school, Dad?" The thought was boggling.

Robert gave one of his old malevolent chuckles. "Someone is *trying* to hassle me."

"Um. Maybe you should talk to your teachers about this. You could show them your Epiphany log of the incident. This is a standard sort of problem they have to deal with."

There was no return fire; the elder Gu just nodded seriously. "I know, I should. I *will.* But it's hard, you know. And given your job, well, you've spent years working on life-and-death versions of these problems, right? You'd have the most expert possible answers."

It was the first time in Bob's life that his old man had said anything nice about his career. *This must be a setup!*

There was silence for a moment as the father waited with apparent patience, and the son tried to think what to say next. Finally, Bob gave a laugh. "Okay, but the military answers would be overkill, Dad. Not because we're that much smarter than a billion teenagers, but because we have the Secure Hardware Environment. Down at the bottom we control all the hardware." *Leaving aside the moonshine fabs and the hardware abusers.*

"The fellow I was talking to this afternoon styled himself 'an all-encompassing cloud of knowingness.' Is that bull? How much can he know about me?"

"If this jerk is willing to break some laws, he can find out a lot about you. That probably includes your medical history, maybe even what you've said to Reed Weber. As for spying on you moment to moment: He can usually watch you in public places, though that depends on your defaults and the density of local coverage. If he has confederates or zombies, he can learn what you do even in deadzones, though that information wouldn't come to him in real time."

"Zombies?"

"Corrupted systems. Remember what things were like when I was a kid? Almost any nastiness we had on home computers, we have on wearables now. The situation would be absolutely intolerable without the SHE." Dad looked blank, or maybe he was Googling. "Don't worry about it, Dad. Your Epiphany gear is about as secure as you'd be comfortable wearing. Just remember that other folks may not be so trustable."

Robert seemed to be digesting what his son had said. "But aren't there other possibilities? Maybe little gadgets the, ah, kids can stick on you?"

"Yes! The little dufuses are no different than I was, but they have more opportunities for mischief." Last semester it had been the crawling-up-your-skirt spidercams. For a while, the gadgets had been a god-damned mechanical infestation. Miri had raged about the invasion for days, and then dropped the issue so abruptly that Bob suspected she'd wrought some terrible revenge. "That's why you should always come into the house through the front hall. We have a good commercial bug trap there. Just you and I talking here is as private as your Epiphany can be. . . . So what exactly is this fellow hitting you up for? You're from so far outside the school scene, I can't imagine you being successfully hassled."

By God, Dad actually looks shifty! "I'm not really sure. I think it's just the hazing a new kid gets"—he gave a little smile—"even when the new kid happens to be an old fart. Thanks for the advice, Son."

"Sure thing."

The old man sidled out of the room. Bob's gaze followed him into the hall and up the stairs to the privacy of his room. Dad was definitely a man with things on his mind. Bob stared at the closed bedroom door for a moment, wondering at life's inversions and wishing he and Alice were like some folks, the ones who snooped on their own miscellaneous dependents.

15

WHEN METAPHORS ARE REAL

For the next week Robert avoided UCSD, just to see if the Mysterious Stranger would react.

He was beginning to feel confident with Epiphany, although he might never be as skillful as kids who grew up wearing. Xiu Xiang was lagging behind him, mainly because of her self-doubts. She had refused to wear for three days after one particularly mistaken gesture had dumped her into—into she refused to say what, but Robert suspected it was some kind of porn view.

The language in the Gu/Orozco project, while not poetry, had risen above the level of egregious noise. Robert had a surprising amount of fun working with video effects and network jitter. If their project had been shown in the 1990s, it would have been taken as a work of genius. That was the power of the libraries of clichés and visual gimmicks that lay in their tools. Juan was properly afraid it wouldn't count for much with Chumlig. "We need some added value or she'll fred us." He Googled up some high schools with manual music programs. "Those kids think it's a tragic form of gaming," he said. In the end, Robert chatted up student musicians in Boston and southern Chile—far enough apart to really exercise his network ideas.

Sharif had returned to Corvallis, but they had several more interviews. Some of the guy's questions were a lot more intelligent than Robert would have expected from their first encounters.

He surfed the web a lot, to study up on security issues and—on occasion—to see what had become of literature. What was art, now that surface perfection was possible? Ah, serious literature was there. Most of it didn't make much money, even with the microroyalty system. But there were men and women who could string words almost as well as the old Robert. *Damn them!*

Still silence from the Stranger. Either he had lost interest, or he understood his power over Robert. *It is so easy to win when your victim is desperate.* It had been a long time since anyone had beaten Robert Gu at a stare-down . . . but then one Saturday he skipped his session with Juan. Instead, he took a car to UCSD.

Sharif showed up on the way. "Thank you for accepting my call, Professor Gu." The image sat down in the car seat, part of its butt disappearing into the cushions. Zulfi didn't look nearly as well put together as recently. "It's been hard to reach you lately."

"I thought we covered a lot of ground on Thursday."

Sharif looked pained.

Robert raised an eyebrow. "You're complaining?"

"Not at all, not at all! But you see, sir, it's possible that perhaps I've allowed my wearable to become, um, perhaps somewhat corrupted. It's possible that I'm subject to some degree of . . . hijacking."

Robert thought back on some of his recent reading. "That's like being a little bit pregnant, isn't it?"

Sharif's image shrank further into the upholstery. "Indeed, sir. I take your point. But frankly, my systems are sometimes subject to a small degree of corruption. I wager that is true of most users. I had thought the situation was manageable, but things have reached the point where . . . well, you see, I did not interview you Thursday. Not at all."

"Ah." So the Mysterious Stranger had had it both ways: bludgeoning Robert with silence at the same time he carried on as another player.

Sharif waited a moment for Robert to say more, then rushed forward with "Please, Professor, I do so very much wish to continue these interviews! Now that we know there is this problem, we can easily work around it. I beg you not to cut me off."

"You could clean up your system."

"Well, yes. In theory. I had to do that once in undergraduate school. Somehow, I ended up the zombie in a cheating conspiracy. Not my fault at all, but the University of Kolkata required me to fry-clean all my clothes." He raised his hands up in open-palmed prayer. "I've never been very good about backups; the debacle cost me more than a semester of progress toward my degree. Please don't make me do that again. It would be even worse now."

Robert looked out at traffic. His car had turned onto Highway 56 and was tooling toward the coast. Up ahead were the first of the bio labs. And perhaps the Mysterious Stranger was there too. By comparison, Sharif was a known quantity. He looked back at the young fellow and said mildly. "Okay, Mr. Sharif. Carry on in your slightly corrupted state." An old memory struck him, how the computer techs at Stanford had always badgered him about the latest antivirus updates. "We'll simply rise above all the petty vandalism."

"Quite so, sir! Thank you so much." Sharif paused, exuding profound relief. "And I'm more eager than ever to proceed. I have my questions here somewhere." Hesitation and a blank stare as he changed mental gears. "Ah, yes. Has there been any progress on the revised *Secrets of the Ages*?"

"No," Robert replied a little shortly. But this was the sort of question you'd expect of the authentic Zulfi Sharif. Robert mellowed his answer with some half truths: "I'm still doing high-level planning, you know." He launched into a long discussion of how, even though Guian poetry was sparse, its creation required infinitely precise planning. He'd said things like that in the old days, but never laid it on quite as thickly as now. Sharif ate it up.

"So over the next few weeks, I'm going to be visiting my old friends—you know, in the library. That will give me some insights into the plight of the, er, vanquished aged. You're welcome to come along. If you watch carefully, you may learn things about how I work. And afterwards, I'd be happy to critique your conclusions."

The younger man nodded eagerly. "Wonderful. Thank you!"

Amazing the thrill it was to have *someone* look up to him, even if it was the sort of no-talent that he had shielded himself against all through his earlier life. *This must be how poor Winnie worked it, using big words and pomposity to fool the even less inspired.* Robert looked away from Sharif's image, and tried to keep his smile from turning predatory. *And when Sharif gets smarter, I'll know it's the Stranger.*

THERE WERE NO demonstrators at the library today, but—surprise—there were lots of in-person students. This was heart-warmingly like his recollections of years past, with the library the center of the university's intellectual life. What good things had happened in the last week? He and virtual Sharif walked through the glass doors and took the elevator to floor six. The building interior was not visible to Robert, even with his new access skills. Okay, look for recent news items. . . . but by then he was on the fifth floor.

Lena --> Juan, Miri, Xiu: <sm>Hey! I've lost the view!</sm>

Juan --> Lena, Miri, Xiu: <sm>The sixth floor isn't publicly searchable today.</sm>

Miri --> Juan, Lena, Xiu: <sm>Maybe if I just ask Robert for forwarding.</sm>

Sharif had faded to a luminescent reddish blob. "I can't see anymore," he said. "And I'll bet you're the only person I can hear."

Robert hesitated, then waved permissions in Sharif's direction. *Let's see what the cabal makes of that.*

Winnie and Carlos Rivera were sitting at the window wall. Tommie was hunched over his laptop.

"*Nǐ hǎo,* Professor Gu!" said Rivera. "Thanks for coming."

Tommie looked up from his laptop. "But I'm not sure we want your little friend."

Sharif got support from an unexpected place. Winston Blount said, "Tommie, I think Sharif might be of some use."

Tommie shook his head. "Not anymore. Now that UCSD is shredded—"

"What?" The stacks were still full of books. Robert stepped back and ran his hand across the spines. "These feel real to me," he said.

"You didn't see the propaganda on the lower floors?"

"No. I took the elevator, and so far I'm not very good at seeing through walls."

Tommie shrugged. "We're on the last unshredded floor. Like we figured, the administration was just waiting for the fuss to die down. Then one night they swooped in with extra shredders. They were done with two floors before we had a clue. By then it was too late."

"Damn!" Robert settled into a chair. "So what's the point of protesting now?"

Winnie said, "It's true that we can't save UCSD. In fact, the clever SOBs have twisted things around so that the Librareome Project is more popular with the students than before. But so far, UCSD has the only library that's been shredded."

Rivera burst into Mandarin: "*Duì, dànshì tāmen xūyào huǐ diào qítāde túshūguǎn, yīnwèi*—" He hesitated, seemed to notice the blank looks. "S-Sorry. I meant to say, they still need to destroy other libraries. For cross-checking. The data reduction and virtual reassembly will be an ongoing project, tending 'asymptotically toward perfect reproduction.' "

Robert noticed that Tommie Parker was watching with a faint smile. "So you do have a plan?"

"I ain't saying nothing while Sharif is here."

Winnie sighed. "Okay, Tommie. Go ahead and shut him down."

Sharif's rosy glow moved a little ways out from the stacks. "It's all right. I don't want to be a prob—" The glow vanished.

Tommie looked up from his laptop. "He's gone. *And* I've deadzoned the sixth floor." He pointed at an LED on the edge of his ancient-looking laptop.

Robert remembered some of Bob's claims: "Even the Homeland Security hardware?"

"Don't tell, Robert." He patted his computer. "Genuine Paraguayan inside, shipped just before they shut the fabs down." He gave them a shifty grin. "Now it's just us, unless one of you is wearing dirty panties."

Blount looked pointedly at Robert. "Or unless one of us is a fink."

Robert sighed. "This isn't Stanford, Winston." But what if the Mysterious Stranger were actually a cop? That should have occurred to him before. He pushed the thought away. "So what's your plan?"

"We've been reading the *Economist,*" said Rivera. "Huertas International is on shaky financial ground. Delays here at

UCSD could force him to dump the whole project." He stared at Robert through his thick spectacles. You could see images flickering around in the things.

"Even though they've shredded almost everything here?"

"*Duì.*" The young man leaned forward, and his T-shirt showed a torrent of worried faces. "It's like this. The Librareome Project isn't just the video capture of premillennium books. It's not just the digitization. It goes beyond Google and company. Huertas intends to combine all classical knowledge into a single, object-situational database with a transparent fee structure."

Object-situational database? This was beyond Robert's newfound nerdliness. He stared over Rivera's head, trying to look up the term. Nothing was coming back. Tommie's deadzone, yeah.

Rivera took his stare as disbelief. "It's really not that much data, Dr. Gu. A few petabytes. The main thing is that it's very heterogeneous compared to similar-size datasets in most applications."

"Of course. Your point?" From the corner of his eye, he saw a smile come to Winnie's face. The guy knew Robert was blowing smoke.

"So," Rivera continued, "the Huertas collection will contain almost all human knowledge up to about twenty years ago. All correlated and connected. It's the reason Huertas is paying the State of California to let him commit this atrocity. Even the first rough compilation could be a gold mine. From the project start six weeks ago, Huertas International has a six-month monopoly on the Librareome they're creating. That's six months with sole access to real insight on the past. There are dozens of questions that such a resource might resolve: Who really ended the Intifada? Who is behind the London art forgeries? Where was the oil money really going in the latter part of the last century? Some answers will only interest obscure historical societies. But some will mean big bucks. And Huertas will have exclusive rights to this oracle for six months."

"But he has to get the data put together," said Winnie. "If Huertas loses a few weeks, there'll be hundreds of organizations that decide they might as well wait till the monopoly runs out—when they can get an even more complete answer for free. It's worse than that. Chinese Informagical has dibs on the British Museum and the British Library, using much better equipment than Huertas has. The Brits have shown more gumption than UCSD, but their digitization is due to begin any time now. If Huertas gets any further behind, he and the Chinese will be in a price war for the sale of first looks."

"A regular death spiral!" Tommie's amusement was without malice. He had always been fascinated by how things come apart. Robert remembered in the 1970 brush fires, teenaged Tommie had been out in East County, helping with communications—but also enjoying every minute of the disaster.

"So, unh . . ." *Why does the Stranger want me in on this?*

Blount chuckled. "Confused, Robert?"

Back at Stanford, Winnie wouldn't have dared such an open gibe, at least not after the first year. But now, the only comebacks Robert could imagine were adolescent sarcasm. So he replied mildly, "Yes, I'm still in the dark."

Blount hesitated, sensing one of the old-Robert traps. "The point is that we're talking about doing Huertas and the Librareome Project serious harm. We're past legal recourse, so anything that depends on *delaying* the enemy must involve criminal behavior. Got it?"

"Yes. We really are conspirators."

Rivera nodded. "And that by itself is a felony."

Tommie laughed. "So what? I just subverted the DHS snoop layer! That's a national-security rap."

"I don't care if we're talking high treason!" said Robert. *If I can get back my song. . . .* "I mean, you know what a lover of books I am."

The others nodded.

"So what *is* the plan?"

Blount gestured to Tommie. The little guy said, "Do you remember our underground hikes?"

"In the 1970s? Yes, they were fun—in a brain-damaged way."

Tommie's grin broadened.

"You're telling me the steam tunnels are still in use?"

"Yup. In the nineties that type of construction went out of

style. There were lots of new buildings that weren't connected. But then in the oughts, folks wanted Extremely High-Rate comms. And the bioscience people wanted automatic specimen transport. These guys had lots of money."

"Even more so, nowadays," said Carlos.

Tommie nodded. "NIR lasers are not for them. They want xlaser and graser gear, trillions of colors per path, and trillions of paths. Nowadays, the 'steam tunnel' network is not for power or heat. Now there are branches extending under Torrey Pines Road to Scripps and Salk. I hear you can walk out under the ocean a short ways, though heaven knows what they're doing there. To the east, you can get into every one of the biotech labs."

Suddenly, Robert saw why the Mysterious Stranger was interested in the Elder Cabal. Aloud, he said, "What does this have to do with the Librareome Project, Tommie?"

"Ah! Well, you know that Max Huertas made his fortune out of biotech. He owns some of the biggest labs in North America—including one just a few thousand feet northeast of us. It was easy for him to modify his genome software to support the Librareome. Okay, so he's storing the shredda in vaults under the north side of campus."

"And?"

"And he's not *done* with them! The shredding got him plenty of images, but the coverage is not complete. He's got to scan and rescan where there were problems in the first pass. Now if there weren't this time limit, he'd be better just to wait till the next victim library goes up in shreds and use *that* for cross-checking, but he's in a rush."

"That storage is also part of the Huertas propaganda," said Winnie. "When they're done with the rescans, the shredda will be 'safely preserved in the Huertas vaults, for the sake of the archaeologists of future generations.' Some of our faculty actually bought into that!"

"Well," said Rivera, "there's a small amount of truth to the claim. The paper will last longer in cool nitrogen than it would on library shelves."

Winnie waved his hand dismissively. "The point is, the books have been destroyed, and Huertas is going to destroy more libraries if he's not stopped. Our plan is—" He looked around, and seemed to realize that he was on the edge of prison time. "Our plan is to break into the steam tunnels and go to where Huertas is storing the shredda. Tommie has come up with a way to make that shredda unreadable."

"What? We're protesting the destruction of the library by destroying what's left?"

"Just temporarily!" said Tommie. "I've found an incredible aerosol glue. Spray it on and the shredda will be like a huge chunk of particleboard. But after a few months, the glue will just sublimate away."

Rivera was nodding. "So we are not making things worse. I wouldn't be here if I thought we were wrecking what's left of the books. Huertas's scheme is unnecessary brutality, trying to grab everything when a slower approach would be just as good. Maybe we can derail him long enough so that the old-time book-friendly digitizers can catch up—and no more libraries will be wrecked." Now his T-shirt was touting the American Library Association.

Robert leaned back and pretended to consider what they were saying. "You say the Chinese are about to shred the British Library?"

Rivera gave a sigh. "Yes, and they're going to whack the Museum, too. But the EU is looking for an excuse to stop them. If we make Huertas look bad . . ."

"I see," Robert said judiciously. He avoided Winnie's eyes. Blount was already suspicious enough. "Okay. The plan seems pretty feeble . . . but I guess it's better than nothing. Count me in."

A grin spread wide across Tommie's face. "Hey, Robert!"

Robert finally looked at Winston Blount. "Now the question is, why do you want me in?"

Blount grimaced. "Another pair of hands. Various errands—"

Tommie rolled his eyes. "The fact is, we couldn't dream of doing this before you showed up."

"Me? Why?"

"Ha. Think what we're talking about: breaking into the steam tunnels, walking a mile across one of the most secure bio labs on Earth. I bet I could get us in. But could I hike us undetected across the bio labs? No way. That only works in old *Star Trek* shows, where the 'ventilation system' was designed mainly to drive idiot plots. This is the real world—and real-world security guys know about tunnels too."

"That still doesn't answer the 'Me? Why?' "

"What? Oh. I'm getting to that! Anyway, after our protest tactics fizzled, I began to do some research." Tommie patted his laptop. "Newsgroups, chat, search engines—I used them all, along with crazy stuff that looks more like online betting than anything else. Maybe the hardest part was to do it all without alerting the feds. That slowed me up, but eventually I got a pretty good picture of the labs' security. It's what you'd expect of a critical national security site. Serious stuff, but clunky. The system is password- and user-intrinsic-oriented, and mostly automatic. The intrinsic is a standard biometric—from certain officers in the U.S. protective services. And guess who happens to be nearby and on the access list?"

"My son."

"Not quite. Your daughter-in-law."

Alice. "That's ridiculous. She's some kind of Asian-affairs expert." *When she's not a mental basket case.* And then he thought about the Mysterious Stranger. "This is all too pat."

Winnie: "Since when are you the security expert, Robert?"

I should keep my mouth shut. They're going in the direction I want! But he'd lost his old skills at verbal maneuver, and he blundered ahead: "Information like this doesn't turn up in a Google search ."

Tommie shook his head. But there was a look of pity in his eyes. "The world has changed, Robert. Nowadays, I can get answers in ways that would have been impossible twenty years ago. A hundred thousand people all over the world collaborated in my search, in little bitty parts of it that no one ever recognized. The biggest risk is that my results are simply bogus. Disinformation is king nowadays. Even when the lies are not deliberate, there are the various fantasy groups out there trying to torque reality around to their latest adventure game. But if we're getting fooled, it's not an ordinary con job. There are details and corroboration that come from too many independent sources."

"Oh." Robert made that sound impressed. In fact, he *was* impressed. Maybe the Stranger could deliver.

O

THEY TALKED FOR another half hour, but nothing more specific was said about the betrayal expected of Robert. Tommie had other tasks for them: They needed some university passwords and some voice fakery. The entrances to the steam tunnels were embedded in concrete now. There was no ground-level entrance as there had been fifty years ago, when construction was under way. And there was a problem with Tommie's "aerosol glue."

"The glue?" Tommie looked faintly embarrassed. "It doesn't exist yet. But it's almost been invented." Tommie had broached the concept on an ornamental gardening forum, crossed that with some VCs. The Ornamental Shrub Society of Japan was even now working with some Argentine biologists to create the final form of the aerosol. The product should exist in less than two weeks, its first showing to be in a Tokyo plant-training exhibit. A liter of advance product was to be UP/Exed to Tommie shortly before that. He looked back at Robert's incredulity. "Hey, this is just what hacking is like nowadays."

It was past 3:00 P.M. The shadow of the library had stretched into the east, drowning nearby buildings. The four conspirators were done for the day.

Tommie stood. "We can do it! We may not even be caught. But if we are, so what? It'll be just like the old days."

Carlos Rivera got up more slowly. "And it's not like we're harming anything."

Tommie put a finger to his lips. "I'm lifting the deadzone, gentlemen." He typed on his laptop, and the LED on the top edge of the case was extinguished.

They were all silent for a moment, trying to think of safe things to say.

"Ah, okay." Rivera glanced at Robert. "Would you like see what we—what the library has done with the empty stacks?"

"You mean, what Tommie said was propaganda?"

Rivera gave a wan smile. "Yes, but it's beautiful in a way. If it had been done after a gentler digitization, I would love it without reservation."

He led them around the floor, past the elevators. "The stairway entrance has the best ambience."

Winnie Blount grimaced, but Robert noticed that he was tagging along.

The stairwell was dimly lit. The naked-eye view showed concrete walls, seamed here and there with the silvery lines he had seen from the outside. As he stepped through the doorway, Robert's view shifted to some kind of standard enhancement: now the lighting came from gas mantle lamps set in the walls. The shadowed concrete was gone. These walls were built from large stones, squared with chisels, fitted together with scarcely room for mortar. Robert reached out to touch the wall, snatched his hand back as he felt slippery stone—not clean concrete!

Rivera laughed. "You're expecting the usual disappointment, right, Dr. Gu?" When touch contradicted visual illusion.

"Yeah." Robert let his hand trail over the stone blocks, trace out the softer patches of lichen.

"University administration has been very clever about this. They enlisted the belief-circle community—and encouraged them to install touchy-feely graffiti. Some of the props are impressive even without the visual overlays."

They went down two flights of stairs. This must be the landing for the fifth-floor entrance, but now the door was carven wood, gleaming darkly in the gaslight. Rivera pulled at the pitted brass handle and the eight-foot-tall door swung open. The light from beyond was actinic violet, wavering from dim to painfully bright. There were sparking sounds. Rivera stuck his head through and chanted something unintelligible. The lighting became more civil and the only sounds were distant voices.

"It's okay," said the librarian. "Come on."

Robert stepped through the half-opened door and looked around. This was not the fifth floor of the Geisel Library, Planet Earth. There *were* books, but they were oversized things, set on timbered racks that stretched up and up. Robert bent back. The violet lights followed the stacks upward, limned their twisted struts. It was like one of those fractal forests in old graphics. At the limits of his vision, there were still more books, tiny with distance.

Whoa. He slipped, felt Tommie steady him with a hand in the small of his back.

"Neat, huh?" said Parker. "I almost wish I was wearing."

"Y-Yeah." Robert steadied himself on a nearby rack. The wood was real, thick, and solid. He brought his gaze down to floor level and looked outward along the aisle. The path through the stacks was twisted—and it didn't end at the external wall that must be there, just thirty or forty feet away. Instead, about where the windows should be, there were sagging wooden steps. It was the sort of ad hoc carpentry he had loved in old used-book stores. Beyond the steps, the stacks themselves seemed to be tilted, as though gravity itself were pointing in a different direction.

"What *is* all this?"

The three were silent for a second. Robert noticed that they seemed to be wearing dark armor. Rivera's outfit had some spiffy insignia. It also looked suspiciously like a T-shirt and Bermuda shorts done in blackened steel plate.

"Don't you get it?" Rivera said finally. "You three are Knights Guardian. And I'm a Librarian Militant. It's all from Jerzy Hacek's *Dangerous Knowledge* stories."

Blount nodded. "You never read any of those, did you, Robert?"

Robert vaguely remembered Hacek from about the time he retired. He sniffed. "I read the important things."

They walked slowly down the narrow aisle. There were side paths. These led not only left and right, but up and down. Snakelike hissing sounds came from some. In others, he saw "Knights Guardian" hunched over tables that were piled with books and parchment; light shone into their faces from the pages of opened books. Illuminated manuscripts indeed. Robert stopped for a closer look. The words were English, printed in a cracked Gothic script. The book was some kind of economics text. One of the readers, a young woman with overgrown eyebrows, glared briefly at the visitors, and then gestured into the air above. High in the stacks, there was a thump, and a four-foot-wide slab of leather and parchment came tumbling down. Robert hopped backward, almost stepping on Tommie. But the falling book came to a hover just within the student's reach. The pages riffled themselves open.

Oh. Robert backed carefully out of the alcove. "I get it. These are the digitizations of what's been destroyed so far."

"The first-pass digitization," said Blount. "Bastard modern administrators got more good press out of this than all the rest of their propaganda put together. Everybody thinks it's so clever and cute. And next week they'll shred the sixth floor."

Rivera led them outward, toward the sagging wooden stairs. "Not everybody is happy. The Geisel estate—Dr. Seuss—didn't go along with the university on this."

"Good for them!" Blount kicked at the timbered stacks. "Our students might as well go to Pyramid Hill."

Robert gestured in the way that was supposed to revert vision to unenhanced reality. But he was still seeing purple light and ancient, leather-bound manuscripts. He tapped the explicit reversion signal. Still no onset of reality. "I'm stuck in this view."

"Yup. Unless you take off your contacts or declare a 911, you can't see what's really here. And that's another reason for not using Epiphany." Tommie waved his open laptop like some talisman. "I can see the illusions, but only when I want them." The little guy walked down another side path, here poking at a book that lay groaning on the floor, there stepping into an alcove to look at what the patrons were doing. "This place is so cool!"

When they reached the wooden stairs, Rivera said, "Be careful. These things are tricky." About halfway down, the steps tilted and the perspective was all askew. Winnie went first. He hesitated at the twist. "I've done this before," he grunted, almost to himself. "I can do it." He stepped forward, started to stumble, and then stood straight—but tilted compared with Robert and company.

When Robert reached the threshold, he closed his eyes. The Epiphany default was to drop all overlays on "eyes-closed," so he was briefly immune to the visual trickery. He stepped forward—and there was no real tilt, just a simple turn!

Tommie came right after him. There was a big grin on his

face. "Welcome to the Escher Wing!" he said. "The kids just eat this up." At the bottom of the stairs there was another ninety-degree turn. Parker said, "Okay, now we're walking back toward the building's utility core, only we have the feeling that we're still wandering through unending books."

Books ahead and behind, and off to the side, hidden in alleys. Books above, like chimneys disappearing in purple light. He could even see books below them, where rickety ladders seemed to drop off into the depths. If Robert looked at them with slightly averted vision, the lettering on the spines and covers gave back a blacklight glow, violet almost too deep to see, but very clear, with the Library of Congress codes cryptic and runelike. The books were the ghosts—or maybe the avatars—of what had been destroyed.

They made sounds, groaning, hissing, whispering. Conspiring. Deep in the alleyways, some of the books were in chains.

"Gotta watch out for *Das Kapital*," said Rivera.

Robert saw one of the tomes—*the word fits for once!*—pulling at its chains, the links ringing loudly on massive eyebolts.

"Yup, Dangerous Knowledge yearns to be free."

Some of the books must be real, touchy-feely props. The students in one alley were piling books together. They stood back and the texts nuzzled into each other in an orgy of flapping pages. "So that's bibliographical synthesis?"

Rivera followed his gaze. "Er, yes. This started out as the scam Dean Blount said, something to endear the shredding project to the public. We represent books as near-living things, creatures that serve and bewitch their readers. Terry Pratchett and then Jerzy Hacek have been playing on that theme for years. But we really didn't appreciate the power of it all. We have some of the best Hacek belief circles helping with this. Every database action has a physical representation here, just as in Hacek's Library Militant stories. Most of our users think this is better than standard reference software."

Winnie looked back at them. He had gotten far enough ahead that he seemed foreshortened, as if they were seeing him through a telescope at some great distance. He waved in disgust. "That's the betrayal, Carlos. You librarians don't approve of the shredding, but look what you've done. These kids will lose all respect for the permanent record of the human heritage."

Tommie Parker was standing behind Robert. He muttered gleefully, "Winnie, the kids had already lost all respect."

Rivera looked down. "I'm sorry, Dean Blount. It's the shredding that's evil, not the digitizing. For the first time in their lives, our students have modern access to premillennium knowledge." He waved at the students down in the alley. "And it's not just here. You can reach the library from the net, just minus the touchy-feely gimmicks. Huertas is allowing limited access without charge, even during his monopoly period. This is just the first-pass digitization, and only HB through HX, but we've had more hits on our premillennium holdings in the last week than we had in the last four years. And much of the new business is from faculty!"

"Hypocritical bastards," said Winnie.

Robert looked at the students in their alcove. The sex-between-books had ended, but now the books floated in the air over the students' heads and the pages sang out in tiny voices to volumes still unsearched. *Metaphor incarnate.*

They trooped back toward the utility core. It turned out to be several times farther than Robert remembered. The staggered aisles must take them around the center of the real fourth floor.

Finally they were in sight of the eight-foot-tall doors. After everything else, the carven wood was quotidian reality. Even the floor had flattened into something solid and normal-looking.

And then that floor shifted under his feet.

"Wha—" Robert flailed out, fell against the wall. Books shifted on their shelves, and he remembered that *some* of those were as real and heavy as they looked.

Lightning flashed in pulsing arcs.

Rivera was shouting in Mandarin, something about a fake earthquake.

Whatever it was, the swaying and shifting were *real.*

A groaning sound came from below, and bats rushed back and forth in the air above. The swaying diminished, cycled around like a dancer doing a little jig.

And then it was over. The floor and walls felt as steady as they had been in Robert's grad-school years.

Tommie climbed back to his feet and helped Winston Blount up. "All okay?" he said.

Blount nodded dumbly, too shaken for sarcasm.

"It's never done that before," said Tommie.

Carlos nodded. *"Āiya, duìbùqǐ, wǒ gāng xiǎng qǐlái tāmen jīntiān shì xīn dōngxī,"* he said, something about trying something new today.

Tommie patted the librarian on the shoulder. "Hey man, you're talking Chinese."

Rivera stared for a moment and then responded, still in Mandarin, but faster and louder.

"It's okay, Carlos. Don't worry." Tommie guided the young man down the stairs. Rivera was still talking, but in bursts, repeating, *"Wǒ zài shuō yīngyǔ ma? Shì yīngyǔ ma?"* Am I speaking English? Is it English?

"Just keep going, Carlos. You'll be okay."

Robert and Winnie brought up the rear. Blount was squinting his eyes in that exaggerated way of his, searching. "Ha!" he said. "The bastards were using the stability servos to shake the building. See."

And for a wonder, Robert did see; all the practice was paying off. "Yes!" The Geisel Library was one of the few buildings not replaced after the Rose Canyon quake. Instead, they built active stabilization into the old frame. "So the admin thought this would give a little extra realism. . . ."

"We could have been killed," said Blount.

They were at the third floor. Coming up the other way was a group of students; at least, Robert assumed they were students, since they were laughing and most had chosen monstrous forms. The two groups slid past each other, the oldsters silent until the students had disappeared above them.

Tommie said, "What triggers the rock and roll, Carlos?"

Rivera weaved around an armoire that was built into the wall. Now he shouted, "Am I speaking English yet? . . . *Yes!* Oh, thank God. Sometimes I dream I get stuck forever." He walked several paces, almost crying with relief. Then the words came streaming out of him. "Yes, yes. I understood your question: I'm not sure what triggers our fake earthquakes. I was at the meeting where we decided to use the stability system this way.

The trigger was supposed to be any attempt to 'open' a book that contains knowledge 'Mankind was not meant to know.' Of course, that's a joke—except when it's so deadly serious that Homeland Security shows up. So I think we just trigger the shakes at random."

They continued downward, Rivera all but babbling: "Our chief librarian is totally committed on this. She's also a big cheese in the local Hacek belief circle. She wants to implement Hacek-appropriate penalties for users who break library rules."

Tommie's look of concern was replaced by technical interest. "Jeez," he said, "Hacek torment pits?"

At the main floor, they stepped out onto the standard carpeting of the library's main foyer. An hour earlier, Robert and Sharif had gone through this area to get to the elevators. Robert had scarcely noticed the clean, open space, the statue of Theodor Seuss Geisel. Now it was a welcoming sanity. They walked through glass doors into the afternoon sunlight.

Winnie turned to look up at the overhanging stories of the library. "They've turned the place into a menace. That earthquake was, was . . ." Abruptly his gaze came down from the sky. "Are you okay, Carlos?"

The librarian waved his hand. "Yes. Sometimes getting stuck is a little like an epileptic seizure." He wiped his face; he was drenched in sweat. "Wow. Maybe this was a bad one. . . ."

"You should get medical attention, Carlos."

"I am. See?" Medical flags had popped up around his head. "I alarmed out on the stairs. There's at least one real doctor watching me now. I—" He hesitated, listening. "Okay, they want me at the clinic. Some kind of brain scan. I'll see you next time." He saw the look on their faces. "Hey, don't worry, guys."

"I'll come along," said Tommie.

"Okay, but don't talk. They're prepping me for the scan." The two walked off toward the west-side traffic circle.

Robert and Winnie stared after them. Blount spoke with uncharacteristic uncertainty. "Maybe I shouldn't have hassled him about the Hacek stuff."

"Is he going to be okay?"

"Probably. Every time another veteran gets permanently

stuck, the VA looks real bad. They'll do their best for him."

Robert thought back to all of Rivera's strangeness. Normally, his Mandarin was just short interjections, almost an affectation. If those had been in Spanish, he might not even have noticed. But now—"What's the matter with him, Winnie?"

Blount's gaze was abstracted. He shrugged. "Carlos is a JITT."

"What's that?"

"Huh? Christ, Gu! Look it up." He glared around the plaza. "Okay. Okay." He gave Robert a forced smile. "Sorry, Robert. JITT's an easy search topic. You'll find lots of good discussion. The important thing is, we have to keep our eyes on the ball. Um, Carlos would want that. A lot depends on you doing the right thing."

"But what is that? What—"

Winnie held up a hand. "We're working on it. We'll get you the details soon enough."

ON THE DRIVE home, Robert looked up "JITT." There were millions of hits, in medicine, in military affairs, in drug enforcement. He picked the GlobalSecurity summary off the top of "respected contrarian" sources:

> JITT, "just-in-time-training" (also, "just-in-time-trainee", when referring to a victim of the procedure). A treatment that combines addressin therapy and intense data exposure, capable of installing large skill sets in less than 100 hours. Most famous for its tragic use in the <link>Sino-American Conflict</link>, when 100,000 U.S. military recruits were trained in Mandarin, Cantonese–

and a list of specialties that Robert had never heard of. In less than ninety days the Americans had made up their military language gap. But then there were problems—

> This talent pool was decisive in ground operations; however, the human price of the procedure was apparent even before the end of the war.

Robert Gu—and perhaps every student—has dreamed of shortcuts. Learn Russian or Latin or Chinese or Spanish, overnight and painlessly! *But be careful what you wish for. . . .* He read the sections on side effects: Learning a language, or a career specialty, *changes* a person. Cram in such skills willy-nilly and you distort the underlying personality. A very few JITTs suffered no side effects. In rare cases, such people could undertake a second hit—even a third—before the damage caught up with them. The rejection process was a kind of internal war between the new viewpoints and the old, manifesting as seizures and altered mental states. Often the JITT was stuck in some diminished form of his/her new skill set. . . . After the war, there was the legacy of the JITT-disabled veterans, and continuing abuse by foolish students everywhere.

Poor Carlos.

And just what is the Mysterious Stranger promising me?

This had definitely been one of those future-shock days. Robert rolled down the window and felt the breeze sweep by. He was driving north on I-15. All around was a dense suburbia much like the most built-up parts of twentieth-century California, except that here the houses were a little drabber and the shopping malls were more like warehouse districts. Strangely, there were real malls, even in this brave new world. He had shopped in a couple of them. Some places had plenty of solid architecture. Shopping "for the old at heart" was their motto; *that* would not have worked in 2000.

Robert pushed away the mysteries (and the fear) and practiced with his Epiphany. *Let's see the minimum adornment.* Robert shrugged the familiar gesture. *Okay so far.* He could see simple labeling. Everything, even the iceplant on the sides of the freeway, had little alphanumeric signs. Another shrug of the shoulder, and he was seeing what the objects he was passing—more accurately, the *owners* of the objects—wanted him to see. There was advertising. The malls had guessed he was an old fart, and tuned their ads accordingly. But there was none of the outright spam of some earlier sessions. Maybe he finally had his filters set right.

Robert leaned back from the window and reached out to wider universes. Colored maps appeared before his eyes. There were realities that were geographically far away, not overlaid upon San

Diego at all. Those must be like the cyberspace crap of the eighties and nineties. Finally he got a window that promised "public local reality only." Yeah. Only two hundred thousand of them for this part of San Diego County. He chose at random. Outside the car, the North County hillsides were swept clean of the subdivisions. The road had only three lanes and the cars were out of the 1960s. He noticed the tag on the windshield of his car (now a Ford Falcon): *San Diego Historical Society.* Bit by bit, they were reconstructing the past. Big hunks of the twentieth century were available for people who wanted those simpler times.

Robert almost stayed with this view. It was so near his own grad-school years. It was so . . . comforting. It also occurred to him that these history fans might be *allies* of the Librareome Project. With Huertas's database in place they could proceed even faster with their reconstructed nostalgia.

He brought up the control window. There was something called "continuous paratime traversal." Or maybe he should pick on a particular writer. There was Jerzy Hacek. No, he'd seen enough of "A Little Knowledge" for today.

How about Terry Pratchett? Okay. The subdivisions were adobe now. His car was an artfully contorted carpet, swooping down a grassy slope that a moment ago had been the grade north of Mountain Meadow Road. In the valley ahead, there were colorful tents with signs painted in a cursive script that made the roman alphabet look vaguely like Arabic calligraphy. There was a scrap of ocean visible in the long, westward-tending valley. And sailing ships?

Robert Gu had read one Pratchett novel. His recollection was that the action mainly took place in a city that resembled medieval London. This was different. He tried to see into the tent city. . . .

Miri --> Lena, Xiu: <sm>I have him again! See?</sm>

Xiu --> Miri, Lena: <sm>Wow. You're driving right next to him?</sm>

Miri --> Lena, Xiu: <sm>No, this is cobbled together from the hills, and various car cams.</sm>

Xiu --> Miri, Lena: <sm>He just seems to be looking around.</sm>

Miri --> Lena, Xiu: <sm>I have a lock on Sharif's persona. We've got Robert all to ourselves.</sm>

Lena --> Miri, Xiu: <sm>This is ridiculous.</sm>

Miri --> Lena, Xiu: <sm>Okay, so now I'm Sharif, sitting right beside Robert . . . oh *darn!*</sm>

Someone gave a polite cough. Robert twisted around.

It was Sharif, sitting on the far end of the passenger seat. "Didn't mean to surprise you, Professor." The vision smiled ingratiatingly. "I tried to reappear earlier, but there were technical difficulties."

"That's fine," said Robert, wondering vaguely if Tommie was still interfering.

Sharif waved at the landscape around them. "So what do you think?"

It was the land of San Diego with a little more water. And a different people, a different civilization. "I thought I was dialing into one of the Terry Pratchett stories."

Sharif gave a shrug. "You got the main Pratchett belief circle all right. At least for San Diego."

"Yes, but—" Robert waved at the grasslands. "Where's Ankh-Morpork? Where are the slums and the dives and the city guard?"

Sharif smiled. "Mainly in London and Beijing, Professor. It's best to fit one's fantasy to follow something like the underlying geography. Pratchett writes of a whole world. This here, is what fits San Diego." Sharif stared for a moment. "Yes, this is Abu Dajeeb. You know, the sultanate he put just south of Sumarbad in *The Fiery Crow.*"

"Oh." *The Fiery Crow?*

"Written after you lost, ah—"

After I lost my marbles, yeah. "It's, it's immense. I can imagine someone writing *about* such a place, but no one man or even a movie company could put together all the—" Robert shrank back from the window as a woman on a winged iguana flew by. (He slipped into the real view, saw a Highway Patrol cruiser speeding past.)

Sharif chuckled. "It's not the work of one man. There's probably a million fans who've contributed to this. Like a lot of the best realities, it was also a commercial effort, the most successful external cinema of 2019. In the years since, it has just gotten better and better, an act of love on the part of the fans."

"Hmm." Robert had always resented the millions that went

into the film industry, and the writers who got rich from it. "I'll bet Pratchett made a pretty penny out of this stuff."

Sharif gave a smirk. "More than Hacek. Not as much as Rowling. But the microroyalties add up. Pratchett owns a rather large part of Scotland."

Robert shifted away from the Pratchett imagery. There were others: Tolkien views, and things he couldn't recognize even from their labels. What was SCA? Oh. In the SCA vision, the suburbs were transformed into villages behind walls, and there were castles atop the higher hills. The county parklands looked fierce and forested.

Sharif seemed to be following his imagery. He jerked a thumb at the Los Pumas Valley park just sliding by on the right. "You should see the RenFaires. They grab the whole park, sometimes run pretend wars between the barons of the hilltops. It's excellent, my man, truly excellent."

Ah. Robert turned and took a close look at Sharif. The match to his earlier appearance was perfect, except for the smartass grin on his face. "And you're not Sharif."

The grin broadened. "I was wondering if you'd *ever* catch on. You really must learn to be more paranoid about identity, Professor. I know, you've met Zulfi Sharif in person. That *is* the graduate student you think it is, and just the groveler he seems. But he doesn't have good control. I can show up as Sharif whenever I please."

"That's not what you said a few minutes ago."

Sharif frowned. "That was different. You've got other fans. One of them is not fully incompetent."

Huh? Robert thought a second, then forced a smile. "Then perhaps you'd better have some password so I don't blurt all your secrets to the wrong Sharif, eh?"

The Mysterious Stranger didn't look amused. "Very well. . . . When I first say 'my man,' that will trigger a certificate exchange. You don't have to do a thing." Now Sharif's face had a faint greenish tinge, and his eyes had a slant that had nothing to do with epicanthic eyefolds. He smiled. "You'll see your djinni and know it's really me. So what did you think of Tommie Parker's plan?"

"Ah . . ."

Sharif—*Stranger-Sharif*—leaned toward him, but there was no feel of motion in the faux leather seat. "I am everywhere, and I appear however I wish, to produce the results that I wish. Despite all Tommie's cleverness, I was there." He stared into Robert's eyes. "Heh. At a loss for words, aren't you, Professor? And that's your whole problem, isn't it? I want to help you with that, but first you'll have to help me."

Robert forced a cool smile. A winning reply was nowhere to be found. The best he could do was "You're promising me a miracle, without showing me a particle of evidence. And if it's JITT you're offering, I'm not buying. That's not what creativity is about."

Sharif sat back. His laugh was open and pleasant. "Very true. JITT is a dread miracle. But happy miracles are possible nowadays. And *I* can make them."

His car had left the freeway. It drove the winding way along Reche Road. They were only a few minutes from West Fallbrook and Bob's place. The Mysterious Stranger seemed to watch the scenery for a few moments. Then: "I really wanted to get a head start on things today, but if you insist on hard evidence . . ." He gestured and something flashed in the air between them. Normally that indicated that data had been passed. "Take a look at those references. And here's proof that I was largely behind the breakthroughs described."

"I'll take a look and get back to you."

"Please don't take too long, Professor. What your merry crew is planning is dead on arrival without your prompt help. And I need that if I am to help you."

His car turned onto Honor Court and slowed to a stop just beyond Bob's house. It wasn't even 4:30, but the ocean haze had moved in and things were getting dark. Little clusters of children were playing here and there along the street. God only knew what they were seeing. Robert stepped into the chill air and—there was Miri pedaling a bicycle up the street toward him. They stared at each other awkwardly. At least, Robert felt awkward. Normally they didn't see each other except with Bob or Alice. *In the old days, I never would have felt an instant's discomfort for blasting this child.* But somehow the concerted anger of Bob and Alice—and Miri's own stiff-necked courtesy—made him very uncomfortable. *I can't stay here, owing children who should owe me.*

Miri slid off her bike and stood beside him. She was looking into the car. Robert glanced at the departing vehicle. He could see Sharif still sitting in the backseat; maybe she could too. "That's Zulfikar Sharif," Robert said, rushing into explanations like the guilty soul he was. "He's interviewing me about the old days."

"Oh." She seemed to lose interest.

"Hey, Miri, I didn't know you had a bike."

She walked the bike along beside him. "Yes," she replied seriously. "It's not good for transportation, but Alice says that I need exercise. I like to ride around Fallbrook and game out the latest realities."

Thanks to the miracle of Epiphany, Robert could guess what she was talking about.

"In fact, it's not really my bike. This is Bob's, from when he was younger than I am."

The tires looked new, but—his eyes traveled over the aluminum frame, the peeling green and yellow paint job. *Lord.* Lena had insisted they buy this bike for the boy. Memories of little Bobby came back, of when he was trying so hard to learn to ride. He had been such a nuisance.

They walked the rest of the way to the door in silence, Robert lagging a bit behind his granddaughter.

16

THE FRONT BATHROOM INCIDENT

Winston Blount called a couple of times during the next few days. His cabal was very anxious to talk further about "what we talked about." Robert put him off and refused to talk privately. He could almost hear Winnie's teeth grinding in frustration—but the guy gave him another week.

Robert had several more interviews with the real—well, he could hope it was the real—Sharif. They were a heartwarming reminder of the Good Years, and totally unlike his encounters with the Mysterious Stranger. The young grad student gushed semi-intelligent enthusiasm, except that sometimes he seemed fond of science fiction. Sometimes. When Robert mentioned this, Sharif looked stricken. *Ah.* The Mysterious Stranger strikes again. Or maybe there were three . . . entities . . . animating the image of Zulfikar Sharif. Robert began to track each word, each nuance.

Juan Orozco's compositions had blossomed. He could write complete sentences intentionally. The boy seemed to think that this made Robert Gu a genius of a teacher. *Yes, and someday soon there will be chimpanzees who look up to me.* But that thought did not escape Robert's lips. Juan Orozco was working to his limits. He was doomed to mediocrity, much as Robert himself, and spreading the pain of such knowledge was not appealing anymore.

The Mysterious Stranger stayed out of sight. Maybe he thought Robert's own need was the best salesman. The bastard. Robert returned again and again to the references the Stranger had given him. They described three medical miracles of the last ten months. One was an effective treatment for malaria. That was not such a big deal, since cheaper cures had existed for years. But the other two breakthroughs related to mood and intellectual disorders. They were not examples of Reed Weber's random "heavenly minefield." Both had been *commissioned* by the customers they cured.

So what? Miracles happened in this modern age. What proof was there the Stranger could create them? He pulled up the documents the Stranger had given him. Their visual represention was as medieval letters of credit, envelopes sealed with wax. If one broke the metaphor, it was easy to look inside and see the lower layers, a few megabytes of encryption. Useless nonsense. But if you followed the metaphor from the top, then you found pointers to magic tools to employ the certificates, and other pointers to the technical papers that explained what these tools actually did with the underlying data.

For three days now, Robert had been digging through those papers. The old Robert would not have had the intellect for this. God had taken away his true and unique genius, and perversely given him this analytical talent in return. Playing with protocols was fun. Okay, another couple of days and he would put it all together—and call the Stranger's bluff.

Meantime, he was falling further behind in his work with Juan for Chumlig's composition class.

"Will you have time to work on my graphics suggestions?" Juan asked one afternoon. "Before tomorrow, I mean." That was when their current *weekly* project was due.

"Yes, sure." The kid had been great about working to Robert's directions. He felt a sliver of shame for not reciprocating. "I mean, I'll try. I've got this problem with some outside things . . ."

"Oh, what? Can I help?"

Lord. "Some security documents. They're supposed to prove that a, um, friend of mine was really involved in solving a . . . game problem." He made one of them visible to Juan.

The kid looked at the wax and gilt and parchment. "Oh! A creditat. I've seen certs like that. You—oops, yours has an outer envelope so only you can do all the steps, but see—" He grabbed the certificate and pointed where Robert should do what. "—you gotta apply your own stamp first, and then you tear along the server line and you'll see a release like this." Phantom transformations spread in the air around him. "And if this friend of yours is not blowing smoke, you'll see bright green here and there'll be a written description of his contribution, backed by Microsoft or Bank of America or whoever."

Then Juan had to go help his mother. As he faded away, Robert studied the examples. He recognized some of the steps from the protocol descriptions, but, "How did you know all that?"

Foolish question. The boy looked a little startled. "It's just—it's just kind of intuitive, you know? I think that's the way the interface is designed." And then he was completely gone.

No one was home right now, so Robert went downstairs and fixed himself a snack. Then he played back the steps the boy had shown him. He had no excuse for further delay. He hesitated a moment more . . . then applied the steps to each of the "creditats."

Bright green. Bright green. Bright green.

THE MYSTERIOUS STRANGER didn't like to come visiting when Robert was indoors at home. Maybe the USMC was not as incompetent as the Stranger claimed. Robert began to look forward to his time away from home with anticipation and dread. Very soon he must decide. Was betrayal a price he could pay for a chance to be his old self once more?

Days passed. Still no contact. *The Stranger wants me ripe for the picking.*

When it finally happened, Robert was walking around the neighborhood, doing another interview with Zulfikar Sharif. The young man hesitated in the middle of a question and looked at him.

Miri --> Juan: <sm>I'm locked out!</sm>

Juan --> Miri: <sm>Again?</sm>

Miri --> Juan: <sm>Yes again!</sm>

Sharif's earnest features took on the sly, greenish cast of the Mysterious Stranger. "How is it going, my man?"

Robert managed a cool response. "Well enough."

The Stranger smiled. "You look a bit peaked, Professor. Perhaps you'd be more comfortable sitting down." A car slid to a stop beside them. The door opened and the phantom graciously waved Robert inside.

"This is more secure?" Robert said as they pulled away from the curb.

"*This* car is. Remember, I have powers far greater than your little friends." He settled in the back-facing seat. "So. Have you convinced yourself that I can help you?"

"Maybe you can," said Robert, a little bit proud of how level his voice sounded. "I checked your creditats. You don't seem to know anything about anything, but you have this knack for bringing the right people together and being around when those people solve serious problems."

The Stranger waved his hand dismissively. "I don't know

anything about anything? You are naive, Professor. Our world is overflowing with technical expertise. Knowledge is piled metaphorical light-years deep. Given that, the truly golden skill is the one I possess—to bring together the knowledge and abilities that make solutions. Your Ms. Chumlig understands that. Schoolkids certainly understand. Even Tommie Parker understands, though he has one important detail backward. In me," another elaborate gesture, his hand flattening against his turtleneck shirt, "in me, you have the far extreme of this ability. I am world-class at 'bringing-together-to-get-answers.' "

And with an ego to match. How does he get his way when he's dealing with the Einsteins and Hawkings of this era? Surely he doesn't have everyone *by the short hairs?*

The Stranger leaned forward. "But enough of me. Winnie Blount and his 'Elder Cabal' are getting desperate. *I'm* not exactly desperate, but if you delay more than another few days, I cannot guarantee an acceptable outcome. So. Are you on board or not?"

"I—Yes. I am." Twenty years ago, betraying Bob would not have bothered him. After all, the idiot was an ingrate. Now, no glib excuse rose to mind, but . . . *I'll do anything to recover what I lost.* "What is this biometric information you want on Alice?"

"Some sonograms we can't take in public. A microgram blood spot." The Mysterious Stranger pointed at a small box that lay on the seat between them. "Take a look."

Robert reached down . . . and his fingers touched something hard and cool. The box was real. That was a first for the Mysterious Stranger. He took a closer look. It was gray plastic without any openings or even virtual labels. Wait, there was the ubiquitous "no user-serviceable parts within."

"So?"

"So, leave that in your front bathroom this evening. It will do the rest."

"I won't do anything to hurt Alice."

The Stranger laughed. "Such paranoia. The point of all this is to pass unnoticed. Alice Gu is in public places several times a week. If ill were wished her, *those* would be the opportunities to take advantage of. But you and the cabal just need biometrics. . . . Any other questions?"

"Not just now." Robert slipped the gray plastic box into his pocket. "I just can't imagine that twenty-first-century military security can be duped by something as simple as a drop of blood and some sonograms."

The Stranger laughed. "Oh, there's much more to it than that. Tommie Parker thinks he's covering the angles, but without my help you four would not even get into the steam tunnels." He looked at Robert's stiff expression and laughed again. "Think of your part as being the user interface." He gave a little bow. "And I am the user."

O

ROBERT MADE A point of taking the Stranger's gadget through the front hallway bug trap. The small box triggered no alarms he could see. So betrayal was as simple as walking into the first-floor bathroom and setting the box down among the bags and aerosols and squeeze tubes that were already piled on the side counter. Modern bed and bath products were a bastion of old-style physical advertising. After all, even the most modern folks had to take off their clothes and their contacts somewhere. But Alice and Bob had no style. They bought the cheapest commodity products they could find. The devil box fit right in.

Robert took a long shower. It would be nice to feel clean. He heard no strange sounds, saw nothing strange through the frosted glass. But when he came out of the shower, he noticed that there was no mysterious gray box either. Even when he pawed around the counter, touching every object there—there was no sign of the intrusion. The bathroom door had been shut the whole time.

Someone knocked on the door, happily following the family rules about not snooping through bathroom walls. "Robert, are you okay?" It was Miri. "Alice says it's dinnertime."

O

DINNER WAS A nightmare.

It was always tense when the four of them ate together. Usually, Robert could avoid such get-togethers, but Alice seemed determined to see him with the whole family at least once a week. Robert knew what she was up to. She was recalibrating, deciding if now she could lower the boom on her father-in-law.

Tonight she was steelier than ever, and it didn't help that Robert had serious things to hide. Maybe she had some special reason to be suspicious. He noticed that Bob and Miri were doing all the running back and forth to the kitchen. Usually Alice helped with that. Tonight she sat herself down in her usual place, and grilled Robert in her merciless, casual way: how was school going, what about the project with Juan. She even asked about his "old friends," for God's sake! And Robert explained and smiled and prayed he was passing the test. *The old Robert never had trouble stringing people along!*

Then Bob and Miri were sitting down to eat. Alice shifted her attention from her villainous father-in-law. She chatted with Miri in the same friendly, interested tones she had used with Robert. Miri replied with precision, a detailed summary of just who and what was good and bad at school.

For a while Robert almost relaxed. After all, they were here to eat. Surely that couldn't give him away.

But something was up, and it wasn't just his imagination. Bob and Alice got into a discussion of San Diego politics, a school-bond issue. But there was an edgy undercurrent; some couples really *argue* politics, but this was the first time Robert had ever heard that from these two. And every so often Alice's clothing *flickered.* Around the house in the real world, Alice Gu wore a dumpy hausfrau dress that wouldn't have been out of place in the 1950s. When she flickered, it was virtual imagery, nothing like Carlos's old-fashioned smart T-shirts. The first time it happened, Robert almost didn't notice—partly because neither Bob or Miri reacted. Half a minute later—as Alice gestured emphatically about some outstandingly trivial election issue—there was another flicker. For an instant she was dressed in something like naval whites, but the collar insignia said "PHS." *PHS?* There were lots of different Google hits on the abbreviation. A minute or two passed, and she was briefly a USMC full colonel. *That,* Robert had seen before, since it was her true rank.

Bob said mildly, "You're emoting, dear."

"It doesn't matter," Alice said curtly. "You know that. The point is"—and she continued chewing on the school-bond issue. But her gaze wandered around the room, eventually riveting on Robert. It was not a friendly gaze, and even though her words were unrelated to Robert Gu there was a sharpness in her voice. Then, for almost two seconds, she was wearing a civilian business suit with an old-fashioned ID lanyard. The ID bore a familiar seal and the letters DHS. Robert knew what *that* meant. It was all he could do not to flinch back. *She can't know everything!* He wondered if Alice and Bob were silently coordinating all the scary signs, conspiring to panic him into confession. Somehow, he didn't think Bob was that adept.

So Robert just nodded and glanced casually around. Miri had been quieter than usual. She was staring off into the distance, and looked as bored as a thirteen-year-old can look when she's trapped at home with her parents rattling on about Things Not Important. But this was Miri Gu, and this was not the twentieth century. Most likely she was surfing, though usually she disguised such absences when she was at the dinner table.

Alice slapped the table, and Robert's eyes jerked back to her. She was glaring at him. "Don't you agree, Robert?"

Even Louise Chumlig couldn't glare more aggressively than that.

"Sorry. My mind wandered, Alice."

She waved her hand abruptly. "It doesn't matter."

And then golden letters spread silently across the air. Miri --> Robert: <sm>Don't worry. She's not mad at you.</sm>

Miri was still gazing into nowhere. Her hands were in plain sight and motionless. She was that good with her clothes. *Okay, but what in hell is going on here?* That was the message he wanted to send back, but short of finger tapping, the best he could do was give her a quizzical look.

Alice rattled on, interrupted occasionally by Bob, but now Robert was not living in stark terror. He waited another three or four minutes, and then excused himself.

Bob looked a little relieved. "We don't have to talk so much about the bond issue, Robert. There are other—"

"No, that's okay. I'm the fellow with homework these days."

Robert pasted on a smile and retreated up the stairs. He felt Alice's rifled gaze following him every step. If not for Miri's silent message, he would have run up the stairs.

And so far, Alice hadn't ventured near the front bathroom.

HE DID HAVE homework. Juan came over and distracted him for almost half an hour with his explanations of immersive outlines. Robert was supposed to have such an outline ready for tomorrow's progress report in Chumlig's class. Juan went away pleased. So was Robert; he had made up for several days of inattention. He fooled around with Juan's templates till he could implement everything. *By God, we should be getting an A for cross-support.* The kid's prose had become almost serviceable—and this immersive *he* had constructed, it was beautiful. He was aware of Miri helping to clean up after dinner and then coming up to her room. Bob and Alice were just sitting in the living room. He set an activity alarm on the first floor, and for a while he forgot himself in the making of more and better refinements to his graphics.

Lord! An hour had passed! He took a quick glance downstairs. Nobody had been to the front john. There was a pending message from Tommie Parker. The cabal wanted to know when or if he was going to come through with his contribution.

He looked downstairs again. Strange. He couldn't see into the living room anymore. Normally that was on the house menu, but now it was as private as the bedrooms. He stood and walked over to the door, quietly eased it open half an inch, snooping the good old-fashioned way.

They were arguing! And Bob was white-hot. His voice grew louder and louder, finally breaking into enraged shouting. "I don't give a fuck if they do need you! It's always just one more time. But this time you've—"

Bob hesitated in midflame. Robert leaned forward, ear to the door. Nothing. Not even the mumble of circumspect speech. Son and daughter-in-law had taken their spat into ethereal realms. But Robert continued to listen. He could hear the two moving around. At one point, there was the sound of a hand slapping down like a pistol shot. Alice whacking the dinner table? There was half a minute of silence and then a door slammed.

Vision returned a second after that. Bob was alone in the living room, staring at the door of the ground-floor den. He stood there for a few moments, then circled the living room and dropped himself down in his favorite chair. He pulled a book off the coffee table. That was one of the three physical books downstairs—and even it was a just-in-time fake.

Robert Gu quietly shut his bedroom door and returned to his chair. He thought a moment, then tapped on his virtual keypad.

Robert --> Miri: <sm>What was that all about?</sm>

Miri was twenty feet down the hall. So why didn't he just walk a few feet and knock on her door? Or present virtually? Maybe it was the habit of staying out of her way. Maybe it was easier to hide behind words.

Maybe he wasn't the only one hiding. It was almost a minute before a reply floated back.

Miri --> Robert: <sm>They're not mad at you.</sm>

Robert --> Miri: <sm>Okay. But what is the problem?</sm>

Miri --> Robert: <sm>There is no problem.</sm> That was the whole message, but then Miri sent another.

Miri --> Robert: <sm>Alice is getting ready for some new job. That's always hard on her. And then Bob gets mad.</sm> There was another pause.

Miri --> Robert: <sm>This is Corps business, Robert. I'm not supposed to know about it. You're even more not. I'm sorry. EOF.</sm>

EOF. That was space cadet for "that's all she wrote." Robert waited; nothing more came. But this had been more real conversation with Miri than he'd had in two months. What did that little girl do with her secrets? They were surely more significant than he had ever guessed. She had better communications facilities than all of twentieth-century civilization, but her prissy standards kept her from sharing her pain. *Or maybe she has friends she can talk to?*

Robert Gu, Sr., didn't have any friends, but he didn't need any; tonight he had plenty of crisis and suspense to distract him. He kept an eye on the front bathroom, and another on the door to the den. Bob was still reading, every so often sliding a look of his own at the den.

"Is now a good time for us to talk, Professor?" The voice came from just behind his shoulder.

The shock all but levitated Robert from his chair. He swung on the sound. "Jeez!"

It was Zulfikar Sharif.

Sharif backed away, startlement in his face.

"You could have knocked," Robert said.

"I did, Professor." Sharif sounded faintly hurt.

"Yes, yes." Robert still hadn't figured out all the quirks of Epiphany's "circle of friends" feature. He gestured for Sharif to stay. "What's on your mind?"

Sharif did a creditable job of sitting on a chair without sinking halfway through. "Well, I was hoping we could just talk." He thought a moment. "I mean, we might continue with my questions about your *Secrets of the Ages.*"

Still no action downstairs. ". . . Very well. Ask." *So who is this?* True-Sharif? Stranger-Sharif? SciFi-Sharif? Or some ungodly combination? Whatever, it was too much coincidence that he showed up just now. Robert sat back to watch and listen.

"Um . . . I don't know." Miserably forgetful? But then Sharif abruptly perked up. "Ah! One thing I'm hoping to get at in my thesis is the balance of worth between the beauty of expression and the beauty of underlying truth. Are they separate?"

A question to be answered in cryptic depth. Robert paused significantly and then launched into flimflam. "You should know by now, Zulfi, even if you can't create poetry yourself, that the issues can't be separated. Beauty captures truth. Read my essay in the *Carolingian. . . .*" *blah blahblah*

Sharif nodded earnestly. "Then do you ever expect an end to one and therefore the other? Beauty and truth, I mean?"

Huh? Now, that was sufficiently bizarre to derail him. Robert parsed and reparsed the stupidity. *Will you run out of beauty? And the answer for me is yes; I can't create beauty anymore.* So maybe this was just Stranger-Sharif jerking him around while they both waited for the little gray box to do its thing.

"I suppose . . . there could be an end." And then he thought about the other half of the question. "Hell, Sharif, truth—new truth—ended long ago. We artists sit atop a midden ten thousand years deep. The diligent ones of us know everything of significance that's ever been done. We churn and churn, and some of us do it brilliantly, but it's just a glittering rehash." *Did I just say that?*

"And if they're linked, then beauty is gone too?" Sharif had leaned forward his elbows on his legs, his chin cupped in his hands. His eyes were large and serious.

Robert looked away. Finally, he choked out, "There is still beauty. I *will* bring it back." *I will regain it.*

Sharif smiled, mistaking Robert's assertion for some general faith in humankind in the future? "That's wonderful, Professor. This goes beyond your essay in the *Carolingian.*"

"Indeed." Robert sat back, wondering just what in heaven's name was going on.

Sharif hesitated a moment, as if uncertain where to go next. "At the UCSD library, how has your project there progressed?"

Still no action downstairs. Robert said, "You see some connection between my art and . . . the Librareome?"

"Well, yes. I don't want to intrude, but ultimately what you do at UCSD seems to be very much a statement about the position of art and literature in the modern world."

Maybe this was SciFi-Sharif, trying to figure out what Stranger-Sharif was up to. *If only I could use one against the other.* He gave his visitor a judicious nod. "I'll talk to my friends about this. Maybe we can arrange something."

That seemed to satisfy whoever-it-was. They set a time for another chat, and then the visitor was gone.

Robert turned off circle-of-friends access. No more surprise visitations tonight.

And downstairs, there was *still* no action. He watched through the walls for almost fifteen minutes. That was certainly a productive use of time. *Think about something else, damn it.*

He blew off the top of the house and looked across West Fallbrook. Unenhanced, the place was very dark, more like an abandoned town than a living suburb. The real San Diego had less skyglow than he remembered from the 1970s. But behind that real view were unending alternatives, all the cyberspace fun Bob's generation could have ever imagined. Hundreds of millions were playing out there tonight. Robert could feel—Epiphany could make him feel—the thrum of it, beckoning. Instead he tapped out a command Chumlig had mentioned; here and there across North County, tiny lights glowed. Those were the other students in his classes, at least the ones who were studying tonight and had any interest in what the others were doing. Twenty little lights. That was more than two-thirds of the class, a special kind of belief circle, one dedicated to pushing up their cooperation scores as far as possible. He hadn't appreciated how hard these little third-raters were working.

Robert ghosted over the suburbs, toward the nearest of the lights. He hadn't tried Epiphany's "out of body" feature before. There was no feeling of air flowing past, or motion. It was just his synthetic viewpoint slewing across the landscape. He could still feel his butt on the chair in his bedroom. And yet he understood why the directions said to do this sitting down. The viewpoint swooped down into a valley with a speed that was dizzying.

He drifted into a welcoming window. Juan Orozco and Mahmoud Kwon and a couple of others were gathered in a family room, marking out possibilities for tomorrow's exchange with Capetown. They looked up and said hi, but Robert could tell they weren't seeing much more than his icon hovering in the room. He could be present virtually, perhaps even look as "real" as Sharif usually did. But Robert just hung in the air, listening to the talk for a few moments and—

Alarm notification!

He cut the connection and was back in his bedroom.

Downstairs, Bob had wandered out of the living room. He stood by Alice's door and knocked gently. As far as Robert could tell there was no answer. After a moment, Bob tucked his chin in and turned away. Robert tracked him up the stairs. The sounds of footsteps came down the hall. Bob knocked on Miri's door, the way he did most evenings. There was mumbled conversation, and Miri's voice saying, "G'night, Daddy." It was the first Robert had heard her call Bob that.

Bob's footsteps came nearer; he paused at Robert's door, but he didn't say anything. Robert watched him through the wall as Bob turned and was swallowed up by the privacy of the master bedroom.

Robert hunched over his desk and stared into the downstairs. Alice hardly ever stayed up much beyond Bob. Of course, tonight was not your usual night. Damn. You screw your courage up to an act of family betrayal—and then fate dumps problems all over your dishonorable intent. But even if Alice camped out in the den, eventually she'd have to use the bathroom. Right?

Twenty minutes passed.

Alice's door opened. She stepped out, turned toward the stairs. *Use the ground-floor bathroom, damn you.* She turned again and paced angrily around the living room. Paced? There was precision and power in every motion, like a dancer or a martial-arts nut. Not like dumpy frumpy Alice Gong Gu, she of the mild round face and the shapeless dress. And yet this was the real view. It was her real face, even if it was tense with pain, and drenched in sweat. Huh? Robert tried to follow her gliding dance in close-up. The woman was dripping sweat. Her dress was soaked, as if she had just finished a long, frantic run.

Like Carlos Rivera.

It couldn't be. Alice never got stuck in a foreign language, or in a particular specialty. In any *one* particular specialty. But he remembered the web discussion of JITT. What about the few strange people who could "train" more than once, who became ever more multitalented, until the side effects finally destroyed them? Where would such wretches get "stuck" if there were dozens of imprints to fall into?

Alice's gliding dance slowed, stopped. She stood for a moment with her head bowed, her shoulders heaving. Then she turned and walked slowly into the front bathroom.

Finally, finally. *And now I should be overcome with relief.* Instead, revelation bounced back and forth in his mind. This explained so many little mysteries. It contradicted several certainties. Maybe Alice hadn't been gunning for him. Maybe she was no more his enemy than anyone in this house.

Sometimes things are not as they seem.

It was very quiet. The old house in Palo Alto had had little squeaks and thumps, and sometimes Bob's PC playing stolen music. Here, tonight . . . yes, there were occasional sounds, the house settling into the cool of the evening. Wait. In the utility view, he saw that one of the water heaters had kicked in. He could hear running water.

Not for the first time, Robert wondered what kind of magic that little gray box was. It had not triggered the house watchdogs. Maybe it wasn't electronic at all, but nineteenth-century gears and cogs driven by a metal spring. Then it had *disappeared* from Robert's own naked eyesight. That was something new, not a visual trick. Maybe the box had sprouted little legs and scurried off. But whatever it was, what would it finally *do?* Maybe the Stranger didn't need a little blood. Maybe a lot of blood would suit him more. Robert sat stock-still for a second and then bolted to his feet—and froze again. *I was so desperate.* Credibility is not important if the victim wants to believe so hard that truth *must* be what the liar claims. So the Stranger had mocked the notion that hurting Alice would be worth such hugger-mugger. *And I, desperate, smiled and was convinced.*

Robert was out of his room, and flying down the stairs. He dashed through the living room and pounded on the bathroom door. "Alice! Al—"

The door opened. Alice was looking at him, a bit wide-eyed. He grabbed her arm and dragged her into the hallway. Alice was not a large woman; she came easily in his grasp. But then she turned, taking him off balance. Somehow his feet got tangled in hers and he slammed into the doorjamb.

"What! Is it?" she said, sounding irritated.

"I—" Robert looked over his shoulder, into the brightly lit bathroom, then back at Alice. She was dressed in a robe now, and her short hair looked as though she had washed it. *And everybody is still in one piece. No pools of blood . . . except maybe where my head hit the doorjamb.*

"Are you okay, Robert?" Concern seemed to rise above her irritation.

Robert felt the back of his head. "Yeah, yes. I'm pretty robust these days." He thought about how he'd come down the stairs. Even when he was seventeen years old, he had never skipped four steps at a time.

"But—" Alice began. Clearly she was more concerned about his mental state than anything else.

It's okay, Daughter-in-Law. I thought I was stopping your murder, and now I find it's a false alarm. Somehow he didn't think that would be a satisfactory explanation. So why was he down here in the middle of the night, pounding on the door? He looked into the bathroom again. "I, um, I just needed to use the John."

Her sympathy frosted over. "Don't let me keep you, Robert." She turned and headed for the stairs.

"Are you okay, Alice?" Bob's voice, from the top of the stairs. Robert didn't have the courage to look, but he could imagine Miri's little face staring down, too. As he stepped into the bathroom and shut the door, he heard his daughter-in-law's tired voice. "Not to worry. It was just Robert."

O

ROBERT SAT ON the can for a few minutes and let the shakes die away. Maybe there was still a bomb here, but if it exploded, none but the guilty would be blown apart.

And neither did he have the little box that was the point of the comedy. When he showed up at the library, he would be empty-handed. *So?* After a moment, Robert stood, and looked into the real glass mirror. He favored his reflection with a twisted smile. Maybe he should just bring them a fake; would Tommie even notice? As for the Mysterious Stranger, perhaps his spell had been broken . . . along with all hope.

His eyes strayed to the countertop. There, sitting away from the clutter, was a small gray box. It hadn't been there when Alice left. He reached down. His fingers touched warm plastic. Not an illusion. A greater mystery than all the flash and glitter that he was just becoming accustomed to.

He slipped the box into his pocket and quietly returned to his room.

17

ALFRED VOLUNTEERS

Günberk Braun and Keiko Mitsuri: They were top officers in their respective services. Vaz had tracked these two since their college days. He knew more about them than they would ever guess. That was one of the benefits of being very old and very well connected. In a sense, he had guided them into their intel careers, though neither they nor their organizations suspected the fact. They weren't traitors to the EU or Japan, but Alfred understood them so well that he could subtly guide them.

So he had thought, and so he still hoped. And yet his two young friends' remorseless efforts to help had become the greatest threat to his plans. As today:

"Yes, yes. There are risks," Vaz was saying. "We knew that from the beginning. But letting a serious YGBM project escape detection would be much more dangerous. We *must* find out what's going on in the San Diego labs. Plan Rabbit can do that."

Keiko Mitsuri shook her head. "Alfred, I have contacts in U.S. intelligence that go back years. These aren't my agents, but they would not tolerate a rogue weapons project. On that, I would trust them with my life. I say we should contact them—very unofficially—and see what they can learn about the San Diego labs."

Alfred leaned forward. "Would you trust them with your country's life? Because that's what we are talking about here. In the worst case, there is not only a YGBM research effort going on in San Diego, but it is supported at the highest levels of the U.S. government. In that case, your friends' best efforts would simply alert their superiors to our suspicions. The evidence would disappear. When it comes to investigating a threat this serious *we simply must do it ourselves.*"

In one form or another, this was an argument that dated from their Barcelona meeting. Today's installment could be decisive.

Keiko sat back and gave a frustrated shrug. She was presenting in more or less her real appearance and location, a thirty-year-old woman sitting at her desk somewhere in Tokyo. She had transformed one side of Vaz's office with her minimalist furniture and a picture-window view of Tokyo's skyline.

Günberk Braun was less prepossessing. His image simply occupied one of Alfred's office chairs. No doubt Günberk figured that the EU swung enough weight that he could afford a mild disposition. Günberk might be the real problem today, but so far he was just listening.

Okay. Alfred spread his hands. "I truly think the course we set in Barcelona is the most prudent one. Can you deny the progress we have made?" He waved at the biographical reports scattered around the table. "We have hands and minds on the scene—all deniable, and ignorant of what is manipulating them. In fact, they totally misunderstand the significance of this operation. Do you doubt this? Do you think that the Americans have any whiff of our investigation?"

Both youngsters shook their heads. Keiko even gave him a rueful smile. "No. Your SHE-based compartmentalization is truly a revolution in military affairs."

"Indeed, and our releasing those methods—even to sister services within the Alliance—shows how seriously we at the EIA view the current necessities. So, please. If we delay more than one hundred hours, we might as well start over. What is your problem with giving the final go-ahead?"

Günberk glanced at his Japanese counterpart. She made an impatient gesture for him to go ahead. "I assume your question is rhetorical, Alfred. The problem with Plan Rabbit is Rabbit. Everything depends on him, and still we know almost nothing about him."

"And neither will the Americans. Deniability is the whole point. Rabbit is everything we could want."

"He is more, Alfred." Günberk's gaze was steady. For all his youth, Braun had the stolid aspect of a turn-of-the-century German. He moved from point to point slowly, inexorably. "In setting up this operation, Rabbit has performed miracles on our behalf. His ability demonstrates that he himself is a threat."

Vaz glanced at the results of Günberk's latest investigation. "But you have discovered critical weaknesses in Rabbit. However much he's tried to disguise it, you've traced all his certificate authority to a single apex." Having a single CA apex was not unusual; that Günberk had managed to discover Rabbit's apex was a triumph. For Alfred—given his own, ah, sensitive relationship with Rabbit—it was miraculously good news.

Günberk nodded. "Credit Suisse. So what?"

"So if Rabbit turns out to be a nightmare, you could pull the plug on Credit Suisse and put him out of business."

"Pull the plug on Credit Suisse CA? Do you have any idea what that would do to the European economy? I'm proud of my people, that they ferreted this secret out—but it's not something we can effectively use."

"We should have dropped Rabbit after that first meeting in Barcelona," said Keiko. "He is too clever."

Vaz raised a hand, "Perhaps, but how could we know?"

"*Ja?* Forgive me, Alfred, but we wonder if you know more about Mr. Rabbit than we."

Damn! "Not at all. Honestly." Alfred leaned back in his chair and took in the nervous postures of his colleagues. "You've been talking behind my back, haven't you?" He gave them a gentle smile. "Do you think Rabbit is really American intelligence? Chinese?" They had spent a lot of time investigating those possibilities. But now Keiko shook her head. "Then what is your theory, my friends?"

"Well," said Günberk, sounding a little embarrassed. "Maybe Mr. Rabbit is not even human. Maybe it's an Artificial Intelligence."

Vaz laughed. He glanced at Keiko Mitsuri. "And you?"

"I think AI is a possibility we should consider. Rabbit's talents are so broad, his work is so effective—and his personality is so juvenile. That last was one of the features the U.S. DARPA thought would be characteristic." She saw the incredulity on Vaz's face. "Not every threat is a cult or conspiracy."

"Of course. But AI monsters? That's a bogeyman out of the twentieth century. Who in the intelligence communities takes that seriously? Ah! That's Pascal Heriot's hobbyhorse, isn't it?"

Alfred's tone became low and serious. "Have you been talking to Pascal about this project?"

"Of course not. But AI is a threat that's been totally overlooked in recent years."

"Correct, because nothing ever came of it. Before the Sino-American war, we know DARPA spent billions on the Little Helper Project. It was almost as much a fiasco as their Space Access Denial initiative."

"Space Denial *worked.*"

Vaz laughed. "It worked against everybody, Keiko, the Americans most of all. But you're right, SAD is not a proper comparison. My point is that some of the smartest people in the world tried to create AI and failed."

"The researchers failed, but surely runnable code survived. The Internet is not the cramped toy it once was. Maybe pieces of DARPA's Little Helper are out there, growing into what it could never be in the low-tech past."

"That *is* science fiction! There was even a movie—"

"More than one, actually," said Günberk. "Alfred, I don't agree with Keiko that programs from years ago could self-organize just because decent resources are available now. But here at the IB, we have been tracking the possibilities. I think Pascal Heriot has a point. Just because most people have dismissed the possibility doesn't mean that it is not real. We are certainly past the crossover point when it comes to computer hardware. Pascal thinks that when it finally happens, it will arise without institutional precursors. It will be like many research developments, but rather more catastrophic." Just another way humankind might fail to survive the century.

"Whatever the explanation," said Keiko, "Rabbit is simply too competent, too anonymous. . . . I'm sorry, Alfred, we think the operation should be shut down. Let's approach our American friends on this."

"But equipment is in place. Our people are in place."

She shrugged. "With Rabbit managing things? That could leave Rabbit with whatever we discover in San Diego. Even if we agreed with you, our bosses would never go along."

She was serious. Alfred glanced at Braun. He was, too. This was bad. "Keiko, Günberk, please. Just balance the risks."

"We are," said Keiko. "Rabbit loose within this grandiose scheme is a cosmic-sized *un*safety!" She could be quite full of modern Japanese bluntness.

Vaz said, "But we could arrange things so Rabbit receives operational information just-in-time as the action evolves."

Fortunately, Günberk shot that down immediately: "Ach, no. Such remote micromanagement, it's a guarantee of disaster."

Vaz hesitated a long moment, tried to look as though he were thinking hard, making some hard decision. "Maybe, maybe there's a way we can have everything—the, uh, 'grandiose scheme' and minimal risk from Rabbit. Suppose we *don't* supply Rabbit with the final details in advance. Suppose we put one of our own people on the ground in Southern California the night of the break-in?"

Mitsuri and Braun stared for a second. "But what about deniability then?" said Keiko. "If we have our own agent breaking in—"

"Think, Keiko. My proposal *risks* tipping off the Americans, which is something yours *guarantees*. And we can keep the risk low. We simply put our own agent nearby, in a well-planned position with essentially zero latencies. What the Americans call a Local Honcho."

Günberk brightened. "Like Alice Gong at Ciudad General Ortiz!"

"—Yes. Exactly." He hadn't been thinking of Alice, but Günberk was right. It had been Alice Gong on the ice at Ortiz, almost single-handedly discovering and stopping the Free Water Front. Maybe the Front would have failed anyway. After all, no one had ever tried to scale a Saturday-night special up to three hundred megatons. But if the bomb had successfully detonated, their "statement of principle" would have poisoned the freshwater mining industry off West Antarctica. Gong remained unknown to the outside world, but she was something of a legend within the intelligence communities. She was one of the good guys.

Thank goodness, neither Braun nor Mitsuri seemed to notice Alfred's discomfort at her name.

"Inserting a Honcho now would be difficult," said Keiko. "Are we talking a credible tourist, or cargo-container roulette?"

Truly black insertions looked like WMD smuggling; they were hair-raising operations for all concerned. "None of my agents-in-place are rated for *this* operation. It will take a special person, special talents, special clearance."

"I have some good people in California," said Günberk, "but none of them are at this level."

"It doesn't matter," said Vaz, his voice filled with steely determination. "I'm quite willing to go, myself."

He had surprised them before, but this was a bombshell. Braun sat for a moment, openmouthed. "Alfred!"

"It's that important," Vaz said. He gave them each his most direct and sincere look.

"But you're a desk jockey like us!"

Alfred shook his head. Today he would have to let a little bit of his background story come unglued. Hopefully, it wouldn't all tear apart. Alfred had spent years "fitting in" as a midlevel bureaucrat at the External Intelligence Agency. If he were unmasked, then at best he'd end up like the prime minister, forced back into high-level political hackery. At worst . . . at worst, Günberk and Keiko might figure out what he was really up to in San Diego.

Vaz --> EIA Inner Office: <sm>Clear Biographical Package Three for joint intelligence viewing.</sm>

Aloud, he said, "I do have field experience. In the U.S. in fact, in the early teens."

Braun and Mitsuri both had a long stare. They were busy browsing. BioPack 3 would show them the operations. It was all consistent with what they had known before, but revealed new depths to their Indian pal. Günberk was the first to recover. "I . . . see." He was silent for a moment, reading more. "You did well. But that was some years ago, Alfred. This will be a heavily network-technical assignment."

Alfred nodded at the criticism. "True. I am not a young man." Mitsuri and Braun thought he was in his early fifties. "On the other hand, my specialty here at the EIA is network issues, so I'm not really out of date."

A surprised grin flashed across Keiko's face. "And you do know this operation better than anyone. So by being on-site you can supply the critical pieces without giving them to Rabbit—"

"Correct."

Günberk was still unhappy: "And yet this is an extraordinarily dangerous operation. We Great Powers compete, that is true. But when it comes to the threat of Weapons, we must stand together. This is the first time in my career that that covenant has been broken."

Alfred nodded solemnly. "We must find out the truth, Günberk. We could be wrong about San Diego. Then we'll thankfully and silently disengage. But whatever the source of this weapon, we must discover it. And if that turns out to be San Diego, the Americans will very likely thank us."

Mitsuri and Braun looked at each other for a long moment. Finally they nodded, and Keiko said, "We'll support the insertion of a Local Honcho, presumably you. I'll put planners on fallback strategies in case you are exposed. We'll provide network and analyst support. It'll be up to you to manage critical data on the ground—"

"—and keep Mr. Rabbit from taking over the whole thing!" said Günberk.

O

ALFRED SAT IN his office for some minutes after his friends departed. That had been too close a thing.

When the stakes are highest, the threats always multiply. Plan Rabbit was the most sensitive operation that the Indian government had ever (knowingly) been a part of; getting the prime minister's support had not been easy. Today Keiko and Günberk had almost shut him down as thoroughly as the PM could have. As for Rabbit—well, AI might be fantasy, but Rabbit was just as much a threat as Günberk and Keiko feared.

Alfred relaxed slightly, allowed himself a smile. Yes, the threats had multiplied like, well, like rabbits. But here today he had collided some of those threats and neutralized them. For weeks he had been plotting his Local Honcho role. In the end, Günberk and Keiko had provided him with the natural excuse to be present on the ground in San Diego.

18

THE MYASTHENIC SPELUNKER SOCIETY

The cabal still met on the sixth floor of the library, but that was a very different place now. Robert came up in the elevator, avoiding the Hacekeans and their Library Militant. Nevertheless, sticking to reality was difficult. Theodor Geisel still held the lobby, but the administration was franchising mind and touch space everywhere else. Scooch-a-mouti characters had infested the basement. H. P. Lovecraft's were said to lurk in the farther underground, in what had been noncirculating storage.

And the sixth floor . . . was empty, stripped to the bare shelving. From the elevator entrance at the middle of the floor, Robert could see through skeletal shelving all the way to the windows. The book shredders had come and gone. In the southeast corner, the conspirators were hunkered down like twentieth-century socialists plotting empire in the midst of their obvious ruin.

"So what's held up the Library Militant invasion?" Robert said, and waved at the stark reality of the empty stacks.

Carlos replied, "A delay in finding the newest haptics is the official explanation. In fact, it's politics. The Scoochi partisans want this floor for their universe. The Library Militant is resisting. The administration may disappoint them both and make this floor a simulation of what libraries were like when they were real."

"But with fake imagery of the books, right?"

"Yup." Tommie was smiling. "What do you expect? Meantime we still have the floor to ourselves."

"We are not defeated, gentlemen." Winnie's face was stern. "We've known for weeks now that this was inevitable. We've lost a major battle. But it is only the first battle in the war." He glanced at Tommie.

Parker pointed at the LED on his computer. "The deadzone is in place. It's time to resume our seriously criminal conspiratizing." He was smiling, but his gaze swept across them, catching each in the eye. "Okay. I've done my research. I can get us into the steam tunnels. I've even arranged festivities that will get the lab staff out of our way. I can get us to the shredda containers, and I have the aerosol glue. We can cause the Librareome Project and Huertas in particular a whole lot of pain. Of course, it won't stop progress on this sort of thing, but it will—"

Winnie gave a grunt. "We've already agreed that a permanent stop is impossible. But if we can block the jerks who use the most destructive methods—well, that will have to suffice."

"Righto, Dean. That's exactly what we can do. It's all set up, just missing one critical ingredient." His gaze slid across to Robert.

Such is the power of common sense that Robert hesitated almost a third of a second. Then he reached into his pocket and retrieved the plastic box the Stranger had provided. "Check this out, Tommie."

Parker's eyebrows went up. "Hey, I'm impressed. I expected a paper napkin or something." He glanced at his laptop's display and then picked up the box. "This looks like a biosample kit." In fact, the box was now showing colorful labels announcing just that function. "How did you do it?"

Yes, how? Robert couldn't think of truth or lie that would make any sense.

Tommie mistook his silence. "No, no don't tell me. I should be able to figure it out for myself." Tommie smiled down at the box for a moment. Then he slipped it into his pocket.

"Okay. We're all set then. Now we've got to decide on a time."

Rivera leaned forward. "Soon. There's too much lab construction between quarters."

"Yup. And there are other constraints. You wouldn't believe the prep I've had to do. I'm netted to consultants up the yinyang. Don't worry, Dean, none of them see more than a small part of what I'm doing. I'm getting to be a real expert at affiliance." Tommie was having a hell of a good time. "I can make this work, guys! Hey, it will be like the good old days—well, maybe not for you, Carlos; you weren't even born back then." He grinned at Winnie and Robert. Robert had gone on those underground hikes often. They'd been impressive enough, trekking through hundreds of feet of tunnel and then popping up in buildings that were dark and empty and largely unfinished. Sometimes there had been stairs in the stairwells, and sometimes not.

Winnie Blount was smiling a little now, too. "Yeah, the Myasthenic Spelunker Society." He frowned, remembering more. "We were lucky we didn't break our necks." That comment was from the side of the desk where Winnie had lived most of his life, the administrator with nightmares about liability and litigation.

"Yup. It was more fun than gaming, and a lot more dangerous. Anyway, that was back before computers—at least as we understand the term now. Today things are way different, but with my research and this bioprofile from Robert, I can get us past all the watchdog automation. At least, if we get the timing right." He typed briefly on his laptop. "Okay, here's the latest. There are three short time slots in the next six weeks when all the security holes line up."

"When is the first?" said Winnie.

"Real soon. A week from next Monday." He spun his laptop around so the others could see. "We'd go in through Pilchner Hall." He launched into an extended discussion of how he would manage the adventure. ". . . And here is where the tunnel forks off campus. Once we get past that, we can walk almost half a mile, out under the old General Genomics site."

"Huertas's labs are just north of that," said Rivera.

"Yup. And ten-to-one odds we can get in there and do our stuff—and maybe even get out!"

Neither Rivera nor Blount seemed discomfited by this prospectus. After a moment, Winnie said, "We really can't postpone things. I vote for a week from Monday."

"Yeah, me too," said Robert.

"*Wǒ tóngyì.* Yes."

"Okay then!" Tommie spun his laptop back and made a notation. "Come wearing, but I'll supply new clothes and all necessary electronics. I—"

Winston Blount interrupted: "There's one other thing, Tommie."

"Uh, oh."

"It's not a big thing, but it could get us the right publicity."

"Hmm."

"I propose that we bring along a remote presence, that Sharif fellow."

"That's *insane!*" Tommie hopped to his feet and then abruptly sat down again. "You want a remote presence? Don't you understand? You won't even be *wearing* down there."

Winnie smiled cajolingly. "But you'll be bringing electronics, Tommie. Couldn't we support his presence through that?"

Parker gargled on his indignation. "How do you think remote presence works, Dean?"

"Um, it's just a kind of overlay."

"As far as display goes, that's true. But it's not local. Behind the pretty imagery, there's high-rate comm and forwarding through ambient microlasers. There are no random networks down in the tunnels. Everything I've planned depends on us being very quiet, in particular not using any lab nodes. What you want is—" He shook his head in disbelief.

Robert looked at Blount. "I don't understand either. Just a couple of weeks ago we shut Sharif out as a security risk."

Winnie's face reddened, just as in the old days when Robert nailed him in a faculty meeting.

Robert raised his hand. "I'm just wondering, Winston. Honest."

After a second, Winnie nodded. "Okay. Look, I was never down on the guy. We've met him in person, right here at the library. He appears to be a sincere student. He's honestly interviewing you, right?"

When he's not the Stranger or Mr. SciFi, yeah. Robert realized that just a word from him now and the whole scheme might be abandoned. He had not imagined that betrayal could be such a full-time job: "Yes. His questions are often foolish, but they're very academic."

"There you are! My point is that if things do not go one hundred percent our way, we want an outsider to present our view, ideally someone who has seen exactly what we're doing. It could mean the difference between going silently to jail—and making an effective moral statement."

"Yes," said Rivera. "You're a security genius, Professor

Parker. But even the best-laid plans can go awry. If you can accommodate Sharif, that would be a . . . a kind of safety net."

Tommie pounded his head gently on the table. "You guys don't know what you're asking."

But for all the histrionics, Tommie had not said no. After a moment, the little guy sat up and glared at them. "You're asking for a miracle. Maybe I can do it and maybe not. Give me a day to think."

"Sure, Professor."

"No problem." Blount was smiling with relief.

Tommie shook his head and hunched down behind his laptop. He seemed just as happy when the other gang members adjourned the meeting and wandered off toward the elevators.

Usually, there was an elevator waiting by the time they got there. Apparently Tommie's deadzone had left even the elevator software in the dark. After a moment spent staring at closed doors, Carlos reached over and punched the ground-floor button. "The virtue of maintaining antique controls," he said with a weak smile.

Winnie was grinning, but it had nothing to do with the elevator. "Don't worry. Tommie will come up with a solution."

Robert nodded. "He always has, hasn't he?"

" 'Yup,' " said Winnie, and they all laughed. And suddenly Robert understood why Winnie and Carlos wanted Sharif on board.

As the elevator doors opened and Rivera and Blount stepped in, Robert said, "Catch you later. Maybe I should see the Library Militant again."

Winnie rolled his eyes. "Suit yourself." And they were gone.

Robert stood for a moment, listening to the sound of the departing elevator. Beyond the stairway door on his left was the descent into the virtual library. There had been no more faux earthquakes, but the Librarians Militant still played with heavy amplifiers. He could hear the sounds of creeping masonry, louder now than the elevator. The floor under his feet trembled to the tune of Jerzy Hacek's fantasies.

He waited a moment more, and then—instead of heading down the stairs—he walked back around the sixth floor to Tommie Parker.

TOMMIE WAS LEANING forward, his nose still buried in his computer. His deadzone LED was still lit. In a very concrete way, he looked like a wizard with a book of ancient lore. No virtual realities needed here. Robert slid into the opposite chair and watched. It was quite possible the guy hadn't even noticed his arrival. He really could get totally absorbed by games and puzzles and cracking schemes.

"I am everywhere, and I appear however I wish, to produce the results that I wish." That was the Mysterious Stranger's brag. After last night, after the miracle in the front bathroom, Robert was willing to believe that whatever the Stranger was, he might be nearly as powerful as he claimed. *I wonder what he has on Winnie and Carlos?*

Finally, Robert broke the silence: "So, Tommie, how badly have we screwed up?"

Blue eyes appeared over the top of the laptop. Tommie's expression seemed to say *what are you doing here?* His gaze turned back to his computer. "Dunno. I just wish you guys would make up your minds." A quick glance back Robert's way. "But you didn't push for this change, did you?"

"I have . . . mixed feelings about it." Now the Stranger would be on-site next Monday, proving again his claim of ubiquity. "I've always believed in letting you tech geniuses get the job done your own way."

Tommie bobbed agreement. "Yup."

Actually, the old Robert had never cared about technology one way or another. Now things were very different. "I remember you were always good at pulling miracles out of your hat, though. Are we asking too much this time, Tommie?"

Parker sat up and gave Robert all his attention. "I . . . I just don't know, Robert. In the old days, there's no way I could swing something like this. I could design super ASICs. I could hack protocols. I could do a dozen things outside my narrow academic specialty. But that doesn't count for so much now. It's that—"

"It's that you're working on problems bigger than any set of specialties."

"Yes! How did you know that?"

Ms. Chumlig told me. Aloud, Robert said, "Nowadays, you deal with completely unrelated specialties."

"Right. Some of my core skills are still important. In those I'm as effective as I ever was. But . . . by the time I retired, I was almost an embarrassment to my department. I was good in certain niche courses, but when I tried to teach the new integrative stuff—well, all my life I'd been way ahead of the students, even in new courses. But toward the end, I was floundering. I got through my last semester by assigning weekly projects, and then having the kids critique each other." He looked seriously embarrassed. Nothing like this had ever happened to the old Robert—*but I could always define what quality and performance meant.*

"Anyway, after I retired, I went back to school—at least inside my head. There's a whole different way of looking at problem solving if you want to solve large problems *fast.* It's like learning to use power tools, except that nowadays your tools aren't just Google and symbolic math packages, they're also the idea boards and future speculations and—"

"And dealing with people?"

"Yup. People were never part of my equations—but that doesn't matter anymore. There are design bureaus that specialize in handling the nicey-nice." Tommie leaned forward, confiding. "Since I started working on this project, *everything* has come together! Getting into the tunnels would be useless if the staff were still in the labs. So I've turned the political maneuvering between the Hacekeans and the Scoochis into the most spectacular media distraction—a clash of belief circles. It'll be so cool! I've found a design coordinator who understands what I'm after. I make the overall concept and he farms it out all over the planet. The detailed plans just grow into place!"

Tommie sat back, his frustration swept away by this vision of his new powers. "And look at my computer!" His hand passed lovingly across the device. The cabinet was nicked and scratched. It looked like it had hosted generations of burglars. The LEDs along the top were set in little pits hacked into the metal. Ol' Tommie didn't believe in "no user-serviceable parts within." "Over the years, I've replaced everything inside. Too often the changes were to satisfy new standards and the damned SHE. But now in the last couple of months, I've put a revolution inside this box. It subverts nontrivial parts of the Secure Hardware Environment. I swear, Robert, I'm hotter than DARPA and CIA ever were in the twentieth century."

Robert was silent for a moment. Then he said, "I'll bet you will figure some way to get Sharif in."

"Ha. That would be the frosting on the cake. The obvious trick is straight out of the twentieth century: We just lay our own cable. That would support decent data rates—enough for Sharif, anyway—and we'd still be all dark and quiet." He glanced at Robert and apparently took his silence for incredulity. "I know, it's a long walk, and the tunnel security will be mostly live. But there's a kind of slimclad optical fiber . . . or there will be after I get done with my design coordinator."

"Yes. Your design coordinator."

"I am everywhere, and I appear however I wish, to produce the results that I wish." The new world was a magical place, but there was a hierarchy of miracles. There was what Juan and Robert could do. There was what Louise Chumlig was trying to teach. There was what Tommie had taught himself. And somewhere above it all, there was what the Mysterious Stranger could do.

19

FAILURE IS AN OPTION

At Fairmont High, final exams were spread across several days. There were some similarities with what he remembered of childhood. The kids were distracted by the upcoming holidays. Worse, the Christmas movie season was something that was beginning to pervade the various shared worlds they lived in.

But finals were different in one profound way from his experience in high school. For Robert Gu, these new exams were *hard.* It was not a foregone conclusion that he would max the tests and outdo everyone around him. The only similar situation from his past was in undergraduate school, when he had briefly been forced into real science courses. In those classes, he had finally met students who were not automatically his inferiors—and he had also met teachers who were not impressed by his genius. Once past the mandatory science curriculum, Robert had avoided such humiliation.

Until now.

Math and formal common sense. Statistics and data mechanics. Search and analysis. Even the S&A exam limited one's opportunity to go out on the net and use the intelligence of others. Though she taught collaboration, Chumlig had always droned about the importance of core competencies. Now all her mismatched platitudes were coming together in one hellweek of testing.

Right after the "common sense" exam, the Mysterious Stranger manifested himself. He was just a voice and a greenish glow. "Having trouble with the exams, my man?"

"I'll get by." In fact, the math had actually been interesting.

Miri --> Juan, Xiu: <sm>He's talking to someone again.</sm>

Xiu --> Juan, Miri: <sm>What is he saying?</sm>

Miri --> Juan, Xiu: <sm>I don't know. Local audio has gone private. Juan! Get out there.</sm>

Juan --> Miri, Xiu: <sm>You're not the boss of me. I was going to talk to Robert now anyway.</sm>

The Stranger chuckled. "At Fairmont High, they don't give automatic A grades, or even automatic passing grades. Failure is an option, but you—"

Relief was in sight. He saw Juan Orozco coming out of the class building, heading his way. The stranger continued, "—and Juan Orozco are not certain F's. You're on a simplified curriculum. You should see the exams they're planning for your granddaughter."

"What about my granddaughter?" If the slimeball brought her into this—

But the voice did not reply.

Juan looked around questioningly. "Were you talking to someone, Robert?"

"Not about school things."

"Because I didn't see anybody." He hesitated, and letters coursed across Robert's view. Juan --> Robert: <sm>It's really important not to collaborate outside of the rules.</sm>

"I understand," Robert replied out loud.

"Okay." Clearly Juan didn't think Robert could pass all the tests. Sometimes it seemed like the poor kid was trying to protect *him.* "See," Juan continued, "the school uses a real good proctor service. Maybe there are some kids who can fool it, but there's a lot more who only think they can."

And then there's the Mysterious Stranger, who seems to have no trouble at all with security. The Stranger was so powerful, yet he still got pleasure from taunting Robert. Could it be some old enemy—someone a good deal brighter than Winnie Blount?

"Anyway, I think we have a chance for an A in our semester demo, Robert." The boy launched into the latest plans for using his writing together with manual music and Robert's network algorithms. It was the blind leading the blind, but after a few moments Robert was absorbed in it.

THINGS WERE VERY tense around the house, and it had nothing to do with final exams. In point of fact, Robert's midnight fracas at the front bathroom amounted to a physical assault. Never mind that he'd been trying to protect Alice—that was scarcely something he could claim. This time there were no threats, no showdowns. But Robert could see an uneasiness in Bob's eyes that hadn't been there before. It was the look of a fellow who begins to wonder if the snake he's been keeping might actually be a black mamba. *That* conclusion would get Robert shipped to Rainbows End faster than any mere boorishness.

Miri gave him a clue as to why this hadn't happened. She caught up with him one afternoon as he wandered around West Fallbrook hoping for contact with some friendly form of Sharif.

Miri rode her old bike along beside him for a few paces, matching his speed, and wobbling wildly. Finally she hopped off and walked the bike. As usual, her posture was schoolmarm straight. She looked at him sideways for a moment. "How are your finals going, Robert?"

"Hi Miri. How are *your* finals going?"

"I asked first! Besides, you know my finals don't start till after the break." Her ebullient bossiness seemed to collide with diplomacy. "So how are you doing?"

"It looks like I'm going to get a C in math."

Her eyes widened. "Oh! I'm sorry."

Robert laughed. "No. That's *good* news. I wouldn't have even understood the problems, back before the Alzheimer's."

She gave him a sickly smile. "Well, that's okay then."

"Hmm. A . . . friend . . . of mine told me that the kids in your classes are really good at these things."

"We know the tools."

"I think I could be a lot better in math," said Robert, almost to himself. "It might even be fun." Of course, if his real plans for the next few days worked out, he would have his poetry back and none of this would matter.

This time Miri's smile was happier. "I'll bet you could! You know . . . I could help you on that. I really like math, and I have all sorts of custom heuristics. Between semesters I could show you how to use them." Her voice slipped into leader mode as she planned out his vacation for him. *That's the Alice in her,* thought Robert. He almost smiled. "Hold on, there's still finals to get through." And he thought about Juan's latest demo plans. The boy was doing okay. It was Robert who was having trouble with his part, the graphics and the interfaces. "That's where I really need help."

Miri's face snapped around, "I will not help you cheat, Robert!"

They both stopped and stared at each other. "That's not what I meant, Miri!" Then he thought about what he had actually said. *Christ. In the old days I insulted people all the time, but I knew when I was doing it.* "Honest. I just meant that finals are a problem, okay?"

Lena --> Miri, Xiu: <sm>Be cool, kiddo. Even *I* don't think Robert's messing with you.</sm>

Xiu --> Lena, Miri: <sm>This is a first for you then.</sm>

Miri glared at him for a second more. Then she made a strange sound that might have been a giggle. "Okay. I should have known a Gu would not cheat. It's just that I get so *mad* at some of the kids in my study group. I tell them what to do. I tell them not to cheat. And yet they are always chiseling at the collab protocols."

She started walking again, and Robert followed along. "Actually," she said, "I was just making conversation. I have a mission, something I should tell you."

"Oh?"

"Yes. Bob wants to send you out-of-state. He figures you tried to beat up Alice." She paused, as if waiting for some defense.

But Robert only nodded, remembering the look in Bob's eyes. So Rainbows End was too close by. "How long do I have?"

"That's what I want to tell you, not to worry. You see—" It turned out that his rescue came from an unlikely source, namely Colonel Alice herself. Apparently, she hadn't felt the least bit threatened by him. "Alice knew you were just desperate, I mean—" Miri made a verbal dance of avoiding insult and gross language: Basically, Alice already thought he was a crazy old man. Crazy old men have to go to the bathroom all the time; they get overly focused on that problem. Furthermore, Alice didn't regard his manhandling of her as assault. Robert remembered how sore his head was after he tripped over her feet and slammed into the doorjamb. Black-belt whatever must be one of Alice's myriad JITTs. Alice was the dangerous one. Poor Alice, poor Bob. Poor Miri.

"Anyway, she told Bob that he was overreacting, and you really need your schooling here. She says you can stay as long as your behavior is . . ." Her voice dwindled into silence, and she looked up at him. She couldn't figure how to pass on the rest diplomatically: *as long as you don't blast my daughter again.*

". . . I understand, Miri. I'll be good."

"Well. Okay." Miri looked around. "I, um, I guess that's all I had to say. I'll let you get on with . . . whatever you're doing. Good luck with finals."

She swung back on her bike and pedaled industriously away. That old bike had only three speeds. Robert shook his head, but he couldn't help smiling.

20

THE OFFICER OF THE WATCH

Robert's finals were over. He had earned a 2.6 average, and a B in Search and Analysis. He had worked harder than he ever had in his life. If it weren't for the imminent irrelevance of it all, he would have been proud of himself.

Now it was Monday afternoon and Robert was counting the hours, almost down to counting the minutes. The Mysterious Stranger had been very scarce lately. The cabal had met a couple of times, with Tommie doling out information on a need-to-know basis. Tommie had read too many spy novels. For now, all Robert knew was that they were meeting at the library at 5:30 tonight.

O

MEANTIME, SOMEWHERE UNDER Camp Pendleton . . .

In theory, being officer of the watch for Continental U.S. Southwest was no different than running a snoop-and-swoop operation anywhere in the world. In theory, there could be world-wrecking conspirators at work here. In fact, this was home, in some of the best-connected real estate in the world. The chances they'd have to swoop were near zero. Nevertheless, for the next four hours Lieutenant Colonel Robert Gu, Jr., would be responsible for protecting about one hundred million of his neighbors from mass destruction.

Gu arrived twenty minutes early, checked in with the current officer of the watch, and then looked for DHS screwups. Those were usually the worst thing about CONUS watches. Through the miracle of virtual bureaucracy, Gu's Marine Expeditionary Group was tonight a part of the Department of Homeland Security. This was how DHS kept its budget so, ahem, small. "Like a modern corporation, DHS seamlessly meshes with whatever organizations are needed at the moment." That was the hype. And tonight—well glory be—there was not a single authorization glitch in sight.

Bob walked around the bunker, transformed the green plastic walls into windows on the Southern California night. The air filled with abstractions, the status of his people and his equipment, the reorganization of his share of the analyst pool. He grabbed some coffee from the machine by the door and settled down at a very ordinary desk just a few feet from the launch area.

"Patrick?"

His second-in-command appeared across the table. "Sir?"

"Who-all have we got tonight?" An unnecessary question, but Patrick Westin produced the official list. The Marine Expeditionary Group consisted of four twelve-marine maneuver teams. Call them squads; everyone else did. Back in the twentieth century, Bob's "command" would have rated a second lieutenant. On the other hand, the MEG controlled thousands of vehicles (though most were the size of model airplanes) and enough firepower to finish almost any war in history. Most important to Bob Gu: Everyone in his group had been through combat training as tough as any in the past. They were marines. Patrick called them all in for a short meeting. The room stretched back from around Bob's desk and for a few moments pretended to be an auditorium. Everyone looked cool; it had been a long time since anything had gone Really Wrong within CONUS. *And we're a big part of the reason why.*

"We'll be here four hours," said Bob. "Hopefully, the time will be a very boring snoop. As long as that's the case, you're free to stay in staff areas adjacent to your vehicles. But most of you have been on my watch before. You know I want you to keep your eyes open. Keep up with the analysts." He waved at the analyst pool. For a CONUS Southwest watch, this amounted to about fifteen hundred dedicated specialists, but with connections leading down to hundreds of thousands of services and millions of embedded processors. Tonight, Alice was in charge of the pool, and already the changes were evident, the three-dimensional rat's nest transformed with a clarity rarely seen outside of managers' dreams. Aside from her marvelous reorganization, the display was completely conventional. Between the humans who had clearance and could communicate directly there were hundreds of color-coded associational threads. The mass of the lower levels was constantly aflicker, weights and assessments and connections shifting from second to second.

Bob pointed at the reddish threat wackos that were always part of the mix. "What have we got to worry about for the next four hours?" The analysts behind the red nodes spewed out their consensus list and supporting pointers.

But even the paranoids didn't have much to say tonight:

- Action issues
  - Possible Anti-Librareome protest at UCSD
    - Belief circle riot a near certainty
    - Possible organized participants
      - Jerzy Hacek belief circle
        - CIA assessment of Indo-European connection
      - Scooch-a-mout belief circle
        - CIA assessment of Central African connection
        - CIA assessment of Sub-Saharan connection
        - CIA assessment of Paraguay connection
        - RIAA report to Congress
      - Commercial entities
    - Possible threats to infrastructure
    - Proximity to Critical National Security Sites
      - General Genomics
      - Huertas International
  - Increased illegal computation imports
      - Orange County
      - Los Angeles County
  - Off-scale low probability estimate linking preceding items
- Law enforcement issues
  - FBI vice raid at Las Vegas Splendor Farm, a near certain event
    - Possible request for intelligence support
  - DEA enhancement-drug raids in Kern County
    - Possible request for intelligence support
    - Possible out-of-area activity
      - Pacific Islander settlements in Alberta

Persons of Interest
- Arizona
- California
  - San Diego County
    - Increased short-term South Asian visitors
    - Others
- Nevada

Recusal advisements

Bob let the list hang for a moment.

"Ha," said one of the gunnies. "At least the policías won't be a problem." Denying the law-enforcement requests should be easy tonight, not like for kidnapping or murder prevention.

A tech sergeant flickered highlights across the UCSD event cluster. "This is what will keep us busy." Her light paused, expanding on definitions. "What? This is a fight *between* belief circles? I never heard of such a thing."

One of the youngest marines laughed. "You're just getting old, Nancy. Cross-belief strife is tragic new."

Bob didn't try to parse the slang, but he'd heard enough from Dad and Miri to get the point. He expanded the description of the expected riot. "It looks like a combination of twentieth-century protest and modern gaming. It should be as safe as most public events. The problem is the location." There was so much bio-lab work near UCSD that any instability was a concern. "This is worth a lot of your attention. Note the stats on foreign interest." He moved on to the links in Persons of Interest. As usual, those expanded into the tens of thousands. At one point or another almost everyone—unless they were dead, in which case they might still count for bioterror paranoia—came under scrutiny. "I'm not going to ask you to dredge through the PoI or this watch will last all year. But follow what the spooks throw up at you—and watch for real-time changes." That last was classic wisdom, proven in dozens of disasters and disasters-avoided so far this century. The analysts always had a million suspicions, but when they hit the hard cold world of real time, success depended on whether the operational folks had been paying attention.

And then there was the item that stood a little down from all the others: Recusal Advisements, that is, team members who might somehow compromise this watch. Normally, that was the most paranoid list of all—but his crew would see no cloud of detail here, not even links. Such advice was Eyes Only for himself and his backups. In practice, if there had been any serious problems there, they would have been taken care of well before this briefing.

"Questions?"

He looked around. There was a moment of silence, marines drinking in the details of the moment, answering a lot of questions for themselves. Then the young slang-slinger spoke up. "Sir, the equipment, is it the same as for a technical-threat overseas mission?"

Bob looked back into the young eyes. "The boost gear is lighter than usual. . . . That's the only difference, Corporal. We're here to protect, but ultimately that means to protect the whole country." *The whole world, some would say.* "So, yes, we're carrying a full strategic load." He leaned back and gave a look that included all his marines. "I don't expect any problems. If we pay attention and do our jobs, this will be just another peaceful evening for the people of California."

He dismissed the crew, and the room shrank to its true dimensions. Patrick Westin had a few follow-up questions about squad deployment, and then his image departed, too. Bob Gu turned down his augmentation and for a brief moment there was just his table and chair, sitting by the coffee machine. On his right was the doorway that led to real hardware. With luck, he wouldn't see any of that tonight.

Bob --> Alice: <sm>Are you cool?</sm>

Alice --> Bob: <sm>Cool and clear. The UCSD thing will be good practice for my lab audit. Talk to you after.</sm> That is, after the watch was complete. Tonight Alice was top analyst; if she weren't currently Trained for the audit, she might have been the operational commander. She was one of only a handful of people qualified for both jobs. In either role, she was a joy to work with—as long as he didn't have to think about the sacrifices that made her performance possible.

He finished his coffee and brought back his visuals, now

fully customized. He checked again with Cheryl Grant. She was ready to go. Okay, for the record:

Gu --> Grant: <sm>I take the watch, ma'am.</sm> He and Grant exchanged salutes. The clock was started. His squads settled into total alertness. They would have to stay that way for four hours—not a long time, but about the longest you could remain watch-alert without drugs.

Bob's job was different. He was like a sheepdog running around the outside of the flock, skittering from topic to topic. He watched where marines and analysts were spending their time. This was partly to stay ahead of hot spots, partly to detect attentional holes. For a moment, he looked down from a popular-press viewpoint over UCSD. This . . . event . . . was going to involve a lot of demonstrators, many of them physically present. And network stats showed that a flash crowd situation was possible on top of that. He wondered if Miri was surfing this.

The thought brought him back to the moment. He looked again at the Recusal Advisements. Half of his marines had relatives enrolled at UCSD. That was the big problem with a local snoop. Three of his people were actually part-time students at UCSD. The slang-slinger had a hobby of Scoochi decoration that involved a number of Bangalore fans. If this hadn't been the kid's duty night, he'd be down there on campus right now. But the analysts had done a minute-by-minute on the young fellow, going back fourteen months. There were some illegalities, some enhancement drug abuse, but nothing that would affect the mission.

Bob had searched the entire recusal tree. Now he ran off its pointers, boring deep. Dad didn't show up. *And I was sure he'd be mixed up in the Librareome thing.* Not that that would be serious grounds for recusal. He was skittering too far afield, a common problem for commanders with latitude—

Xiu Xiang? The name was vaguely familiar, but it wouldn't have popped out at him if his own name hadn't been in the item. Xiang was one of about three hundred thousand people in CONUS Southwest who were currently of interest for tinkering with hardware. Much of that was illegal, of course; such people could be thrown to the FBI. But it was more productive simply to track them. Most of these people were benign hobbyists or intellectual-property cheats. Some were the hands for terrorist cults. And some were the analyst smarts *behind* those cults. Xiang had the intelligence and training to be in this last category, but so far the most interesting thing about her was the range of toys she had built, a regular museum of oddball electronics. And she was in one of Dad's classes. That connection was marked "tenuous."

But there was also a reference to Rainbows End Rest Home. . . . This woman was Mom's roomie! And all this time he'd worried about how dull life must be for Mom nowadays. What a team: the mad scientist and his mother the shrink and—*What's this?* Weeks of do-it-yourself snooping that Miri and Mom and this Xiang had run on Dad. A dozen surmises rose to mind, and—*Mission, mission, keep your eyes on the mission.* He resolutely pushed all the personal issues aside. The main thing this proved was the stupidity of running watches with local personnel.

Bob grabbed another coffee and settled back to watch the views of UCSD and the night's other hot spots. In the modern military, losing concentration was much the same sin as falling asleep on duty. It was time to get in the groove.

And still, a tiny internal voice did its best to distract: *What in heaven's name have Miri and Mom been up to?*

MONDAY, 5:00 P.M. *Finally.*

Twilight was still colorful in the sky over La Jolla Shores when Robert drove into the traffic loop north of Warschawski Hall. He headed east on foot, toward the Geisel Library.

"Ready for the big night, my man?" That was the Stranger-Sharif, walking beside him. Passersby didn't seem to see his green-faced companion.

Robert gave the Stranger a sour look. "I'm ready to see you deliver."

"Don't worry. If we succeed tonight, you'll have your peculiar genius fully back, my word on it."

Robert grunted. Not for the first time he speculated on the lunacy of the terminally desperate.

"And don't look so discouraged, Professor. You've already done your hardest part. Tonight it's mainly Tommie Parker who has to get things straight."

"Tommie? I wonder."

"You wonder?" The Stranger's smile broadened. "So you've identified Tommie's 'miracle design bureau'? Poor Tommie. He's the only one of you who thinks he's running free. In fact, he thinks I'm just one of his best collaborators. See, I can be nice when that's absolutely necessary."

There were as many people here as Robert had ever seen on a campus evening in his grad-school days. Up ahead, in the direction of the library, light hung in the sky, brighter than the twilight behind them. Looking down from the tops of the eucalyptus trees, Robert could see crowds along the esplanades south and east of the library. There seemed to be several groups, not mixing. "What's going on?" That must be the distraction Tommie had promised; it was far larger than Winnie's Librareome demonstration.

"Heh. I've planned extraordinary festivities around the library tonight; almost everybody's invited, especially staff from General Genomics labs. But not you. I suggest we detour around the library."

"But that was the rendezvous point—"

"It's already too busy. We'll head for Pilchner Hall direct. This way, please." The Stranger pointed to the right, into dark eucalyptus trees.

O

MEANTIME, IN THE GenGen labs . . .

Sheila Hanson popped up half an hour into the night shift. "You ready, Tim?"

Tim Huynh sat back from his desk, and gestured up his little helpers. "We're ready, boss." He stepped into the corridor and followed Hanson's come-hither arrows up the stairs. She and the rest of her lab techs were already gathered round the surface entrance. Four or five were recent graduates. The rest—like Timothy Huynh himself—were work-study students. "You're sure this isn't going to lose us our jobs?" Belief-circle gaming was all very well outside of work, but Huynh would never have considered this adventure if his own supervisor hadn't suggested it.

Hanson laughed. "I told you. GenGen regards this battle as a form of public service. Besides, it will embarrass Huertas International." Her glance took in all of them, GenGen' s entire night crew except for regulomics. Sheila's explanation was enough for Tim. Once upon a time, he had really looked forward to working at GenGen. How many people got to see—in person—the lab equipment that their college majors were built upon? But more often than not, his job came down to unwedging overenthusiastic cleaning robots, and hauling non-prepped cargo. Yes, sometimes there were real problems, problems where you got to consult with users and help customize their experiment setup. But then you spent days devising automation so *that* wouldn't happen again. Not one of the crew members, even the ones who weren't Scooch-a-moutis, looked unhappy about tonight's little diversion.

"Okay, everybody," said Sheila, "let's see you look properly formed." They slipped into their Scoochi characters. There were pofu-longs and dwelbs, and a great big shima-ping. The shima-ping was Sheila. She glanced at Huynh. "You can't be the Scooch-a-mout, Tim. That's reserved."

"But I'm commanding the critters." He waved at the helper bots that had followed him up the stairs.

"You're *guiding* them, Tim. You can be a Lesser Scooch-a-mout."

"Okay." He shifted form. These were all world-class designs, not seen before tonight. He doubted very much that any of them would remain reserved for long, but if Sheila wanted to play the beliefs strictly, he wasn't going to be the one to break the circle.

They trooped out the doors, into the evening twilight. There was still color in the tops of the eucalyptus. South, across the ravines, their goal was a vast double pyramid, glassy-faceted on top, dark and be-vined below. And that was the real, naked-eye view! The Geisel Library. As they moved along, Sheila and others were fitting their vision over the world. This hadn't been rehearsed. It was designed as a surprise for the Hacekeans, but even more as a surprise for the world that would soon be coming down to watch. One by one, the eucs made little popping noises and suddenly were transformed into moonflower trees, their leaves fluorescent in the twilight.

"We have been noticed," someone said.

"Of course. We're all over. There are s'nice and got-a-runs coming from the Lit Building."

"There's fweks and liba-loos flying from our basement at the library!"

And every appearance sent a tiny fraction of a penny winging back up the Scoochi tree of creation. For once, Tim didn't mind the rip-off. The Scooch-a-mout affiliance was as broad as any. Even hardware illegals at the edge of the world would benefit from the royalties.

Hanson --> Night Crew: <sm>Keep our gear out of sight, long as you can.</sm> The real view from local cams would show that some of the Scoochi images wrapped real critters. So for the moment, Sheila wanted all the privacy she could get on that. What the Hacekeans learned would have to come from public viewpoints and their own naked eyes. Huynh let Rick Smale and the others handle that. He concentrated on running the critters: all the lab bots with enough range and flexibility to walk to the library. These gadgets did routine cleaning and module swapouts. They weren't designed for running around in the wild out-of-doors.

But GenGen had cleared them to go, and Timothy Huynh was having a ball. First, he laid down a consensus for the robots' appearance. There were queeps and chirps, spitting and shooting in all directions. In reality, these were his four hundred mobile manipulators—known as "tweezer bots" in the business. They were barely fast enough to keep up with the humans. But he also had mapped megamunches and xoroshows and salsipueds—these onto his cleaner bots and sample carriers. Behind them lurked the two largest mechs in Huynh's lab, combination forklifts and heavy-equipment installers; for now, they were tricked out as gray-masted blue ionipods. He had supplied the physical specs two weeks ago, when the prospect of this adventure had first floated around the labs. The resulting visual designs were spectacular, and meshed with the reality of the underlying robots and the touchy-feely gear that Huynh had at-d to the bots' hulls. If you patted the xoroshow on its haunches, you'd feel muscle sliding lithely under silky fur, just what your eyes were telling you. As long as they were confronted by only a few pairs of human hands, the haptics were fast enough to maintain the illusion. They were better than anything he'd ever touched on Pyramid Hill. Of course, the remote audience would benefit very little from that, but it would boost the morale of the Scoochis here in person, and undermine their opposite numbers among the Hacekeans.

And that enemy was already forming up. Five Knights Guardian stood on the library's east terrace, and a Librarian lurked by the Snake Path.

"That's all they have?"

"So far," said Sheila the shima-ping. "I'm just hoping we aren't too fragmented."

"Yeah." That was the virtue and the weakness of the Scoochi worldview. Scooch-a-mout was distributed in bits and pieces. It was customized to the wishes of children, not just in the Great Powers, but also in the failed states at the edge of the world. The Scoochis had so *many* different creations. The Hacekeans had the notion of knowledge conquering outward, a vision that claimed consistency over everything. And just now that fit their near-total control of the library.

The shima-ping bounced up and down on its three feet. Sheila was shouting at the enemy with what must have been an external speaker, since Huynh could feel the loudness all over. "Get out of our way!"

"We want our floor space!"

"We want our Library!"

"And most of all, we want our REAL books!" That last demand made for a good chant, even if it didn't quite fit with Scoochi's edge-of-the-world background.

Sheila's gang raced forward with the battle cries. But now dozens of Hacekeans joined the five Knights Guardian. Surely most were virtual, but the blending was perfection. No surprise; both sides knew this was coming. This was a collision of belief circles. The point was to convince the wider world by belief and images that Scooch-a-mout's was the greater vision.

Both sides *thought* they knew what was coming. In fact, Tim's had something special planned:

The Hacekeans roared their threats at the Scoochi army, at the chirps and queeps, and the larger, vaguely seen things that lumbered along behind them. They thought it was all clever imagery and human players. Then the first of the gray-masted blue ionipods crunched onto asphalt, and the Hacek people realized that the sound it made was *real.* At the same time one of the salsipueds—a sample carrier—raced out and bit a Knight on the ankle. It was just a small electric shock really, but the Hacekeans recoiled, wailing, "Cheaters! Cheaters!"

And it was cheating, really, but Huynh saw from the network stats that support for his side had doubled. *Besides, we're doing it for a good cause.* Timothy Huynh never used the physical library that much, but what had happened there rankled.

The terrace was clear for the moment, but Sheila hesitated.

Hanson --> Night Crew: <sm>I don't like the straight run in. I think they have something planned.</sm>

"Yes! See!" Smale shouted aloud, and pointed them to views from above the library's entrance. Those cams showed spider-like somethings guarding the final approach to the library doors. The creatures were so thick they almost hid the stone mosaic. Then the views went offline.

"Jeez, were those critters real?"

". . . I think some of them were," said Sheila.

"Can't be. Even Electrical Engineering doesn't have that many robots. In this contest, *we* are the ones with mechanical superiority!"

But what if the enemy had bought a mob of hobby bots? If even half of those mechs were real—

Sheila paused, listening to advice that might be coming from anywhere on earth. Then she roared, "Into the trees!"

They gave a ragged shout. What came out of the synthetics was an answering roar, loud and baroque and totally Scoochi. They pounded off into the bushes southeast of the library. Virtual imagery faded into an artful blur that disguised the patchy network coverage.

The smaller mechs, the cleaners and sample carriers and

tweezer bots, had little trouble with the mulchy ground cover. It was the forklifts that were the problem. They sank into the softness. Huynh ran around them, giving a push here and moving a stone there. The monsters slowly shuffled forward. It was not so different from some of the work he had to do down in the lab. But now was the time for some out-of-band complaining:

Huynh --> Hanson: <sm>This doesn't help, Sheila. The spider bots will just follow us here.</sm>

Hanson --> Huynh: <sm>Bear with me. This detour will work. Watch what I</sm>

A little yip of surprise came from Sheila's lips, and her sentence hung uncompleted. The virtual Scoochis blundered on for a pace or two, depending on their various latencies, but the GenGen night crew stumbled to an abrupt stop. Everybody milled around for a moment, images coalescing as they threaded routes out of the thicket.

But that was not the reason for the sudden stop. They were all staring at—a man and a rabbit. The first real, the second virtual. The two weren't exactly hiding; they were standing in a clearing. But there was brush all around, and until the Scoochis came stumbling in, there had been no camera viewpoint on this spot.

The rabbit was nothing special, a toonish chimera. It had a nicely impudent leer, you had to give it that.

Sheila the shima-ping hesitated a second, then took a couple of threatening steps toward the rabbit. "You're out of place."

The critter took a chomp out of its carrot and waggled an ear. "What's it to ya, Doc?"

"I'm not a doctor—yet," said the shima-ping.

The rabbit laughed. "In your dreams, then. I'm here to remind you that it's not just you and Hacek in collision tonight. There are other, greater powers at work." It wailed the last words and swept a carrot-clutching white-furred paw at the sky.

Huynh --> Night Crew: <sm>C'mon, Sheila, there are always bystanders.</sm>

Smale --> Night Crew: <sm>Stopping here just dilutes our reputation.</sm>

But Sheila ignored the objections. She sidled around the impudent rabbit and stepped close to the physically present human. *That* guy . . . looked aggressively normal: in his fifties, maybe Hispanic, dressed in dark work clothes. He was the perfect picture of UCSD faculty, though a bit overdressed. He was wearing, but very low-key, not even showing courtesy info. His eyes followed the shima-ping with a sure calmness that—now that Huynh noticed—was a little unnerving.

Then Huynh saw what Sheila was seeing. The stranger was projecting imagery. It was a subtle thing, the sort of far-lavender shades that you almost can't see. They were a mist that drifted up from the stranger's shoes and seemed even brighter as they flowed into the trees.

Hanson --> Night Crew: <sm>Switch to utility view.</sm>

GenGen's utility diagnostics were tricky to use outside of a lab, but they were much more sophisticated than what came with Epiphany outfits. In the utility view . . . you could see that this guy was heavily equipped. The lavender hinted at that, but now Huynh could see the scintillation of the high-rate laser links coming from the guy's clothes.

Without the lavender clue, they might never have noticed. Sometimes the highest form of showmanship is to pretend at unsuccessfully pretending to be innocuous.

Smale --> Night Crew: <sm>Hey! This guy—he's hooked into the Bollywood people here on campus.</sm>

They stared at each other with joyous surmise. This must be a genuine Bollywood mogul. Belief circles were the fuel that sustained the movie industry.

Hanson --> Night Crew: <sm>I told you, battling the Hacekeans would mean big recognition.</sm>

Booting Hacekean ass out of the library was more important than ever. "Onward!" shouted Hanson, now out loud and across all the world. "Down with Hacek! Down with the Librareome Menace!"

The virtuals and almost all the night crew continued on through the forest. Huynh stayed behind a few seconds, making sure that no queep or chirp was stuck in the leaves, making sure that the forklifts had enough space between the trees. And then they were all pounding along again.

"We want our floor space!"
"We want our library!"
"And most of all, we want our REAL books!"
Huynh did not expect that the spider bots would be caught by surprise. What did Sheila have up her shima-ping sleeve?

21

WHEN BELIEF CIRCLES COLLIDE

Alfred Vaz watched the departing crazies.

Beside him, Rabbit swayed in time to their battle cries. For once, the critter seemed impressed by someone other than itself. Or maybe not. "Heh," it said, giving a little carroty salute. "I can't wait to see their faces when they discover who's fighting for the other side."

Vaz looked down at the furry ears. "Turn off your public presence." The goal was to *not* attract attention.

"You worry too much." But the rabbit took a last chomp and tossed the carrot green aside. This one vanished before it hit the ground. "Okay, Doc. I'm for your eyes only. What next?"

Vaz grunted and started off toward the south. In fact, he was more irritated than worried by Rabbit's impudence. If things went properly tonight, the Americans would not connect the operation with Rabbit, much less with the Indo-European Alliance. If the Americans started seriously looking, they would quickly pick out Alfred's role here—whether or not he and Rabbit were actually seen together. Keiko's people had worked out an elaborate decision program—a "contingency tree"—that described just what could still be denied and what could still be achieved in the face of various glitches. Twenty years ago, Alfred would have laughed at such automated planning, but no more. His secret analyst teams had developed his own contingency tree. It grew out from Keiko's, reaching all the way to ultimate worst cases—such as the unmasking of his YGBM project.

Alfred emerged from the densest part of the eucalyptus grove. All around him, his tiny bots unobtrusively kept pace. Every one was in violation of local law, containing not a single chip in thrall to the U.S. Department of Homeland Security. While Vaz continued to play Bollywood exec through the public net, these devices provided him with his own network and countermeasures. There were places in the contingency tree where they could be very useful.

Meantime, a tiny stealthed aerobot followed along above, accepting his local network's traffic and flickering it at a thousand points in the westward sky. The energy in any pulse would be undetectable except to someone very alert and very close by, but the ensemble—correlated with the right time synch—should be visible to Keiko's antenna array out over the Pacific. It was their very own military net. That was the theory. In fact, Alfred had been out of touch for nearly three minutes. He knew Alice Gong was on watch tonight, probably as an analyst. He had launched his attack on her just before he lost milnet access. Very soon her surveillance duties would bring her to a lab file containing an innocuous moiré pattern—only the pattern would not be innocuous for her. *Has that happened yet?* Maybe he should snoop it out via the public net.

"Come on, Doc, come ona come on." Rabbit danced a little jig. Its voice had a mocking lilt that Alfred had first heard some eighty years earlier. "Is there some kinda problem?"

"No problem," said Vaz. "Are your agents in place?"

"Never fear. All but Rivera and Gu are at the start point. I'm guiding them around the riot even as we speak. But if you want to snoop the fiber, you better hurry up."

The ground was firm and level. There was a surfaced path. Now their speed was limited by how fast his mechs could make their stealthy way.

There were crowds here, but almost everyone was walking toward the library. He caught a glimpse of Rivera and Gu. And, once, he saw two children on bicycles. Where did that fit with Hacekeans and Scoochis? He would have put the question to his analyst pool—if only he had his milnet link.

O

THE MYSTERIOUS STRANGER hustled Robert off the surface path, down past where administration bungalows used to be. Robert kept a virtual light on the rough ground. The view was up-to-the-second and clearer than a flashlight might have given him, but keeping up with the Stranger didn't leave time to ghost around the library. "Those are real lights back there," he said. "Even more than before. What—?"

"The Hacek people got a little too enthusiastic. They've destroyed some camera infrastructure. They *need* real light." He was chuckling. "Don't worry. No one will be hurt, and it's a diversion that will be . . . useful."

The Stranger slowed. Robert looked away from the ground for a moment. Over the hill, he got a look—from a point high in the trees—at the people on the ground. In true view, they were students shouting at each other, a few involved in real scuffles. But shift a little away from strict reality, and the imagery became what one group or another wanted you to see. There were Hacek Knights and Librarians tussling with fluffy, colorful critters that might have been big-eyed mammals or—"Ah! So it's the Scooch-a-mout fans going after the Hacekeans?"

"Mostly." The Stranger seemed to be listening for something. Somebody was coming down the hill on an intercept course. A Librarian Militant. Carlos Rivera. The chubby librarian nodded at Stranger-Sharif and Robert. "What a mess."

"But a useful mess," said the Stranger.

"Yeah." Carlos dropped his costume: the Librarian's hat reverted to an everyday baseball cap worn backward, and now his plate armor was just Bermuda shorts and the Rivera standard T-shirt. "I just hope this fighting doesn't become a tradition."

The Mysterious Stranger waved them on through the brush. "A tradition?" he said. "But that would be a plus. Like panty raids and putting automobiles on top of administration buildings. The sort of thing that made American universities great."

Rivera puffed along. "Maybe. We've had a lot more business since the library went virtual, but—"

Robert was still watching the mobs beyond the hill. "I thought the whole point of belief circles was that they can coexist in the same space."

"In principle," said Rivera. They took a big detour around a space that was dark even in the virtual. Sharif's image seemed to flicker and jerk. So few people walked through this area that the random network was sparse and your wearable had to make way too many guesses.

"But," Rivera continued, "the library is a tight fit. In principle we can morph to support the multiple beliefs, like on Pyramid Hill. In fact, our environment is often too close for conflicting haptics. So the administration tried to satisfy the Scoochis by giving them some space underground." Rivera paused, and Robert almost ran him over. "You knew that wouldn't work, didn't you?" Carlos was looking at Stranger-Sharif, or what Robert saw as Stranger-Sharif.

The Stranger turned and smiled. "I gave you the best advice I had, dear boy."

"Yeah." Rivera sounded close to surly. He looked over his shoulder at Robert. "What does he have on you, Professor?"

"I—"

"Ah, ah, ah!" interrupted the Stranger. "I think we'd all be more comfortable without such revelations."

"Okay," said both victims.

"In any case," said the Stranger, "I'm rather proud of how I've morphed the Librareome controversy into this conflict between belief circles. This riot will distract people who would otherwise be paying attention to other things—such as what we're doing."

They were well south of the library now, out of the trees and coming down a steep slope. Just ahead was Gilman Drive. Carlos walked heedlessly into the street. The cars slowed or speeded up or changed lanes so there was always a wide bubble of empty space around him. Robert hesitated, looking for a crosswalk. *Damn.* Finally he scooted after Carlos, out into traffic.

MIRI STOPPED ON the north side of Gilman Drive.

"So where are they going?" said Juan.

"They're coming down to Gilman Drive." Viewpoints in the eucalyptus showed Robert and the librarian, Carlos Rivera, walking through deep brush. The pictures were fragmentary since there weren't many cameras there, but Miri was sure no one was pulling a swap on her. The two would reach the roadway in a couple of minutes.

"But that's true of anyone coming south."

Miri stopped her bike, put a foot on the ground. "Look! You want me to say I don't know where they're going, is that it?"

The Orozco kid stopped his wikiBay bike beside her. "Honest, I'm just wondering."

Xiu Xiang popped into existence, and a moment later, so did a young version of Lena Gu. Their images were Barbie-doll stiff, but every day they got better. For instance, Lena had mastered facial expressions—and right now her look was stern. "Juan isn't the only one with this question, young lady. If you don't *know,* you should say so."

Xiu just sounded anxious. "Lena and I are driving around the north side of campus. Maybe my research was all wrong. How can we help if the action is on the south?"

Miri struggled to make her own voice serene. "I think you got it right, Dr. Xiang. Juan and I have been following Robert closely, but now . . . I guess I don't know where he's going. That makes it even more important that we stay spread out. Please Dr. Xiang, if you and Lena can stay on the north side, that would be best." Over the last few days, Xiu had done some good detective work; she could be really smart when she wasn't doubting herself. They knew that Huertas kept the Librareome shredda in his labs on the north side. If Robert's friends planned a "direct protest," that would be the sensible place for them to break in. *So why aren't Robert and the others heading that way?* Big boogers of uncertainty were beginning to form.

But Dr. Xiang nodded, and not even Juan Orozco asked the obvious embarrassing questions. This was still the Miri Gang. For better or worse.

The treetop cams had lost sight of Robert and Mr. Rivera. Miri dropped those viewpoints and glanced up the hillside, almost with a naked-eye perspective. The other two were still out of sight. They could come out on Gilman Drive almost anywhere.

Miri licked her lips. "The main thing is to keep these—"

"—crazy fools—" said Lena.

"—from doing anything too destructive."

"Yeah," said Juan, nodding. "Who do you think that remote guy is, the one who's walking with them?"

"What?" Juan was a mostly clueless kid, but sometimes he was accidentally very sharp. Miri played back her last images of Robert and Mr. Rivera. Those pics were fragmentary, but Juan was right. The two were looking at a consistent location that drifted along with them—and granting it a certain amount of open space. So. A private presence.

Juan said, "I'll bet they're seeing Zulfi Sharif."

"I'll bet you're right." Not for the first time tonight, she tried to bring up her Sharif control. Still no response.

So do something! "C'mon, Juan." She walked her bike out onto Gilman Drive, crossing the lanes slowly enough not to get a ticket.

Xiu and Lena drifted along. "Traffic is heavy," said Lena.

"It's the belief-circles clash. People are attending in person." The gaming buzz had come out of the blue, but Miri could not imagine that it was coincidence. Setting this up must have involved deep coordination. Even though the clash was still just rumor, there was a huge turnout. The cars around them were dropping off passengers. People were laughing and shouting and talking, and walking toward the library. The sidewalks on the other side of Gilman Drive were all but empty.

She reached the far curb and looked back. "Come *on,* Juan!"

Now the sky above the library was twisting violet, a very nice fractal effect from some art co-op in northern China. She glanced at network status. . . . It wasn't just automobile traffic that was heavy. She could see network trunks lighting up all over California. There were millions of viewpoints being exported from UCSD's campus. There were hundreds of thousands of virtual participants. As Juan caught up with her, she said, "It's a whirlwind. Like a big game first-day."

The boy nodded, but he wasn't paying attention. "Look what I found in the street."

The gadget was half crushed. Metal fibers hung from one side.

She waved for him to drop it. "Roadkill. So?" If a node lost connectivity and then got into the street—well, something that small would get run over.

"I think it's still online, but I can't get a catalog match."

Miri looked closer. There was spiky flickering, but no response. "It's pingless wreckage, Juan."

Juan shrugged, then dropped the gadget into his bike bag. He had a blank look. He was still searching. "It looks like a Cisco 33, but—"

Fortunately, Orozco had not distracted everyone. Lena said, "Miri. I've found Robert and the Rivera fellow." There was a pause while Lena got the camera ID. There! Robert and Rivera were crossing the roadway a quarter mile west of them.

"We're on it, Lena!"

O

IN ROBERT'S TIME, this side of Gilman Drive had been Quonset huts. In later years, classic University of California concrete had housed the medical school. Now there was Pilchner Hall, which like almost everything else on campus looked as temporary as the old Quonsets.

The Mysterious Stranger led Robert and Carlos into the building. Real light followed them in concentrated pools, while farther down the hall the view was virtual. There might have been other people in the building, but the Stranger avoided them. He headed down a stairway, into a warren of tiny rooms. In places the floor was dusty. Elsewhere it was polished clean, or covered with streaky scrape marks. "Heh," said the Stranger, pointing at the scrapes. "Tommie has been at work. This whole floor has been rearranged for tonight. And there are parts that just won't show on the university's security plan."

Their path was now a trek through the maze. Finally, the Mysterious Stranger stopped at a closed door. He paused and spoke soberly. "As you may know, Professor Parker is not fully on board. For the sake of your various goals, I suggest you be careful not to enlighten him."

Robert and Carlos nodded.

The Mysterious Stranger turned and mimed knocking on the plastic door. His hand sounded like a hammer pounding heavy wood. After a moment, the door opened and Winston Blount peered out. "Hello, Carlos." His gaze passed less favorably over Robert and the Stranger. He waved them in.

The room was a triangular wedge trapped between slanting

walls. A concrete caisson took up most of the floor space. Tommie Parker sat on the floor beside a handcart that was filled with plastic bags and backpacks. "Hiya, guys. You're right on time." He glanced at his laptop. "You'll be pleased to know that press and police did not notice your arrival. At the moment we're standing in a room that doesn't even exist. This—" he slapped the caisson "—is still visible to the university, but it will happily lie about what we're doing."

Robert edged round the blocky structure. "I remember this." In the 1970s, the caisson had been out-of-doors, covered with a wooden lid. He looked over the edge. Yes, just as before: iron ladder rungs marched downward into darkness.

Tommie stood up. He had his laptop in a sling that left the keyboard and display accessible, but also freed him to move about. In his own way, Tommie Parker had arrived at wearable computing.

Tommie reached into the handcart and lifted out two plastic bags. "Time to leave your Epiphanies behind, guys. I've got new clothes for you."

"You really meant it," said Rivera.

"Yup. Your old clothes will help me fake your location. Meantime the real you will be with me, and using far better equipment."

"Not laptops, I hope," said Winnie, giving Parker's laptop sling a doubtful look. But he and the others shed shirts and pants and shoes. They still had their contact lenses, but now there was nothing to drive them. The real lighting was bright enough, but without external sound and vision, the room felt like a coffin.

Tommie seemed genuinely embarrassed by all the naked flab. But not for long. He pulled open one of the plastic bags and passed around pants and shirts. They looked like plain gray fabric, working clothes. Carlos held his new shirt up to the light and peered at the weave. He folded it between his hands and rubbed the sides together. "These clothes are dumb."

"Yup. No infrared microlasers, no processor nodes. Just the good cotton as God meant us to wear it."

"But—"

"Don't worry, I have processors."

"I was joking about laptops, Tommie."

Tommie shook his head. "No, not laptops, either. I have Hurd boxes."

Huh? Without his wearable, Robert was stumped.

Carlos looked just as blank, but then some errant natural memory must have popped up: "Oh! Hurd OS! But isn't that obsolete?"

Tommie was rummaging in the second plastic bag. He did not look up. "Not obsolete. Just illegal. . . . Ah, here they are. Genuine *Hecho en Paraguay.*" He handed each of his co-conspirators a black plastic box about the size and shape of a paperback book. There was a real keypad on one side and a metallic clip on the other. "Just snap it on your waistband. Make sure the metal tab is actually touching your skin."

Robert's new pants were too short, and the shirt fit like a tent. He slipped the criminal computer on his waistband and felt the cold touch of metal on his skin. He could see a faint overlay now. It was a picture of a keypad, and when his hand rested on the box at his waist, he saw markers corresponding to his fingertips. What a pitiful interface.

"Don't cover the box with your shirt, Carlos. All the comm ports are on it."

Winnie: "You mean we have to turn in just the right direction to make a connection?"

"Yup. While we're below, our only external routing will be through my laptop. And my laptop's only uplink will be through this." Tommie held up something that looked like a prayer wheel. He gave it a little spin. There was a glint in the air, sliding along a thread too fine to see, to a connector Tommie held in his other hand. He turned and plugged that into a box on the handcart. "Check it out."

Robert pulled his shirt back from his waistband, and turned so the box had a clear view of Tommie's laptop. Nothing. He entered a simple command, and now he could see through the walls again! North of Gilman Drive, there were even more people heading toward the library. Indoors . . . he drifted back up the hallway. Still deserted. *No!* There was a fellow walking purposefully down toward their "secret" room. Then he lost the viewpoint.

"Hey, Tommie—"

"What?"

The Stranger's voice sounded in Robert's ear. The audio was as bad as his old view-page, but he clearly heard: "You didn't see a thing, my man."

"I—" Robert swallowed. "Your fiber link is working fine, Tommie."

"Good, good." Parker walked among them, making sure that everyone could receive and transmit. "Okay. You're all equipped. That was the fun part. Now here's the pack-mule part." He pointed at the backpacks in the handcart.

Robert's pack weighed something like forty pounds. Carlos's looked about the same. Tommie and Winnie had smaller packs. Even so, Blount struggled with his load. *Winnie's like an old man.* Yeah, Reed Weber's heavenly minefield. Robert looked away before Winnie could take offense. He shrugged his own pack into a more comfortable position and complained, "I thought this was the future, Tommie. Where's the miniaturization? Or at least the automatic freight handlers?"

"Where we're going, the infrastructure ain't friendly, Robert." Tommie glanced at his laptop's display. "Hello, Mr. Sharif. Okay, it looks like we're all ready to go." He bowed them toward the dark hole in the middle of the room. "After you, gentlemen."

22

THE BICYCLE ATTACK

Alfred waited a decent time before entering the room. No sense in making noise that Rabbit's stooges might hear.

"What did I tell you, Doc! We're in. We're in!" Rabbit danced a merry jig around the caisson. The optical fiber that was giving Rabbit such joy was invisibly thin except when the light caught it just right.

Vaz nodded. He had a different communications success to celebrate; he had reestablished his milnet link across the Pacific.

Braun --> Mitsuri, Vaz: <sm>U.S. Homeland Security looks

calm, Alfred.</sm> Alfred watched the stats streaming by. They were from the Alliance's listening posts. The national-security scene was indeed calm, even though the library disturbance had brought crowds to the UCSD campus. Rabbit had created the perfect paradoxical distraction. *Almost* perfect; the affair was growing too large.

Vaz knelt beside the box that marked the termination point of Thomas Parker's fiber link. The box was a scamful bridge. On one side, it accepted the uncertified data streams from Parker's criminal computers. On the other, it was a "good citizen," running under the government-required Secure Hardware Environment. It hid Parker's data in innocent packages wrapped in all the licenses and permissions needed to survive on the SHE of the Internet. Altogether it was not as secure as Vaz's milnet, but it would suffice for most regions of the contingency tree.

Alfred tweaked the box, and now he was getting Parker's video direct. At last, he was truly a Local Honcho.

The video from Parker's laptop bounced around without a bit of program control. But Vaz recognized the equipment in the walls, and some of the physical signage. Rabbit's stooges had breached bio-lab security. Even more impressive, the delicate game of fooling the lab's automatic security was a continuing success.

"How far are they from Goal A?" Alfred asked Rabbit. In fact, that was the site of his private research program. He would pretend to inspect it along with the others.

"Almost there." Rabbit waved airily. "They'll start dropping off equipment in less than ten minutes. Don't worry about a thing."

Alfred looked out through his surface viewpoints. "Most of my mobiles are trapped on the north side of Gilman Drive." In conventional combat, his bots would have simply seized the local infrastructure and come storming across. Instead, they were balked by the human and automobile traffic along the roadway. At least one had been struck by an auto.

Rabbit spread its paws in mock sympathy. At least it didn't bring out another carrot. "You can't have everything. Hacek and Scoochi fans have done everything we could pray for: The human staff is out of the labs. The riot is sucking in the local comm resources. It'll be a regular black hole by the time it peaks. *And it all looks totally innocent.* Don't tell me you could mask this operation any better."

Vaz let that brag go unanswered. He'd come to realize that irritation was the kindliest emotion he could feel for Rabbit. He sat with his back to the concrete caisson and tracked ongoing developments. He could see that the Department of Homeland Security people were watching closely, but they were watching the wrong places. Analyst consensus was that Rabbit had tuned things to match DHS paranoia perfectly. Maybe Alice Gong had been taken down, but undetected by Alliance monitors? Underground, Rabbit's stooges had almost reached Goal A. In ten minutes the "investigation" of that site would begin. In another half hour, he could begin to report his doctored results . . . and after that it was simply a matter of getting out and letting the stooges be captured. Things were going so smoothly, he could have stayed back in Mumbai. Not that he was complaining!

Analyst red flag. Someone reviewing stale video had noticed something. Alfred brought up the flag report. It was a ten-second snippet from one of his mobiles on the north side of Gilman Drive: Two children with bicycles. They were standing by the roadway and looking at something that might have been a crushed mech. *Those are the two I saw earlier.* Queries spread outward: Who were the children? Was the mobile one of Alfred's?

Ugly answers came back.

Rabbit didn't have access to the Indo-European analysts, but suddenly the creature sat up and gave an admiring whistle. "Well, I'll be dipped! We've got company, Doc."

O

MIRI LEFT HER bike in the rack outside Pilchner Hall. Juan insisted on bringing his fancy foldup into the building. When Miri pointed out the absurdity of this, the boy just shrugged. "My bike is special."

Lena and Xiu were no longer visible, but Lena's voice followed them through the wide-open doors. "There should be better security, Miri. I don't like this."

"It's the emergency overload behavior, Lena. Unoccupied rooms stay locked. The others are open."

Lena said, "And we can't see you anymore."

The sudden drop in data was very strange, but Miri wasn't going to say that. Instead: "I bet high-rate forwarding isn't supported except for around the library."

Xiu said, "Yes, we still have spectacular views from there."

The main corridors in Pilchner Hall had searchable viewpoints. There were glimpses of Robert's recent passage. That was enough to guide them downstairs. But now there were places where Juan and Miri could talk only to each other.

"It's like a haunted house." Juan's voice was hushed. His hand reached out and grasped hers; she didn't shake him loose. She needed him to keep cool. Certainly losing connectivity in the middle of an office building *was* an eerie thing.

They came around a corner, and there was a glimmer of connectivity, enough for sming:

Miri --> Miri Gang: <sm>I think we're getting close.</sm>

Lena --> Miri Gang: <sm>First we lost video. Now we can barely talk. Get out of there.</sm>

Miri --> Miri Gang: <sm>It's just temporary. I'm sure wikiBell is shifting extra coverage into place.</sm> How bad could an entertainment riot get?

Miri imagined Lena was having a similar discussion with Dr. Xiang in a certain car driving around the north side of campus. Grandmother seemed truly anxious.

Xiu --> Miri Gang: <sm>I agree with Miri. But give Lena and me regular reports.</sm>

Lena --> Miri Gang: <sm>Yes! Even if that means you have to backtrack. Where is Robert now?</sm>

Miri --> Miri Gang: <sm>Real close. I can ping him direct.</sm>

The twisty hallway was brightly lit, just what you'd expect during a network brownout. Juan's bike coasted along almost silently, all folded up into portability mode. He only had to give it a push every so often. Their footsteps and the faint snicking of its tires were the only sounds. They took another corner. The hall was narrower, with intersections every few feet. This was one of those temporary makeovers that crazy architects-for-a-day liked to do.

For a few dozen feet they had high-rate connectivity. Ads and announcements appeared on the walls; someone's medical research project loomed like a monster on the left. She gave Lena and Xiu a continuous video as they turned another corner—and lost all outside connectivity.

Juan slowed, drew Miri to a stop. "This place is really dead."

"Yeah," said Miri. They walked forward a few more paces. Except for her point-to-point link with Juan, she might as well have been on the far side of the moon. And there was another corner ahead. She pulled Juan forward.

Around the corner, the corridor ended at a closed door. "I can't ping your grandpa anymore, Miri."

Miri looked at the map she had cached. "This has to be where they are, Juan. If we can't get through, we'll just pound on the door." Suddenly she didn't care too much about embarrassing Robert and his friends. This was too strange.

But then the door opened and a man in dark clothes stepped out. He might have been a janitor, or a professor. Either way, he didn't look friendly. "May I help you?" he said.

O

"HOW DID THEY find us?"

Rabbit a made warning gesture. "Not out loud, Doc," it hissed. "They might actually hear you." It seemed to look over Alfred's shoulder. "I'd say they're following the girl's grandfather."

Vaz glanced at the heap of clothes that lay by the caisson. He sminged back, voice format: "Those clothes are still transmitting?"

"Well, of course. To the outside, it looks like the old guys are just sitting around, maybe playing cards. I'm faking everything, even their medicals."

Alfred realized he was grinding his teeth.

"That Gu kid is such an pain," Rabbit continued. "Sometimes I think she—"

Alfred waved his hand and the creature disappeared—along with all public network communication. There was now a deep local silence, a hard deadzone.

But his milnet link was still in place, a fragile chain that led through his mobiles to his stealthed aerobot and thence across the Pacific. Alfred's analyst pool in Mumbai was estimating sixty seconds till the deadzone got serious attention from the campus police and fire departments.

Braun --> Mitsuri, Vaz: <sm>This can't be sustained, Alfred.</sm>

Vaz --> Braun, Mitsuri: <sm>I'll clear the deadzone in a few seconds.</sm> This was why successful missions had a Local Honcho. He probed the mobiles that had made it into the building: the children were about thirty feet away, well inside the deadzone, and still coming. He could hear them, right through the plastic wall. He glanced at the door; it was locked. Maybe he could pretend to be empty air while they pounded on the door. No, they'd just back off and call the police.

Okay, time for direct action. Alfred set the two nearest mobiles into motion. These were network-superiority bots with essentially no antipersonnel capacity, but they would be a distraction. Then he opened the door and stepped out into the hall, confronting two children and a folded-up bicycle.

"May I help you?"

O

MIRI TRIED TO glare at the old fellow. Self-righteous indignation came hard when you were trespassing and trying to think of a good lie. And her link to the outside world was still fully dead.

Juan stepped forward and just blathered out the truth. "We're looking for Miri's grandfather. We ping him somewhere behind you."

The janitor/professor/whatever shrugged. "There's no one here but myself. As you know, network connections are very unreliable this evening. The building shouldn't have allowed you down here. I'll have to ask you to go back to the public area." There was a sign by the door now, one of the standard biohazard symbols that covered a lot of the classrooms and labs in Pilchner Hall. You might think the public net was coming back up—except that Miri still couldn't probe beyond her line of sight.

Juan nodded as if the old man made perfect sense. He walked forward a couple more steps, at the same time relaying what he saw back to Miri. The room beyond was brightly lit. There was some kind of *hole* in the floor, and she could see the top of a metal ladder.

"Okay," said Juan agreeably. He was fiddling with something on his bike. But point-to-point, his words were on fire:

Juan --> Miri: <sm>See the clothes!</sm> piled on the floor beside the pit.

Miri --> Juan: <sm>Time to go.</sm> Get outside, get where they could call the cops. She shrugged, as casually as she could, and said, "We'll be on our way then."

The stranger sighed. "No, it's too late for that." He started toward them. Behind her there was the snick of something hard on the floor and she saw dark things scuttling toward her.

There was no way back and no way forward.

And then Juan made a way forward. He bounced his bike toward the stranger. There was a screech of rubber. The wheels spun up with all the power from the regen brakes, and the bike exploded across the room, smashing into the stranger and the equipment behind him. Miri ran forward, toward the pit. "C'-mon, Juan!" She knew where Robert must be, and how she could put out the alarm.

She scrambled over the edge, saw metal rungs. "Juan!"

Mr. Janitor/Professor was back on his feet and staggering forward. He had something pointy in his hand. Miri was frozen for an instant, watching the pointy thing swing toward her.

Orozco was such a runt. He couldn't stop someone like that. But he tried. The bad guy staggered back and the thing in his hand made a bright purple flash. Miri felt a numbing tingle all across her side. She tipped over the edge of the pit, managed to grab a ladder rung with the hand that still had feeling. But her feet swung through emptiness. She pawed with her numb hand, missed, and fell onto very hard concrete.

All her imagery was gone; maybe her Epiphany was fried. But she could see the circle of light above, and she could hear.

"Run Miri! Run—" Juan's shout was cut off by a meaty crunching sound.

Miri ran.

23

IN THE CATHEDRAL

The UCSD library riot was the news of the evening. No doubt it would be echoing back and forth across the world for the next few weeks, a new twist in the trajectory of public entertainment. It was also a bright spot on Bob Gu's situation board. Too bright. Bob watched the analysts—even people with specialties as remote as forensic virology—cluster around that single locus in Southern California.

There are other things going on tonight, guys. The DEA raid in Kern County had triggered real violence in the Canadian North. *That* was outside of Bob's watch area—but it might indicate that something more than simple enhancement drugs was involved. If not for the library riot, he'd be seeing dozens of theories floating up: Maybe the Kern County business was a cover for immigrant bashing. Maybe something more lethal than enhancements was involved. Analysts were great at such wild conjectures, and equally great at feeding on them, reducing them to rubble—or finding solid evidence and drawing in the firepower that Bob Gu commanded.

But tonight—well, the UCSD riot did have the taint of a classic diversion, covering something big and bad and elsewhere in CONUS Southwest. Alice had doubled the size of the analyst pool. Now there were specialists from the Centers for Disease Control, even folks from other watches. Normally, she would have groomed her unruly mob of specialists; she had the breadth and the depth and the charisma to bring even academic civilians into line. But tonight, Alice was part of the problem. Every time he redirected the group into a wider view, she drew it back. She was the one who had diverted the virologists. There was a tight little cluster of bioscience types that grew brighter and closer, bandwidths rising. Alice was not studying the riot per se, but its connections to the bioscience labs that surrounded the school. Except for the diversion of their night staff, the labs showed all green. And the harder she pounded on the lab network security, the cleaner it looked.

It's the damn JITT. Alice had just completed her Training for the bio-lab audit. That had been the most extensive JITT she had ever undertaken. At this moment, he'd guess there wasn't anyone in the world with more knowledge of lab automation and associated research. *I should talk to her direct, no more polite redirections. . . . Hell, if she won't back off, I should relieve her!* And those thoughts were much too like their recent fights at home.

So it was Bob who drew back. He sat and watched the correlations, the statistical outliers. He moved his group members away from San Diego issues. They would be the tripwires if UCSD was a diversion.

The bioscience pool just got brighter. Alice had preempted CDC's genomics division. He would hear about *that* in the after-action meetings. He had a cold intuition. Tonight could be the night. The thing he personally feared as much as anything in the world, the possibility Alice always denied. *Is she slipping away?* What would a full-sized JITT collapse be like for someone who had Trained a dozen times more than the worst JITT-head in a VA hospital?

O

"DID YOU HEAR something?"

"Like what, Tommie?"

"You know, like a distant thump."

They stopped and looked back. Winnie made an indignant noise. This was like the old days, when Tommie was always working to increase the suspense of their illicit expeditions.

Tommie hesitated. He was leading from behind so that the fine fiber he was paying out wouldn't get trampled by the others. He listened for a moment more, and then turned to catch up. "Maybe it was nothing . . . but the fiber went dead for moment, too." He glanced down at his laptop. "It looks okay now." He waved them up the tunnel, into the dark beyond their little pool of light. "Keep going."

The first part of the tunnel had been very familiar, an eerie walk down memory lane. There was a time, now more than fifty years past, when all of them but Carlos had explored the tunnels. Tommie Parker had been a smartass freshman showing off to a couple of grad students who often wondered how they had been inveigled into such harebrained expeditions.

As they walked farther on, things became less familiar. Glassy tubes ran along the walls. Robert saw signs printed on the walls, cryptic physical backup for nodes that wouldn't respond to his computer box. *Thunk.* Something white and the size of a volleyball whizzed by in one tube. *Thunk, thunk.* Similar traffic in the opposite direction. Pneumatic tubes had once been a sign of the brave new world. When Robert was a child, he'd seen such things in dying department stores. "Why the pneumo tubes, Tommie?"

"Well, this is where theory meets reality. Proteomics, genomics, regulomics—you name the 'omic,' and it's here. These labs are *huge.* The local data traffic is a million times what you have on a public trunk, with the latencies of a home network. But they still need to look at real biologicals. Sometimes they gotta move samples—transport trays for short moves, pneumos for longer ones. GenGen even has its own UP/Express launcher, for shipping parcels to other labs around the world."

Now Robert heard sounds from the darkness ahead of them, voices that never quite made recognizable words, clicking that might have been old-time typewriters. *This is science?*

Carlos said, "When I try to probe the local net, all I see are the bare walls."

"I told you. Talking to the labnet would make this scam way too complicated."

"The tunnel must know we're here." They walked in a small pool of light. Behind and ahead of them, the tunnel was dark.

"Yup. It knows we're here. But you might say that's only at a subconscious level."

Robert was in the lead. He pointed at the wall just at the front edge of the light. "What about these signs?" The letters were physically painted on the wall:

5PBps:Prot<->Geno. 10PBps:Multi

That brought Tommie forward. "Maybe it's the General Genomics crossbar!" He held his prayer wheel high, waving the fiber out and away from the others. The Stranger was visible beside Tommie, but down here the monster couldn't quite locate itself. Its feet floated above the floor, and its gaze was wrong by ninety degrees.

Tommie pointed his laptop so its camera could see the lettering. "I have to admit, this fiber link is handy. I can send video out to my consultancy." Invisible to Tommie, the Mysterious Stranger jerked a thumb at itself and grinned. Tommie studied his laptop's display for a moment. "Yes! We have reached the GenGen optical crossbar." He pointed down the side tunnel. "This is where things get tricky."

Within fifty feet, the side tunnel had opened into a wider . . . cavernous . . . space. In the shadows, something slanted into the heights. "See that tower?" said Tommie. "That's GenGen's private launcher. These guys don't bother with the launchers in East County."

The clickety sound was all around them now. It came from the tops of equipment cabinets; it had a pattern, like poetry scanned purely for stress. At the end of a stanza, things actually *moved.* Light glittered from deep within matted crystals. Some of the cabinets had a physical label:

Mus MCog.

The Stranger danced among them, a fantasy from Tommie's laptop and the fiber behind them. But the fantasy was watching through the laptop's camera, and talking—at least to Robert. The Stranger pointed in the general direction of the crystals. "The wonders of nano-fluidics. A decade of old-time bioscience done in every shifting of the lights. How do you represent a trillion samples, and a billion trillion analyses? How can art deal with that?" It hesitated as if truly anxious for an answer, and then it was gone again. But it left behind its own labels and explanations.

Robert looked at the ranks of machines, the tower almost lost in the distant dark. The place was a machine cathedral. But how to represent it, when it would take him years to have even shallow understanding? The massed crystal was not spectacularly colored; most of the fluid paths were microscopic and hidden within appliances that might have been oversized refrigerators. The Stranger's labels floated randomly about, ghostly subtitles to some transcendent process. And yet, it almost made him remember what he had lost; words burbled up within his imagination, words striving to capture the awe he felt.

They walked down the narrow aisles, turning only when Tommie told them to turn. Every minute or so, he would stop their progress and grab a few more gadgets from the backpacks.

"We gotta install these just right, guys. Staying invisible here is a lot harder than in the tunnel." Tommie wanted the gadgets set near comm nodes, which turned out to be way back within the fluidics crystals. Robert did most of the "installing." Carlos would boost him up over the top of the cabinet. Robert would wiggle back, so near the glassworks that he could hear tiny, tiny clicks and the fluid hissing so faintly it might have been seepage. In their millions, those sounds added up to the larger atmosphere of the room.

In one case, Robert lingered, and noticed that the gadget itself took care of final installation, sliding away from him, deeper into the glassworks—*as if its underside were a miniature transport tray.*

"What are you laughing at, Gu?" Blount's voice came from below.

"Nothing!" Robert crawled off the cabinet and dropped to the floor. "I just figured out a little mystery."

They continued on. Most of the cabinets were labeled *Dros MCog* now. They were making faster progress, mainly because Carlos and Robert had figured out the gymnastics of the operation.

"That's the last of them, guys!" Tommie's gaze shifted from his laptop to the fluidics crystals. "You know, it's really weird that all the node locations were so deep in the lab equipment," he said.

The Mysterious Stranger slipped in front of Tommie and waggled greenish fingers at Robert and Carlos and Winnie Blount. "That's not a mystery to follow up on. Why doesn't someone suggest that we get on with Tommie's great plan, eh?"

No one said anything for a moment, but Robert guessed two things about what they had just done: It was what they had really come here for. It was how the Stranger might make good on his promises. Maybe Carlos and Winnie realized something similar, because suddenly all of them were talking. Blount waved the others silent and turned to Parker. "Who knows, Tommie? You said this was subtle. It might take weeks to figure out just how everything fits together."

"Yup, yup," Tommie nodded, oblivious of the Stranger's satisfied look. "Time for analysis later!" He glanced down at his laptop. "In any case this was the hard part. Now we have a clear run to where Huertas stores the shredda."

THEY DIDN'T SET down any more gadgets. Tommie's laptop advised speed, and therefore so did Tommie. Whatever the Mysterious Stranger planned for GenGen no longer needed them. Robert glanced back. Winnie was out of breath, almost trotting. The Stranger must have given him some special encouragement. And behind Carlos, Tommie spun his prayer wheel, drifting the spider thread out behind them.

Suddenly the concrete floor gave way to something that bounced back against their feet. And the sound of their steps was like tapping on a vast and tightly fitted drum.

"When does a tunnel fly?" said Tommie. "When it's really a tunnel in the sky!" And suddenly, Robert realized where they were. This was one of the enclosed walkways that came off the side of Rose Canyon, just north of campus. Right now they were standing in a tube seventy feet above the brush- and manzanita-covered hillside.

Then they were back on concrete. Ahead was another cavern, and this one was almost empty. Huertas country.

MIRI RAN, BUT a spotlight followed. No, that was just normal tunnel lighting. She slowed, stopped, slid up against the wall . . . and looked back. No human followed. The entrance hole was the only other light, and now it was some distance behind her. *Juan!*

She watched it and listened. If no one was coming after her, that might mean that UCSD security was still working down here.

She tried to probe the walls. She called 911. Again. Nothing. Maybe the Badguy had permanently zapped her Epiphany. She shrugged up some test routines. No, it wasn't dead. She could see her files, but every local node was ignoring her. Then she noticed the pink flicker at the edge of the diagnostic, a wireless response that her Epiphany would normally have discarded as too distant, too erratic. A second passed, heaven knew how many retries, and she got an ID. It was Juan, his wearable.

Miri --> Juan: <sm>Please answer!</sm>

No reply came back, and she couldn't check his medicals without more access rights. Abruptly Juan's light flared, died. Miri sucked in a breath. Mr. Janitor/Professor was still up there. He had whacked poor Juan again. No, be precise: He had whacked Juan's gear again, maybe just to prevent Miri from forwarding out through it. For a moment, Miri drew in on herself. It was not a good thing that all her planning and leadership could come to this. Alice never seemed to have these problems. She always knew what to do next. Bob . . . sometimes Bob made mistakes. He was the one who always seemed uneasy about certainty. *I wonder what Bob would think of all this? . . . I wonder what Juan would do?*

Miri looked down the tunnel, away from the entrance. It was dark, but it wasn't perfectly quiet. There might be voices, chatting conversationally, never quite making words. Robert and his library friends were down here, surely being run as cat's-paws by Mr. Janitor/Professor. *How can I wreck his plan?* Miri got to her feet and ran quietly up the tunnel, still trapped in her own private pool of light. No sign of Robert, and none of the mumbled voices sounded quite right. She passed occasional cross tunnels. Small things whizzed down transparent tubes.

○

SOME MINUTES LATER, and still no sign of Robert.

Miri read as she ran along; she had cached plenty about

UCSD and the biotechs. There was proprietary and security stuff she couldn't know, but . . . the cross tunnels led off to particular labs. Three hundred acres in seventeen separate chambers!

Miri's run slowed to a walk, then came to a miserable stop. Robert could be anywhere. How much control did the Badguys have down here? *Maybe I should just start shouting.*

Faintly, behind her, there came a new kind of sound. Soft hammers pounding on a metal drum. But the cadence was like footsteps. And suddenly she had a very good idea of where the others were. Now if only she could match that to where *she* was. Miri turned and headed back.

24

THE LIBRARY CHOOSES

Sheila Hanson's night crew came out of the forest on the path of the great snake of knowledge, just east of the library. The Hacek spiders were already there, and they had the high ground. Tim Huynh rolled and walked his bottish army right to the edge of the enemy force.

Huynh --> Night Crew: <sm>Jeez. They're all real!</sm> The spiders, that is. Most of the humans were real, too. Hacekean Knights and Libarians were thick behind their robots.

Round the north side of the library came more Scoochi reinforcements, supporters from the Oceanography Library at Scripps Institute. But the Hacekeans had their own reinforcements. From cameras flying above the library, Huynh could see those latest arrivals chasing the Scripps people. So far there had been little property damage. The mechs looked sinister enough, and the humans were mostly milling and shouting. Sheila was still doing pretty well with her "We want our REAL books!" chant.

Something big and virtual came rushing out of the

Hacekean side and onto the bottish no-man's-land. It was twelve feet tall, the best Dangerous Knowledge that Timothy Huynh had ever seen. Half Librarian, half Knight Guardian, the creature was Hacek's central paradox. Now it capered almost to the edge of the Scoochi lines and made a grotesque face, tongue long and pointy like a Maori daemon. And when it shouted, every Scoochi heard, but the message was customized to the listener:

"Hoy, Timothy Huynh, you think you's a Lesser Scooch-a-mout. Lesser indeed! All you Scoochi moppets be trashy children's things, shallow and unworthy before our Depth!" Dangerous Knowledge waved at the Hacek critters around and behind it.

That was the usual slur against the Scooch-a-mout mythos, and it always made the Scoochis mad, since naive outsiders might be deceived by the claim. There were counterchants from the Scoochi ranks:

"Hacek is just counterfeit Pratchett!" And that set the *Hacek* people into a rage, since of course it was only the simple truth.

Huynh pushed past Sheila and Smale and the rest of the night crew, till he stood at the forward edge of his army. Up close, this Dangerous Knowledge was even more spectacularly detailed. Its taloned boots were artfully sunk in the muck beside the serpent's path. Spider bots hummed and hopped around their patron.

The spider bots were real. Where had the Hacekeans gotten such clever things, and on such short notice? He pinged them; not surprisingly, nothing came back. There was an almost living suppleness about the way they scrambled over one another, surging and retreating. The gadgets looked like custom melds of the latest Intel and Legend models. GenGen regulomics was upgrading to something like this. He pinged them again, this time with his GenGen technician's authority.

Holy shit!

"Hey!" Huynh shouted. "The Hacek bums have stolen GenGen equipment!" And now that he looked closely at the other side, he recognized fellow employees! There was Katie Rosenbaum. She waved her battle axe and leered at him.

Rosenbaum --> Huynh: <sm>We just borrowed them, dearie!</sm>

He'd had lunch with Katie and her friends only yesterday. He knew there were Hacek sympathizers in regulomics, so of course his crew had kept their plans under wraps. And all the while the treacherous Hacekeans had been doing the same!

Dangerous Knowledge continued its merry dance through the spider troops, mocking the Scoochis' surprise. It shouted, "Indignant, be ye now, wee Huynhling? Could it be ye just cheated with too little imagination? What ye brought is old and slow, well matched to the petty concept of your imagery!"

The art behind Dangerous Knowledge was astoundingly good, without precursors. But whoever was pulling the strings was even more impressive, certainly a world-class professional actor. For a moment the Scoochi ranks wavered and their mob of virtual supporters began to melt away. In the view from above, Huynh saw still more Hacekeans piling up around the other sides of the library. If the balance shifted too far, the Scoochi cause would end in humiliation and defeat.

Then Sheila Hanson's voice came loud on the public venue, audible across the entire participating world. "Look! The Greater Scooch-a-mout!"

Behind Huynh, one of the forklift mechs stirred to life. Ah! That was just the thing Huynh should have thought to do. Thank goodness Sheila was on the ball.

The forklift stepped forward as delicately as could be imagined for a machine that was twelve feet tall, with a center of gravity that now was over six feet up. It certainly wasn't running autonomously, but he hadn't thought Sheila could drive it this well.

Its foot-platters descended slowly, giving humans and chirps and salsipueds plenty of time to clear out of the way. It was impressive, but it was just a forklift. Then Huynh realized he was still watching it with his driver's view. Meshing with the belief-circle view it was—

Sheila had morphed the blue ioniped into something even more spectacular than Dangerous Knowledge. Now it was the Greater Scooch-a-mout, the most popular of the Scoochi critters. In its short career, the Greater Scooch had been the subject of refurbishments, spinoffs, spinups, mergers, and attempted government takeovers. It was the maximum hero to millions of schoolchildren across the poorest lands of Africa and South America, the champion of little people improving their place in the world. And this vision of it, tonight, topped everything in sight.

What's more, this vision, tonight, had four tons of haptic truth clunking along inside.

The Greater Scooch-a-mout reached the edge of the Scoochi lines, and advanced into spider-bot territory. Now it moved *fast,* as fast as its stabilizers and motors would carry it. *Whoa, who is driving that thing?* It danced through the Hacek robots and bellowed insults at Dangerous Knowledge.

Knights and Librarians, pofu-longs and dwelbs and baba llagas—everybody on both sides went wild. Special effects blossomed in the air above them. And then the shouting got even louder. The robots surged into combat. Huynh looked at the melee of robotic special effects. Megamunches and xoroshows were coming out from the bushes; Sheila was throwing their reserves into the maw of battle.

This mech battle was real! When the Greater Scooch-a-mout tap-danced on the backs of spider bots, fragments of carapace and leg flew into the air. In his technician's view he could see damage reports. Twenty regulomics spiders were listed as "nonresponsive" on the lab's real-time roster. Dozens of his tweezer bots were destroyed. Three of the sample carriers had lost mobility.

Huynh --> Hanson: <sm>Borrowing robots is one thing, Sheila. But lots of these are going back as junk.</sm>

Sheila was at the other end of the front. It looked like she was trying to get the robots to advance into the Knights and Librarians. On Tim's end, the Greater Scooch-a-mout had already accomplished some of that by dancing toward the edge of the real human players.

Hanson --> Huynh: <sm>Not to worry! Management is happy! Take a look at the publicity, Tim.</sm>

His coworkers and the virtual thousands pushed forward. In

the network view . . . jeez, GenGen was getting coverage like you couldn't pay for, better than in the twentieth century when millions were forced to watch just what the few had decided was Important. There were backbone routers in the UCSD area that had run out of capacity! That wouldn't last long, since there were endless ad hoc routers and dark fiber everywhere. But the whole world was here tonight.

Step by step, the Scoochis advanced.

"We want our floor space!"

"We want our library!"

"And most of all, we want our REAL books!"

Belief circles normally competed from within, based on their own popularity. Here, tonight, was a grand exception: belief circles fighting each other directly for attention and respect. In minutes they might burn up months of creativity, but reach an audience beyond all their earlier dreams.

And whoever was driving the Greater Scooch-a-mout chatted with Huynh directly:

Greater Scooch-a-mout --> Lesser Scooch-a-mout: <sm>Your mechs are the thing, my man! Bring them on!</sm>

Okay! Huynh fired up the other forklift. He often dreamed of kicking ass with one of these monsters. He walked carefully through friendly lines, drawing the smaller robots along behind him. From somewhere across the world, Scoochi artists draped the forklift every bit as brilliantly as the Greater Scooch-a-mout. But this vision was mercurial as smoke: Huynh's forklift was tricked out as Mind Sum, the ambiguous spirit that sometimes helped Scooch-a-mout when enemies were at their wiliest. Its vapors both lagged and led the real device. Dozens of helpers and helper programs made sure that the effect was always in place. The forklift's hull was dark composite plastic. Unless you looked carefully in the real view, you couldn't be sure just where the robot might really be.

Tim Huynh took advantage of all this, stomping like a steel mist across the bottish battle zone, high-fiving the Greater Scooch-a-mout . . . and treading with ambiguous location toward the Knights and Librarians. The Scoochi chant boomed from the forklift's speakers:

"We want our floor space!"

"We want our library!"

"And most of all, we want our REAL books!"

The advance was a combination of beauty, surprise, and physical intimidation. The Hacek forces fell back and Huynh's chirps and salsipueds hustled forward to claim new ground. But Katie Rosenbaum's critters still outnumbered them and were far more agile. The spider bots raced backward, keeping a battle zone between the contending human forces.

Smale --> Night Crew: <sm>Keep after them!</sm>

As Huynh walked forward behind his forklift Mind Sum, he was also looking down from above and tracking the reviews. There were more than a hundred million people watching what the two belief circles had created. Not quite a game, not quite a work of art, this was a contest where you won with imagination and calculation and impudence. So far, the world thought that the two sides were matched as to imagination, but the Scoochis were way ahead on calculation and impudence. They had created real physical destruction—all around and among real humans!

Yard by yard, the battle moved round the library. The Scoochis now occupied parts of the south esplanade, the principal axis of the campus. On the roads around campus, cars were bringing people from all over town, the physical counterpart of the far more numerous virtuals. Forty percent of the backbone routers were saturated. The audience had surged past two hundred million. Hundreds of thousands were players, tricked out with new imagery from the depths of Hacek and Scoochi design. The participants, real and virtual, spread out around the central hub that was the university library. Seen from journalist viewpoints a thousand feet up, the conflict looked like a strange spiral galaxy, its arms glowing the brightest where the battle was the fiercest.

There were others present, invisible but for the reporting of the entertainment-trade journalists: the movie and game people, maybe a hundred thousand professionals. Some watched the watchers, sampling and polling. Others were down in the bottish battles, collecting designs. He could see the spoor of

SpielbergRowling, GameHappenings, Rio Magic, and the big Bollywood studios.

Tim Huynh could see more. After all, he was running Gen-Gen equipment. He could see nets that merged with the background, collecting and collecting—then subtly affecting. Those must belong to the Fantasists Guild, the richest artists' cooperative in the world. (Their motto: "We don't need no stinking middlemen!")

And of course the police were here, a half-dozen jurisdictions from campus cops up to the FBI.

Greater Scooch-a-mout --> Lesser Scooch-a-mout: <sm>Hey, my man! We have ten minutes to win belief and decision. Then they're going to start shutting us down.</sm>

ALFRED WATCHED IT all from under Pilchner Hall. Rabbit's riot had emptied the bio labs. The Indo-European inspection equipment was in place, and already sending back results (faked results, but that was Alfred's doing). The stooges who had installed that equipment were now well away from the Gen-Gen area, off where their eventual arrest would provoke diversionary suspicions. But—

"We need at least fifteen minutes more," said Alfred. The faked data stream from the investigation would complete sooner than that, but cleaning up and getting out would take additional time.

Rabbit shrugged. "Don't worry, old fellow. I told Huynh ten minutes just to keep him on his toes. Even after the campus police crack down, you'll have another half hour before the Gen-Gen crew begins to trickle back underground."

Mitsuri --> Braun, Vaz: <sm>I think Rabbit is right about the timing. His library operation is a masterpiece. We couldn't have organized a distraction like this without pressing every red button in the Americans' security apparatus.</sm>

Braun --> Mitsuri, Vaz: <sm>The riot has grown too large.</sm> The traffic still blocked their mobiles. Without sufficient mechs on-site, they hadn't been able to fully control Pilchner Hall—and two unwelcome children had created the first real problem of the evening. Now one of those children lay unconscious by the caisson, right where Alfred had brought him down.

Vaz glanced at where Rabbit sat on the edge of the pit, its furry feet dangling into the dark. "What about the girl, Rabbit? Right now she is running around in the tunnels, out of control."

Rabbit smiled broadly. "So call me the lord god of unintended consequences. When things get complicated, there are side effects, and Miri Gu is just one of them. *You're* the Local Honcho. Why don't you go after her?"

Braun --> Mitsuri, Vaz: <sm>No. That would put you well outside of our contingency plans.</sm>

In fact, Alfred was tempted. Instead, he had sent down just one mobile to track the girl. It might be enough to distract her. And if she caught up with the stooges, why then they had another option available, something that should surprise Rabbit. Out loud, Vaz said, "I don't think so. Do you have any other suggestions?"

"The obvious, old fellow: Be flexible, like me. Who knows what opportunities may develop? You can't locate Miri Gu, but big deal. That must mean she's nowhere that interests you and your friends, right?" He waggled his ears inquisitively.

Braun --> Mitsuri, Vaz: <sm>I want Mr. Rabbit out of there. He is trying to coopt *us,* and all the time distracting us with his impudence.</sm>

And that could be very distracting. Rabbit had started on another carrot. The creature grinned around large incisors as it chomped away, as if to say "Don't mind me; sming all you please!"

From far beyond the walls, Alfred could hear the sounds of Rabbit's diversionary riot. Counterforce analysts reported that Homeland Security was watching UCSD with intense interest, but was otherwise calm. Günberk and Keiko took that as good news. *But does that mean Alice Gong is still functioning?* For Alfred, that was the question of the moment, far more important than his run-in with the two children.

In any case, it was time to get the inquisitive rabbit out of here. It had to be done without making Günberk and Keiko suspicious. Fortunately, Günberk was already pushing in the right direction. Braun floated a needs-and-goals matrix into view.

The colors were shaded to reflect probability, but it was strikingly pure: for the library riot, Rabbit-critical items glowed bright red, a hundred tasks that only he could do if the diversion were to proceed. For the underground labs, there were a dozen Rabbit-critical items, mainly involving getting the stooges underground, guiding them around, and getting them out of the operational area. And every one of those was some shade of green.

Vaz --> Braun, Mitsuri: <sm>Good point, Günberk.</sm>

Mitsuri --> Braun, Vaz: <sm>Okay. Cut Rabbit loose, but gently. I suggest you blame this move on your obnoxious remote colleagues <grin/>.</sm>

Alfred gave Rabbit a smile. "You are right, Mr. Rabbit. Some of us are sadly inflexible."

"Hey, no problem." Rabbit waved magnanimously.

"In fact, you have made things so safe for us down here, my bosses want you to concentrate on topside operations."

"What are you doing—Hey!"

Vaz reached down and unclipped the fiber-optic line from its scamful bridge.

For a moment the image of the Rabbit was frozen, like some dumb graphic that had lost its remote source. Of course, Rabbit still had its Internet link to here; this pause was a moment of simple astonishment. When it passed, the creature hopped to its feet. "Why did you do that?" Its voice and facial expression were almost without affect. Apparently, Rabbit had never conceived the possibility of having to confront *real* surprise and embarrassment.

The fiber-optic plug dangled loose in Alfred's hand. It took an effort of will not to flash a gloating smile at the creature. He slipped the line into a transceiver on his belt. What went in and out the fiber would now go through his private milnet.

Braun --> Mitsuri, Vaz: <sm>Bravo, Alfred!</sm>

Mitsuri --> Braun, Vaz: <sm>Be nice! We still need him for the riot.</sm>

Rabbit paced along the edge of the hole, its paws waving in a blur that might have been fists. "You are breaking our agreement." The voice was still flat.

Alfred put on his kindliest expression and spoke without a

hint of triumph. "Please, Mr. Rabbit, look at our agreement. We both need the other to profit—and we are each best in our own domain. The equipment is now inserted in the labs. If you will maintain the riot environment for a few more minutes, you will have everything we promised you."

The Rabbit stared expressionlessly. "You need me down in the labs. Surely . . ."

He isn't all-knowing! "Conceivably. I'll keep you apprised of our situation. What do you say?"

There was a sudden cascade of expression across Rabbit's face: anger, then a knowing smile quickly covered up as though the operator had not wanted it seen, then an elaborate, overly patient sigh. Yes, the long-suffering Rabbit. "Ah, paranoia triumphant. Very well, I will bow to your wishes—" which it did elaborately, dancing on the edge of the pit "—and retreat to keeping you safe from surface threats." A flash of unherbivorous teeth: "But I do expect all the agreed payoffs. You know my capabilities."

"I do. And I realize there may still be complications," *and attempts by you to create complications.* "One of our people will run liaison with you and your surface ops."

Vaz --> Braun, Mitsuri: <sm>Keiko?</sm>

Mitsuri --> Braun, Vaz: <sm>I'm on it.</sm>

Rabbit gave a last flippant wave, and suddenly the little room with the plastic walls and the concrete floor was free of all taint of Rabbit. Alfred shut down the remaining Internet links. Now there was just the pile of old clothes, the handcart, the hole in the middle of the floor . . . and their one human casualty.

The comforting sounds of mayhem continued to waft down the hill from the library.

Vaz --> Braun: <sm>How does the lab data look?</sm> The inspection equipment had been transmitting for some minutes now. Were the lies being believed? Could Günberk give up his precious theories?

Braun --> Vaz: <sm>They're seventy percent complete. We have a lot of post-analysis to do, but at first glance these labs look innocent.</sm>

Yes!

GREATER SCOOCH-A-MOUT --> Lesser Scooch-a-mout: <sm> Forward, now, my man! The Hacek bastards are giving way! </sm>

And Hacekeans were falling back, at least in the area ahead of Timothy Huynh. He walked his forklift into the gap, crushing what spider bots got in the way. The arc of contention had shifted round till he was almost due south of the library's main entrance. Here the enemy was in retreat. The Scoochis had more real people on the ground and that meant more backup for the visual effects. But the Hacekeans had perhaps two hundred thousand folk from afar compared with half that many virtual Scoochis. On the far side of the library, on the hill by the loading dock, there was no room for a real human mob. Over there, Hacek—the worldwide belief—was in ascendance. Dangerous Knowledge hung out there, more spectacular than ever, orchestrating a sky show that boomed over the north-side valley. His reinforcements swarmed downward on lances of light.

Tim did his best to follow the big picture, though just now he was very busy stomping on every spider bot that he could lay a foot-platter on. He had seen marvels on both sides tonight, things that their belief circles could feast on for at least the next year. And yet there was still room for a clear win. Tonight Scooch-a-mout could transcend what had been a fringe market and reach the same worldwide big time as the Hacek and the Pratchett and the Bollywood empires. They needed something awesome, something that would put clear sky between them and the Hacekeans. He marched his Mind Sum, his being of mist and steel, back and forth across the front, crushing all that remained of the spider bots. He could think of nothing more spectacular to do. *Damn.*

But there was a world of Scoochis out there, and cleverness to match.

Greater Scooch-a-mout --> Lesser Scooch-a-mout: <sm>Release the overrides on my forklift.</sm>

Huynh did so.

The figure of the Greater Scooch-a-mout was motionless for a moment, but in his technician's view, Huynh could see its power cells charging capacitors well into the burnout range.

And then the Greater Scooch-a-mout sprinted forward like a human athlete and . . . by God *broad-jumped* thirty feet, to the lawn by the Snake Path. It looked over the north-side valley and shouted down at Dangerous Knowledge in a voice that was both virtual and real. And the real was noise unto pain.

"Hey there! Little Bitty Knowledge! We're equally matched, don't you think?"

From the valley by the loading dock, Dangerous Knowledge shook his fist at the teetering forklift. "Too equally matched!"

"But one of us should clearly win, don't you think?"

"Of course! And that would be meself, as all the world knows." Dangerous Knowledge waved at its virtual—millions! (But a big part of that count was faked images, Tim could tell.)

"Maybe." The Greater Scooch-a-mout jumped again, this time to the edge of the drop-off over the loading dock. There was something awesome in the maneuver, knowing the tons of real machine behind it. "But what is this whole conflict about?" It waved its arms, a cheerleader god, and Scoochis screamed with all the amplification they could muster:

"We want our floor space!"

"We want our library!"

"And most of all, we want our REAL books!"

"YES!" said the Scooch-a-mout. "It's the Library we're all fighting about. It's the Library that should decide!"

And with that all the Scoochi sound effects chopped to nothing. An uncertain silence spread across the Scoochis. Sometimes the belief thing got caught in its own metaphors and wound up spouting nonsense. Huynh looked back and forth, gauging the reaction the Greater Scooch had provoked. It sounded good to enlist the library itself, but what did that *mean?*

Down in the north-side valley, there was a flare of laughter. The enemy had come to the same conclusion. *We are screwed,* thought Huynh. But then he noticed that Dangerous Knowledge was not laughing. The creature came partway up the hill, confronted the Greater Scooch-a-mout eye-to-eye. And now there was eerie silence on all sides.

Somehow, Dangerous Knowledge knew what the Scooch-a-mout was talking about. "So," the Hacek godling said at last, and its voice had a silken tone even though it echoed off the library and settled deep in the mind of every one in the world who was watching. "Ye want the Library itself to decide who should care for it and who should have its space?"

"And how real the books should really be," the Greater Scooch-a-mout said, with a smile that seemed almost friendly. "I propose that we put the question to the library—and whichever of us *it* chooses will be deemed the blessed."

"Ah!" Now Dangerous Knowledge was smiling, too, but it was a fierce stretching of the face. The creature backed down the hillside, but grew with each step so that its eyes stayed on a level with the Greater Scooch-a-mout. Ordinarily, such a cheap visual wouldn't have earned any respect, but the move seemed to fit the moment. Besides, whoever was behind the creature's design had saved some marvelous fractal armor for just this extension of height.

Dangerous Knowledge turned to face the virtual millions behind him. "The challenge is just. I say to all Followers of Knowledge: Join me in a final torque upon the enemy. Show the Library that we are its future and its greatest supporters. And let the Library show its choice to the world!"

The silence was ended as the millions discovered new amplifiers on campus—or somehow usurped and reused the ones that the Scooch-a-mout had appropriated.

The galaxy of players—mechs and humans, real and virtual—all came alive in renewed conflict. Knights and Librarians dumped fire on the Scoochi side. Huynh's Mind Sum was once again stomping and kicking. The ensemble resumed its vasty turn about the university library, and the spiral arms of the battlefront flared even brighter than before. But now the battle cries were appeals to the Library itself. And the library glowed in a light that seemed to come from infinitely high above. That light was purely virtual, but it was seen in every view.

As Huynh tromped along with the screaming multitudes, he was almost totally taken by the moment. Almost. This had gone farther and higher than he had ever imagined. Part of the success was simply the audience, a significant part of the waking world. Part of it was the unexpected acquiescence of GenGen and the UCSD administration, and the awesome possibility of future revenue that might come streaming in from the various entertainment producers that now lurked all around. And none of that would have happened if not for the content that had suddenly appeared when they went to battle. Content from both sides, content that was as artistic as new designs and as physical as what they had done with their bottish legions.

But now everyone's hopes, Hacek and Scoochi, were hostage to the impossible. If the Library did not "reply," or if the reply was simply more imagery, then in about another thirty seconds, the momentum would begin to dissipate and a very large number of people—among them Timothy Huynh—would begin to feel a little foolish. It was the fate of many flash crowds, especially those that at first seemed the most successful. Big promises earned big rewards, up to the point that the promises had to come true.

What could the Greater Scooch-a-mout have in mind? Huynh used his technician's view and his artist's. He looked out from Scoochi cams, from the aerobots above, even GenGen utilities. The best *he* could imagine was some pallid surprise, something to distract everyone from the promise that could not be kept.

As the battlefronts tightened around the library, point and counterpoint came from the opposing armies and together made a concerted rhythm. Music seeped into the shouting. After a few moments, every local voice was synched to the sound and everyone was swaying to the beat. It came louder and louder, and Huynh noticed that the amplifiers included police and fire-department equipment. Someone had committed real vandalism to make this even more spectacular.

It would be for nothing without some definite result.

In fact, the singing held together just a few more seconds. Then it faltered as nothing more happened, and no one could imagine anything more happening. But . . . there was another sound, a trembling vibration that crept up from the ground. Ten years ago, Timothy Huynh had felt something similar. The Rose Canyon earthquake.

Huynh freaked, dropping all the fantasy overlays. He stared out in panic with his own naked eyes. Real lights flashed back and forth, flickering across the faces of the thousands of real rioters, picking out the angular bodies of the larger mechs. Now there was no pillar of light from heaven. The library was occasionally lit, but more often a silhouette against the lights on the other side.

The trembling in the earth grew stronger. The walls and overhanging floors of the library seemed to shiver. The magnificent double pyramid that had survived the decades, that had survived the Rose Canyon quake—it was shaking, all the thousands of tons of real concrete.

In time to the rising music.

There were screams. Lots of people remembered Rose Canyon. But lots of others were taken by the spectacle—and their singing resumed and was picked up by the vision of the night and blasted out across the world.

The library swayed. Parts dipped; parts rose. It was not shaking as much as it was dancing. Not a bouncy riverdance. The building was dancing like a man with feet planted firmly in the ground. And Huynh realized there was no earthquake; somebody had hijacked the building's stabilization system. He had once read that a well-powered building could survive almost any quake short of a great crack opening up beneath it. But here that power was being turned upon itself.

The rhythmic swaying became more pronounced, twelve feet left and right, and up and down, with parts of the building shifting away and together. The shrugging, swaying dance of the overhanging floors shifted to the outlying pillars. There was a sound that might have been real and might have been ingenious invention. It might have been both. It was the sound of mountains being torn from their roots.

The pillars shifted and the library . . . walked. It was not as spectacular as fake imagery could be, but Huynh was seeing it with his naked eyes. In halting cadence, first one fifty-foot pillar and then another rose visibly from the ground, moved several yards in the direction of the Greater Scooch-a-mout, and descended with the sound of rock penetrating rock. The rest of the building shifted with them, twisting on the utility core that was the library's central axis.

The Greater Scooch-a-mout stepped forward and embraced a corner of the nearest pillar. The music became triumphal. Cheering blasted across the world, wondering and still a bit frightened.

Hanson --> Night Crew: <sm>Hey is this an Event or is this an Event?</sm>

The Library had chosen.

25

YOU CAN'T ASK ALICE ANYMORE

Braun --> Mitsuri, Vaz: <sm>By damn! Homeland Security will respond to this. Has Mr. Rabbit gone mad?</sm>

Mitsuri --> Braun, Vaz: <sm>He claims his 'library dance' will only trigger FBI intervention, and all together give us more time.</sm>

Braun --> Mitsuri, Vaz: <sm>Okay then. I have the complete dump from our inspection equipment. God willing, that's everything we need to prove what's been going on in these labs.</sm>

Alfred was already working through the exit checklist. He had fooled his friends, but . . . what of his attack on Alice Gong? If she was still functioning, it might not matter what he did.

"FBI REQUESTS CLEARANCE to take charge of the riot area."

"On what grounds?" Bob Gu spoke without looking away from the library. Even the unfudged video was remarkable. This was a 1900s concrete behemoth, originally as dumb as snot. Yet it had moved without collapsing.

"The grounds are the frank evidence of violation of federal

law, namely—" A stream of legal references spewed across Bob's vision. "FBI argues that this is effectively an attack on a federal building."

Bob hesitated. There were criminal violations here, though UCSD had made no formal complaint. At this point, there was no watch-related service FBI could render; they would simply be law enforcement. The watch priority—*his* priority—was to snoop and swoop. Snoop, then swoop. What might this disorder be a cover for? He glanced at the bio-lab status. Still all green. Finally he replied, "Request denied. There is an ongoing Homeland Security investigation here. However, give the first layer of our analysis to San Diego Police and Rescue and the UCSD campus police. Be prepared to support emergency networking."

"Layer one to SDPD and campus police. Yes, sir."

Bob's eyes turned back to the library. It was still standing, but this was damn dangerous foolishness.

His analyst pool certainly thought so. In the last thirty seconds, the node structure had come close to turning inside out. For the moment, Alice let the engineers dominate. The text clouds were full of gibber about how the library "walk" had been accomplished and the dangers there might be for the people in and around it. USMC nodes were lodged deep in the discussions, his own people thoroughly caught up in the excitement. That was not acceptable.

Bob leaned forward and spoke: "All squads! Move to Launch Alert." The chances of an actual launch were still near zero, but this would get his people into their assault craft. More important, it got their attention. The USMC nodes moved away from all the speculation and into the tight coordination of marines in a launch prep. Bob stared at the distracted analyst pool for a moment more. Alice was already drawing them away from the library. The structural engineers were no longer the center of the tangle. The library had walked. So what might that be covering? His marines' duty was to guard against the deadliest grand surprises. For instance, were the bio labs still secure? What was going on in the rest of CONUS Southwest?

He turned and jogged out of his bunker, into the narrow tunnel that led to his own launcher. The analyst display followed along, hanging just to his right. Alice had grabbed another fifteen hundred analysts, more bioscience and drug research people.

The ceiling curved low at the end of the tunnel. His assault craft was a tiny vehicle, its design a compromise between time to target and the desire to make the local combat manager invisible. From the ingress tunnel all that was visible of it was the open hatch and a portion of the dead black fuselage. He settled into his place, but did not zip up.

What is Alice doing? He watched the analyst pool grow, now larger than for most worldwide operations. But all the attention was on the bioscience labs around UCSD. True, the situation there was strange. Even though lab security was in the green, the staff was topside in the riot. That justified some attention, but it also made lab surveillance even easier. *Damn!* Now Alice was stealing analysts tasked with cargo tracking throughout all of CONUS Southwest.

Squelching your top analyst was a black mark on everyone, but there was no help for it. Even in combat, this sort of monomania would be bizarre.

As it happened, Alice acted first. Emergency flags came up in every view. The assault craft's hatch slid shut and his acceleration pod zipped tight. *LAUNCH LAUNCH LAUNCH* flashed in his eyes, and a launch clock appeared, counting down from thirty seconds. This was analyst preemption, the sort of drama that happens when analysts realize that their own forces are about to be nuked in their bunkers. Everything would go at once and sort itself out in midflight.

But the analyst pool showed no such threat.

The launch target was UCSD.

The gee pod was inflating tight around him. The countdown clock showed twenty-five seconds. He brought up a view of his top analyst. "Alice! Advise reason for launch."

Alice's eyes were wide. "It's very simple. Onset was slow, but now insight has saturated. This one is undergoing threatful integration. Neuromodulator pathway Gat77 has been subverted. Signaling cascade has too many control points for MCog analysis, but reference"—some kind of arXiv pointer—"demonstrates the progression." She frowned at him, and suddenly she was shouting: "Don't you understand? This one is failing! Conformational changes are preventing adaptive response! This one—"

Ten seconds to launch. Alice Gu's medicals were off the chart.

Eight seconds to launch. Bob overrode the launch order and relieved his top analyst: *STANDDOWN STANDDOWN STANDDOWN.* The gee pod relaxed around him. He scarcely noticed. Alice's head was down, but she was still talking, desperate. Drool spattered her blouse. And he couldn't notice that either. He promoted her second-in-analysis, a CIA spook who'd been far too passive tonight. But then what could one do when a star like Alice crashed?

The spook was trying her best. "I'll have us up in two minutes, sir."

In the meantime, Bob Gu was blinded and the watch was just a mob of bright people watching a million data feeds. One of those feeds was medical: Alice had suffered a JITT stick, the most violent and sudden of her career. Despite all her desperation to communicate, she was stuck in molecular biology.

The CIA analyst was back. "Sir, are you all right?"

"I—I'm fine." Bob considered the analyst display. The spook had hung the operation off the rest of the CONUS watches. There was close backup now. Big chunks of Alice's network were improperly connected, but the spook was healing it, forcing connections and possible correlations. Maybe she was still too heavy on UCSD. She seemed to think that Alice's last words pointed to enemy action there. Okay, after everything else tonight, that had to be followed up. "I'm fine."

○

OVER THE PAST twelve weeks, Rabbit had learned a lot; he had *grown,* you might say. Tonight it all came together. Topside, the riot was at climax—better than sex could ever be, Rabbit was sure. *I am the reality arm of the Scoochi belief circles, yeah!*

There were surprises, too. The affair had called into existence (or simply into his notice?) a creature who might be his equal. Rabbit had played both sides through the first part of the riot . . . but now Dangerous Knowledge had been taken over by something very creative, something who was having as much fun tonight as Rabbit himself. So he had millions of new affiliates, some of them as capable as a human could ever be. And he'd found a special new friend, to boot.

His riot fully outclassed the espionage hugger-mugger it was designed to protect. It was amusing that despite the carrot greens and all the other generous clues Rabbit had provided, Alfred & Co had not realized whence his powers came, or how great they were. But something told Rabbit that in the long run, what was happening underground was important too. Alfred was playing out his mysterious game down there. Now was the time Rabbit had planned to find out just what Alfred was looking for—hey, and maybe get a piece of it.

Now was the time, but Rabbit was locked out. *Damn Alfred.* The fiber link was behind Alfred's milnet. Short of tipping off DHS—and destroying the wonderful jape Rabbit had so carefully planned—Rabbit was balked. Heh! But what did Alfred's milnet talk to? Why, just a few thousand very clever Indo-European analysts! And they didn't get to be so clever by hiding in government holes. They each had their own creative lives. Rabbit hopped from Brussels to Nice, to Mumbai and Tokyo, and—natch—listened to his own inner self. Now that he needed to think about it, he saw how the tricks he had used with American security might be applied. Rabbit tweaked a thousand affiliances, and he listened to a million conversations that he really had no intention of consciously reviewing. One last piece of SHE magic, and *viola*:

Rabbit was into the milnet! He zipped down through Alfred's stealthed aerobot and . . . once again he was in Vaz's glorious command center in Pilchner Hall. Rabbit took a look at the medicals on the Orozco kid. Still alive. Ol'Alfred wasn't a monster, except when principle demanded it. What was he after? *And can I get some?*

Rabbit tiptoed down Alfred's connections into the labs. No surprise, Alfred Vaz was making good use of the devices Rabbit's little friends had planted in the GenGen area, sending oodles of data out to his colleagues in Japan and the EU. Rabbit watched quietly; one doesn't ask pointed questions when one is trying to be invisible. He captured the raw encryption, noted what was talking to what within Alfred's GenGen domain.

Even so . . . it didn't make sense. The exported data did not match what was locally observed. And then suddenly a big lightbulb went off in Rabbit's mind. Alfred was not searching for anything! He was making sure his Alliance friends did not see what was already there! *Alfred, you old devil, running your own program on American equipment and keeping it secret from everybody.* And what could be worth such secrecy and such a wild-ass cover-up? Figuring that out was still a guessing game—but Rabbit was the grand master of guessing, better than any Indo-European analyst pool, better even than Alice Gu and all *her* analysts.

Oops. Something told him Alice was in deep trouble. Rabbit had dutifully played messenger boy for Alfred's mysterious snooping on Alice. That must have been the setup for Alice's downfall. But how had he done it? Suddenly, the underground was more intriguing than ever.

The heart of Alfred's research empire was in a corner of the Molecular Biology of Cognition area. The data from everywhere else was truthful reporting on innocent proprietary research. Rabbit looked more carefully at the lies coming out of the MCog area. The phrase "animal model" leaked from gaps in the encryption. Animal model, animal model. The term usually referred to animals possessing an analog of some human condition—usually a disease to cure. Somehow, Rabbit didn't think Alfred was trying to cure anything. And there were lots of animals in the MCog area. Of course most were bugs. Gallons of fruit flies, and every itsy-bitsy one labeled and probed. Rabbit dipped into some of the local databases. It looked like Alfred was messing with YGBM, but the details were not easy to understand. Rabbit was not *always* fast. For hard problems, he was like lesser beings; he had to sleep on the question. Then in the morning, the old intuition would deliver remarkable insights.

In this case, tomorrow would be too late. Five minutes from now might be too late. Alfred's show was almost over, and with it access to the snooper nodes; heck, the gadgets would probably fry themselves. Rabbit hesitated and listened to his inner self. He had a gut feeling about this. Modern intelligence services existed to prevent terrorism. But Alfred . . . with whatever he was creating here, the dwit might proceed *beyond* Grand Terror into realms no man was meant to go.

So maybe I should just call DHS. Even without Alice Gu, they could shut down Alfred in five minutes. Rabbit gave the possibility the serious thought it deserved . . . about two seconds' worth. And then a big grin spread across his concept of face.

Rabbit was full of ideas. And there was one that had been pounding on him since the moment he'd broken into Alfred's milnet. *Besides having the greater intellect, I now have the physical advantage!* Alfred was on the scene with very low latencies, very high bit rates, and more hard data. Nevertheless, he was stuck in his little room and all but one of his mechs were topside. But the "Elder Cabal" was still down in the labs. True, they were not in the GenGen area, but they were still reachable at the end of a fiber link. *And hello, what's this?* The slightly-overweight-Chinese-ninja princess. She was definitely not part of the original plan, but bless her, there she was. What a strange and marvelous girl.

Back to business. He was already preparing contingency plans, contingency documents. *And if I'm very careful, very quiet, I can sneak out along the fiber, tell Robert and Winnie and Carlos and Tommie the right stories. And then I'll have my own physical hands.*

What Alfred was planning might go beyond Grand Terror. *But that same power in my hands . . . well, that could be glorious fun!*

26

HOW-TO-SURVIVE-THE-NEXT-THIRTY-MINUTES.PDF

I told you my planning would pay off! Didn't I?" Tommie Parker stood knee-deep in the remains of the library book collection. The shredda towered behind him like dirty snow, flakes as big as your hand. They had found the Librareome storage at the back of Max Huertas's cavern, just where Tommie had said. It was stored in rows of sturdy cargo containers labeled "Rescued Data." The containers had been no match for Tommie's cutter. He had flooded the floor with the contents of "A-BX." This had been most of the fifth-floor stacks. *It seems so much smaller when it's in shreds,* thought Robert.

Tommie waved at the drifts of shredded paper. "You guys ready to start with the glue? This will jam Huertas's operation up the wazoo. And where's your reporter guy? I haven't seen Sharif in a while." He went around, handing out spray cans.

Finally, he seemed to notice his pals' silence. "We don't really need Sharif, do we? I mean, we've got our own record." He lifted the laptop in its sling.

Robert looked at Carlos and Winston. Winnie gave a little shake of his head. So none of them had heard from the Mysterious Stranger. "Sure, Tommie," Robert said. "That's—"

"That will be fine, Professor Parker." Sharif's voice from Tommie's laptop. "Perhaps you could have Professor Gu act as cameraman?"

They untangled the laptop from its sling, and the voice directed Robert around to the side. The voice was very picky about where it wanted the laptop pointed, across the edge of the shredda, almost in line with their path into this vacant hall.

Then Robert noticed letters painting silently across his field of view. It was sming . . . and the letters were green.

Mysterious Stranger --> Robert: <sm>Hey, my man!</sm>

"I—"

Mysterious Stranger --> Robert: <sm>Ah, ah, ah! Be discreet. We don't want Alfred to know I've come back to help you.</sm>

Alfred? thought Robert, but he kept quiet.

No one else seemed to notice the Stranger's arrival. Tommie walked back into the drifts of paper, tossing them up in the air, squirting them with his spray can. "Is the camera getting this, Robert?"

Robert looked down at the laptop's screen. ". . . Yes."

Any other time, the effect of Tommie's aerosol glue would have been a showstopper. He threw another armful of loose shredda into the air, and sprayed a mist of glue. Where mist and paper met, the page fragments were suddenly tumbling as one. The mass drifted slowly to earth. Most of the frags never actually touched the ground, but hung permanently in the air. Tommie laughed and pushed at the hazy something. The ensemble of scattered papers rocked back and forth, like bits of fruit in invisible Jell-O.

Tommie whooped. "Try it yourselves. Just don't squirt each other." He threw another armful up, and another. Arches of paper and mist grew around him.

Robert hung back, playing cameraman.

Mysterious Stranger --> Robert: <sm>Look where Alfred has you pointing the camera. See the light? Coming out of the dark?</sm>

There was a tiny pool of light, someone running down the steps into the Huertas cavern.

It was Miri. The girl came pounding across the floor shouting, "Robert! Robert!"

Tommie and the others turned to watch, openmouthed.

Miri came around the edge of the shredda. She was gasping for breath.

Winston looked her up and down and then looked at Robert. "This is another Gu, isn't it?"

"Um, my granddaughter."

"I thought we agreed to keep this among ourselves!" Winnie's glare was as good as any high-tech messaging: *You're going to ruin this for all of us.*

But Tommie was more astounded than any of them. "How

could she get through security? The cops should be all over."

"No, no." Miri managed to speak between gasps for breath. "Must *call* police!"

The laptop had its say, too: "Pay no attention to this child. Remember why you are here."

Robert shoved the laptop at Winnie and reached for Miri. "How did you find us, kiddo?"

Her arms went around his middle. "It was Juan and me, and—" She hesitated, looked up at him with her eyes wide. Gone was her usual assurance. Horror looked out. "—somebody's using you, Robert. I think they maybe, maybe killed Juan!"

"Not so," said the laptop. "Uh—" The voice hesitated.

Mysterious Stranger --> Robert: <sm>Heh. Alfred put ForgetIt gas in your belt boxes, and now he's wondering why you're still standing.</sm>

"Gentlemen," the voice resumed, "I advise you to remember why you are *really* here."

Tommie had come out from his fountains of paper. His spray can dangled unnoticed from his fingers. He looked at Carlos and Winston and Robert. "Yes, what is it that we're supposed to remember? Why are we *really* here?"

Carlos and Winnie wouldn't look him in the eye. Carlos mumbled something in Mandarin.

"We did what we thought was right," Winston said.

Yes, each our own vision of what was right, but . . . Juan murdered? He looked back at Tommie. "We tricked you, Tommie. Someone else is behind this."

Tommie walked back to the pile, kicked aimlessly at his masterpiece. "But . . . I thought I had my touch back." He glanced at Miri and seemed to be putting together all the inconsistencies. His shoulders slumped. "Okay. I was an old idiot. Who was boosting me along, Robert?"

"I don't know."

Mysterious Stranger --> Robert: <sm>I could tell you. Maybe I will someday.</sm>

Apparently, Winnie and Carlos were not seeing the sming.

Miri's chin came up. "We've got to get word out."

And the laptop said, "It's not safe to move. Stay where you are."

Mysterious Stranger --> Robert: <sm>Actually, I would recommend the same. But right now I'm peeved with Alfred. Do what you please, my man.</sm>

Tommie Parker looked off into the emptiness of the Huertas cavern. He was shaking his spray can, almost an idle gesture. "The gear we planted in GenGen, I thought *I* made that. Me, the big genius. It could be anything . . . bombs, poison, some kind of takeover hardware. But we're at the north edge of the complex." He waved at the wall that loomed from the dimness just beyond the shredda containers. "That overlooks Sorrento Valley. There are some old entrances. We could have used them instead, except my research said the alarms would be harder to disable—but now I don't care if busting through them sets off alarms!"

"Stay where you are," said the laptop. "You are surrounded by lethal weapons!"

Something small and black sidled out of the darkness.

"I saw one of those on Gilman Drive." Miri took a step toward it. The robot turned toward her. There was a metallic click that sounded very much like a round being chambered.

"Miri—" Robert held her arm, but Tommie was coming around from the other side and the robot turned toward him.

Parker stopped about seven feet from the critter. Some of his old cockiness returned. "I'll bet it's just a network-superiority bot. Most of the payload is communications and counternode gear. It's not much use all by itself."

"There are hundreds on the floor," said the laptop. "Don't force us to act."

Miri slipped loose of Robert. "I didn't see any others," she said, moving closer to the robot.

Mysterious Stranger --> Robert: <sm>There's only the one, but</sm>

And then several things happened at once: Robert pulled Miri behind him. Tommie stepped forward in a fencer's lunge that brought his spray can within a foot of the mech. The robot flipped up like a sprung rat trap. Tommie screamed and fell forward.

Robert ran toward the robot and grabbed—hard air. The hardened froth was barely visible, but it held the robot beyond his reach. He spun the gel around, looking for some point closer to the enemy. There! He slammed the carapace into the concrete floor. Again. It was in pieces now, each still embedded in the mist. There was sound of tiny motors, whining to be free. Then Miri and Carlos were stomping on what remained. Sparks flew within the mist, and Robert felt a tingling that raised the hairs on his arms.

And then the robot was just dead composites, the pieces hanging motionless in blocks of invisible fluff.

The only sound was Tommie gasping. Winnie had rolled the little guy on his side. Tommie's face was bluish, his mouth a gaping grimace of pain.

"What happened, Tommie?"

Parker's back arched. "Bastard . . . fried . . . my pacemaker."

Carlos was on his knees. He touched Tommie's shoulder. "*Wǒmen shāsǐ le nàgè jīqìrén.* We killed the robot, Dr. Parker."

Tommie grunted acknowledgment, even as he rocked back and forth on the ground.

"We'll get you out of here, Tommie," said Blount. He looked up at Robert. "No more games."

Mysterious Stranger --> Robert: <sm>Oh, damn. Parker was such an interesting wannabe. Okay, I'll help you get him out. And if you help me after that, I can still make good on my part of the bargain. How's that?</sm>

Robert looked past the greenish letters and nodded to Winston Blount. "No more games."

Tommie still lay twisting in pain. His voice came out between spasms. "Keycard . . . in my pocket."

Mysterious Stranger --> Robert: <sm>Heh. Magical me, that ancient keycard will actually work. My little surprise present for Alfred.</sm>

The voice from the laptop—Alfred?—was silent.

Carlos looked down at where the laptop sat on the concrete floor. "We should break this. It's the eye of the enemy."

Miri walked around the antique computer. "I think if we pull the plug on that fiber, the bad guys are gone."

"Yup . . . unplugit!"

Mysterious Stranger --> Robert: <sm>Hey wait. Where do you think *I'm* coming from! So what if Alfred can still snoop? It's me you need. If you cut me off then well damn I'll have to</sm>

Miri picked up the laptop and turned it on edge. She studied the unfamiliar physical connectors for a moment, then reached down—

Mysterious Stranger --> Robert: <sm>I hate Miri.</sm>

—and popped the optical fiber out of the laptop.

For a moment they grinned at each other like idiots. Tommie squeezed out a weak laugh. "We're . . . off the leash." He gasped for a few seconds. "Gotta carry me, guys. . . . Sorry. I'll . . . show you the exit."

Winnie looked down at Tommie. "We'll get you out, Tommie. You'll be okay." He lifted Parker under the shoulders, then reached to support him under the knees. Parker didn't weigh that much, but Blount was staggering.

Robert reached out. "I can carry him, Winnie."

Blount glared back, and Robert shut up. Then Winnie's hands slipped and Tommie almost crashed to the ground. "I got him, I got him!"

Miri ran around Blount and slipped her hands under where he was holding Tommie's left arm. Winnie didn't object; maybe it was because she didn't ask. Robert took both legs and they started off along the wall. Carlos followed, carrying the cutter and what other gear might still be of use.

Nothing more followed, nothing they could see. For what it might be worth, Robert's dumb little waist box showed only utility glimmers in the empty cavern.

Tommie's breathing was a raspy wheeze. Every few paces he twisted within their grasp. "About hundred yards more. . . ." He shuddered and went limp.

"Tommie?" Winston hesitated, bringing them almost to a halt.

"Keep going . . . keep going." And then after a moment, "So our Librareome protest was . . . fraud from the beginning, huh?"

"I don't know, Tommie. I knew it was silly, but it seemed

worthwhile." Blount looked across at Robert. "I thought it would lead to something I really want."

"Me too," said Carlos, his voice faint. "In the end, Sharif-whoever got to all of us, didn't he?"

"All but Tommie."

Miri was watching the back-and-forth silently, but her eyes were wide. Well, she had earned the right to listen.

Robert said, "So what did he promise you, Winston?"

Winnie's lips pulled back from his teeth. "I sure as hell won't tell you." He hesitated and the snarl became a twisted smile. "But I bet I know what your deal-with-the-devil was." When Robert didn't reply, Blount's smile broadened and he continued, "You tried to disguise it, Gu. All the times we met in the library, and never once did you pull your old tricks. At first I just figured you were setting me up for one of your extreme traps. After I learned about Sharif, I thought maybe *you* were running *him*." Winnie laughed. "But then I began to suspect the truth. You've lost your killer edge, the way you could look inside people and see what would hurt them the most, and then do it to them. You've lost that, haven't you, Robert?"

Robert lowered his head. "Yes." The word came out softly, without anger, almost a sigh.

"And I bet you can't write poetry anymore, either."

"It's the poetry I want back, Winnie."

"Oh."

Tommie twisted in their grasp, trying to suck in breath. "Shut up . . . the north gate should be in . . . next hundred feet."

They walked in silence, eyes straining for some sign on the unmarked wall.

And now that Robert was looking, he saw something else. Not more green lettering, but a blinking icon that meant pending mail. One last message before Miri had cut the fiber link. Almost without thinking, he shifted his grip on Tommie's leg, and tapped a go-ahead on his waist box.

A pdf, by God. He hadn't seen anything like this since his teaching days. The table of contents floated in the air above him. The critic in him couldn't resist scanning down the page. The ToC was impeccably formatted, with perfect spelling (at least, if you ignored context). The bullet headers were a mish-mash of unparallel constructions and grammatical infelicities. It looked as if it had been thrown together by a gang of paraliterates in a hell of a hurry.

But what it said was . . . important:

While We are out of Touch
or
How to Survive and Prosper during the Next Thirty Minutes

by Your Friend, the Mysterious Stranger

Dedication:

To the idiots among you who cut the fiber link. Now Alfred can't see you, but I'm cut off, too. Hence, I'm breaking my stealthy cover and shipping down this bolus of bits before Miri pops the connector.

Executive Summary

[none provided]

Table of Contents

Introduction.. page iv
- How to use this document

Chapter 1, Saving Tommie Parker .... page 1
- The Huertas back door
- The keycard that should not work, but does!

Chapter 2, Your beknighted wearables........... page 3
- Not really *hecho en Paraguay,* unfortunately for you
- The knockout gas—ah, but I already told you about that
- What you can and cannot trust about these gadgets

Chapter 3, What Alfred is up to...................... page 5
- And why you really don't want Alfred to succeed

Robert looked at Miri. She was concentrating on holding up Tommie's shoulder. For the moment all her nerdly interests seemed far away. *But we need the nerd as much as ever.*

Robert --> Miri: <file type=´pdf´/> And he pushed the Stranger's file across to her.

TOMMIE DID HIS best to count Winnie's paces. But there were distractions. There was this rock concert playing in Tommie's chest, and every screech of the beat sent fire across his shoulders and down his arms. This wasn't a real heart attack. This was just his pacemaker fallen into wild chaos. The last few years, Tommie hadn't been too envious of other people's diddling medical miracles. So what if his vascular system was falling apart; the pacemaker would keep him going till classic science-fictional immortality arrived. But now all his plans for living forever were in trouble. *Count the paces. Count the paces!*

And then there would be seconds when the pain would let up, and his heart was a butterfly flutter in his chest. For a few seconds his thoughts would clear, and then he would black out. . . . They were carrying him still, though the ride was bumpy. Ol' Robert was shifting around like he had business with the box on his belt.

"Okay. Stop," he whispered. He would have shouted, but the whisper was all he had just now.

They heard him. And then he was lying on the cold, hard concrete.

Winston's voice came down from high above him. "So where is the door? . . . I see!" Sounds of Winston fumbling with the keycard. Something big slid aside and there was a wall of faint light, maybe the night sky. He felt cool breeze on his face. The sound of the freeway was like distant surf.

"No alarms," said Winston.

"Maybe . . . silent alarms?" he managed to wheeze. This exit had been such a wild-ass escape option in his original plan.

Winston was a shadow against the sky. He was tapping at his keypad. "I got 911, Tommie!" Now he was talking to someone Tommie could not hear, telling them about a man down with a heart attack.

"They're on the way, Tommie! They want your med log."

The rock concert was back, whacking a new tune in his chest. "Bet . . . med log . . . is fried." He twisted onto his elbows. There were more important things. "Tell'em about the labs, Win!"

"I told them. I just called 911 myself." That was Robert's granddaughter. Her feet were right beside his head. Now she stepped away, became a second shadow, beside Winston. She turned this way and that, the way kids do when they're playing games with their wearables. "I don't like this," she said after a moment.

"You heard the Highway Patrol, kid." Winston's voice was tight, like he was worried as hell. "They're sending a car. We just have to sit tight for a few moments."

Tommie's pacemaker was working upward to the next crescendo. Okay, give it a few seconds more and the pain would lessen—or maybe this time, his heart would break.

The girl's words floated in and out of hearing: "—is an emergency. They should airlift. And the net is screwy. I can't route to my . . . friends, not even sming. I think someone's spoofed the local nodes and—" Tommie rolled from side to side, pain blotting out the rest of the sentence.

Someone was cradling his shoulders. Carlos? "It'll be okay, Professor Parker." The voice turned away from him. "I'm having some access problems, too. But the error messages make sense. I think the library riot is soaking up too much resource."

The little girl's voice was scornful. "So much that I can't even sming?"

"How about laser direct to the freeway?" That was Robert.

The girl's shadow repeated the strange little dance. "I can't quite reach it from here." She was silent for a moment. "We're just playing into the Badguys' hands. Here. Take a look at this pdf."

Winston again: "There will *be* a car! If one doesn't show up in five minutes, we'll—we'll carry Tommie down the hill ourselves."

Tommie's heart had stopped. No, it was back in butterfly mode. He'd have a few seconds of clarity. The girl was probably right, but there was no way he was going down that hill. The others should go, see if they could get far enough to put out a real alarm. Or maybe they should go back *into* the labs and give the enemy a big surprise. Darkness was rising inside him. In a moment or two this would not be his problem. And his friends were too stupid to leave him here. Maybe he could set some of them loose.

Listen to me! But Tommie's words came out scarcely louder than a sigh: "Guys . . . we gotta split up." And then the darkness had him.

27

THE REVOCATION ATTACK

Xiu Xiang looked out from their car, at the dark hillsides. "I feel pretty useless, Lena."

"*You* feel useless?" Lena Gu shifted irritably in her wheelchair.

Their plan had been to be a mobile presence across the places where Robert was most likely to show up. Tonight they would be *on the scene* and no one could balk them. But now, all the action was elsewhere! Even the transportation was uncooperative, operating under "special event rules" in all areas near UCSD. Their car was moving as slowly as they could make it go, but in another thirty seconds it would reach the south end of this old bit of asphalt, at which point—no matter how loudly they demanded otherwise—it would turn left at the little T-intersection, away from the hillside, and take them back to the freeway. Then, if they wished, it would drive north to the Ted Williams Expressway, turn and come down here still again.

Xiu stared into the dark of the hillside. And saw nothing. "I've practiced so much, and still I can't make my contacts work right."

Lena said, "Actually, there isn't a whole lot to see here. This hillside has to be the dumbest public land near campus."

There was some real light. It silhouetted the hilltops and lit the low overcast; around the library, insanity still reigned. A few minutes earlier, Lena had guided Xiu through some of the views. Celebration, riot, whatever it was, the network stats were impressive. Now Xiu couldn't see any of it.

Okay, I confess defeat. She reached into the backpack on the floor by her feet. The pack contained her shop-class projects. She had told herself they might come in handy tonight. How, she couldn't really imagine, but the gadgets did prove that X. Xiang could still create. There was something useful there, even if it wasn't one of her gadgets. She pulled out her viewpage, sat back, and enjoyed the clunky comfort of its old-fashioned interface. What a fall from grace this was—but just now, she was too nervous for Epiphany.

Lena abruptly said, "We have more audio from Juan!"

The boy's voice was almost a whisper: "We're still in Pilchner Hall. We're waiting for Miri's grandpa to come back from the basement." Miri's voice came faintly to the microphone: "They're not doing *anything*."

"Lemme talk to Miri," said Lena.

Xiu listened to the two for a moment. They couldn't get any video, and Miri's Epiphany had suffered a 3030 error. (Xiu had looked that up; "3030" was a catchall code for a system deadlock caused by licensing conflicts.) Meantime all they had were these very occasional, very brief voice messages through Juan.

"Gotta go," whispered Juan, and the session was ended.

Lena was silent a moment, just watching the familiar dark landscape slide by. "I want to see those kids. They're needing a smart grilling. . . . Any chance the link was faked?"

"Juan is a careful boy. It would be almost impossible to fake his Epiphany's cert—"

Lena harrumphed. "And as far as I can tell that was their voices, but talking in whispers and not saying much except that everything is boringly safe."

It was strange, if the children needed stealth and a low bit rate, that they had not used silent messaging. Maybe someone thought they could fool a pair of old ladies. In fact, *with Juan's wearable, I could fake sessions like this!* She glanced at Lena. "Maybe you should call in the marines." Bob and Alice.

"Yes, but if it's a small emergency, they can't do anything more than you or I. And if it's a big emergency—well, they might have to do something awful." Lena hummed a few bars of something nervous. "And Miri says everything is fine. Just fine."

"Maybe we should call the police."

"Ha! Nowadays you don't have to call the police; they just happen to you." Lena was staring at the hillside, her fingers trembling against her lips.

The last couple of months, Lena Gu had been such a reliable source of certainty. *What if we both wimp out?* Xiu thought.

Now, that was a frightening idea. She tried to think of something really forceful to say: "Um, your ex has been 'doing nothing' for almost half an hour. Don't you think that's too long?"

Lena's head bowed, and she said softly, almost to herself, "Oh, Robert. You're up to something terribly stupid, aren't you?" She stared into the dark. "Let's give Miri five more minutes. Then we'll call 911."

"Okay." They tooled along the valley floor, slowly enough that the windows could roll down. The resinous scent of manzanita drifted in. On their left was southbound Highway 5, a lightless torrent of fast-moving vehicles, edged by the blaze of the manual lanes. On their right were steep, dark hills, violet light flickering along the ridgelines. Xiang brought up a local network view, looked back and forth between that and the physical world.

Their little automobile was speeding up again. A pleasant male voice spoke within the passenger cabin: "This portion of Valley Bottom Drive is misfunctioning. You may return after ten A.M. tomorrow."

"What? Now we can't even circle back! There has to be some override, Xiu."

Xiang shook her head. This would be their last drive through here tonight. Xiu had helped design the hardware security layer. It solved so many problems. It made the Internet a safe and workable system. Now she was its victim. . . . She thought again of the bag of tricks that sat on the floor beside her feet. She had spent the whole semester building those gadgets, her mechanical daydreams. Maybe—

"Xiu! Traffic!" Lena was pointing up the hillside.

Xiu leaned over and looked out Lena's side. She saw two spears of light that just now were turning away from them. "It looks like a car on manual," or maybe it was on automatic, but driving on unimproved roadway.

"It must be on the service road." Lena paused, and a map appeared on Xiu's view-page, showing the road they hadn't been able to get on. The road that led to Huertas's old back entrance.

The lights turned back toward them, then disappeared behind an outcropping. Xiu's view-page didn't even show a nav marker for the other vehicle.

"What are they up to?" said Lena.

Their own car was almost to the T-intersection.

"Car!" said Lena. "Turn right."

"Sorry. That's not an existing road. The only legal turn is left."

"Turn right! Turn right!"

"I'm sorry. I'll have you in safe traffic in less than five minutes. Please think about giving me an ultimate destination." Xiu bet herself that company logic had decided it was dealing with a DUI customer. If they didn't come up with something sensible, the vehicle would take them all the way back to Rainbows End.

Lena sucked in a breath. "We're so close. Wait. I got a ping response. It's from Thomas Parker's outfit. They *are* up there!" And then much louder: "Hey, car, I wanna speak to your supervisor—I mean a *human being!*"

"Certainly, twenty seconds please." Twenty seconds would put them past the T-intersection.

Lena Gu seemed to shrink down in her wheelchair. Her gaze swept back and forth between the hillside and the approaching intersection. "We've got to stop them, Xiu. I'll wager they could tell us what's going on."

"You'd come out from cover? Let You-Know-Who see you?"

"I'd lurk in the background."

But the question was moot. The intersection was just fifty yards ahead. In a few seconds they'd turn left, and be conveyed ignominiously away.

Or . . . maybe not. Xiu lifted her backpack onto the seat beside her. She picked up the curved tube with the can of diamond flakes; she had improved her first shop-class project out of all resemblance to the original transport tray. This new model was very much designed with destruction in mind; sometimes you needed to get the machines' attention. She knelt on the back-facing seat and set the tip of the cutter against the dashboard. Given Robert Gu's example, she had a good idea of what to expect.

Oops. "Lena, scrunch down!"

Lena looked at the tube in Xiu's hands. "Yes!" She laughed even as she tried to flatten herself out of Xiang's way.

Xiu pressed the start button—a real physical button!—and a

roar ripped through the cabin. Her transport tray, now a very fine accelerator, drove three thousand diamond flecks into the dashboard every second. The recoil was a soft, steady push. It was easy to keep the tip pointed. Some of the diamonds bounced up, embedding in the acoustic ceiling, but most drove straight into the dashboard. She wobbled the cutter's tip and the hole widened. Now she was drilling through drive internals.

The car slowed smoothly to a stop, parking itself just short of the intersection. "System failure," it said. "Emergency backup engaged. Please depart the vehicle and await emergency assistance."

The doors popped ajar on all sides.

"Hah!" said Lena. "I was hoping for a real crash, and you having to cut the doors open." But she was already backing out of the car.

Xiu was speechless. *Did I really do this? Timid little X. Xiang?*

Lena wheeled around to the front of the car. "We have a hill to climb," she said.

O

FOR ALFRED VAZ, there had been various pieces of good news. He had completed his fake investigation of the GenGen labs and provided Günberk's clever analysts with evidence that would eventually lead them far away. And *finally* Alice Gu had collapsed. That had come very late, but it was more spectacular than Alfred had expected; Keiko's people claimed that DHS surveillance was blinded, in chaos. That chaos was unexplained good fortune to her and Günberk. For Alfred, it could mean complete success. Give him a few more minutes and his private research program would be safe not only from Günberk and Keiko, but also from the inevitable American investigations.

And then things went very wrong:

Miri Gu had found the stooges. He had lost his one mech in the labs, and also his fiber link to the stooges. And now—

Braun --> Mitsuri, Vaz: <sm>Mr. Rabbit has penetrated our milnet.</sm>

It was a fantastic claim—and manifestly true. For the last ten minutes there had been minor comm glitches, error retry packets happening a little too often. The statistics were well below the level of reasonable suspicion. But then in a grand gesture—typical Rabbit madness—the creature had sent a two-megabyte jumbogram straight through the milnet and off the end of the fiber.

Braun --> Mitsuri, Vaz: <sm>Just before we lost the fiber, it seemed the local stooges intended on escape. How much time does that leave us?</sm>

Numerical estimates floated up for "Time till stooges can reach 911" and "Time till DHS responds." But Keiko's people had an idea:

Mitsuri --> Braun, Vaz: <sm>For the moment, DHS is distracted. I can be very crude. I can fool the stooges into believing *I'm* the local police.</sm> Such a masquerade would mean hijacking a significant part of the local net. Within the highly regulated networks of the modern world, that was about as subtle as an infantry assault. DHS was truly in disarray.

For several minutes, there was no manager-level traffic. Alfred was aware of Keiko masquerading as the California Highway Patrol. His own attention was on a number of tasks he hadn't dared try while Alice Gong was still around. Günberk's analysts were assessing how deeply Rabbit's intrusion had gone. Their conclusions were tagged a soothing green.

Braun --> Mitsuri, Vaz: <sm>I wonder what Rabbit was doing?</sm> There were much easier ways of betraying the operation than this. As far as the network analysts could tell, Rabbit had managed little more than to rattle the metaphorical doorknobs of their milnet. The psych people had their explanation: Rabbit was known for its childish ego. It simply couldn't pass up a chance to show off—hence the jumbogram. Such antics could not be taken as a sign of overall betrayal. After all, Rabbit was still doing a magnificent job with the library riot.

Some analysts had more paranoid theories. The current favorite was that Rabbit was China; that would make tonight a perfect Keystone Kops comedy, all the Great Powers chasing after each other. But there were also nightmare speculations:

Maybe Rabbit had fooled the network analysts and all the lesser paranoids. After all, the jumbogram had been sent just before the fiberlink was broken. Maybe Rabbit was a Grand Terrorist, who had used the Alliance as *its* stooge, installing its own interests within the labs, a quick conversion of the entire establishment into a death factory. And there was that UP/Ex launcher in the GenGen area, what amounted to a delivery system.

Alfred sighed to himself. In the long run, he feared Rabbit as much as the extreme paranoids did, but tonight—well, if they looked too closely, they might see Alfred's own operation lurking in the shadows. It was best to calm things down.

Vaz --> Braun, Mitsuri: <sm>I'm with the greens on this. Yes, Rabbit has exceeded our worst estimates. He has broken into our operation's milnet. But we have hard limits on his bandwidth and my people still control the changes being made. Just look at the consistency checks. Short of having physical troops on the ground there, we *own* the MCog area.</sm>

Mitsuri --> Braun, Vaz: <sm>We also have good control of the topside operation, no sign of Rabbit funny business. The important</sm> <wait-on-message-pause/>

Red doubt was hemorrhaging across the analyst pool, spreading from a statistical analysis team at Moscow-Capetown. These were the same chaps who had been consistently right about the Soybean Futures Plot. They had credibility . . . and they claimed that the views from the north side of the GenGen area were corrupt. Those were not views Alfred had subverted. For better or worse, his colleagues had discovered some *other* deception.

Now the signals and stat people in all the analyst pools had precedence. A thousand specialists, who a second ago might have been looking at a dozen other problems, were suddenly watching the same data. Computing resources shifted from a myriad drudge tasks, began correlating data from the accessible sensors in the labs. It was as if Indo-European intelligence were an immense cat suddenly come alert, listening and watching for sign of its prey.

Only one of the area cams was offline, but others were subtly misregistered. The inconsistencies were scattered all across the area that the Alliance controlled . . . but analysis made the Moscow-Capetown guess more and more a certainty. A blotch of deception was moving into the GenGen area at the speed of a fast walk.

There! A fleeting glimpse of the Gu child. The analysts pounced on the location, dredged two sets of footsteps out of the lying silence. So Rabbit did have troops on the ground.

Mitsuri --> Braun, Vaz: <sm>That damned bunny. We can't stop him. He just keeps coming and coming and *coming.*</sm>

For a moment there was no conversation. Then:

Braun --> Mitsuri, Vaz: <sm>I can stop him. I can pull the plug on Credit Suisse.</sm>

There was another long pause. Yes. Günberk's discovery that Rabbit depended on a single apex certificate authority. All power in the modern world, from flying the largest aircraft to moving bytes between components in a single processor, it all came down to the exchange of appropriate markers of trust, as enforced by the Secure Hardware Environment. And far at the top of Rabbit's operations, via billions of unknown paths, there was a single source, Credit Suisse CA. Revoking that authority would disarm Rabbit. It would likely destroy the fellow's access to his own most personal files, leaving nothing but what the creature held in his natural mind (unless Rabbit really was an AI, in which case nothing would be left). But the collateral damage would be enormous. Shutting down a top-level certificate authority was a metaphorical weapon of mass destruction. And now it was all that was left to them.

Braun --> Mitsuri, Vaz: <sm>Mr. Rabbit must be stopped. . . . I have begun the proceedings. Credit Suisse will begin issuing global revocations in fifteen seconds.</sm>

Mitsuri --> Braun, Vaz: <sm>I'm sorry, Günberk.</sm> Ten percent of the trust apparatus of Europe would slide into chaos in the next half hour. The aftershocks would rattle the world. Whatever else came out of their mission here, for Günberk Braun it was a career-ending failure.

Another kind of failure threatened Alfred Vaz. Shooting

down Rabbit had been one of his fondest hopes, but *not just now!* Alfred dipped back into the GenGen viewpoints. Downing Rabbit had eliminated all the slack from the schedule. *And I need that time for my own cover-up.* He was reduced to emergency measures: Alfred brought two more secret teams online. One would use the fruit-fly scam to divert what was left of Rabbit. The other would destroy his lab-within-a-lab, destroy Alfred's work of years. But they would also outship his secret lab's greatest prize through GenGen's UP/Ex launcher.

For Alfred Vaz, some form of success was still possible.

GU THE ELDEST and Gu the Youngest hiked southward out of the Huertas cavern. Behind them the shredda containers and the north entrance were swallowed by darkness. The light that traveled above them shone just a few yards in all directions.

"How far till we're in enemy territory?" said Robert.

Miri held a finger up to her lips. She gestured, and silent messaging paraded across his vision.

Miri --> Robert: <sm>Your pdf says they only control a small part of GenGen. But I bet they can hear a long ways. Stick with silent messaging.</sm>

Robert fumbled with the box at his belt. The keypad display helped, but typing was tedious. All the tricks that Juan had taught him were nearly useless without Epiphany.

Robert --> Miri: <sm>Ok.</sm>

Miri walked in almost perfect silence, and Robert tried to imitate her. In fact, with Winston and the others gone, things were very quiet in Huertas country. Maybe they were as alone as the Mysterious Stranger had claimed, shielded from friends and enemies alike.

Miri must have been reading as they walked. More sming appeared.

Miri --> Robert: <sm>I didn't know about "Alfred."</sm>

It was curious that she didn't wonder about the Mysterious Stranger.

He tapped a few cramped words. Robert --> Miri: <sm>Wht cn we do?</sm>

Miri --> Robert: <sm>Well, there's Mr. Smart-Aleck's list.</sm> She waved at the air, and a page of the Stranger's pdf popped into view:

Page 17

What you can do to defeat Alfred

First off, even I, your mysterious friend, am not sure exactly what Alfred is up to (but I am afire with curiosity). Here are some possibilities.

(1) To blow up the bio labs, classic straightforward terrorism. But don't you think he went to rather a lot of trouble if that's all he wants to do? It would be a gross under-employment of everyone's talent.
If this is the scam, you will be the heroes of the day, my hands in disabling those little boxes you and your friends planted—but your fame will likely be posthumous. My condolences!

(2) To sabotage some component of the labs, maybe in a way that won't become evident till much later disasters. This is almost as stupid as (1).

(3) To install (or cover) some fiendishly clever Man-in-the-Middle software that gives Alfred de facto ownership of research done in that part of lab that you, Robert, infested for him. This would be cool, and it is my personal favorite (see my discussion of fruit flies in Chapter 3). Unfortunately for Alfred, this caper is so far blown that I doubt it will survive the audits that will surely come raining down. In this case, you two can help by grabbing anything that Alfred has not yet hidden.

(4) In the failure of case (3), or perhaps as his original plan, Alfred may take advantage of your cabal's efforts and outship biologically interesting materials from the labs.

[Diagram of the pneumo tube transport system]

[Picture of GenGen's UP/Ex launcher]

> To what end? Oh, the usual terrorist possibilities—but more likely, something weird and interesting. I'm confident I can identify such activity, and you—my loyal hands—can physically prevent the loading and outshipment.

For the moment we are all in the dark about this. But once you enter the perverted GenGen area, I should be able to contact you again. Be careful, be quiet, and Watch for Me in Your Sky!

Miri's words were overwriting the text even before Robert finished reading it.

Miri --> Robert: <sm>This guy is always so modest.</sm>

Robert grinned. Then he read her message a second time. And he thought back to all his conversations with Sharif, to the mystery of True-Sharif and Stranger-Sharif and . . . SciFi-Sharif. *Oh, my God.*

Robert --> Miri: <sm>How much of sharif ws u?</sm>

She glanced up at him and for an instant her intensity was transformed into a dazzling smile. Miri --> Robert: <sm>I'm not sure. Sometimes we were all mixed together with the real Zulfi. That was almost fun, hearing what the others asked and what you answered. But way too often, I was frozen out and it was just Mr. Smart-Aleck.</sm>

Robert --> Miri: <sm>The Mysterious Stranger.</sm>

Miri --> Robert: <sm>Do you really call him that? Why?</sm>

Robert --> Miri: <sm>Yes.</sm>

Because of the magic he promised. But he didn't type that out.

Miri --> Robert: <sm>Well, I think he's nothing without us.</sm>

Everything was still dark beyond their little pool of light, but now the walls were closer. They were almost back to the sky tunnel.

Robert --> Miri: <sm>Whn will yr mom and dad gt here?</sm> Kids spying on family members and reporting to the government—that feature of tyranny is so much simpler when the family itself is mainly government agents.

Miri --> Robert: <sm>I don't know. I didn't tell them.</sm>

Where is tyranny when you need it! For a moment, Robert couldn't think of anything to say.

Robert --> Miri: <sm>But why?</sm>

Miri stopped for a second, looked up at him with that patented stubborn stare.

Miri --> Robert: <sm>Because you're my grandfather. I knew you never meant to hurt me. I knew you must be hurting inside. I knew Bob must be wrong about you. I figured that if I could help you out from a different direction, you'd get better. And you did get better, didn't you?</sm>

Robert managed a nod. Miri turned and marched on.

Miri --> Robert: <sm>But I messed up. I thought Smart-Aleck was all I had to worry about. Wherever you broke in, I thought there'd be instant alarms—and me and Juan being there might make things go better for you. Now Juan is</sm>

She hesitated, then reached out to grasp his hand.

Miri --> Robert: <sm>Juan is hurt *bad.*</sm> Her hand trapped his fingers. No matter. Robert had no sensible reply except to squeeze back.

Miri --> Robert: <sm>But Dr. Xiang is out there. She'll call for help. And Mr. Blount should be calling the real 911 by now. Meantime, it's up to you and me down here.</sm>

There were surprises in almost every one of Miri's sentences, and if he could have spoken aloud or typed freely he would have asked a hundred questions. Juan? Xiu Xiang? Miri? So many friends, doing so much to save an incompetent old fool and his fellow fools.

The ground bounced elastically against their feet. They were passing through the sky tunnel, back into GenGen territory.

28

THE ANIMAL MODEL?

Even on a slow day, thousands of certificates got revoked every hour. It was a messy process, but a necessary consequence of frauds detected, court orders executed, and credit denied. All but a handful of revocations were short cascades of denied transactions, involving a single individual and his/her immediate certificate authority, or a small company and its CA. Perhaps once a year there would be a significant cascade, usually when a large company ran into uncompromising creditors and a court order was delivered to a midlevel CA. Even more rarely, a revocation might be part of a military action, as in the fall of South Ossetia. In theory, the revocation protocols worked with arbitrarily large CAs . . . but until this night, no apex certificate authority had ever issued global revocations. And Credit Suisse was one of the ten largest CAs in the world. Most of its business was in Europe, but its certificates bound webs of unmeasured complexity all over the planet, affecting the interactions of people who might speak no European language.

Tonight all those unknowing customers would learn of their connection.

The failures spread as timeouts on certificates from intermediate CAs and—where time-critical trust was involved—as direct notifications. In Europe, airplanes and trains came smoothly to a stop, without a single accident or fatality. A billion failures were noted, and emergency services moved—with varying success—into action.

The U.S. Department of Homeland Security noticed the failures and the growing collateral damage. Analyst pools in the U.S. reached out to the other Great Powers and conferred under emergency protocols established years ago. Chinese Public Safety, the Indo-European intelligence services, the U.S. DHS—they all agreed that a category-one disaster was in progress, a really *bad* software failure or a novel terrorist attack.

In certain corners of Indo-European intelligence, understanding was more precise. Considerably more precise.

Braun --> Mitsuri, Vaz: <sm>So I have done it. Has it had any effect on Rabbit?</sm>

So far there were only small failures at UCSD, just a few certificates timing out. That was enough to make some projections: The crowds had not consciously noticed the changes, but the library riot was due for an abrupt and ignominious end. Even more than the analysts had guessed, Rabbit had been behind what they had seen tonight, and now that support was rotting away.

Down in the labs, Rabbit had been an almost invisible intruder. Confirming the *absence* of that intrusion was not easy, but Alfred's analysts had a consensus:

Vaz --> Braun, Mitsuri: <sm>Communication failures are up, but not in our core operation. Rabbit is still here, but he's losing flexiblity.</sm>

Braun --> Mitsuri, Vaz: <sm>Losing flexibility? By damn, we need more than that. What about his two agents? What are they doing?</sm>

Vaz --> Braun, Mitsuri: <sm>They've wandered out of our area.</sm> That wasn't precisely true, but the Gus and what remained of Rabbit were properly diverted. *Now I just need a few more minutes.*

RABBIT WAS UNDER pressure. He always told himself that he performed best under pressure—though usually the pressure was not so immediate, nor his opponents so powerful and humorless. Other than some of the low-ranking analysts, Rabbit didn't know anyone on the Indo-European side who could take a joke.

Rabbit looked out through a dozen cameras, everything that Alfred had suborned in the MCog area. His hands had entered the area just a few moments before; maybe that was what had panicked his enemies into their massive revocation attack. With a small and dwindling part of his attention he followed the wonderful riot around the library. Sigh. Alfred & Co had never guessed his connection with Scooch-a-mout, and yet . . . Who'd'a thunk they'd detect his affection for Credit Suisse CA? Or that the EU had such power over the certificate authority of a sovereign country? . . . Or that his own dependence was as broad as he was now discovering?

Rabbit had other apex CAs, though none so useful as Credit Suisse. They would suffice for a few more minutes. Where they didn't, he had legal programs posting appeals against the most destructive of the revocations.

Meantime, focus on the fun things: What was Alfred trying to do? Sheer destruction? Intellectual theft? Rabbit was beginning to feel mean. He had been willing to settle for a secret back door into Alfred's operation. Now, well, now he meant to steal it all. Starting with the fruit flies.

Rabbit reached out for his hands.

O

ROBERT REMEMBERED THIS area. They were back in the heart of GenGen country, the unending rows of gray cabinets, the crystal forests that connected them, the pneumo tubes. But up ahead was a sound like cardboard boxes being crushed.

The Stranger's pdf had explanations for the abbreviations that were printed on the sides of the cabinets:

Dros MCog

Robert --> Miri: <sm>Fruit flies?</sm> This was where he had set down almost a third of the little boxes, having to crawl over above and between the cabinets.

Miri --> Robert: <sm>Yes. Did you read what Smart-Aleck claims about this? I don't believe it.</sm>

"Hey, hey, my man!" And there was the Mysterious Stranger, Miri's Mr. Smart-Aleck. His skin was practically glowing green, even in the shadows. The face was Sharif's but the smile was inhumanly wide. "Talk as you please. Alfred discovered us here several minutes ago." The Stranger looked around, as if expecting a visible enemy. "So now I don't care if he hears you. Or me! What can you do, Alfred? You're shutting me down, but I wager I'll last another minute or two. Oh, I suppose you could shut down your own operation, too. I'd be instantly gone then." He glanced back at Miri and Robert, and continued sotto voce. "If he does that, he's truly desperate. And it won't help him a bit, since you still have my pdf. *You'll* still be here to destroy his underhanded plans."

The Mysterious Stranger waved for them to follow. "Did you get to this part of my explanation?" He waved at the cabinets. "Molecular Biology of Cognition. MCog. And Alfred's people have created the ideal animal model for their research."

"Fruit flies?" said Robert.

"I don't believe it," said Miri. "Fruit flies can't think. What could your 'Alfred'—or you—do with them?"

The Stranger gave out one of its dismissive laughs, and Robert noticed Miri's face jerk up. She might do better with this manipulator than Robert. After all, she wasn't desperate for his help.

"Ah, Miri, you read but you don't understand. If you had access just now to the wider net—and a few hundred hours of research—perhaps you'd understand that molecular biology depends more on data depth and analysis than it does on the particular class of organism. In his *Drosophila melanogaster alfredii*—is that what you call them, Alfred?—we have the metabolic pathways that are the basis for all animal cognition."

Minus the editorial comments, this did look like some of the pdf.

They rounded a corner and saw the source of the sounds.

"*Viola,* Alfred's three hundred thousand fruit flies, now being folded into convenient shipping cartridges." The Stranger's face and body bore less and less resemblance to the original Sharif. "But I must confess—I know what these little bugs are, but I don't really know what Alfred has planned for them. Surely there are some marvelous diseases—cognitive diseases?—that might come out of such research. Or maybe he wants to get a head start on all the enhancement-drug people. Or maybe he's into YGBM. But I do know—"

The fruit-fly arrays were being folded on a large transport table, much bigger than anything in Ron Williams's shop class. The shipping cylinders rolled across the table, right through the

Stranger's body. The creature noticed this a half second late, but did a creditable hop back from the table.

"But I do know that he's trying to ship them off-site."

"So you claim."

"Hey, trust me, Miss Miri. You've *met* Alfred. He's the fellow who tried to kill Juan Orozco. The guy's an evil loon. Ping the labels on these packages if you don't believe me."

Yes. UP/Ex labels with an encrypted destination. The first of the cylinders was sliding off the table, headed toward the nearest pneumo tube.

Now the Stranger was hopping from one foot to the other. "Only you can save mankind! Just knock the cylinders onto the lower tray. Don't let Alfred win!"

That seemed to convince Miri. She rushed to the table, grabbed the package out of the pneumo tube lock, and tossed it to Robert. He caught it and the next and the next and now his arms were full. The white cylinders were as light as foam.

The Stranger's image froze for a second. Abruptly, animation returned. "Heh! Excellently done." He waved vaguely at the walls. "See that, Alfred? It doesn't pay to cross the Rabbit!" *Rabbit?* The creature turned back in their general direction; by God, it did look a little bit like a rabbit. "That was a near thing, but I won! I mean, we saved mankind." It drew itself up, but its whole body was tilted. "Damn Alfred. He is shutting me down a piece at time. Maybe I should exit with my impression of the Wicked Witch of the West. Dying, that is."

The creature spun around, giving out melodramatic moans, its body dissolving around it. It hesitated, and said offhandedly to Robert, "Oh, don't let the cylinders go untreated. Just drop them onto the lower tray."

Robert didn't move.

"I mean it!" said the Stranger, something like a serious tone creeping into its voice. It flailed about—more dramatic dying, or looking for an explanation? "If the bugs are disease vectors, you're at ground zero! The lower tray will send them to an incinerator, all safe and tidy."

Miri shook her head. "No. That's an alternate path to the UP/Ex launcher."

"Look at my pdf, you fool. The map."

"I looked at *my* map, the one I cached this afternoon." Miri's smile was triumphant.

There was a two-second lag. Then the creature turned and looked almost straight at Miri. "I hate you, Miri Gu. You evil thing. Everything was going so well till you started meddling. I'll get you for this."

Then it was shouting. "Meantime, I'm gonna get *you,* Alfred. If I'm out of action, so are you! I'm blowing the whistle on you. I'm—"

The figure stopped moving. There was a moment of silence; then Robert heard a single word, faint and faraway: ". . . help."

The creature vanished. Robert and Miri stared at each other. It was just the two of them, and the ranks of cabinets.

"Do you think he's *really* gone, Miri?"

"I . . . don't know."

Miri --> Robert: <sm>But if Smart-Aleck wasn't lying about everything, then this Alfred guy *is* still around.</sm> Aloud, her words were timid. "Maybe we should stay here and wait for the police."

"Okay."

Miri plunked herself down on the floor. She was very quiet for a moment, both publicly and privately. Robert set the packages down and stared off into the dark, looking this way and that. Supposedly there were no more enemy robots. What could "Alfred" do with the fruit flies now? What could the fellow do to Miri and Robert himself?

Miri --> Robert: <sm>Things don't sound the same.</sm>

Robert looked a question at her. Miri drew a golden arrow at right angles to the corridor they had arrived from.

Miri --> Robert: <sm>I kept track of everything I heard when I was following you. There's something new going on, most likely in the mouse arrays. Did you do anything over that way?</sm> She quietly came back to her feet.

Robert tapped at his keypad:

Robert --> Miri: <sm>Thts whr we put most of our eqt.</sm>

Miri's chin came up.

Miri --> Robert: <sm>The sounds are like what we heard *here.* Someone's packaging another shipment out.</sm>

29

DR. XIANG TAKES CHARGE

Günberk and Keiko and Alfred each had their own analyst pools. Ten seconds ago those analysts had agreed: As an active threat, Rabbit was gone, both topside and in the operation's milnet. Dissent clusters hung around the opinion, but they were related to collateral-damage prediction.

Braun --> Mitsuri, Vaz: <sm>God willing, we've stopped the monster.</sm>

Mitsuri --> Braun, Vaz: <sm>And we have the inspection data we came for. Now it's time to get the hell out!</sm> She brought up a zoomed picture of the contingency tree. They were way out on a limb that led to full loss of deniability. And yet, until they knew for sure the results of their investigation, they needed the Americans kept ignorant.

Alfred presented his latest extraction schedule, the times padded just enough to cover his outshipment activities.

Mitsuri --> Braun, Vaz: <sm>Eight minutes! That much?</sm> Keiko still had things covered on the north side of the labs. And the views of the riot showed the Bollywood team still in place by the library . . . but that affair was descending into civil disorder, the sort of thing that brings a direct police response. Meshing Alfred back into the Bollywood people should be easy now; very soon it would be impossible.

Vaz --> Braun, Mitsuri: <sm>I'll trim every second I can, Keiko.</sm>

Mitsuri --> Braun, Vaz: <sm>You'd better! Five minutes is the most I can guarantee.</sm>

Alfred smiled at Keiko's impolitely constrained panic. She and Günberk would do their best. And in some ways, this chaos was helpful. Fooling Günberk and Keiko had always been Alfred's biggest problem. His outshipment would've been impossible if they weren't so distracted.

Two minutes passed. Three. His secret team had completed

most of the fakery. They had updated the logs to satisfy both Alliance and future U.S. investigators. Now they were working with one small section of the *Mus musculus* arrays, his true animal model. Alfred hopped from viewpoint to viewpoint, swooping over cabinets that looked like office blocks in some bland, utilitarian city. He couldn't take more than a few of the mice, just a few of those conceived since the last update. His team had already shut down the in-progress experiments and started destruct operations. Now they detached the chosen arrays and began prepping them for launch. Other members of the team were already sending shipping cartridges to the pneumo port atop the cabinet. He could fit one twenty-by-thirty array—six hundred mice—into each cartridge.

Mitsuri --> Braun, Vaz: <sm>Alfred! The public net is failing.</sm>

Vaz swore and glanced at the topside analysis. This wasn't even close to Keiko's deadline.

Braun --> Mitsuri, Vaz: <sm>It's a full system failure. Mr. Rabbit has screwed us.</sm>

The analysts were boiling with contrary opinions. Failures like this happened a couple of times a year somewhere in the world, the price that civilization paid for complexity. But here there was a more sinister suspicion, that *this* failure was collateral damage from the revocation. Maybe Rabbit's riot magic depended on his commandeering the embedded computer systems of the public environment. Now that his certificates were revoked, there was a cascade of failures working through almost everything, just as fast as the certificates failed.

Mitsuri --> Braun, Vaz: <sm>Alfred! Clean up and get out!</sm>

The second and third cartridges would be ready in a moment. Alfred glanced at the UP/Ex status. The launcher was close to the MCog area. Most important, it was locally managed, unaffected by the crash outside. He entered a destination in Guatemala—and selected a launch vehicle that he'd emplaced some weeks before. It ought to be stealthy enough to get out of U.S. airspace.

Vaz --> Braun, Mitsuri: <sm>One minute. Can you give me that?</sm>

Mitsuri --> Braun, Vaz: <sm>I will try.</sm>

The topside analysts were hard into contingency planning and probability estimates. A thousand little changes were being made across the UCSD landscape, wherever the Indo-European operation had influence. The Bollywood presence would survive as long as any up there.

Alfred forced his attention back into the labs. The second cartridge was loading. The first cartridge was shooting down the pneumo, taking its little passengers to the launcher.

Alfred froze. The Gus were gone from the fruit-fly area. There was movement in another window, at the edge of the mice arrays. A girl and a man running toward the camera. They hadn't been fooled by the fruit flies.

Alfred leaned forward. Okay. One minute. What could his people cook up in that time?

LENA'S WHEELCHAIR WAS no hiking machine. It did well enough on the asphalt, even going uphill; Xiu had to trot to keep up. But where the asphalt was carved by gullies, the chair had to walk. The going got very slow.

"Can you even see the road, Lena?" Her view-page was as dark as the natural view.

"No. I think someone has turned off the hillside. Side effect of the riot, maybe." She moved to the middle of the road. "Sst! They're still coming." She waved at Xiu to come forward. "How can we stop them? One way or another, we have to find out what's happening."

"Robert will see you."

"Damnation!" Lena dithered, caught in a dilemma.

"Go back to the side of the road. I can stop them more safely, anyway."

"Hmph," said Lena. But she retreated.

Xiu stood still for a moment. There were the distant sounds of the freeway. From over the hilltop there were noises that might have been chanting. But nearby were just insect sounds, the feel of air cooling in the night, the narrow roadway jumbled and rocky under her feet. She saw light sweep across the outcroppings above her.

"I can hear them, Xiu."

Xiu could, too, the crunch of tires and now the faint whine of electric motors. The mystery car came around a last, unseen bend in the road, and she tensed to dive out of the way.

But on this road, cars could not speed. Its headlights slowly bore down on her. "Make way, make way." The words were loud, and the view-page in her hand came alight with flashing warnings about the penalties for interfering with the California Highway Patrol.

Xiu started to give way, and then she thought, *But it's the CHP I want to talk to.*

She waved for the car to stop. The vehicle slowed still more, then turned and tried to edge past her on the left. "Make way, make way."

"No!" she shouted and hopped back in front of it. "You stop!"

The car moved even more slowly. "Make way, make way." And it tried to pass her on the other side. Xiu jumped in the way again, this time flailing her backpack as though it could do some damage.

The auto backed up a yard or two, and turned slyly as if preparing an end run. Xiu wondered if she really wanted to jump in front of what happened next.

WITH EVERY HEARTBEAT, pain spiked through Tommie. After a moment he realized that was *good* news. He raised his head, saw that he was stretched out on the backseat of a passenger car. That was Winston and Carlos in the facing seats.

"Where's Robert and his little girl?"

Winston Blount shook his head. "They stayed behind."

"We split up, Professor Parker."

Scary memories were coming back. "Oh . . . yeah. Where's my laptop? We gotta call 911."

"We called, Tommie. Everything's okay now, this is a CHP vehicle."

Despite his haziness, that didn't make sense. "It sure doesn't look like one."

"It's got all the insignia, Tommie," but there was dawning uncertainty in Winston's voice.

Tommie slid his legs from the seat and pushed himself into a half-sitting position. The pain squeezed tight on his chest, clawed out along his arms. He almost blacked out again, and would have fallen forward if not for Carlos.

"Hold . . . hold me up!" Tommie looked forward. The car's headlights were on. The road was steep and narrow, with scattered remnants of asphalt surfacing, the sort of thing you might see in the East County, or in short stretches along the coast, a disconnected remnant of lost roadway. They slowed, negotiating deeply shadowed gullies. Bushes swept close around them. And now ahead he saw someone standing in the middle of the road. The car slowed to a crawl just five yards short of—it was a young woman.

"Make way, make way." Their car said over and over, trying to get by on one side and then the other.

The woman hopped from side to side, blocking them. She was shouting, and swinging a good-sized backpack at them.

Their car backed up a few feet, and Tommie heard the faint squeal of a capacitor preparing for something drastic. The wheels turned a few degrees—and the woman jumped in front of them again. Her face was bright in the headlights. It was a pretty Asian face . . . if you added thirty years to it, you got the face from some very distasteful turn-of-the-century papers in *Secure Computing*. She was the last person he'd ever expect to play "block the tanks at Tiananmen Square."

The headlights went out. The car jolted forward. Then the brakes engaged and they slid halfway into the ditch. There was a muffled explosion that might have been that capacitor slagging itself. The doors on both sides of the vehicle popped open and Tommie slid partway into the cool night air.

"You okay, Professor Parker?" That was Carlos's voice, coming from close behind his head.

"Not dead yet." He heard footsteps on the roadway. A light flared in a small hand, and the woman said loudly, "It's Winston Blount and Carlos Rivera—" and then more conversationally,

"—and Thomas Parker. Y-You probably don't know me, Dr. Parker, but I have admired your work."

Tommie didn't know what to say to that.

"Let us pass," said Winston. "This is an emergency."

He was interrupted by the sound of wheels—but not from another car. A voice spoke from the darkness: "Where's Miri? Where's Robert?"

Carlos said, "They're still inside. They're trying to stop the—We're afraid that someone is taking over the labs."

Motors whined. It was a wheelchair, carrying someone all hunched over. But the voice was strong and irritated. "Damn it. Lab security would prevent that."

"Maybe not." Winnie sounded like he was chewing on broken glass. "We think that someone has . . . subverted security. We called 911. That's what you're interfering with." He waved at their car. It was halfway into the ditch, unmoving.

Tommie looked at the darkened passenger car. "No," he said. "That's a fake. Please. You call 911."

The wheelchair rolled nearer. "I'm trying to! But we're in some kind of a deadzone. We should go down the hill, find something we can latch on to."

"Duì!" said Carlos. He was staring all around, the way kids do when their contacts fail.

The redoubtable Dr. Xiang waved her little handlight, light and shade sweeping up around her. Strange. There was a kind of hesitancy about her. X. Xiang was one of the true Bad Guys of the present era, at least one of the people who had made the Bad Guy regimes possible. You could never tell it by looking at her. She doused the light, and stood silently for a moment. "I-I don't think we're in a local deadzone."

"Sure it is!" said Winnie. "I'm wearing, and I can't see a thing except the real view. We have to get to the freeway, or at least get a line of sight on it."

And now Tommie remembered what Gu's granddaughter had said. Maybe the local nodes were being spoofed. Xiang had another theory:

"I mean the deadzone is not just here. Listen."

"I don't hear a thing—oh."

There were little sounds, insects maybe. There was faint

shouting from over the hills. Okay, that must be the belief-circle diversion. What else? The freeway sounded . . . strange, not the constant, throbbing surf of wheels on road. Now there was only the faintest sound, a dying sigh. Tommie had never heard such a thing, but he knew how stuff worked. "Failure shutdown," he said.

"Everything? *Stopped?*" said Carlos, horror climbing up into his voice.

"Yup!" Tommie's chest pain beat toward a crescendo. *But hey, let me live long enough to learn what's going on!*

The voice from the wheelchair said, "Even if we can't get word out, someone will notice."

"Maybe not," Tommie gasped out. If the blackout was large and spotty, with the appearance of natural disaster—why, it might cover something really big going on underground.

"And there's nothing we can do to help," said Winston.

"Maybe not." Xiang's words echoed Tommie's, but her voice was thoughtful, distant. She flicked her light at the backpack. "I've had a lot of fun in shop class. You can make so many interesting things now."

Tommie managed, "Yeah. And they all obey the law."

X. Xiang's laugh was soft. "That fact can be used against itself, especially if the parts don't know the big picture."

A lot of Tommie's old friends talked that way; it was mostly idle talk. But this was X. Xiang.

She pulled out a clunky-looking gadget. It looked like an old-time coffee can, open at one end. She held the coffee can where it could see her view-page. "Lots of gadgets are still working, they just can't find enough nodes to get a route out. But there's a big military base just north of here."

From the wheelchair: "Camp Pendleton is about thirty miles thataway." Maybe the speaker gestured, but Tommie couldn't see.

Xiang scanned her coffee can across the starless sky.

"This is crazy," said Winston. "How can you know there are nodes in your line of sight?"

"I don't. I'm going to shine signals off the sky haze. I'm calling in the marines." And then she was talking to her view-page.

BOB GU AND his marines logged more time in training systems than they ever did in combat or on watch. Training managers were legendary for creating impossible emergencies—and then topping them with something even more unbelievable.

Tonight the real world was outdoing the craziest of the trainers.

Alice had been moved to Intensive Care. Bob would have gone with her—except that whatever had taken her down was enemy action, and not the end of it.

The analyst display had sprouted new nodes and a dozen long-shot associations: Credit Suisse CA had just collapsed, a major disaster for Europe. The certificate revocations would have effects even in California. Bob took a closer look. The Credit Suisse collapse was so abrupt that it had to be a sophisticated attack. *So what was a distraction from what?*

The DoD/DHS combined Earth Watch was involved now. Tonight's action could be something new, a Grand Terror that ran simultaneously through the U.S.A. and the Indo-European Alliance, profiting from the gaps created by national sovereignties. Looking at the analysis above him, Bob could see only the broadest outlines, but it was evident that the intelligence agencies of the U.S.A., the Alliance, and China were collaborating to hunt down the source of the threat.

In CONUS Southwest, his new top analyst was doing her best. His analyst pool was still crippled, but folks were talking productively. Their structures of conjecture and conclusion were growing. The new top analyst took voice: "Colonel, the revocation storm is very intense at UCSD."

The traffic display showed that the demonstration around the library had ground to a halt. The new failures were not due to backbone router saturation. Participants were being decertified by the thousands. Millions of support programs were balked. If nothing else, this showed that massive foreign involvement in tonight's festivities had not been some analyst pipe dream. Whatever had hit Europe was intimately involved here.

But the bio labs still showed green. Even the participation of the night crews in the library demonstrations had worked out for the best. Maybe productivity and performance would be down for this shift, but that was a commercial issue. In fact, the departure of the human crews had simplified the lab situation. There was nothing there but automation—and it showed all was well.

"FBI again requests clearance to take over."

Bob shook his head irritably. "Denied. As before."

Hmm. More than riot participants were being decertified. Three analysts from the Southern California utilities reported infrastructure failures in the campus area. Why would local infrastructure depend on certs from Credit Suisse?

"Correlation of systems failures with the revocation storm is ninety-five percent, Colonel."

No kidding. Even if the labs were clean, there was some kind of deadly interference here. Bob tapped the command he had been contemplating these last few minutes:

LAUNCH ALERT

"Analysts update contingency nine and give me a launch mark," he said.

There was a pause as the request was reviewed by the DoD/DHS combined Earth Watch. His CONUS Southwest watch was on a very short leash since Alice's breakdown:

But clearance came back in just five seconds.

Bob scarcely noticed his gee pod inflate. He would be the last out of the barn, so there was a lot to watch.

LAUNCH LAUNCH LAUNCH

"Uncrewed vehicles launched."

His displays showed thirty canisters of combat network-munitions shot high into the Southern California night. The uncrews were from the north side of the base, twenty kilometers away. Farther north, from MCAS Edwards, more primitive weapons rose into the heavens. Their manifest was a catalog of extreme possibilities: rescue lances (500), damage-suppression fogs (100), HEIR lasers (10), thermal flechettes/isolation variant (100) . . . and then the last three, the nightmares—sterilization-fog dispensers (10 by 10), HERF area munitions

(20 by 20 by 4), strategic nuclear munitions (10 by 10 by 2). *Analysts are paid to think worst-case . . . but Lord.* The bio labs were the only excuse for these items.

But in truth—if you discounted the absence of follow-up equipment—this was a fairly conventional load for a modern expeditionary force. Three times in Bob's career, such launches had ended in real combat. But those had been half a world away, in Almaty, in Ciudad General Ortiz, and in Asunción. The most terrible weapons had never been used, though Asunción had been a very near thing.

Tonight he was aiming all this hardware at his own neighbors, just thirty miles south of Camp Pendleton. Full force in an urban area was like going after rats in your kitchen with a machine gun. *Keep your head down, Miri.*

"FBI again requests clearance to take over."

"Denied. The situation has escalated." For the moment, hopefully just for the moment. If police and rescue could bring the system back up, then all the hardware that Bob had just boosted over Southern California would simply be an expensive exercise. But one good thing about being locked and loaded was that he had lots more call on resources: Gu grabbed analyst teams from all across the national workshift and pushed the intel and sensor backlog at them. Priority questions: Are the San Diego labs secure? What is the prognosis for the current system failures?

Meantime, Bob's launches had soared to the top of their trajectories. He tweaked the Edwards munitions still higher, delaying them behind the gear from Pendleton. If nothing was resolved soon, he would have to light the uncrews' jets. *I need answers, guys!*

But the analyst mob was still busy connecting a billion dots, looking for patterns and conspiracies. Then a single observation changed everything. A weather-service geek doing her monthly reserve duty grabbed a very high priority: "Twenty seconds ago. I see ad hoc signaling in the backscatter above *here*"—and she drew an ellipse over San Diego North County, covering much of Camp Pendleton. Somebody was making their own communications, simply blinking a light into the sky haze! The long axis of the scatter ellipse pointed right back toward UCSD. The words of the intercepted message streamed across Bob's vision:

Xiu Xiang --> anyone clever enough to notice me in the backscatter: <sm>GenGen laboratory automation has been corrupted. The system is attacking anyone opposing it. This is not a game. This is not a joke. What? Yes, I'll tell them. There are two people still in the labs. They are good guys! They are trying to help.</sm>

The NOAA analyst spoke over the script display: "The message is a one-second burst, retransmitted twelve times. What you're seeing is the summed cleanup."

It was clear enough. Bob Gu's fingers tapped in their gloves, launching his marines.

Then his own gee pod came tight and—

—for a moment Bob Gu was not paying attention. For a moment he *could not* pay attention. Battle commit put the combat CO himself into the fray. In this case, launch took his landing dart almost horizontally out of Pendleton. *Maybe this is not a good idea,* he thought muzzily. But he always thought that coming out of a twenty-gee railgun launch.

Now he had to recollect his wits and context. His team and equipment were on schedule. The unthinkable Last Resorts were still high overhead, flexible to the last. The network munitions were already at UCSD. And the bio labs *still* showed green, all secure and peaceful.

His own landing dart was seconds away from the UCSD.

There was something else that was important, something in the last few seconds. Xiu Xiang? Bob's recollection came unsquished just as a DHS analyst team presented its own form of the insight: Xiu Xiang. A not uncommon name. But in all of Southern California there probably weren't more than three or four who owned that name. And one lived at Rainbows End with Lena Gu.

Suddenly he had a good idea just who was in the crosshairs of all that he commanded.

30

WHEN THE NETWORK STOPS

The Library had chosen.

For an instant, Timothy Huynh and all the night crew were silent. The crowds of real humans were quiet, and even the millions of virtuals took part in a coordinated stillness.

The Library had chosen—and it had chosen the Scoochis.

On the Hacek side you could see the realization of defeat spreading. The triumph was real. How would the Hacekeans take it? There had been a few debacles in the late teens, when major belief structures had produced some awful art. Some were so bad that the circles themselves had shriveled and died. Who heard of Tines anymore, or the Zones of Thought? But tonight the Hacekeans had lost at the hands of others; they must do *something* . . . maybe even something gracious.

The silent stillness of the mob continued a second more. Then Dangerous Knowledge suddenly turned away from the library. Its gaze swept fiercely across them all. After all, playing loser wasn't in its repertoire. But whoever was behind all the creativity was flexible: After a moment, Dangerous smiled gently and turned back to the library. Its voice made concession sound like the granting of a favor: "We bow to the wishes of the Library. Here you have won, O Scooch-a-mout."

Wails arose from the Hacek side, but Dangerous raised a hand and continued. "We give up our claims here. We remain as guests only."

Sheila --> Night Crew: <sm>The Hacek people are in heavy discussion with the university administration. They're begging for whatever scraps they can get.</sm>

And the Greater Scooch-a-mout was conciliatory in victory, though it didn't step away from its embrace of the library. "You are welcome as guests, in a library with *real* books."

Hanson --> Night Crew: <sm>Admin is squealing about that, but the publicity should pay for extra floor space. We've won, gang!</sm>

For some minutes, everything was cool. Ending a riot without a police confrontation or a physical debacle was a little bit anticlimactic, but the riot designers had even more special effects to wind things down. Katie Rosenbaum gathered the spider bots all together, then sent them out to Huynh's mechs for a bizarre "peace dance"—that incidentally cleaned up most of the night's garbage. Tim sensed negotiations going on between the two sides, things being traded, promises made. Dangerous Knowledge retreated into the sky, and both sides played with special effects that were new on this night.

But now, when things should have been getting smoother, there were network problems. Here and there, service was unusably slow or all jittery. It made everyone look bad. Scooch-a-mout still stood by the library, embracing the pillar that had "walked." You hold a heroic gesture that long and you just look stupid. Huynh looked at his mech status board. There hadn't been a Scoochi update for almost seven seconds. That was no way to drive a mech.

Huynh --> Hanson: <sm>Hey, Sheila. Who's driving the Greater Scooch-a-mout?</sm>

Hanson --> Huynh: <sm>Dunno. He was good, but now he's dropped the ball. It's okay, we're winding down now. Just take control and walk the robot out. No need to look cool.</sm> Then she was messaging the whole night crew, trying to tidy up and get all her GenGen people and gear back where they belonged.

Huynh drove his forklift toward the Greater Scooch-a-mout mech. He walked along behind and tried to figure some nice way to get the two off the field. His robot's "Mind Sum" mists weren't matching its movements anymore; they looked like crap. Okay. He'd take control of the Greater Scooch-a-mout, and have the two robots give a last high five, and then rumble out together. That would be cool, if not fully so.

Maybe it didn't matter. The network problems were getting a *lot* worse. There were strange latencies, maybe real partitions. Blocks of the virtual audience were being run on cache. Single-hop still mostly worked, but routed communication was in trouble. Huynh stepped a few feet to the side and managed to find a good diagnostic source. There were certificate failures at the lowest levels. He had *never* seen that before.

Even the localizer mesh was failing.

Like the holes in threadbare carpet, splotches of plain reality grew around him, eating out the mists and crowds, revealing the armies of everyday lab mechs. Where there had been hundreds of thousands of players, now there were open stretches of dark lawn, and the crowds of real humans, standing in shock.

"Tim! Your forklift!" The shout was real sound, from Sheila Hanson, just a few feet away.

Huynh turned back toward the library. He had lost contact with Mind Sum! He ran toward the mech. The forklift had continued autonomously for just a couple of steps. But this was not a flat lab floor, and the localizer mesh was failing around it. The robot had tripped on one of the ornamental boulders that fringed the terrace. It teetered off-balance, shrieking location queries in all directions. But now the mesh was gone, and the forklift was in trouble. Its onboard systems were designed to cope with instability: the failure mode consisted of stepping quickly into the fall, lowering its center of gravity, and dropping stability limbs. That would have worked down in the clean environment of the labs. Here, its lunge took it to the edge of the north-side grade—and there was no localizer mesh to alert it to the drop. The stability limb settled into thin air, and the forklift tipped over the edge.

There were screams.

Huynh ran out onto the robot battlefield. All the epic imagery was gone, but the robots still had local coordination. They rolled out of his way. He scarcely noticed. All his attention was on his forklift. He had direct contact now. He surfed across the forklift's cameras . . . and felt sick. There was someone pinned underneath. He climbed down the hillside and fell to his knees. The woman was trapped there, still screaming. Her leg, up to above the knee, was crushed by forklift composite.

Someone scrambled down beside him. Sheila. She wriggled under the blades of the forklift, reached down to grasp the woman's hand. "We'll get you out. Don't worry. We'll get you out."

"Yes!" said Tim. He had full control now. Between his own vision and the cameras, he could see how it had fallen, and where the woman was pinned. *Be cool and everything will be okay.* The forklift put its weight on knees that didn't touch the woman. There was solid support, no surprises. From under the blades he could hear Sheila comforting the woman.

Okay, just shift the weight back, push off into a low sitting posture. Easy . . .

But now there were other screams, and the sounds of people running.

Smale --> Huynh: <sm>Help us, Tim!</sm>

Huynh glanced through a camera on the other end of the forklift: The robot that had been the Greater Scooch-a-mout was still standing by the library, but now its center of gravity was absurdly high and someone had overridden all its safeties, to *push* against the nearest pillar. The mech's foot pads were grinding into the concrete cladding of the terrace. There was the sound of motors on emergency burn, but in an off/on/off rhythm that sounded almost musical. The robot looked like a child trying to prop up a teetering bookcase.

Huynh turned the camera to look up and up . . . at the sixth-floor overhang, almost directly overhead. There were gaps in the concrete, and places where the floors tilted and swayed. It was a building that had the smarts to stabilize itself, even to move a little. But now that intelligence was cut off from location information. Like Timothy Huynh's forklift, the library was doing its best to remain standing . . . and on its own vast scale, it was failing.

31

BOB CONTEMPLATES NUCLEAR CARPET-BOMBING

Bob coasted across the UCSD campus, his landing dart now as slow and quiet as the network munitions that were raining out of the sky. This was a classic network-superiority assault, absent significant defenses. There were many many things to do and only seconds to do them, but for these few moments he had a paradoxical sense of security. There weren't many places in the modern world where a human could be as self-sufficient—if only temporarily—as when in command of such an assault. Bob Gu's expeditionary group had its own network, its own power supplies, its own sensors. Even if all his remote analysts were to disappear, his marines would still be in business.

At the moment, thousands of assault nodes were nestling into trees and bushes, fastening themselves to vehicles and ledges and the sides of buildings. Even before they touched down, they asserted primacy over what civilian network hardware still functioned. That takeover was almost complete. He already had access to almost all the embedded controllers in the area. In combat, those local systems were often unsalvageable. Here, there were a few seconds of intense interrogation, DHS authority was asserted, and he had control. The cars and wearables, the medicals, the viewpoints and financials and police systems, they were all responding. Police and rescue workers were reconnecting via the combat net. Already he could hear their voices picking up the operation. With just a little luck, there would be no loss of life, just a very bad and strange network outage. He would leave the combat net in place, just as in a foreign operation. Over the coming days it would be replaced—not by administrative forces but by the gradual reassertion of the civil system.

None of that was really important. "The labs. Have they responded?"

"Yes, sir," came Patrick Westin's reply. He was on the ground with the first squad, near the GenGen main entrance. "We have access to the labs' backup security. It's agreeing with the primary, claims the underground is secure, no sign of perver—"

Civilian status alarm: *Building Failure.* The letters streamed across a corner of Bob's view. The university library was going down. In combat bad things happen, but tonight the cause looked like stupidity plus bad luck—first the rioters making their library "dance," then network outage destroying its smarts. Whatever the reason, people would end up just as dead.

Bob threw the problem to his reserve squad, which just now was four hundred meters up, coming down with assorted hardware . . . including the rescue lances. He was vaguely aware of the lance canisters popping their fins, turning to point down into the library. There was the flash of a hundred tiny rockets, and as many hardened nodes were rammed downward through the concrete and steel of the elderly building. Inside, action would be faster than any human attention, the composite flechettes guiding themselves between walls, doing their best to minimize damage to old-style wired utilities. Once in place, they would displace the control codes of the dead building system, and attempt to contact the stability servos. Waves of compute and recompute flickered from the squad's status board. Success depended on just what had survived and how fast it could engage the marines' localizer mesh.

But rescue was not the mission. His attention was on Patrick Westin—

"Understood," Gu said. "Make it clear to biotech management and automation: They are to stand down and seal off the labs. Nothing goes in or out."

"Warn and embargo. Yes, sir."

Maybe the Xiang message was some bizarre fraud. Maybe, yeah. He gave Westin another squad and engaged police backup. CDC inspectors would be here from Denver in about thirty minutes and then they could contemplate making a safe entrance into the labs.

Bob glided in a silent arc around the south side of the campus. It was time to land himself and his third squad. Where?

If this was enemy action, there should be Local Honchos on the enemy side. He popped up the suspect lists. There was the usual population of foreign students. The interesting ones would be interviewed by the end of the evening. The library festivities had been almost a total surprise to the press—so why had that Bollywood contingent just happened to be in town and on-site? Surely the Indo-European Alliance wouldn't try anything really destructive. But the European cert collapse seemed at the heart of the destruction here in San Diego. The analysts and Bob's own intuition put the Bollywood crew at the top of his interest list.

He stalled his dart in a clearing among the eucs, and crunched down on a litter of branches and dead leaves. The third squad dropped at twenty-meter intervals east and west from his position. There were shouts and lights from up the hill toward the library. The building was still out of plumb, but stability servos were engaged and—if nothing else failed—it should maintain a standing state. Police vehicles had come alive; direct loudspeakers were making calming announcements. If things worked out, they might even be able to disguise the fact that there had been a military response. Local public safety could pat itself on the back for heading off one of those rare but inevitable system glitches. . . . Just ahead was the cluster of game and film people from Bollywood. They had already received a hold notice. None of them were attempting to leave. *Just a few words with you, ladies and gentlemen, that's all we want.*

GenGen said the labs were sealed tight, ready for the proper authorities—when? Ha! The CDC inspectors were ahead of schedule; somehow they had gotten superballistic transport. They'd be on the ground in ten minutes. He had support extending up the chain of command. And downward, too. Some very large, very competent groups were reworking the odds that the labs had been converted to factory-of-death mode. They agreed that the probability was less than one percent—that is, science fiction.

Now his analyst pool was larger than Bob Gu had ever seen, perhaps fifteen percent of the analytical power of the entire U.S. intelligence community. All that support should have been comforting, yet there were places where the connectivity looked thin. Maybe that was just the way the associations flowed when a crisis was totally bizarre.

Others thought it strange, too. He saw lots of paranoid colors. Finally someone got desperate:

<point-of-order>I have a sanity check. We've lost communication with five percent of our original threat analysts since the revocation attack began. This should be impossible.</point-of-order> All analysts were internal to the U.S. intelligence community. If Credit Suisse certificates were necessary for any of those participants to maintain connectivity, then there was at least a design failure . . . and maybe the enemy had been part of Bob's own support staff.

There was an immediate counterargument:

<point-of-order>You're mistaking loss of connectivity for loss of trustability.</point-of-order>

Then parts of the analyst pool got jammed in the controversy. It was the kind of deadlock that only a miracle-worker could quickly untangle—*and Alice is off in some hospital ward.*

Another alarm flashed across the lower part of his vision. His combat network lay all across campus now, and it did more than manage communication. Altogether, it was a two-thousand-meter-wide snooper-scope, and its report: *GenGen's private UP/Ex launcher has just gone hot.* A counter showed sixty seconds till cargo boosted out of the labs.

Even as USMC sensed the launch capacitor charging up, GenGen's own network continued to assure the world that all was safely sealed.

Something was trying to break out of GenGen.

This is way too much like Asunción.

Bob glanced at the nukes and death-fog dispensers and HERFs and HEIRs floating down through 10,000 meters. To the journalists, those weapons should look like random aerobots—but they gave Lieutenant Colonel Robert Gu, Jr., the physical power to annihilate *any* threat in this corner of the U.S.A.

So what was the Minimum Sufficient Response?

Thirty seconds till UP/Ex launch. Chaos still reigned in the land of the analysts.

Verified contact with DoD/DHS had been lost.

Sometimes decisions come down to one poor slob on the ground.

32

THE MINIMUM SUFFICIENT RESPONSE

M*us MCog*

The Stranger's pdf said that "Mus" was short for "Mus musculus." *Mice! The mouse arrays stretched away into the dark. If anything, the place seemed even bigger than it had the first time Robert had been here. So where to go?*

Miri hesitated only a second, then ran in the direction of the loudest noises. They trotted down two aisles and over one. Yes! Here was a cabinet with doors swung wide. Pneumos were delivering white cylinders into the crystal forest on top.

Miri skidded to a stop in front of the opened doors. Inside the cabinet were glassy racks; it was like some kind of old-time snack dispenser. The slots behind the glass were a silvery honeycomb, hundreds of perfect hexagonal cells. Hundreds of tiny faces looked out of the cabinet. Tiny faces with tiny pink eyes, on tiny furry white heads. A high-pitched chittering came through the glass.

"They can't move, they're wedged in so tight," said Miri. "Their rear ends must be plugged into little—" She paused, perhaps looking up background on her local cache? "—little sucking diapers." For a little girl who had no interest in pets, there was a strange sadness in her voice. "It's a standard thing really."

Miri tore her gaze away from the array of chittering faces. "Each of these cabinets has mice cells arranged twenty by thirty by ten. So there are nine more arrays behind this one we're looking at. Hear the crunching noise? Smart-Aleck's friends are wrapping up some of them for shipment."

"But where?" None of the mouse cells were moving.

"That must be in back—"

There was a sound like a goblet breaking. Colored mist floated down from the crystal forest. It barely wet his face. But Miri was standing right beside the cabinet. He reached out and drew her back. Above them, the rest of the fluidics shattered. There was the faint scent of unwashed socks. Robert moved them farther back, stepping on the broken glass. "Miri, that could be nerve gas."

Miri was silent for a second and then her voice piped up confidently: "They're trying to scare us. This part of the lab isn't designed for simple poisons." But Robert remembered the shipping cartridges just arriving here. *We were suckered into stopping at this cabinet.*

Miri slipped out from behind him and ran around the cabinet. "Ha! There *is* a transport tray back here." By the time he caught up, she was hosing the tray with aerosol glue. Tiny motors whined, unable to load from the cabinet. Miri reached out, patted the almost invisible boundaries of the gel. After a moment the crunching sounds within the cabinet came to an untidy stop. "Nothing's going out from here!"

They stood, listening . . . and now the familiar sound of cargo prep came from all over the cavern.

"How many mouse arrays are there, Miri?"

"Eight hundred and seventeen when I cached the lab description." She looked up at him. "But there's no way Smart-Aleck's friends could be using more than a few arrays. There's too much security and too many other projects down here. . . ." The sounds of packaging grew louder. Dozens of cabinets were playing the game of Come Stop Me. Miri stepped back and gazed into the distance. The lab was a miniature city, its alleys laid out in a rectangular grid, stretching off into the dark beyond their single streetlamp. "I've got a good map, but . . . what can we do, Robert?"

Robert looked at her map. "I came through here with Tommie. We set down gadgets by particular cabinets."

"Yes! Which ones?"

Robert looked again at the map floating in the air before him. The place was a maze, and the cabal had come in from a different direction. "I, uh—" In 2010, Robert had gotten lost in a shopping-mall parking lot. After an hour, he still couldn't find his car; he'd ended up at mall security. That had been the first undeniable encounter with his mental decline. *But the new me shouldn't have trouble remembering!* "The nearest is two rows thataway, then jog right."

They raced past two aisles, then over one to the right. Almost all the cabinet doors were open, their transport trays working to prep cargo. Miri waved at the pneumo tubes that branched above the cabinets. "But see, nothing is actually shipping from here. Where's the next place?"

And they were running again, off toward his best guess.

Ahead of them something loomed against the ceiling. The GenGen launcher.

Miri skittered to a stop, and began shaking her spray can. "Which one, Robert?" All the cabinets around her were behaving like suspects.

"It's still two more rows, then five cabinets down."

"But I thought you said—never mind." Miri walked past two more rows. Robert followed.

She looked up at him.

"I . . . I'm not sure." He glared over the tops of the cabinets, trying to orient on the launcher, trying to force memory.

She hesitated and then touched his arm. "It's okay, Robert. Sometimes, you can't remember. But things will get better for you."

"Wait," he said. "I'm sure this is right." The pneumo tube behind the nearest had just received a shipping cartridge. Mouse boxes were rolling on board.

"So that means, um"—and Miri's hand slipped from his arm. She looked around and then up at him: "Where are we?"

Maybe it hadn't been nerve gas. Maybe it was something worse. *And Miri got the bigger dose.* Above the cabinet the pneumo hatch had closed. There was a pillowed thud and the cartridge sped away.

Another cartridge pulled into the siding above the cabinet. Another batch of mice rolled to meet it. It was out of reach, *But I still understand what has to be done.* Robert looked down at Miri and did his best to smile and lie. "Oh, we're just on a tour, Miri. How about it, would you like to climb on top of that cabinet?"

She looked up past him. "I'm not a little girl, Robert. I don't climb on other people's property."

Robert nodded, and tried to hold his smile. "But Miri, this . . . this is just a game. And . . . if we can stop the white thing with your, your game gun, then we win. You want to win, right?"

Now that brought a smile, full of pert intelligence. "Of course. Why didn't you say it was a game. Huh. This looks like some kind of bioscience lab. Nice!" She looked at where the transport was sliding the mouse boxes along. "So what do you want me to do?"

Once she's up there she'll forget all over again. "I'll tell you when you get up there." He lifted from beneath her arms. "Reach up! Grab the edge and I'll push."

Miri giggled, but she did reach up, and Robert did push. She slid through the gap beneath the siding. Her spray can was just inches from the transport tray.

"Now what?" her voice came down to him.

Yes, now what? You go to all the trouble to do something, and then you forget the point. Only this time, he knew the point was something very important. Robert flailed, beginning to panic. "Cara, I don't know—"

"Hey, I'm not Cara. My name is Miri!"

Not my sister, my granddaughter. Robert stepped back from the cabinet and tried to make sense: "Just shoot the spray can at the moving things, Miri."

"Okay! No problem."

A sound that was pain spiked into his head. Over the cabinet, he had a glimpse of a strange hole that split the side of the UP/Ex launcher. *Nothing to do with Miri!* The thought had barely registered when he was slammed backward.

ARRAY ONE WAS in the GenGen launcher! The stealthed launch vehicle had a good chance of making it out of the U.S.

cordon. Array Two? Alfred's cameras showed that his strategy with the Gus was working. Somehow they had found the one *Mus* cabinet that really mattered, but his improvised gas attack was taking effect. The two were moving with a kind of aimless uncertainty.

He had time to prep the second load; he could get both out!

Mitsuri --> Braun, Vaz: <sm>USMC elint has detected ballistic launcher power-up in the labs! What can that be, Alfred?</sm>

Damn USMC. Alfred's analysts hadn't thought American electronic intelligence would be so sensitive.

Vaz --> Braun, Mitsuri: <sm>It's just bad luck. The GenGen launcher is cycling through its nightly calibration.</sm> That was a lie, but Alfred had his story ready. He launched a flurry of faked analysis, showering conclusions across Keiko and Günberk's teams. After the fact, he'd blame the launch on a resurrected Rabbit.

Mitsuri --> Braun, Vaz: <sm>But will the Americans believe that?</sm> She popped up some windows, her best estimate of just when and how the USMC might respond to the launch prep.

No time for the third cartridge. The GenGen launcher was loaded, the capacitor within forty-five seconds of launch. If only the Americans would just dither a bit.

Vaz --> Braun, Mitsuri: <sm>I'm finished with cleanup. Heading for rendezvous.</sm> Alfred took a last glance around. In fact, all his checklists were finally green. Across the room, the Orozco boy was sleeping peacefully. He would remember nothing of tonight, and his personal log had been artfully corrupted.

Alfred stepped out of the room, and proceeded down the hallway. There was lots of area lighting, the sort of thing you'd expect in a major system failure. *Ah!* The marines had finally detected his network. They had killed his stealthed aerobot. He still had contact with half a dozen mobiles scattered in the brush to the north. They were hunkered low, mainly trying to be very quiet and still maintain a net. The American assault grid was sweeping the area, destroying them one by one. The USMC mechs drifted down like a kind of black snow, unnoticed by the crowds, and visible to his robots only in the last instant before their destruction.

He came out of the stairway, onto the first floor. Ahead was the main entrance.

Five seconds till UP/Ex launch! He could imagine the chaos on the American side, losing their top analyst right at the crisis point. This was sniper warfare, brought into modern times, and three more seconds' delay would—

His milspec contacts lost transparency and he felt a flash of heat on his face. Alfred dived for the floor. When the shock hit, the building swayed, barely stable in its uncommunicating configuration. He lay still for a moment, watching.

That had been a High Energy Infra-Red laser, punching straight through the roof of the GenGen lab some two thousand meters away. He had a single direct view, a glimpse of trees silhouetted against a pearly glow, a rising cloud of steam and fog. Part of the haze was zapped vegetation. Most was damage-suppression mist, designed to soak up the knife edges of reflected death. The Americans had fired thirty times in less than a second. Glints from those blasts would have splattered kilometers in all directions, invisible to the naked eye, but potentially blinding and blistering those same eyes.

A second viewpoint came online. The target hillside looked like a miniature Mauna Loa, a river of flowing rock that slumped down into the hillside. Flashes of light marked the ongoing work of thermal flechettes. Thunder pounded.

So the American response had been prompt and decisive, cauterizing and sealing the launcher area, with minimum collateral damage. *And all my dreams are ashes.*

His contacts had transparency again. Alfred came to his feet and ran out of Pilchner Hall.

Ahead of him people swirled in panic, first stunned by network failure, now dazzled by HEIR laser glints. *Get into the crowd.* Even though he was shoulder-to-shoulder with humanity, for the first time this evening Alfred felt really alone. Some people around him stared upward; some were temporarily blinded. People were crying. Others were counseling the sensible thing: Get under cover, keep your gaze down and away from reflectors. In the midst of network failure, these people were reduced to literal word of mouth. But that word was spreading. More and more people realized that for only the third or fourth time in recent history, their own country was under a military assault. So far none of them had guessed that it was their own military's doing.

Alfred kept his head down, his face covered. It wasn't a suspicious posture; hundreds of others were cowering similarly. He shrank his communications down to a fuzzy static that conveyed only a few bits per second and that routed chaotically through his mechs. His ops gear was heavily shielded; to the USMC probes it would seem like just another Epiphany unit struggling to cope with the sudden failure of the public nets.

All that might buy him ten more minutes. Long before then, the DHS analyst pool should recover from Alice's collapse and run a *retrospective* surveillance of the local video streams. Analysts obsessing on a dataset that small were deadly effective. He could imagine their gleeful pursuit: See how the enemy mechs are clumped across from Pilchner Hall? Scan back to early in the evening; who-all has been near that building? Why, there's Gu's daughter going in, and a few minutes earlier, an Indian-looking fellow doing the same. Scan forward; no action till a minute ago, when that same Indian-looking fellow comes running out. Track him forward to the present—and my, my, there he is, trying his damnedest to seem an innocent bystander.

In any case, tonight's Indo-European operation was beyond all deniability. And that was the minor disaster. For a few seconds, Alfred Vaz drifted in uncharacteristic despair. *What about all my years of planning? What about saving the world?* He had heard enough to know that Rabbit's accusations were in the pdf sent to Parker's laptop. Alfred would never complete his research program. Indeed, Rabbit had been the Next Very Bad Thing. The carrot greens in Mumbai had made the point, but *I willfully ignored the evidence, so hoping I was to win with my plan.*

And yet . . . what of Rabbit now? Quite possibly its *substantive* evidence was indecipherable garbage. Conceivably the minds behind Rabbit were reduced to ignorance. *Then maybe, maybe, with all my leverage at External Intelligence, I can survive to try again.*

Alfred moved back to the edge of the crowd and cautiously reached out to his network. He'd lost his link into the labs. For half a minute there was nothing except a deadly *snick* and *snack* that sounded privately in his ears, marking the steady extermination of his little army.

There. A route through his surviving devices, back into Pilchner Hall. Tiny windows popped up and . . . he found a viewpoint, a single lab camera that had survived the HEIR attack and looked down upon the *Mus* array cabinet. The camera had suffered glitter damage, swaths of stuck pixels, but he could see enough.

Collateral damage could be your friend; there might be nothing here to prove Rabbit's accusations! The blast from the Americans' attack on the launcher had knocked over his very special cabinet. The last group of mice had fallen along with it. Best of all, the Yanks' thermal bombs had flooded the area around the launcher with molten overburden. The lava had closed off the hole created by the attack, just as intended, but it had not stopped there. The glowing, tarry tide had pushed out along the aisles and piled almost two meters deep in places. Its farthest extent lapped the fallen cabinet and covered all but a corner of that final batch of mouse boxes.

There was no sign of the Gus. Before the laser attack, they had been standing just beyond the current destruction. If he'd had more viewpoints, he might have tracked them down—but would that matter? Their jumbled memories were a still a threat, but that was now beyond his control. Suddenly, Alfred realized he was smiling. Strange how in the midst of disaster, he could be pleased that his two most persistent antagonists—*not counting Rabbit, may he burn in hell*—had probably survived.

He was closer to the library now. Civilian rescue workers were in evidence, though the network support was probably provided by the marines. Interrogation teams were not yet in action. And he'd found a backup aerobot to relay through! He got one fresh message before it was lost:

Mitsuri --> Vaz: <sm>Günberk's analysis is almost complete. Please give us a few more minutes' cover, Alfred. USMC is still focused on the labs. You have a clear run to your Bollywood team.</sm> She marked a map with the cinema team's current location, on the north edge of the crowds, in the eucalyptus. The Bollywood crew and its automation were well prepared for tonight's operation, though the on-site people were not knowing participants.

Alfred took a final check all around himself. He walked a few paces through the trees . . . and he was in midst of his Bollywood crew.

"Mr. Ramachandran! We have lost all connectivity." The video tech's eyes were wide. "Everything was fine, but now it is so very terrible!" The crew were experts on the spectacular, but not the real.

Alfred shifted into the persona of harried cinema exec. "You have your cached videos, do you not? You forwarded the earlier contexts back home, did you not?"

"Yes, but—" They wanted to rush out from the trees, to help the injured down by the library. That was for the best; in moments, Vaz would be one of the group again. Perhaps the DHS analysts were still in chaos. It would be amusing (and amazing, too) if this cover got him past the USMC cordon and out of California. As he followed his cinema crew out into the open space around the library, he had only one remaining link to his milnet. It was past time to drop that bit of incrimination.

But there was still intelligence streaming in. Terrible, chilling words that Alfred would never have been burdened with if he hadn't still been linked.

"Please. Please don't do this to her. She's just a little girl."

Gu. Alfred searched wildly in his only remaining view. Back in his physical person, he stumbled.

The video tech grabbed his elbow, steadying him. "Mr. Ramachandran! Are you quite well? Were you blinded in the attack?"

Alfred had the presence of mind not to shake her off. "I'm

sorry, it's just all this destruction. We must help these poor people."

"Yes! But you must stay safe yourself." The tech guided him down to where the rest of the Bollywood crew was already helping the emergency workers. Her aid gave him cover to look carefully out from his underground viewpoint. The damage to the camera had partially healed; some of the stuck pixels were flickering, and now he could see a little beyond the left of the fallen cabinet. . . . The elder Gu was pinned beneath. Lord, where was the other one?

I didn't mean for this. He should say nothing, but his body betrayed him:

Anonymous --> Robert Gu: <sm>Where is your little girl?</sm>

"Who is this?" the voice screamed in his ear, then continued more quietly, more desperately. "She's right here. Unconscious. *And I can't move her out of the way.*"

Anonymous --> Robert Gu: <sm>I'm sorry.</sm> Alfred couldn't think of anything more to say. Dead, these two might marginally improve his own prospects. He looked angrily away from the viewpoint. *Damn me.* He had accomplished nothing this night except destroy good people. But how could he safely save them?

"Please. Just tell the police. Don't let her burn."

O

MORE SPIKES OF overpressure, the sound of a thousand fragile things breaking, of heavy plastic tearing, bones being crushed. Robert didn't really hear it all. The bones getting crushed, that was distracting. Even the follow-up explosions and the heat went more or less unnoticed.

Robert surfaced from introspection that might as well have been unconsciousness, except that it hurt a lot more. Miri was on her hands and knees. She was wailing. "Grandpa! Grandpa! Say something, *please.* Grandpa!"

He twitched a hand, and she grabbed it. "I'm so sorry," she said. "I didn't mean to knock things over. Are you hurt?"

It was one of those questions that had an easy answer. Agony the size of an elephant was sitting on his right leg. "Yes," but the rest of a clever answer was lost in the pain.

Miri was crying, choking, very un-Miri-like. She turned and pushed at the cabinet that had him pinned.

Robert took a deep breath, but that mainly made him dizzy. "The cabinet's too heavy, Miri. Stay back from it." Why was the air so hot? The steady light was gone. Something like an open furnace glowed beyond the fallen equipment, where the sounds were all of popping and hissing.

"Cara—*Miri!*—come back from there!"

The little girl hesitated. Under the cabinet were the crushed remains of the mouse array that had been about to load. It wasn't going anywhere now. Miri reached down into the broken glass. Robert cricked his neck and saw a tiny face peering back into his, a mouse loose from its suction trap in the array.

"Oo," Miri's voice squeaked. "Hi, little guy." A laugh mixed with a sob. "And you, too. You each get a free pass." Robert saw more tiny faces as she freed other mice. The heads bobbed this way and that. They didn't seem to see him, and after a moment, they found something that was much more important in the mousely order of things: freedom. They ran around the girl's hands and away from the heat.

Now Robert could see what caused the heat. A glowing white gob of syrup dripped over the wreckage, hissed into redness as it oozed down the side of the fallen cabinet.

Cara gave a panicked cry and came back to him. "What is that?"

The hissing and spattering. If it could make it over that barrier, it must be dammed up several feet deep. "I don't know, but you've got to get away."

"Yes! Come on!" The girl pulled at his shoulders. He pushed with her, ignoring the tearing pain in his leg. That moved him four or five inches; then he was stuck more solidly than before. And now the heat was even more distracting than the crushed leg. Robert's mind hopped from one horror to the other, trying to keep its sanity.

He looked across at his crying sister. "I'm sorry I made you cry, Cara." She just cried harder. "You've got to run now."

She didn't reply, but the crying stopped. She looked at him, uncomprehending, then slid back from the furnace heat. *Go! Go!* But then she said, "I don't feel good," and lay down just beyond his reach.

Robert looked back at the oozing rock. It had swamped the bottom of the cabinet. Another inch or two and it would slop onto his little sister. He reached out, snagged a long shard of—ceramic?—and wedged it against the glowing tide.

There were more explosions, but not so loud. Up close there was just the smell and sound of things cooking. He tried to remember how he had come to be here. Someone had done this to him and Cara, and surely they must be listening now.

"Please," he said into the glowing dark. "Please don't do this to her. She's just a little girl."

No reply, just the terrible sounds, and the pain. And then the strangest thing, letters scrolling across his gaze:

Anonymous --> Robert Gu: <sm>Where is your little girl?</sm>

"Who is this? She's right here. Unconscious. *And I can't move her out of the way.*"

Anonymous --> Robert Gu: <sm>I'm sorry.</sm>

He waited, saw nothing more.

"Please. Just tell the police. Don't let her burn."

But the silent watcher was gone. Cara lay unmoving. *Can't she feel the heat?* It took everything he had to hold the shard in place.

Then: "Professor Gu? Is that you?"

It was some pestering student! There were so many afterimages, he couldn't be sure, but someone was there, partly submerged in the molten ooze.

"It's me, Zulfi Sharif, sir."

That name *was* familiar, a weaselly arrogant student. But now his skin wasn't green. That meant something, didn't it?

"I've been trying for some hours to call you, sir. It's never been this bad before. I . . . I fear I may have been truly hijacked. I'm so sorry." He was mostly submerged in the glowing rock. A ghost.

"You're injured!" said the ghost.

"Call the police," said Robert.

"Yes, sir! But where are you? Never mind, I see! I'll get help straight—"

The glowing rock dribbled over Robert's makeshift dam, onto his arm. He descended into a pit of mindless pain.

33

FREEDOM ON A VERY LONG LEASH

The New Annex to Crick's Clinic was less than five years old, but the spirit of the place was straight out of the last century, when hospitals were great imposing places where people had to go for a chance at survival. There was still some need for such places: the most extreme intensive-care units were not something you could pack into a first-aid box and sell to home users. And of course, there were always tragic cases of incurable, debilitating diseases; some small portion of humanity might always end up in extended-care nursing homes.

The New Annex satisfied certain other needs. Those occurred to Lieutenant Colonel Robert Gu, Jr., every day when he drove onto the hospital grounds. Every day since the debacle at UCSD, he'd pull into the Crick's traffic circle, get out, and look down along the cliffs and beaches toward La Jolla. The clinic was just a short hike up the hill from some of the most fashionable resort properties in the world. Just a few miles inland were the biotech labs that ringed UCSD, perhaps the most prestigious source of medical magic in the world. Of course, those labs could have been on the other side of the world for all that their location made any real difference. But psychologically and traditionally, this joint nearness to resort luxury and magical cure was a lure for the very richest of the very ill.

Bob Gu's wife, daughter, and father were not stuck here because they were rich. Once you walked past the imposing—

and totally real—main entrance, you had privacy. In this case, the privacy was a combination of the clinic's basic design and the fact that Uncle Sam had taken a special interest in certain patients.

What better place to keep sensitive cases hidden from contact than in a resort hospital. The press flitted around beyond the walls and speculated—without having grounds for a civil-liberties complaint. It could be a very good cover.

Bob hesitated just outside the main entrance.

Oh Alice! For years, he had lived in fear that JITT would take her. For years, he and she had fought about the limits of duty and honor, and the meaning of Chicago. Now the long-imagined worst had happened . . . and he found himself quite unprepared. He visited her every day. The doctors were not encouraging. Alice Gu was stuck under more layers of JITT than these guys had ever seen. So what did they know? Alice was conscious. She talked to him, desperate gibberish. He held her in his arms and begged her to come back. For unlike Dad and Miri, Alice was not a federal detainee. Alice was a prisoner in her own mind.

○

TODAY BOB HAD an official assignment at Crick's. The last of the detainee interrogations—that is, the last of the *debriefings*—were complete. Dad was scheduled to be awake by noon, Miri an hour later. Bob could spend some time with them, in the virtual company of Eve Mallory, a DHS officer who fronted for the investigation teams.

At 1200 hours, Bob was standing in front of a very old-fashioned-looking wooden door. By now he knew that such things were never faked at Crick's. And he'd have to turn the doorknob if he wanted to go in.

Eve --> Bob: <sm>We're especially interested in this interview, Colonel. But keep it short. Stick to the points in our memo.</sm>

Bob nodded. For a moment he didn't know who he was most angry at, his father or the jerks from DHS. He contented himself with pulling the door open without knocking, and stepping abruptly into the hospital suite.

Robert Gu, Sr., was pacing the windowless room like a caged teenager. You'd never guess he'd recently had one leg crushed and the other fractured; the docs were good at fixing that kind of thing. As for the rest, well, his burns were hidden by medical pajamas.

The old man's gaze snapped up as Bob came in the room, but his words were more desperate than angry. "Son! Is Miri okay?"

Eve --> Bob: <sm>Speak up, Colonel. You can tell him everything about your daughter.</sm>

". . . Miri is fine, Dad." He waved at the plush chairs by the table at the side of the suite.

But the old man just kept bouncing around the room. "Thank God, thank God. The last I remember was the heat and lava crawling toward her." He looked down at his pajamas, and suddenly seemed very distracted by what he saw.

"You're at Crick's in La Jolla, Dad. Miri wasn't hurt in the fire. Your left arm was pretty much destroyed." The flesh had burned down to the bone in places, burned all the way *through* the lower forearm.

Robert Senior touched the loose sleeve. "Yes, the doctors told me." He turned and dropped into one of the chairs. "That's about all they've told me. You're sure Miri's okay? You saw her?"

The old man never behaved like this. There was strain all around his eyes. *Or maybe he's just reacting to the look on my face.* Bob sat down across from this father. "I've seen her. I'll be talking to her later this afternoon. Her worst problem is some mental confusion about what happened in the labs."

"Oh." Then more softly, "Oh." He sat mulling the news, and then he was fidgeting again. "How long have I been out? There's so much you need to know, Bob. . . . Maybe you should get some of your law-enforcement buddies in here."

Eve --> Bob: <sm>So he doesn't remember the debrief? I didn't think we were that good.</sm>

"There's no need, Dad. There may be follow-up questioning about particular points, but we've dredged up all the dirty little secrets. You've been under interrogation for several days."

His father's eyes widened slightly. After a moment, he gave a nod. "Yeah, all those weird dreams. . . . So that means you know about, about my own problems?"

"Yes."

Robert looked away. "There are strange bad guys out there, Bob. The Mysterious Stranger—the one who hijacked Zulfi Sharif—he was on my case all the time. I've never known anyone who could manipulate me as he did. Can you imagine someone riding on your shoulder all the time, telling you what to do?"

Eve --> Bob: <sm>Just as well not to follow up on the Rabbit.</sm>

Bob nodded. Rabbit—that was the name they had pried out of the Indo-Europeans—might be something new under the sun. Rabbit had compromised the SHE. Scenario-building *within* the DHS and USMC had actually been in support of Rabbit. The Indians and the Europeans and the Japanese had a lot to answer for, but Rabbit's scam might never have been detected if they hadn't launched their revocation attack against the creature. But how had Rabbit managed its trick? What else could it do?

Those were burning questions, but not ones to discuss with your traitorous father. "We're taking care of the loose ends, Dad. Meantime, you have results and consequences to catch up on."

"Yes. Consequences." Robert's right hand played nervously with the chair's fine upholstery. "Prison?" The words came out softly, almost a request.

Eve --> Bob: <sm>No way. We want this guy running loose.</sm>

"No jail time, Dad. Officially, you and your pals were part of a campus demonstration that got wildly out of hand. Less officially—well, the rumor we're peddling is that you helped stop terrorist lab sabotage." That would be another job for the ever-useful Friends of Privacy.

Robert shook his head. "Stopping the bad guys, that part was Miri's idea."

"Yes, it was." He gave his father a stony look. "I was officer of the watch that night."

Eve --> Bob: <sm>Careful, Colonel.</sm> But the warning was empty. The interrogation strategists had agreed that Robert should learn part of this. The only problem was how to tell Dad without putting a fist into his face.

"Here? In San Diego?"

Bob nodded. "For CONUS Southwest, but all our action was here. Alice was my top analyst that night." He hesitated, trying to hold down his rage. "Did you ever guess that it was Alice who kept me from booting your ass out of the house?"

"I—" He swept his hand through unruly hair. "She always seems so remote."

"Do you know what JITT stick is, Dad?"

An abrupt nod: "Yes. Carlos Rivera gets stuck in Chinese. Is he okay?" The old man looked up and his face turned ashen. *"Alice?"*

"Alice collapsed right in the middle of your adventure. We have good evidence that the—"

Eve --> Bob: <sm>No details, please.</sm>

Bob continued with barely a hesitation, "She's still stuck."

"Bob . . . I never meant her any harm. I was just so desperate. But maybe, maybe I set her up." He looked into Bob's eyes and then away.

"We know, Dad. It came out in your debrief. And yes, you *did* set her up." DHS had investigated the Gu home and personal logs as much as they had anything at UCSD; they even had pictures of the bot Dad had used in the front bathroom. *But we still don't know exactly what it did.* India and Japan and Europe blamed Rabbit, and Rabbit had been reduced to rumors and unreadable chunks of stale cache.

Eve --> Bob: <sm>Heh. We'll figure it out. A network attack on a bio-prepped victim—that's a technology that's *way* too interesting to ignore.</sm>

Dad's head was bowed. "I'm sorry. I'm so sorry."

Bob stood up abruptly. It was something of an achievement that his voice came out calm and steady. "You'll be out of here later today. Meantime, get something to wear and catch up with the outside world. For a while, you'll still live with us in Fallbrook. We want you to take up . . . right where you left off. I'll tell Miri about Alice—"

"Bob, it won't work. Miri could never forgive—"

"That's probably true. But she's going to get the abbreviated version. After all, your part in the attack on Alice is circumstantial. And it's hidden behind security that even Miri Gu is unlikely to penetrate. I . . . strongly suggest . . . that you don't spell things out for her."

And so Lieutenant Colonel Robert Gu, Jr., had performed the duty that he'd been assigned here. And now he could get out. He walked across the room, reached for the door. Something made him turn and look back.

Robert Gu, Sr., was watching with anguish in his eyes. It was a look Bob had seen before, on other faces. There had been times over the years, when youngsters in his command had fucked totally up. Young people get desperate. Young people do terrible, foolish, selfish things—sometimes with terrible consequences.

But this is my old man! There was no desperation, no inexperience that could excuse him.

And yet . . . Bob had watched the CDC team's video as they followed Sharif's direction down into the labs. He had seen his father and daughter lying on the floor, just beyond the UP/Ex crater. He had seen the way Robert's arm was extended, how it dammed the curdling stone just inches from Miri's face. And so, despite the old man's monstrous fuckup, there was still something left to say:

"Thanks for saving her, Dad."

O

"TAKE UP JUST where you left off," Bob had said. At Fairmont High, that was almost feasible. Juan and Robert had already taken their written final exams, then been out of action through Christmas and New Year's. Now they were back, and just in time for what most students considered the scariest part of the semester: the Parents' Night demonstration of their team projects. Problems of life and death and horrid guilt devolved to worrying about making a fool of oneself in front of some children and their parents.

Amazingly, Juan Orozco was still talking to him. Juan didn't know quite what had happened at UCSD. His memories had been gutted even more systematically than Miri's. Now he was piecing things together from the news, trying his best to separate the truth from Friends of Privacy lies.

"I don't remember anything after Miri and I got to campus. And the police are still holding what I wore. I can't even see the last few minutes of my diary!" The kid waved his arms with the same desperation Robert had seen in him the first day they met.

Robert patted his shoulder. "They still have Miri's log, too."

"I *know!* I asked her." Tears welled up in the boy's eyes. "She doesn't remember either. We were getting to be friends, Robert. We wouldn't have gone after you together if she couldn't trust me."

"Sure."

"Well, now she treats me like when we first met—pushing me away. She thinks I must have chickened out and that's why she had to find you by herself. And maybe I was chicken. I don't *remember!*"

Lena --> Juan, Xiu: <sm>Give her time, Juan. Miri's distracted by what's happened, especially to her mother. I think she blames herself for that, and maybe all of us. *I* know you wouldn't chicken out.</sm>

Lena --> Xiu: <sm>But why he's asking the SOB for comfort is beyond me.</sm>

Juan looked away from Robert for a moment, gradually seemed to get himself back together.

Robert gave the boy an awkward pat on the back. Comforting others was definitely not part of his former résumé. "She'll come around, Juan. She didn't call you a coward when we were underground. She was very worried about you. Just give her some time." He cast around for some distraction. "Meantime, do you want to waste all the work we put in this semester? What about the kids in Boston and down South? We have to catch up on our demo preparation."

Lena --> Xiu: <sm>Can you believe this jerk? All he wants is to trick some more help out of the boy.</sm>

Robert's attempt at humor was feeble, but Juan looked up at Robert and gave a creditable smile. "Yes. Gotta keep track of the important things!"

O

Bob and Miri didn't come to Fairmont High for the vocational-track demos. At least they weren't physically visible—and Robert could tell that Juan Orozco was searching hard.

"Miri's at Crick's Clinic tonight, Juan. Her mother should be coming home from the hospital." Bob had seemed just as happy that Robert had another commitment this evening.

The boy brightened. "But maybe she'll peek in here, right?"

In fact this was rather a big deal for Fairmont, but not for good reasons. The popular press had built an enormous pile of speculation around the events at UCSD, and Friends of Privacy lies surrounded and embedded those speculations in conspiracies unending. The rumors contaminated everything and everyone associated with that night. Robert had dredged the public record—first to try to discover what had happened to him that night under UCSD, and then to see what people *thought* had happened. Robert and the cabal showed up in most of the theories, often as the picaresque heroes Bob had mentioned. But there were other theories. Robert had never heard of Timothy Huynh, but there were journalists who claimed that Huynh and Robert had engineered everything that happened in the riot and the underground!

Robert had become very good at blocking paparazzi mail, but now the notoriety was blowing over; his ratings were declining with a half-life of about five days. Nevertheless, he spent a lot of time at Fairmont High, where the school rules banned the most intrusive visibles.

Tonight, at the demos, that ban was in force. The bleachers were jammed with ticketed visitors—families of students and their guests, including virtual presences. Most of these people had no interest in Robert Gu. But if you looked at the network stats, a *lot* of people were invisibly watching.

The vocational program was not the gem of Fairmont High. Most of these kids could not master the latest, cutting-edge applications (and most of the retread students were even less competent). On the other hand, Chumlig had asserted in an unguarded moment that parents preferred the vocational demos, mainly because they made more sense to them than what other children were doing.

The teams were duos and trios, but they were allowed to use solutions dredged from all over the world. Demo night didn't begin until after sunset, so meshing overlays with reality would be relatively easy. Chumlig wouldn't have given the regular students such a crutch. Those demos lasted two days—and would not begin until a week after the vocational-track students had done their best. That was a kindly interval, a week for the vocational students to bask in their achievements.

Tonight, the audience sat on the west side of the soccer field, leaving the east free for whatever grandiose imagery might be created.

Robert sat with Juan Orozco right down on the sidelines, with the other performers. They all knew the order of their execution, er, performance. Their private views hung little signs over the field showing how much time remained in the current demo and who was up next. There had been no democratic choosing of the performance order. Louise Chumlig and the other teachers had their own ideas, and they ruled. Robert smiled to himself. In this, his old people-sense hadn't deserted him. Even without knowing the details of each project, he knew who had a strong project and who did not. He knew who was the most frightened of getting out in public and in person. . . . So did Chumlig. Her play order was an orchestration, exercising each kid to his or her limits.

Amazingly, that ordering also produced a pretty good show.

The Radner twins started out. For these two, the east side of the campus was not enough. They had some kind of wacky suspension bridge—it looked like the Firth of Forth Railway Bridge, but scaled up—that put down steel caissons on each side of the bleachers, and then climbed higher and higher into the northeast till it broke into the departing daylight. Seconds passed—and the construction reappeared out of the *southwest,* their nineteenth-century masterpiece making a virtual orbit of the Earth. The climax was the roaring passage of vast, steam-powered trains across the sky. The bleachers shook with the apparent power of the locomotives.

"Hey!" said Juan, and gave Robert a nudge. "That's new. They must have figured out some of the building maintenance protocols." If the Radners had not been targeted by the Library Riot rumor mill before, they were now. Robert guessed that would please the twins just fine.

Most of the demos were arty, visual things. But there were also students who had built gadgets. Doris Schley and Mahmoud Kwon had built a ground-effect vehicle that could walk up the steps of the bleachers. They tipped it over the top; there was an explosion of sound, and then it touched down without breaking anything. Juan stood up from his place at the bottom of the bleachers to turn and watch with his own eyes. He cheered Schley and Kwon, then plunked himself back down. "Wow, a ground-effect parachute. But I bet Ms. Chumlig doesn't give'm more than a B." His voice rose into a standard Louise Chumlig imitation: " 'What you did was scarcely more than off-the-shelf engineering.' " But he was still grinning. They both knew that a B was better than what most of the image plays were going to get.

There were even kids who tried for the cutting edge, projects that seemed a little like what Miri said her friends did. There were two new-materials demos, an extreme elastic band, and some kind of water filter. The elastic was not spectacular—until you realized there was no trick imagery. Two boys that Robert hardly knew did the demo. They stood twenty feet apart, swinging a large doll between them. The mannikin was suspended from a strand of their magical glop. The strand wasn't simply a strong composite. Somehow the boys could change its physical characteristics by the way they squeezed the ends. Sometimes it behaved like a giant spring, whipping the doll back to the center line. Other times, it stretched like taffy, and they swung the dummy in wide arcs. Their demo got the biggest cheers of all.

On the other hand, the water-filter demo was just a magnified image of a garden hose feeding into the filter. Above them, the students had floated an enormous graphic that showed just how their programmable zeolite could search for user-specified impurities. There were no sound effects, and the graphics were slow-moving and crude. Robert looked up into the sky and then back at the girls. “They’re going to get an A, aren’t they?”

Juan rocked back on his elbows. He was smiling, but enviously. “Yeah. It’s the sort of thing Chumlig likes.” And then his basic honesty forced him to add, “Lisa and Sandi never bother to polish their graphics, but I heard they’ve got a *buyer* for that water filter. I bet they’re the only vocational kids who make real money off their demo.”

“WE’RE NEXT, KIDDO,” said Robert.

The only evidence that Juan understood was the way his gaze fixed on their private clock.

Xiu --> Juan: <sm>You’ll do fine, Juan.</sm>

Juan --> Xiu: <sm>Is Miri watching?</sm>

Juan and Robert were last, the only part of the schedule that was really beyond Chumlig’s control. That had not been due to any Juan/Robert cleverness. It had been a consequence of the fact that their demo involved outside groups who had their own scheduling problems.

Juan hesitated a second more. Then he was running out onto the soccer field, waving up a phantom stage parallel to and facing the bleachers. Their performers filed in from both sides of the stage. The imagery was subdued, with no impossibilities. These were real people and real musical instruments, as Juan’s magnified voice explained to the audience.

“Hello, hello, *hello!*” Juan was huckster enthusiastic, and—to Robert’s ears—clearly panicked out of his mind. Robert could have handled the emcee role, or they could have recorded this spiel, maybe have had Juan lip-synch it—but that was just another way to lose points with Chumlig. So Juan made do with his live, cracking voice and words that came out with awkward pauses and forced bravado. “Ladies and gentlemen! Meet the Orchestra of the Americas, created especially for you this evening from the Charles River High School orchestra and chorus, cheapnet live from Boston and—" he waved to his left "—the Gimnasio Clásico de Magallanes, also cheapnet live but from Punta Arenas, Chile!"

Both sides of the stage were full now, two hundred teenagers in school uniforms of red on the north and checkered green on the south: students who had their own "far cooperation" requirements to satisfy. Altogether they comprised parts of two choruses and two orchestras, seven thousand miles apart, with only cheapnet in between. Persuading them to try this scheme had been a miracle in itself. Success would look mundane to outsiders, yet failure was a real possibility. *Well, things didn't go too badly in rehearsal.*

"And now—" Juan grabbed for still greater import "—and now, ladies and gentlemen, the Orchestra of the Americas will perform their very own adaptation of Beethoven's EU Anthem, with lyrics by Orozco and Gu, and network synchrony by Gu and Orozco!" He gave a hammy bow and ran back to the sidelines to sit by Robert. Sweat was streaming down his face, and he looked pale.

"You did good, kid," said Robert.

Juan just nodded, shaking.

The hybrid orchestra began to play. Now it was up to these kids and Robert's jitter algorithm. The sounds of cellos and basses rose from the young musicians in Boston and from the other end of the world. The kids' adaptation had a faster beat than the usual EU style. And every note came across hundreds of hops of randomly changing networkery, with delays that could vary by several hundred milliseconds.

There was the same synchronization problem that had made Winnie's choir at the library such a noisy affair.

Juan's lyrics climbed up, the chorus from the north singing his English version, and the one from the south his Spanish. Their student collaborators had created a flexible work with its own conductor interface; that helped some. Plus they were surprisingly good musicians and singers. But the performance still needed the magic of the adaptive delays that Robert's scheme injected into the transmissions (well, okay, and maybe also the far deeper magic that was Beethoven's).

Robert listened. His contribution was not perfect. In fact, this was worse than the rehearsals. Too many people were watching, and *too suddenly.* He'd been afraid this might happen. The problem was not bandwidth. He glanced at the variance plot he had put in his private view. It showed the presence of several million people suddenly observing, grabbing resources so fast that they confused his poor little prediction program—and changed the nature of what was observed.

And yet, the synch survived. The hybrid did not fragment.

Ten seconds to go. The performance hit some slightly ragged crescendos, and then, by some miracle, everything came together for the last two seconds. Juan's lyrics ended, and the central melody swept into silence.

The joint orchestra/chorus looked out at the audience. They were smiling, some perhaps a little embarrassed—but they had brought it off!

There was applause, wildly enthusiastic from some quarters.

Poor Juan looked absolutely drained. Fortunately, he didn't have to venture out on the field to wind things up. The performers were making their bows and trooping to the north and south ends of the stage—back to their respective corners of the world. Juan's smile was a little sickly as he waved to the local audience. His voice came sideways to Robert. "Hey, I don't care what grade it gets. We did it and we're done!"

34

THE BRITISH MUSEUM AND THE BRITISH LIBRARY

The kids rushed off the bleachers, only slightly impeded by the fact that Chumlig & Co could review the evening and determine just who had been unacceptably bumptious. Juan and Robert were slower, hanging with the other demo students and exchanging congratulations. Grades for the demos wouldn't be available for another twenty hours or so. They would have plenty of time to agonize over their failings. Nevertheless, Louise Chumlig looked quite cheerful, giving each student her congratulations—and deflecting all manner of questions about whether this or that deficit should truly be of any grading significance.

Still no sign of Miri or Bob. Robert's attention was filled with the kids and Chumlig and Juan Orozco—this last person alternating between hysterical relief and the conviction of failure.

So it was without forewarning that Robert found himself face-to-face—almost nose-to-nose—with Winston Blount. Behind the former dean, Tommie Parker was standing hand-in-hand with Xiu Xiang. Now, that was surely the strangest pairing to come out of this adventure! The little guy was grinning ear-to-ear. He flashed a thumbs-up at Robert.

But for the moment, Blount had all his attention. Robert had seen little of Tommie and Winnie since that night at UCSD. They and Carlos had spent several days at Crick's Clinic. As far as Robert could tell, certain deals had been made, much as in his own case. And now they were loose. The official story was just what Bob had said: The cabal activity had been a protest that got out of hand, but they had never intended to damage laboratory equipment and they were all terribly sorry for that. The unofficial tales of heroic sacrifice helped explain why the university and the bio labs seemed happy not to pursue the matter. If the Elder Cabal kept its collective mouth shut, there would be no Consequences.

Just now there was an odd smile on Winnie's face. He nodded to Juan and reached out to shake Robert's hand. "Even though I've dropped out of Fairmont, I still I have family here. Doris Schley is my great-grandniece."

"Oh! She did well, Winston!"

"Thank you, thank you. And you—" Winnie hesitated. In years past, praise for Robert Gu came from all quarters and it had often been used as a club to beat down Winston Blount. "—you wrote something wonderful there, Robert. Those lyrics. I would never have imagined such a thing riding on Beethoven and in English and Spanish. It was . . . art." He shrugged, as if waiting for a sarcastic putdown.

"It wasn't my work, Winston." *And maybe this is a putdown, but I don't mean it that way.* "Juan here did the lyrics. We collaborated all through the semester, but on this I let him go, just critiqued the final effort. Honestly—and this Chumlig character is the death of lies—honestly, Juan is responsible."

"Oh?" Winnie rocked back, then really seemed to notice Juan. He reached over to shake the boy's hand. "It was beautiful, son." And a sideways, still incredulous, glance at Robert. "Do you know, Robert, in its way, that was as good as what you did in the old days?"

Robert thought a second, listening to Juan's lyrics with his imagination the way he used to listen to his own poetry. *No, I was better than that.* Much better. But not better like being in a different world. If the old Robert could have seen these lyrics . . . well, the old Robert couldn't abide second-raters. Given half an excuse, he would have made sure that Juan's art died aborning. "You're right. Juan made a beautiful thing." He hesitated. "I don't know what . . . the years have done, Winston."

Juan looked back and forth between them. There was the beginning of shining pride on his face, though he seemed to guess that there were words unspoken going between Winnie and Robert.

Winnie nodded. "Yes. Lots of things have changed." The crowd was diminishing, but that just meant that some of the kids thought they could run around even faster. They were getting jostled by the flow of bodies and the ever louder shouting and laughter. "So if you didn't do the lyrics, what was your contribution, Robert?"

"Aha! I did the time-lag synchronization." *As much as it could be done.*

"Really?" Winnie was trying to be polite, but even after his own choir experience, he didn't seem especially impressed. Well, it had been a bit ragged.

Xiu --> Lena: <sm>For God's sake, say something to him, Lena!</sm>

Lena --> Xiu: <sm>Buzz off, you!</sm>

Xiu --> Lena: <sm>Then I will speak for you.</sm>

After a few more pleasantries, Winnie took off in the direction of the Schley family, Tommie and Xiu Xiang in tow. But Robert noticed a line of golden text drifting out behind Xiang.

Xiu --> Robert: <sm>That was great, Robert.</sm>

Juan was oblivious of Xiang's silent message. "Dean Blount didn't understand your part in our project, did he?"

"No. But he liked what he did understand. It doesn't matter. You and I both did better than we thought we could."

"Yes, we really did."

Juan led him back along the bleachers. Even if Bob and Miri weren't here, Juan's own parents were. Greetings and congratulations all around, though the Orozcos still didn't know what to make of Robert Gu.

O

A CLOT OF family and friends remained on the soccer field for some time. More than anything else, the parents seemed faintly surprised by their children. They loved the little klutzes, but they thought they knew their limits. Somehow Chumlig had transformed them—not into supermen, but into clever creatures who could do things the parents themselves had never mastered. It was a time for pride and a little uneasiness.

Miri was still out of sight. Poor Juan. And *I hope Alice got home okay.* One-armed, he wasn't quite good enough to check that in mid-flight.

Robert pressed into the densest part of the crowd, the folks swirling close around Louise Chumlig. She looked happy and tired, and mostly she denied responsibility. "I just showed my students how to use what they have and what the world has."

He reached across, managed to catch her hand. "Thanks."

Chumlig looked up at him, a crooked smile on her face. She held on to his hand for a moment. "You! My very strangest child. You were almost the reverse of the problem I had with the others."

"How's that?"

"For everyone else, I had to make them reach out to learn what they were. But you . . . first you had give up what you had been." Her smile was fleetingly sad. "Be sorry for what you lost, Robert, but be happy with what you are."

All along, she knew! But someone else had her attention, and she was gaily assuring them all that the rest of the school year would be even more exciting than what had gone before.

ROBERT LEFT JUAN and the others when speculation turned to what the regular demos would be like. The kids didn't want to believe that they could be outdone, not after tonight.

Robert spotted two familiar figures on his walk back to the traffic circle. "I thought you were with Winston," he said.

"We were," said Tommie, "but we came back. Wanted to congratulate you on your music-synch gimmick."

Xiu Xiang nodded agreement. Of the two, only she was wearing. A congrats logo floated out from her. Poor Tommie was still lugging around his laptop, though whatever remained inside surely belonged to the secret police.

"Thanks. I'm proud of it, but emphasize the word 'gimmick.' No one really needs to synch manual music across thousands of miles of cheapnet. And basically, I just took advantage of routing predictabilities plus knowledge of the music being played."

"Plus some timing analysis of the individual performers. Right, right?" said Tommie.

"Yes."

"Plus some counter-jitter you inserted," said Xiu.

Robert hesitated. "You know, it was *fun.*"

Tommie laughed. "You should do some ego surfing. Your hack was noticed. Back when I was young, you could have got a patent off it. Nowadays—"

Xiu patted Tommie's shoulder. "Nowadays, it should be worth a decent grade in a high-school class. You and I—we have things to learn, Thomas."

Tommie made a grumbling noise. "She means I should be learning to wear." He glanced at the young-looking woman. "I never dreamed that X. Xiang would end up saving my life. But of course she did it by getting us all arrested!"

Lena --> Xiu: <sm>Parker is afraid to try new things, even when he brags about the future.</sm>

They walked in silence for a few steps. There were more golden words from Xiang; she was getting better and better at silent messaging.

Xiu --> Robert: <sm><sigh/>Tommie is old, and all the medicine hasn't helped him that much. He's afraid to try new things."</sm>

Robert stifled a startled glance at the woman. Since when had the geek become a parlor shrink? . . . But she could be right about Tommie.

Tommie was surely oblivious of all the sming, but a familiar crafty grin was spreading across his face.

"What?" Robert finally said.

"Just thinking. Our UCSD op was the biggest and most dangerous I've ever been part of. We got used, yeah. But you know, it was like of lot of these modern whatsits—these affiliances. We contributed, and in one way, we got what we were aiming for."

Robert thought of the Stranger's promises. "How is that?"

"We nailed the Huertas Librareome Project."

"But the library books are all consumed."

Tommie shrugged. "I kind of like the Library Militant vision. The point is, we terminally embarrassed Huertas."

"That's a triumph?"

They were walking along the traffic circle now, followed by a hopeful automobile.

"Yup. You can't stop progress, but we stopped Huertas long enough for other events to come to our rescue." He glanced at Robert. "You haven't heard? You wear all that fancy equipment and you can't keep up with news."

Tommie didn't wait for a reply: "Y'see, Huertas was in such an awful rush for a reason. It turns out, the Chinese were chewing up the British Museum and Library faster than we ever guessed. And the Chinese have years of experience in semi-nondestructive digitization. They're positively gentle compared to Huertas's shredder operation. They made the San Diego effort look foolish, and they even got haptic data off non-book exhibits. There's clear sky between them and everyone else, including the Google archives. Anyway, we stalled Huertas by a few days, long enough that he can't claim any sort of priority.

And it was long enough so that the Chinese were able to frost the cake."

Tommie reached into his jacket and pulled out a three-inch-square piece of plastic. "Here. A present for you, that cost me all of $19.99."

Robert held up the dark plastic. It looked a lot like the diskettes he'd used on his old PC at the turn of the century. He pointed a query at it. Labels floated in the air: *Data Card. 128PB capacity. 97% in use.* There was more, but Robert just looked back at Tommie. "Do people still use removables like this?"

"Just paranoid propertarian old farts like me. It's a nuisance to carry around, but I have a reader right here in my laptop." Of course. "The data is all online, along with a lot of cross-analysis that the Chinese will be charging you extra for. But even if you don't have a card reader, I thought you'd be interested in holding this in your own hot little hands."

"Ah." Robert peeked at the top directory. It was like standing on a very high mountaintop. "So this is—?"

"The British Museum and Library, as digitized and databased by the Chinese Informagical Coalition. The haptics and artifact data are lo-res, to make it all fit on one data card. But the library section is twenty times as big as what Max Huertas sucked out of UCSD. Leaving aside things that never got into a library, that's essentially the record of humanity up through 2000. The whole premodern world."

Robert hefted the plastic card. "It doesn't seem like very much."

Tommie laughed. "Well, it's not!"

Robert started to hand it back, but Tommie waved him off. "Like I said, it's a present. Put it on the wall where you can remind yourself that it's all we ever were. But if you really want to see it, just look on the net. The Chinese have it pretty well meshed. And their special servers are really clever."

Tommie stepped back and motioned to the car that was trailing them. The rear door opened and he waved Xiu in ahead of him. For a weird instant Tommie looked like an old rake with some sweet young thing. Just another image from the past that had nothing to do with the truth.

"So Huertas is out of the shredding business, and the Chinese promise their follow-ups will be even gentler than what they did to the British Library. Imagine soft pinky robot hands, patiently picking over all the libraries and museums of the world. They'll be cross-checking, scanning for annotations—giving whole new generations of academic types like Zulfi Sharif something to hang their degrees on." He waved at Robert. "Hi ho!"

O

IT WAS ALMOST midnight when Xiu Xiang got back to Rainbows End. Lena was still up. She was in the kitchen, fixing some kind of snack. Lena's osteoporosis forced her to lean so far forward that her face was just a few inches off the table. It looked strange, but the wheelchair and the kitchen's design gave her plenty of freedom to maneuver.

Xiu eased into the room, feeling entirely embarrassed. "Sorry for cutting you out, Lena—"

The other twisted around to give her a direct look. There was a lopsided grin on her face. "Hey, no problem. You young people need your privacy." She waved for Xiu to sit down and have something to eat.

"Yes. Well, Tommie isn't really so young." She felt a blush coming on. "I, um, don't mean physically. He wants to keep up with progress, but he just can't cope with everything that means."

Lena shrugged. "Tommie's mind is better than some." She grabbed a sandwich off her plate and gave it a munch.

"Do you think he'll ever get his edge back?"

"Could be. Science marches on. And even if that doesn't help in Parker's case, we can give him pushes in the right direction. A big part of his problem is that life was too easy for him when he was young. He's too ornery to try anything that's really hard for him." She jabbed a hand in Xiu's direction. "Eat up."

Xiu nodded and reached for a sandwich. They had been over this before. In fact, it had been such discussions that had made all the difference for a certain Dr. X. Xiang. But maybe she had more on the ball than Tommie. Her chief problem in the near future might be in avoiding government "job offers."

Xiu bit into the sandwich. Peanut butter and jelly. But not bad really. "Have you had a chance to do your thing with the various people we saw today?"

"Play shrink, you mean? Yeah, I reviewed your Epiphany log; I posted some anonymous consults. The advice we gave Carlos Rivera was fine. He's got an ongoing problem, but that's life. As for Juan, we've done our best there, at least for the moment."

Xiu smiled around a mouthful of peanut butter and jelly. It had taken her some time to realize what a genius Lena was. After all, psychiatry was such a soft specialty. Lena said little Miri loved to view her grandmother as a some kind of female wizard. She claimed to know that even though the girl never announced the fact. Now Xiu had realized Lena was everything Miri imagined, at least metaphorically. *I've never understood other people, but with Lena seeing out of my eyes and chatting in my ear, I am learning.*

There were still mysteries: "I don't understand why your granddaughter is pushing Juan away. Sure, the kids don't remember what really happened in Pilchner Hall, but we know they were coming to be friends. If we could only get Miri's logs"—what the government was still withholding.

Lena didn't answer directly. "You know Alice is home from hospital?"

"Yes! I caught the fact from you, no details."

"There won't be any details. 'Alice was sick and now she's better.' In fact, I've known for a long time that Alice plays dice for her own soul. She nearly lost it this time, and somehow that's related to my ex-husband's grand screwup at UCSD. I think Alice will recover. That should help Juan with Miri." Lena sat back in her chair. Or rather, she let the chair tilt into a different posture. On her own, Lena couldn't really straighten up. "We've talked about this before. Miri can be stubborn to the point of being an asshole. She inherited that trait from the SOB, skipping a generation over Bob. And now that stubbornness has latched on to some deep-down guilt: subconsciously Miri feels that she and Juan messed up and did this terrible thing to Alice."

"Um, that doesn't really sound like science, Lena."

"I'm sparing you the technicalities."

Xiu nodded. "You get results. There are people at Fairmont High who think I'm some sort of human-relations genius. Me!"

Lena reached her hand a few inches across the table, as far as her twisted bones could go. Xiu took the hand gently in her own. "We've made a good team, haven't we?" said Lena.

"Yes." It wasn't just Lena's way with people. It wasn't just saving Tommie and his friends. There had been those dark days at the beginning of her time at Fairmont, when she was sure she could never come back—and Lena wasn't so happy-go-lucky either. Together they had climbed into the daylight. Xiu looked at the little old lady who was ten years younger than herself. *Together, Lena and I have become something rather remarkable.* Apart . . . ?

"Lena, do you think I'll ever be good at seeing into people the way you do?"

Lena shrugged and gave a little smile. "Oh, I don't know."

Xiu cocked her head, remembering little incidents here and there across the last few months. Lena Gu almost never lied outright. She seemed to realize what that would do to her credibility. But Lena could deceive, even in the face of a direct question. "Do you know, Lena, when you say 'oh, I don't know' and shrug—that means you're thinking 'not in a million years'?"

Lena's eyes widened. She gave Xiu's hand a squeeze. "Um. Well, there you go. Maybe in this case it won't take a million years!"

"Good. Because I want to tell you, Lena . . . I don't think Robert is the SOB you remember. I think he's really changed."

Lena's hand slipped away from hers. "I take it back. In your case, a million years may not be enough."

Xiu reached out, but Lena's hand was back in her lap. Never mind. There were things that had to be said. "Robert was brutal in the beginning, but look how he has helped Juan. I have a theory." She flicked the *Nature* citation across the table at Lena. This wasn't really her own theory. "Robert has had the equivalent of major trauma, the sort of thing that rebuilds a personality's worldview."

"You read too much crap science, Xiu. Leave that to us professionals."

"It's as if he's been all unwound. He has his memories, but physically he's just a young man. He has a second chance to get things right. Can't you see that, Lena?"

Lena flinched at the words, then hunched forward even more. She was silent for a long moment, staring down at her twisted body, her head swaying in gentle negation. Finally she cranked her gaze up to Xiu's. Something that might have been a tear glinted in her eye. "You have a lot to learn, my girl."

And with that Lena backed away from the table, her chair making an agile rise and turn. "'Fraid I'm done for the evening." She rolled off toward her bedroom.

Xiu took care of the dishes. Usually Lena insisted on doing the kitchen work. "That's something I can still do with my own hands," she often said. Not tonight. *And if I were just a little more clever about people,* thought Xiu, *I might know why.*

35

THE MISSING APOSTROPHE

Zulfikar Sharif was no longer in the graduate program at Oregon State. Robert encountered a very old-fashioned error message: "No longer a registered student, no longer at OSU." Even Sharif's enum was a stub labeled "vacated." That was a little scary. Robert hunted around. Worldwide, there were about a thousand matches for "Z* Sharif." None of the accessible ones were a good match. The rest were people trying with various degrees of competence to keep their privacy.

But the Zulfi Sharif whom Robert sought was still a technobumpkin. After an hour or two, Robert had tracked him down to the University of Kolkata.

Sharif was very subdued. "Professor Blandings dimissed me."

"From the OSU graduate program? In my time, we professors were not so powerful."

"Professor Blandings had help from your authorities. I spent several weeks trying to explain myself to some very insistent U.S. government agents. They couldn't believe that I was an innocent who had succeeded in being multiply hijacked."

"Hmm." Robert looked away from Zulfi Sharif, at the city all around them. The day looked hot and muggy. Just beyond their small table, crowds swirled, young people laughing and smiling. The skyline had its share of tall and ivory towers. It was the Kolkata of modern Indian vision. For a moment he was tempted to open a second, naysayer channel and try to figure out what was real and what was hype. *No, concentrate on figuring what part of Zulfi Sharif is real and what is hype.* "I suppose the best evidence the cops think you're innocent is that they let you return to India."

"Indeed so, though sometimes I wonder if I'm not just a fish on a very long line." He gave a wan smile. "I really did want to do my thesis about you, Professor Gu. In the beginning, it was academic desperation. You were the trophy I could sell to Annie Blandings. But the more we talked, the more I—"

"How much was you, Sharif? How many—?"

"I wondered that too! There were at least two besides myself. It was a most frustrating experience, sir, especially at the beginning. I would be in the middle of speaking with you, going through the questions that I knew would impress Professor Blandings—and then at a whack I was a mere bystander!"

"So you could still hear and see?"

"Yes, often that was so! So often that I think the others were using me to generate some questions for inspiration, and then warping them to their own purposes. In the end—and my confessing this to your police was a great mistake—in the end, I came to treasure these bizarre interventions. My dear hijackers were asking questions I would never have conceived. So I hung around throughout your Librareome conspiracy, and in the end I looked the perfect foreign provocateur."

"And if you hadn't been there the night of the riot, my Miri would have died. What did you see, Zulfi?"

"What? Well, I had been most thoroughly locked out that evening. The other players on my persona had agendas that did not include any discussion of literature. But I kept trying to get through. The police claimed I never would have succeeded without terrorist assistance. In any case, for a few seconds I could see you lying there on the floor. You asked for my help. The lava was creeping up against your arm. . . ." He shivered. "In truth, I couldn't see any more than that."

Robert remembered that conversation. It was one of the sharpest fragments in the jumble.

The two of them, eight thousand miles apart, sat in silence for a few moments. Then Sharif cocked his head quizzically. "Now I am well quit of my perilous literary research. And yet, I cannot resist asking: You are at the beginning of your new life, Professor. Can we expect something new under the sun? For the first time in human history, a new Secret of the Ages?"

Ah. "You're right, there is room for something more. But you know—some secrets are beyond the expression of those who experience them."

"Not beyond you, sir!"

Robert found himself smiling back. Sharif deserved the truth. "I could write something, but it would not be poetry. I got a new life, but the Alzheimer's cure . . . it destroyed my talent."

"Oh no! I had heard of Alzheimer failures, but I honestly never suspected you. Thinking there might be another canto of the *Secrets* was about the only good thing I still hoped to come out of this adventure. I am so sorry."

"Don't be too sorry. I wasn't . . . a very nice person."

Sharif looked down and then back at Robert. "I had heard that. In the days I couldn't get through to you, I interviewed your former colleagues at Stanford, even Winston Blount when he wasn't making conspiracies."

"But—"

"It doesn't matter, sir. I eventually realized that you had lost your sadistic edge."

"Then surely you would have guessed the rest!"

"Do you think so? Do you think your talent and your malevolence were a package deal?" Sharif leaned forward, engaged in a way that Robert had not seen since their interviews of weeks before. "I . . . doubt that. But researching the issue would be intriguing. For that matter, I have long wondered—and been too timid to ask—what really changed in you? Were you a decent fellow from the time of your dementia cure? Or was the change as in Dickens' 'A Christmas Carol,' with new experience making you kindlier?" He rocked back. "I could make such a splendid thesis out of this!" His eyes swept back to Robert, questioning.

"No way!"

"Yes, yes," said Sharif, nodding. "It is such a great opportunity that I almost forgot my resolutions. And the first of those resolutions is no more activities that get me mixed up with the security authorities." He looked up, as if at unseen watchers. "Do you hear that? I am clean, clean in body and soul and even in my fresh fried clothes!" And then addressing Robert once more: "In fact, I have a new academic major."

"Oh?"

"Yes. It will take several semesters of prerequisite fulfillment, but that will be worth it. You see, the University of Kolkata is starting a new department with new faculty, real go-getters. We have a long way to go considering the competition from the universities in Mumbai—but the people here have funding, and they're willing to take on fresh faces such as myself." He grinned enthusiasm at Robert's puzzled look. "It's our new Institute of Bollywood Studies! A combination of cinema and literature. I'll be studying the influence of twentieth-century lit on the latest Indian arts. And much as I regret our lost opportunities, Professor Gu, I am so happy to be in a major that will keep me out of further trouble with the authorities!"

O

ROBERT WAS ACTUALLY busy between semesters. His contrived synch hack had raised him to the lowest level of guruhood. He'd been noticed by a small company called Comms-R-Us. In a way it was a traditional firm. It was old (five years old), and it had three full-time employees. So it wasn't as nimble as some operations, but it had managed several innovations in concurrent communications. Comms-R-Us had paid Robert to consult for a period of three weeks. And though it was clear that the "consult" was mainly an opportunity for Comms-R-Us to decide if Robert Gu had any future, Robert jumped at the chance.

For the first time since he lost his marbles, he was creating something that others valued.

Otherwise, things were not going entirely smoothly. Juan Orozco was gone; his parents had taken him on vacation to Puebla, where they were visiting his mother's grandfather. Juan still showed up occasionally, but Miri was not talking to him.

"I'm trying not to care, Robert. Maybe if I stop bothering her, Miri will let me start over with her." Nevertheless, Robert had the feeling the boy might have camped out on their front steps if his parents had not dragged him away.

"I'll talk to her, Juan. I promise."

Juan had looked at him doubtfully. "But don't make her think I put you up to it!"

"I won't. I'll choose the time carefully."

Robert had decades of experience in choosing the right time to strike. This should have been easy. Miri had wangled an Incomplete grade on her demo project. That meant that when she finally did perform, at the end of the next semester, she would have even higher standards to meet. For now, she was a busybody around the house, mainly taking care of her mother. Alice Gu was a ghost of her former self. The steel of the last fifteen weeks of their acquaintance had been torn out of her. The result was . . . charming. More evenings than not, Alice and Miri were down in the kitchen, attempting to make hard work out of modern cookery. His daughter-in-law was distant, but her smile wasn't the meaningless reflex it had often seemed before.

Then Bob was out of town again, and Miri seemed to be

busier than ever. Every day, she had some news for him about her searches on burns and limb rehabilitation. Real soon now he should use that as an excuse to set her straight about Juan . . . and about himself.

○

MAYBE TONIGHT WAS the right night. Bob was still out of town. Alice had retired to the ground-floor den shortly after dinner. None of Miri's "board games" tonight. They were fun, one of the nicer things about life since that terrible night at UCSD—but tonight Robert had finally seen his way through some of his Comms-R-Us problems. Working on them, he lost track of the time. When he came up for air, he had some results, maybe things worth showing his employers. What a good night!

Downstairs, a door slammed. His eyes were still on his work, but he heard Miri come pounding up the stairs. She raced down the hallway and into her bedroom.

A few minutes later she came out. There was a knock on his bedroom door. "Hi Robert, can I show you some things I discovered today?"

"Sure."

She bounced into the room and grabbed a chair. "I found three more projects that could help your arm."

In fact, the medical condition of Robert Gu's left arm was best characterized by its absence. It was completely burned off at the lower forearm. There were two places near the shoulder where all that was left was a strip of flesh. His "prosthesis" was more like an old-style plaster cast. But interestingly, the medics had passed on the opportunity to whack the thing off and fit him with some modern miracle. Reed Weber—the physician's assistant had resurfaced now that the MDs needed someone to front for them—had explained the situation, though perhaps not in quite the way the doctors would like: "You're a victim of the new field of 'prospective medicine,' Robert. You see, we have prosthetics with five-finger motor control, and with almost the durability of a natural arm. But they're a little heavy and the sensor system is nowhere near the real thing. On the other hand, there are clear trends in nerve-

and bone-regeneration tech. Even though no one knows quite how it will happen—or if it will happen—the *odds* are that in eighteen months they'll be able to grow out from what you have now, into an effective natural arm. And the MDs are afraid that debriding what's left of your arm for a prosthesis might make the later solution much more expensive. So for a while you are stuck with a solution that wouldn't have impressed your own grandfather."

And Robert had nodded and not complained. Every day with this dead weight on his shoulder was a small penance, a reminder of how close his foolishness had come to destroying lives.

Miri was oblivious of all that. In fact, she had dismissed "prospective medicine" as stupidity. Miri believed in making her own medical solutions. "So there are these three teams, Robert. One of them has grown a complete monkey's paw, another is into whole-limb prosthesis, but very lightweight, and the third has some improvements in neurocoding. I bet your Comms-R-Us friends would put you up as a fast-track guinea pig. What do you think?"

Robert touched the plastic shell that held the remains of his arm. "Ah, I think a deal involving a monkey's paw is too risky for me."

"No, no, *you* wouldn't have a monkey's paw. The monkey's paw was just—" Then she got a Googling look. "Robert! I'm not talking about some old story. I'm trying to help you. I want to more than ever. I owe you."

Yeah, tonight was definitely the night to set her straight. "You don't owe me."

"Hey, I can't remember it, but Bob told me what he saw. You put your arm in the way of molten rock. You held it there." Her face twisted with imagined pain. "You saved me, Robert."

"I saved you, kiddo. Yes. But I created the problem. I played ball with something evil." Or something very strange.

"You were desperate. I knew that. I just didn't know how deep things would get. So we both made a mess."

It really was time to get down on his knees and beg forgiveness. But first let her know why this was beyond forgiveness. The words were hard to say: "Miri, you made a mess trying to fix things. But I . . . I was the guy who set up your mother for what practically killed her." There. It was said.

Miri sat very still. After a moment, her gaze fell. She said softly, "I know."

Now they both were very still. "Bob told you?"

"No. Alice did." She looked up. "And she told me they still can't figure out how what you did could have brought her down. It's okay, Robert."

Then abruptly, she was crying. And Robert did get on his knees. His granddaughter threw her arms around his neck. She was in full bawl now, her body shaking. She pounded his back with her fists.

"I'm so sorry, Miri. I—"

Miri's wail got even louder, but she stopped beating on him. After half a minute, her weeping trailed off into choking sobs, and then silence. But she still held on to him. Her words were halting and muffled. "I just found out that . . . Alice is . . . Alice is back *in Training*."

Oh.

"She's not even recovered!" Miri was sobbing again.

"What does your father say?"

"Bob is out of touch tonight."

"Out of touch?" In this day and age?

Miri pushed him back. She started to wipe her face on her sleeve, then grabbed from the box of tissues he set beside her. "Really out of touch. Tactical blackout. D-Don't you follow the news, Robert?"

"Um."

"Read between the lines. Bob is off somewhere making places and things glow in the dark." She wiped energetically at her face, and her voice returned to something like its usual tones. "Okay, maybe not literally. Bob talks that way when he has to do things he really doesn't want to do. But I watch the rumor mills and I watch Bob and Alice. Between the three I'm a pretty good guesser. Sometimes Bob is out of touch, and I read about something wonderful or something terrible happening in another country. Sometimes Alice goes into Training, and I know that somebody needs help or else very bad things may happen. Right now Bob is away *and* Alice is back in Training." She hid behind her hands for a moment, then resumed wiping her face. "My g-guess is that the top rumors are right. Something awful happened at the Library Riot, worse than the GenGen takeover. Now all the superpowers are running scared. They think someone has figured how to crack their security. A-Alice almost admitted that tonight. That was her *excuse!*"

Robert sat down again, but on the edge of his chair. His great confession had vanished into the abyss. "You should talk to Bob when he gets back."

"I will. And he'll argue with her. You've heard that yourself. But in the end he can't stop her."

"This time, maybe he can go over her head, or get the doctors to back him up."

Miri hesitated, seemed to relax a fraction. "Yes. This time *is* different. . . . I-I'm glad we can talk, Robert."

"Any time, kiddo."

But then she was quiet.

Finally, Robert said, "Are you conspiring, or just Googling?"

Miri shook her head. "N-Neither. I tried to call someone . . . but they're not answering."

Ah! "You know, Miri, Juan is in Puebla visiting his great-grandfather. He may not be wearing all the time."

"Juan? I wouldn't call him. He's not very bright, and when the crunch came in Pilchner Hall, he was useless."

"You can't know that!"

"I know I was down in the tunnels by myself."

"Miri, I've talked to Juan almost every day since I started at Fairmont. He wouldn't let you down. Think back to the times you *do* remember. You two must have conspired a lot to keep track of me. I'll bet he played fair. He could be your good friend, another person you could talk to."

For once, Miri's chin came down. "You know I can't talk to him about these things. I couldn't talk to you, except you already know."

"That's true. There are things you can't tell him. But . . . I think he deserves better from you."

Miri's eyes flicked up to meet his, but she didn't speak.

"Remember how I told you, you remind me of your great-aunt Cara?"

Miri nodded.

"You were happy to learn that. But I think you know how I treated Cara. It was like the Ezra Pound Incident, over and over again, for years. I never had a chance to make up for that; she died when she was not much older than Alice is now."

Tears were back in Miri's eyes, but she held the tissues tight on her lap.

"I went through my whole life like that, Miri. I married a wonderful lady who loved me very much. Lena put up with more than I ever dumped on Cara, and for years longer. Even after I drove her away, you know how she helped me at Rainbows End. And now she is dead, too." Robert looked down, and for a moment all he could think of was lost opportunities. *Where was I? Oh:* "So . . . I think you owe Juan. Dumping on him isn't in the same league as my screwups. But *you* still have a chance to set things right."

He looked at Miri. Her shoulders were hunched. She was shredding the tissues she held in her hands. "Just think about it, okay, Miri? I didn't mean to get carried away."

Finally, she spoke: "Have you ever broken a solemn promise, Robert?"

Where did that come from? But before he could get his mouth in gear, Miri continued:

"Well, *I* just did!" And with that, she grabbed the box of tissues and ran from the room.

"Miri!" By the time he got into the hall, Miri had disappeared into her room.

Robert dithered for a moment. He could go down and pound on her door. Or maybe he should message her.

He stepped back into his room, turned—and saw the golden light on the table, right beside where Miri had been sitting. It was an enum, granting some kind of limited message capability. But he already had that and more for Miri. He opened the golden enum and looked inside.

This one was for Lena Llewelyn Gu.

ROBERT SAT BESIDE the enum for almost half an hour. He studied it. He studied the documentation. It was exactly what he thought. *Lena lives.*

There was no physical address, but he could write her a simple message. It took him only two hours to do so. Less than two hundred words. They were the most important words that Robert Gu had ever written.

Robert couldn't sleep that night. Morning came, then afternoon.

There was no reply.

Epilogue

Six weeks passed.

Robert was watching the news more now; he had learned that the world can bite you. He and Miri compared notes on what they saw. The raids at the edge of the world were allegedly over. Rumors held that little had been discovered. Rumors—and some real news—spoke of scandals in the EU, Indian, and Japanese intelligence services. All the Great Powers remained very nervous about insert-your-favorite-crazyass-theory-here.

On the home front, Bob was back! Robert and Miri took that to mean that some disaster theories were much less likely. Others remained scarily viable. Indeed, Bob blew his stack when he learned about Alice. Things got very tense around the house. Both Robert and Miri sensed heartbreaking battles hiding behind the looks and silences. Miri had years of putting together the clues. Her best guess was that Bob *had* appealed to the doctors, that he *had* complained far up the chain of command. None of it mattered. Alice remained in Training.

Somewhere in all of this, Juan returned from Puebla. Miri didn't have much to say about him, but they were talking. The boy was smiling more.

From Lena there was . . . silence. She lived. His messages didn't bounce and her enum remained accessible. It was like talking into an infinite void. And Robert did keep talking, a message every day—and wondering what more he should do.

Xiu Xiang had left Rainbows End.

"Lena asked me to leave," Xiu told him. "Maybe I pushed her too hard." *But I know where she lives now! I could go there. I could make her see how much I've changed.* And maybe that would just prove that he had changed in all the ways that didn't matter. So Robert didn't drive out to Rainbows End; he didn't snoop the public cams there. But he continued to write her. And when he was outside, he often imagined that besides the 7-by-24 attention of the security authorities, perhaps there was another watcher, one who would someday forgive him.

Meantime, he threw himself into schoolwork. There was so much to learn. And the rest of his time was spent with Comms-R-Us. They liked his work.

Two months after the Great Library Riot, Robert returned to UCSD. He had lost track of Winston and Carlos. It was strange when he thought about it. For a few days the cabal had been such a tight conspiracy, but now they never spoke. The easiest explanation was mutual shame. They had been used, and their various agendas had come close to killing a lot of people. There was truth in all that, but for Robert there was another explanation, something weirder and almost as unsettling: the cabal was like a childhood clique, the animosities and closeness now vanished as his childlike attention morphed in new directions. Sometimes the desperation of the fall semester seemed almost as remote as his life in the twentieth century. There were so *many* things he wanted to learn and do and be, and they had so little do with what had previously consumed him.

In the end, it was his project with Comms-R-Us that brought him back to campus. Jitter and latency were bad problems in video protocols, worse in voice, and absolute death for touchy-feely interfaces. Haptic robots were getting better and better—but they were almost useless when run over the net. Now, Comms-R-Us wanted Robert to try his crazy synch schemes on haptics.

In the aftermath of the Librareome and the riot, the UCSD administration had dumped further bushel-baskets of cash on the library. In some ways its touchy-feely experience was better than commercial parks like Pyramid Hill. The question was, how could you export *that* across the net? He had done plenty of reading, studied the design of touchy-feely bots, but until the problem was solved there would be no substitute for firsthand experience. He took a car down to UCSD.

O

TWO MONTHS. NOT really a long time. The server shacks on the north side of Warschawski Hall had merged. There was a soccer field where the Software Engineering Department had been. Robert could see that this wasn't destruction related to the Library Riot or the Marine landings; it was the normal churn of any modern institution.

He took the footpath through the eucalyptus. As always, coming out of the trees gave the naked eye a sudden vision across miles of tableland, into the mountains. And there, standing before it all, was still the Geisel Library.

It was by far the oldest building at UCSD, one of the twenty percent that had been rebuilt after the Rose Canyon quake. But that damage had been nothing compared with what befell it during the riot, when the cabal's sponsors literally ripped the east side from its foundations. Any other building on campus would have been razed after such trauma, perhaps restored if it was of sufficient historical value. But neither had happened in the case of the Geisel Library.

Robert walked around the north side of the library, down past the loading dock. He had seen views of the structure immediately after the riot, the floors sloping and sagging, the ad hoc buttresses that the fire department had added as the internal servos burned out, the chunks of twentieth-century concrete that littered the terrace.

Those signs of destruction were gone. The overhanging floors were level once more.

The university had not undertaken a simple restoration. On the west it looked almost unchanged, but there was perceptible distortion above the loading dock, and on the east there was a graceful *twisting* of the building's great pillars. Where those pillars had moved, where the library had "walked," now the pillars were set. At the base was grass and smooth concrete, the tiled path that was the snake of knowledge. Looking upward, lush ivy followed the curving twist of the concrete. Where the ivy ended, there were lines of colored pebbles set in the pillars, making bands like stress fringes in illuminated crystal. And then above that, the rectangle of each floor was slightly turned from the one beneath it.

From the building specifications, Robert could see that some of the pillars were carbon fibers embedded in lightweight composite. Yet the building was as real and solid as it looked to the naked eye; more than any building on campus, this was real. This building lived.

O

HE TOOK THE stairs, stopping at each floor to look around. He recognized the Hacek domain. There were still Librarians Militant here. *But I thought their circle got booted out?* In other places, there was craziness he recognized as Scooch-a-mouti. The Scoochi mythos was eclectic nonsense that he had never figured out. How it fit with library metaphors was beyond him. But the Scoochis had "won" the riot and the library.

In other places, *both* belief circles were running in parallel. You could choose which you wanted, or neither.

Robert concentrated on management and naked-eye views. After all, he was here to study the touchy-feely support. There were haptic robots everywhere—not as many as at Pyramid Hill, but the university had crammed almost as much parallel variety into a few floors of a single building. UCSD had spent an enormous amount of money on the gadgets. There were some free-running models, but most were surface-mounted. These were fast. As quick as a Librarian Militant could reach for the vision of a book, a robot would slide into position, altering its surface just where it would meet the reacher's hand.

Robert stood for a few moments, watching the action. The naked-eye view was like nothing in his experience. When the student—that's what she was without her "Librarian Militant" cover—turned the book in her hands, the haptics flipped in coordination, never losing contact or slipping in a way different from the vision it was supporting. When she set it on a table, the haptics moved instantly to another task—this supporting some Scoochi client in even more unintelligible maneuvering.

He noticed that the girl was staring at him. "Sorry, sorry! I just haven't seen all this before."

"Tragic, not?" and she gave him a wide grin.

"Yes, uh, tragic." Somewhere on a high protocol layer, all this involved books and the contents of books. At the physical layer it was even . . . more . . . fascinating. He wandered along, his mind far away, trying to imagine how the intricate dance of the haptics could be replicated on robots that were at some distance on the network. If both sides had human players it would be infernally hard. But if it was an asymmetric service, maybe—

"Hey, Professor Gu! Look up here."

Robert looked in the direction of the voice. The ceiling above him had become transparent, as had the one above that. His view had tunneled through to the sixth floor. Carlos Rivera was looking back down at him, a happy smile on his face. "Long time no see, Professor. Come on up, why don't you?"

"Sure." Robert found his way back to the stairwell. The stairs were free of haptic diversions . . .

. . . as was the sixth floor. But there were no more books either. Someone had set up some offices.

Rivera gave him a tour. He seemed to be just about the only one on the floor. "Right now, the team is spread all over. Some of them are working on the new extensions underground."

"So what's your job now? Still library staff, I assume?"

Carlos hesitated. "Well, I have several titles now. It's a long story. Hey, come into my office."

His office was on the southeast corner, with windows overlooking the Snake Path and the esplanades. In fact, this was just where the cabal had held its meetings. Carlos waved him to a seat, and sat behind a wide desk. Carlos himself . . . he was still overweight, still wore the bottle-glass spectacles and the old-fashioned T-shirt. But there was a difference. This Carlos seemed relaxed, energetic . . . happy with whatever he was doing. "I was hoping we could talk, but things have just been so busy since—you know, since we almost fucked things up beyond all recognition."

"Yes, I know what you mean. We were . . . very lucky, Carlos." He glanced around the office. Nowadays, rank could be hard to see in visible things, but much of the furniture and plants were really what they seemed. "You were going to tell me about your job."

"Yes! It's a little embarrassing. I'm the new Director of Library Support. That's the title the university recognizes. In some circles that's not the important title. Downstairs and across the world, you'll find that I'm other things—like Dangerous Knowledge and the Greatest Lesser Scooch-a-mout."

"But those are two different belief circles. I thought—"

"You read that the Scoochis won it all, right? Not quite. When the dust settled, there was a very bizarre—well, 'compromise' isn't quite the right word. 'Alliance' or 'distanced merger' might be better." He leaned back in his chair. "It's scary how close we came to blowing up this end of San Diego. But we stopped just short. And that crazy riot made more money than a new cinema release. More important, it sucked money and creativity from all over, and the school administration was smart enough to take advantage." He hesitated, a little sadness creeping into his voice. "So we failed in everything we told each other we were trying to do. The books are gone. Physically gone. But the Geisel Library lives, and these two crazy belief circles are driving its content all over the world. But you've seen that, right? That's why you came down here?"

"I came down to study your haptics, actually." Robert explained his interest in distanced interactive touch.

"Hey, that's great! Both groups have been beating on me to extend our reach. But at a higher level, what did you think of what they're doing to the library experience?"

"Um, the Librarian Militants look the same as before, I guess. It's an amusing interface, if you like that sort of thing. The Scoochis . . . I tried to see what they're doing, but it doesn't make sense. It's so scattered, almost as if each individual book is its own consensual reality."

"Almost. The Scoochis have always been eclectic. Now that they have a librareome, they're building game consensus down to fine-grained topic levels, often down to individual paragraphs. It's much more subtle than the Hacek stuff, though children pick up on it very quickly. Their real power is that Scoochis can *blend* realities. That's what's happened with them and the Hacekeans. The Scoochis come from all over, even from the failed states. Now they're feeding the digitizations back outward. Wherever it fits, the Hacek people are running things. Other places, other visions—but all with access to the entire body of the library. If you can crack the problem of remote interactive touch, it should make their attraction even greater." Carlos looked around his office, where the cabal had plotted for such very different ends. "An awful lot has changed in just two months."

"What do you think really happened that night, Carlos? Was the riot intended to distract from what we four were doing—or was it the other way around?"

"I've thought about that a lot. I think the riot was a diversion, but one that got way out of hand and ended up causing immense—what's the opposite of collateral damage? Collateral benefit? Sharif-whoever—he was more often a rabbit to me—was a merry madman."

Rabbit. That was what his interrogators had called the Mysterious Stranger. It was also what the Stranger had called itself there at the end. "Well, *our* part of the business was darker. Rabbit manipulated all of us, each according to our own weaknesses."

Carlos nodded. "Yes."

"Rabbit promised each of us our secret wish, then defaulted after we had committed the necessary treachery." Though to be honest, Robert was pretty sure the critter was kaput. Maybe things would have been different if it had survived. His burning hope in the Stranger's promise had powered Robert's treason. That was cold ashes now. Thank God.

Carlos leaned forward. Behind the bottle-glass specs, his eyes looked skeptical.

"Okay," said Robert, "maybe Rabbit didn't promise everyone something. I think the power-assisted scheming was its own reward for Tommie."

"That's probably so." But the librarian did not look convinced.

"Look, we'd know if any of the promises came true. It would be spectacular. I'll bet Winston wanted to—Where *is* Winnie these days?" He was looking up the answer, but Carlos already had it:

"Dean Blount was hired by the university last month, in the Division of Arts and Letters."

Robert's gaze skittered across his search result. "But as an entry-level administrative assistant!"

"Yes, it's bizarre. The current Dean of A and L is Jessica Laskowicz. She's another medical retread. Back in the oughts, she was a secretary in the division. Nowadays, the career track for admin assistants doesn't have any ceiling, but Winston is starting awfully far down—and the best gossip is that he and Laskowicz never got along."

Oh my. "I guess maybe Winston finally made peace with his dreams." *Like me.* In any case, it meant the Mysterious Stranger was really gone, his extravagant promises dead. He looked up at Carlos Rivera. And felt the stirring of a vast surprise. Robert had very little of his old people-sense; nowadays, the obvious had to beat him over the head with a club. "What . . . what about *you*?"

"Do you notice anything different about me, Professor?"

Robert gave him a close look, then glanced again around the real-plush office. Carlos had done well for himself, but Robert had never thought that worldly success would be his demand of the Stranger. "You seem happier, more confident, more articulate." *Bingo.* "You haven't said one word of Mandarin. Not a single JITT slip!"

Carlos's reply was a smile of purest joy.

"So you've lost the language?"

"No. *Qí shí wǒ hái kěyǐ shuō zhōngwén, búguò búxiàng yǐqián nàme liúlì le.* And I haven't had a seizure in more than six weeks! The JITT doesn't rule me. Now I can enjoy the language. It has been a great help in working with the Chinese Informagical people. We'll be merging their capture of the British Library with what came out of Huertas's default."

Robert was silent for a long moment. Then he said, "Your cure, it could be coincidence."

"I've . . . wondered. This is a medical breakthrough that came out of groups in Turkey and Indonesia. It had nothing to do with the Veterans Administration or institutional research programs. But that's the way of most medical breakthroughs these days. And I've had no gloating messages from Rabbit. Everything is in the open, even if the news hasn't got much traction. You see, this treatment for JITT syndrome isn't effective for most victims. They contacted me through Yellow Ribbons because I'm smack in the middle of the likeliest genotypes." He shrugged. "I guess that could be a coincidence."

"Yes." The heavenly minefield.

"But it's an awfully *big* coincidence," Rivera continued. "I got what I asked for, just a few weeks after I did my part of the bargain. And some of my Scoochi progress has been strange. I've made agreements in weeks that should have taken a year. Somebody's helping me along. I think you're wrong about Rabbit. Maybe he's just lying low. Maybe he can't do all the miracles at once—Professor? Are you okay?"

Robert had turned away, and pressed his forehead against the cool window glass. *I don't need this. I am happy with the new me!* He opened his eyes and looked out through tears. Down below was the familiar footpath, the snake of knowledge wriggling up the hillside toward the library. Perhaps the Mysterious Stranger really was a god, or had grown to be one. A trickster god.

"Professor?"

"I'm okay, Carlos. Maybe you're right."

They chatted a few minutes more. Robert wasn't quite sure what they said, though he remembered that Carlos seemed a little worried for him, perhaps mistaking Robert's raw confusion for some kind of medical emergency.

Then he was down the elevator and back on the sunny plaza. And hovering immanent all around him were the worlds of art and science that humankind was busy building. *What if I can have it all?*

The End

ABOUT THE AUTHOR

Vernor Vinge is a four-time Hugo Award winner (for novels *A Deepness in the Sky* and *A Fire Upon the Deep,* and novellas "Fast Times at Fairmont High" and "The Cookie Monster") and a four-time Nebula Award finalist. He's one of the bestselling authors in the field and has been featured in such diverse venues as *Rolling Stone, Wired, The New York Times, Esquire,* and NPR's "Fresh Air."

Highly regarded by scientists, journalists, and business leaders—as well as readers—for his concept of the technological singularity, Vinge has spoken all over the world on scientific subjects. For many years a mathematician and computer-science professor at San Diego State University, he's now a full-time author. He lives in San Diego, California.